The Bloody Branch

The Bloody Branch

BRIGID LOWE

1 3 5 7 9 10 8 6 4 2

Harvill, an imprint of Vintage, is part of the Penguin
Random House group of companies

Vintage, Penguin Random House UK, One Embassy Gardens,
8 Viaduct Gardens, London SW11 7BW

penguin.co.uk/vintage
global.penguinrandomhouse.com

First published by Harvill in 2026

Copyright © Brigid Lowe 2026

The moral right of the author has been asserted

Map by Bill Donohoe

Penguin Random House values and supports copyright. Copyright fuels creativity, encourages diverse voices, promotes freedom of expression and supports a vibrant culture. Thank you for purchasing an authorised edition of this book and for respecting intellectual property laws by not reproducing, scanning or distributing any part of it by any means without permission. You are supporting authors and enabling Penguin Random House to continue to publish books for everyone. No part of this book may be used or reproduced in any manner for the purpose of training artificial intelligence technologies or systems. In accordance with Article 4(3) of the DSM Directive 2019/790, Penguin Random House expressly reserves this work from the text and data mining exception.

Typeset in 11.7/16pt Calluna by Jouve (UK), Milton Keynes
Printed and bound in Great Britain by Clays Ltd, Elcograf S.p.A.

The authorised representative in the EEA is Penguin Random House
Ireland, Morrison Chambers, 32 Nassau Street, Dublin D02 YH68

A CIP catalogue record for this book is available from the British Library

HB ISBN 9781787305250
TPB ISBN 9781787305267

Penguin Random House is committed to a sustainable future
for our business, our readers and our planet. This book is made
from Forest Stewardship Council® certified paper.

am Ynys Môn, Mam Cymru

This book contains depictions of sexual and other violence which some readers may find troubling.

Contents

Dramatis Personae   viii
Note on Language   ix
Map   x

BOOK ONE – FLOWERS   1
BOOK TWO – SEED   191
BOOK THREE – WAR   293
Afterwards   357

Note on the Text: The Collective Imagination   361
Acknowledgements   365

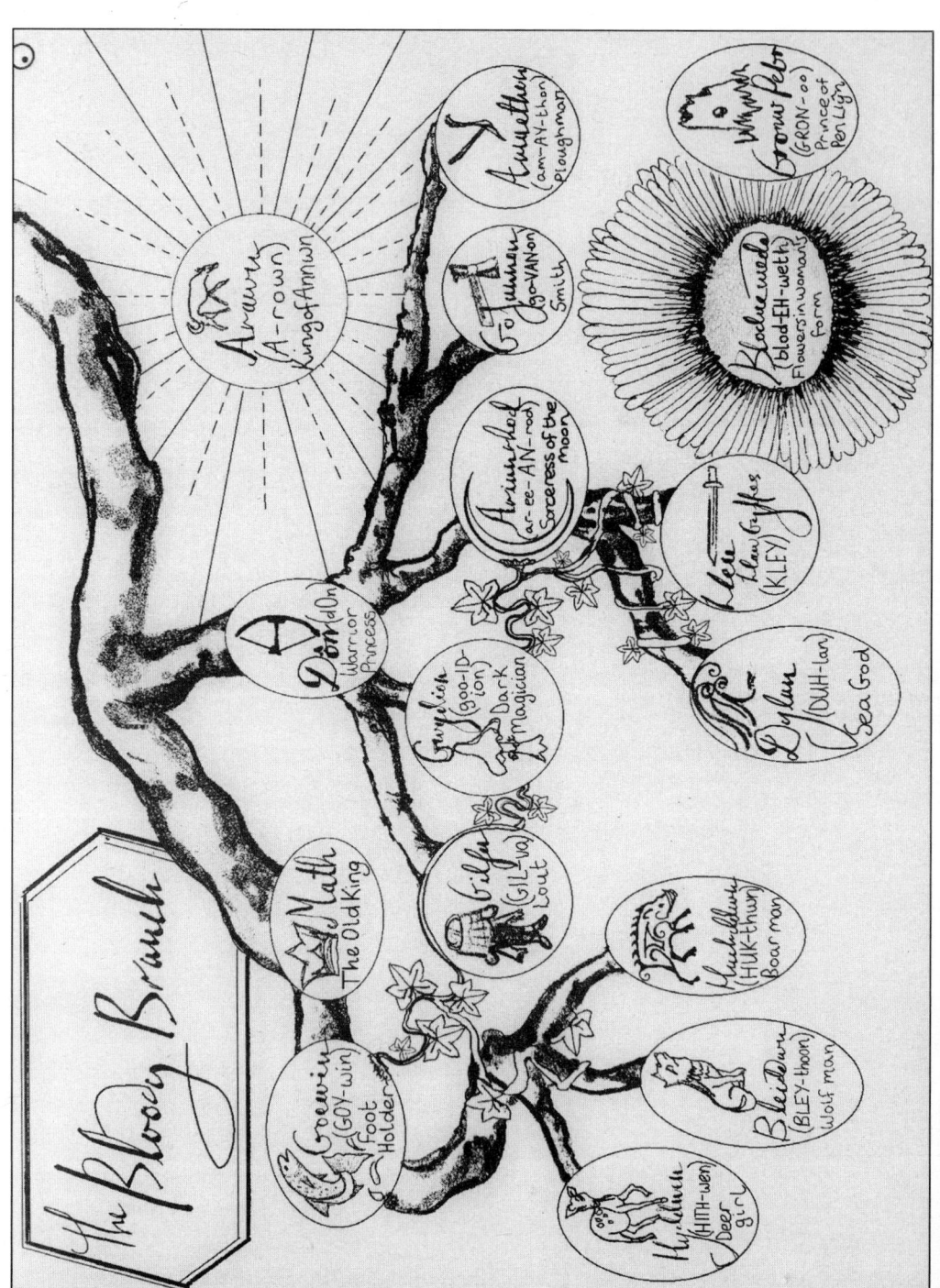

Note on Language

Welsh is pronounced phonetically, with the stress of the word almost always on the penultimate syllable. Welsh 'dd' sounds like the hard 'th' in 'the'; 'u' makes a sound closest to 'ee'; a single 'f' sounds like 'v'; and 'll' makes a sound quite unlike anything in other European languages, but closest to a 'k'.

BOOK ONE
FLOWERS

GOEWIN

I

Dewi! . . . Play a different song!

I'm sick to death of the Battles of Bendigeidfran, aren't you, friend? What – never heard of them? You really must have come from the back end of nowhere.

But I love this one they're starting now. The wind sings in the rushes beside the well – there's a bitter herb and a honey bee and a parting at a stile; a curlew and a corncrake, a muddy brook and a heartbreak. If I made a song, I'd put all that in. But also – knees and arms and thighs and breasts and heads and backsides. Mine, mainly, but other people's too. The story of my life revolves around a ticklish little body part we all look down upon.

In those days I sat there, in the great hall, every minute of the day. And all night. I'd be woken by blackbirds at dawn, and look down and see *them* there, in my lap. I'd doze off again, until levered at last from my dream by the shaft from the window. And there they'd be still, plain as daisies.

Feet. Not mine. Feet I know better than my own.

His very existence depended on me holding those feet in my lap. Ever since the curse, that was how it had to be, all day and every day. It was as though I nursed a solemn, stolid newborn I would never see grow up.

There I sat, before the old man's chair. He loved my black hair, which he said was a shade only seen amongst the forest clans. When he thought my spirits were depressed, which they sometimes were, he would braid it for me. His old fingers would knead their way to the bottom of a tress, and when the time came to tie it off, he'd click those fingers with a snap as brisk as though they were young – and then pull out from behind my ear a chain of turquoise damselflies, their wings blotched black where he'd pinched them between thumb and forefinger. Fluttering about my head, they'd lightly knot the ends of the braids and bind them around my temples into a dark crown, before flying off through the window.

Perhaps not every hero has feet of clay, but I doubt any has feet that are a pleasure to cradle all day long. Clay would've been better, frankly. The lord was never sure whether it showed greater consideration to me to keep his feet naked or shod – but as he was a very large man, and I a small girl, his boots were heavy in my lap, and so he generally kept them bare.

Math's feet were those of an old man who'd known many battles. The skin of his arches was fine as crepe silk, with shining violet scars, but the nails were curled and yellow, the soles thick and cracked as a griddle cake. Truth be told, they smelt, too. Math was ashamed of this, and would sometimes cast a spell to shroud them in a cloud of saffron and honeysuckle. There was something to be said for this, but knowing the truth, I seemed to smell fungus ripen in the flowers, and that was worse than the foot smell.

Still worse was the day he cast stronger magic, so that his feet appeared in every way like those of a young man who spent little time standing. The smooth, plump flesh not only seemed to deepen the creases of the rest of his old man's body, but was somehow repulsive in itself, so that, despite myself, I shrank away and let his feet fall. In an instant the curse began to tell on him, and I saw his being visibly thin out a shade, and was sorry, and bundled them hastily back into my lap.

You've really never heard all this? Stories every kid in Wales knows? I can tell you – how it all happened, and how the likes of me wound up here – if you really want to know. It's strange; even though I have everything, can do anything I want, I've got no one to listen to my side of the tale. People nod and smile when I talk, but if I look them in the eyes, I can see they're looking mainly at their own image in mine. They're wondering whether they're pleasing me, whether they can get into my good books, smooth the way to a better holding or position, or even – the cocky ones – get into my bed, which they imagine would guarantee everything.

So I never tell my own story. But for some reason I trust you, stranger. And this flower wine has gone to my head.

It'll go to yours, too, slow but sure. Likely you won't remember half of what I tell you – perhaps not even so much as that. Just tawdry shreds to snarl up the smooth thread of some dream. Well, no bad thing that. You won't be able to hold it against me. I'd want to tell it anyway. We all have a right to tell our story, if not to expect to be heard out sober.

So be it then. Cenwyn! Fresh water for the dogs! Their dish is warm already. On a day like this every beast deserves a well-cold draught. You'll need to fill your glass, stranger. Fill mine too.

If you stand and look from the portal you can just see my own island out there, across the water. After all these years, it still feels my home. I go there pretty often – there is a high court at Llys Rhosyr – but people wouldn't like it if I lived there. It's not quite . . . of this world. Between Wales and Erin, but between this world and Annwn, the fairy world, too.

That, there – behind the bare back of the sandbank, and before the high ridge with the great barrow – that's my own blue hill. From a tree there I looked out this way, and thought of the business of men that went on here, certain it would never be anything to me. My father had died, and my mother – gone – so it was just me, cared for by my father's sister. She did her duty – more than. But we didn't know each other. I kept company with the creatures of the wood and home meadows: the badger and the mistle thrush, the squirrels and slow worms.

One morning I went out before dawn to watch the hares. It had been a long winter, and they were more full of chase than I'd ever seen. I knew they'd be up with the sun. The sky was yellow as a barley-bird beneath the silver silt of night still sifting down. Light hung in the grass. I made dark prints in the dew, my skirts soaking up the glisten. I liked to think I might save it for later. I spread my cloak in a hollow that smelt of nettle sweat, like a form of my own where my shape would be hidden, and set to watch.

It seemed the hares were sleeping in, but the sun rose strengthened. It was a summer day in April. I slipped off my shoes, and angled my soles to catch the beams. I felt the sun's thumb on the thin skin of my arches, letting my feet wave on their stems with the buttercups.

And then! – three hares bolted into sight. Two against one – but she looked unstoppable, the males lagging, as though the cowslips were catching at their ankles. One crossed the corner to cut her off. She doubled, crossing the path of her other pursuer, and drove straight in my direction.

Hares gallop. In movement, they are pure sinew, a pulse of energy. Three now bounded fast towards me, each leap the compound impetus of the last.

I froze. I confused the hammer of their feet with my own pulse – with the hurtling of the coming spring. I was not sure I could roll aside in time.

She veered. Both pursuers anticipated her, closing the gap.

The faster touched her flying heel with his, and a puff of fluff drifted my way, clinging at last to my face, oil-soft between my fingers and my cheek.

She was still well ahead, but her rhythm was broken. Desperation gave her speed. The gap widened – she had space to make it to the bramble break. But then she stumbled, and at once there were strong paws on her back.

She turned and clattered him round the head. Have you ever seen hares box? It's brutal. He was knocked sideways, but reared instantly to hit her back. Now his fur flew, as with chin back she beat him with both fists, hitting his shoulders and neck mostly but sometimes getting a smack in to his face. She had the best of it, but fur streamed downwind of them like thistledown.

She punched again – he gave a twisting leap, and stretched high for a lengthened moment in the air, before smashing down across her back.

And then they were a whirling knot, rising and sinking together as they span, like clay on a wheel. She broke away, but he was straight after her, and almost immediately on her.

And now she was still. Still enough for me to watch the show-holes of her eyes focused on nothing; her ears pressed back, like twin razor shells in their sand hollow. The tide of the morning seemed to ebb away, leaving only the quicksand shiver in the loins of the male hare.

And then I heard them calling me, and crept away.

The walk back to the house was the last freedom I would know for a long while. The grass was just long enough to make the way across the top meadow into a path again. The first swallow of the year swooped by my knee, sticking close above the narrow margins of the track, as though it craved a flying challenge greater than the freedom of the air. The bird – sloe-blue harpoon – sped away from me, like that moment itself; so much force in a small fleet thing. I longed for power over time, so that I could meet my life coming, rather than always watching it go . . . always ready to stroke the swallow's glassy back as it passed, and feel the sharp wire styles of its tail soften to feathered shadow against my waiting palm.

As I came in sight of the stockade around the village, I was surprised to see a rush of something pale in the green shade of the wood. A pack of hounds – now coursing towards me, like creatures from a tapestry, making silver horseshoes of their backs and stretching out until their ribs showed like harp strings as they bounded through the fern. I heard a chorus of barks and yelps, but as they drew nearer it died away. By the time they were close upon me the whole wood was quieter than night.

The breed was new to me. Their coats had a frosty bloom, and their ears and paws were red. When they reached me, they pelted around in a tightening circle, until the innermost leapt up against me – some at my shoulder, and some licking my face. I wrapped my arms around their stretching necks. They trotted around me as we approached the hall, as though I was one of the pack, sometimes looking up at me with gentle eyes.

As we entered the enclosure, I saw that the others shrank away from the dogs, and a way cleared for us towards the hall.

A party of horsemen shifted there. I'd seen a war party set out many times, bright and loud as jays in oiled leather and bronze. As a little child I'd run to them at the last moment with an apron full of starflowers to drop into their wine and tuck into their belts for courage. The last time I saw my father, I peered into his cup to see the blue stars floating in the dark wine, and then up into his face, where his eyes seemed their swimming reflection.

These men . . . did not look like that. Their horses' coats were matted with dust and splashed with – something – down to the gaskins. Below that they were clean – from wading through a river, I guessed. The sheen of muscled legs emphasised the filth above of horse and riders both.

The horsemen had dented and split helms, and clothes torn, stained and full of leaves and other muck. Some of the dark slicks on clothes and saddle could not be mistaken, however hard I tried – bright blood, brown blood, black blood, blood clotted and choked with . . . but have you seen it? Don't try to imagine. To watch human beings hack each other to portions, like butchers hard at work, may be even worse, but the aftermath, in the clear spring light, is bad enough, you take my word, friend. As I understood what I saw, I smelt the blood and shit, trailing sickly sweet and warm across the spring air, and wished I could close my nostrils like a water shrew.

There was one clean figure amongst them, who rode a tall grey. He wore a white hood and cloak, lifted by the air as though made of spider's silk. The hounds now ran between myself and his horse's legs – it was clear who had brought them here. At last he leant to stroke the nose of one who jumped up to his hand, and his hood fell back. The flowing lines of his mist-pale face seemed to ripple and shift, as though they had been shadows cast by supple branches bending to a breeze, though the silver birches had all been rooted up from this part of the village many years since. It was clear he did not belong in this loud yard; almost as though his eyes looked right through it, to another world behind. That is the look of a fairy – a look I know well – a look I have been told is a buried part of my inheritance, and which I sometimes show in myself. But I could tell this man was pure *tylwyth teg* – perhaps the fairy of fairies – and I wondered what business could be of such significance to this world and the other both that he might be brought to show himself for what he was in the dusty daylight of the village.

By his side was one I could not fail to know from many a description. King Math, his huge head bare; his eyes showing blue in a thicket of hair and beard, tangled with the strips of leather and beads that had made him magnificent as he rode out, but now hung like the last blighted leaves and fruit on a gnarled apple tree after a November storm. For all this, he seemed just as certain to see out as many winters as might come. He was not quite a giant, but he was the next thing to it. The bones of his cheek and brow and jaw were level under his brown skin, a stark geometry of decision and execution. The soul behind his eyes must have been as hard and cold as slate that they gleamed so cool in such a burnished, weathered face. His sword was twice the size of any carried by the rest – as tall as I was. And he had a shoulder to match it, like a hill. But he was old, and his was the strength of awesome reputation. He had no need to brandish it.

Behind him were two much younger men, whose family resemblance emphasised their very different manners and physique. The larger handled his horse with exhibition, tangling with the bridle so that the mare sidled and reared in the narrow space, just for him to bring her up close again with a display of mastery. He acted like a boy of seven years old, who had only ever sat an ass before, and was puffed up with pride to have a bigger animal between his legs. His sword was uncleaned, bloody up to and over the hilt. From his saddle hung sacks, stained dark and filled with bulging rounds. He looked at me from the height of his saddle, and tossed his mare's head again, so that I saw the white of her eye, and was presented with a wall of gore-caked flank.

The other youth, whom I took for his brother, sat his horse

as still as any fishing heron. My attention still magnetised by revulsion, I noticed that his clothes were less thickly soiled than his brother's, and his sword wiped with methodic if not solicitous care. His face was lean and aquiline. His eyes were as self-contented as his brother's were anxious for admiration. They rested beneath fine brows, which made his only movement. A hair's-breadth adjustment of them was his only acknowledgement of me. And yet – I might have read the story of my later years in that angling, had I known how. From this day on, that thin man would keep me in his narrow sight until the time to strike.

The other horsemen, as I could see by their rich saddles and the ease with which they sat them, were famous warriors in their own right. Yet they handled their mounts so that they always kept their place behind these leading four. I saw more stained and bulging sacks across their horse's back, patterned skin, and whips of hair stuck with sweat to bare and brawny bloodied arms. I had heard their voices loud and rough with male excitement as I approached, but they were quiet now. When I saw the dirty energy of those men and their horses – the pride and skill and muscle and blood – and saw how it was kept in check behind the king, I looked at him again, and was afraid.

I could have shrunk back when I saw he meant to get down to speak with me. He swung from his saddle with the creaking confidence of one who'd ridden five times as many days as I had been alive. His approach to me was gentle however, and he took both my hands in his without a word.

I thought of the dark stains on the horses, saw how they obscured the fine needlework of Math's clothes too, and imagined so clearly some of the things his hand must have done in the last days that I wanted to snatch my fingers away. But the feel of his skin gave me another picture – of how he had washed and dried his hands in anticipation of this moment. I looked into his face, and though I shook before the blue purpose in his eyes, I let him hold me.

'My girl. Forgive all this. I wouldn't be coming in such a state . . . and bringing these ruffians with me, unwashed . . . if I had any choice. And what I'm about to tell – it'll be just as rough and strange as we must look – even stranger, if you can fancy it.'

And now I saw his purpose flicker – as impossibly as if the wind that swelled a clear blue sky had lulled and let it shiver slack a moment. For an instant he looked down, as though in search of inspiration in the mud and stones.

I was more alarmed by his hesitation than his decisiveness. But soon his gaze was level as a spear again, and he continued.

'We've been fighting raiders from Erin. And as, thank the gods, happens often enough, we beat our enemies, and beat them sound. But – at a cost. This nephew here of mine,' and he gestured back at the large young man bridling up his horse, 'slaughtered the four sons of an Irish queen – brought them to earth like badgers.'

Here the restless horseman gave a boastful thwack to the sack across his saddle. It oozed. I looked down.

'In her rage, the queen, she placed a curse upon me, as the leader of the army who had been making such merry hell among the Irish youth. In the usual course of things I'd use magic of my own to smooth away such a sticking point. But the curse of a mother who's just been burying her children – burying their bodies without their heads – that can be more of a challenge. And she knew what she was doing – a subtle piece of magic it is, I do admit, despite the crazy incoherence of it; she didn't overreach herself.'

For a split second again I thought I saw a ripple in his face from that threatened dying of the wind. But now he spoke louder, and with greater conviction.

'She vowed this: as I had . . . inverted nature . . . in forcing a mother to bury her sons, from now the very conditions of my existence, if I was to exist, must be backwards. In my age I must depend again upon a mother, but that mother must be a virgin. And as I came into the world head first from my mother's womb, the only thing that would keep me from going out of it was to have my feet in the womb of a virgin.

Hear me out.

The words she used were vague, and so we do still have a little room to find a way through. In my experience of curses – and it's wide; folk are always cursing me for some reason, or these damn nephews of mine, for reasons clear enough – fate takes it all the same, between a woman's womb, and the lap where she holds the baby, night and day, once it's born. A virgin to nurse my feet in her lap would fulfil the terms and keep me alive – for the sake of the realm. It needs me sorely still, so it does, as you will see.

Though there was no virgin at hand when the curse was cast, you can see I've hardly flickered out of existence. Here I stand still, all seven feet, all three hundredweight of me. While I'm at war, that is in itself enough to make me a man. A virgin to hold my feet while I'm at peace is all I need.'

And now he looked earnestly into my face – eyes blue, and cool, and hard and kind. 'I watched the starlings fly their text over the *cors* for many an hour last night, and they sent me here, to you. They know you, it seems, and call you the brave little one. This is your fate, and you must take to it bravely.'

I had withdrawn my hands in confusion by now, but he kept on speaking to the end, while I hardly knew how to look. This story was absurd – humiliating to him of course, though that he should ever be humiliated seemed quite against nature. I dared not look at him in case he should read my eyes. Though I felt his weakness, I was yet frighteningly conscious of his strength. He had shown me no anger; but he was king of Gwynedd. Had he come to take me now into this preposterous service by force? I tried to find words to protest, to plead, to pray.

But now the dogs, with their lovely silken ears, red as the rising sun in winter, were close to me again. One jumped up with gentle weight and had its velvet nose against my neck – the warmest, softest thing that I had felt for many a year. Their eyes were mild and wide in their pale faces. Lost looking into them, I jumped at the sound of Math's voice.

'I can stay still, at peace, not a moment longer. We have fugitives to bring to heel yet, and without the drive of the fight I can feel the curse of that angry mother gaining on me, and it's no good feeling. But these hounds shall stay with you, and come with you on the road to Tre'r Ceiri – which must be before tomorrow noon, so you're certain to be there by the time I return myself, you hear? Say your goodbyes, to everyone you love – it may be long enough before you're here again. We'll be leaving a horse for you to ride. Her name is Eponwen. She is a true mare – the seventh filly of her mother, and the sister of a king – and no harm may come to anyone who rides a horse like that. You'll find she knows the way.'

The dogs clung around me, and still I did not speak. I gasped for words, watching Math swing himself back into his saddle, and turn his mountainous shoulder to me, and then his back. How could I now yell out after the back of a king?

As the dirty men filed away, I saw that behind them all this time had stood my true mare. A pure white horse. Her neck curved like a crescent moon and her coat shone like that dew on the grass before dawn. Her mane and tail seemed made of light. She let me take her bridle and look her in the face.

Her eyes were black springs. I was sure I could have read the whole future in them, if I'd known how, but all I saw was sorrow, a brimming pail of tears hauled from the deepest well. If I looked too long I felt I would tumble in; but her long lashes seemed to blink love, and I hid my face in her neck, grateful.

I was so captivated by the mare that by the time I turned again, Math and his train were almost out of sight. Last, a way behind the others, rode the quieter of the two brothers, and I could see his head turned back at me for some time, before he set to look ahead. Something in the way he rode away reminded me of a falcon, which rows quietly from the scene on pointed wings, and might well pass for but another gentle dove, quite like the one he just now tore from out the sky.

But I beg your pardon. This messenger, it seems, has instructions to speak with me alone. He doesn't know that a stranger like you is a very grave for secrets.

Well. You might have heard all that – though it was delivered with deep looks enough. It seems that I – the queen of Gwynedd – am . . . summoned. Summoned to a folly castle on a crag that cuts out so far into the sea that all have expected the waves to swallow it these two decades past. And by Arianrhod, the one they call a sorceress.

Of course I needn't go. But I will. I don't know why I've been asked, but there seems only one way to find out, and I'm tired of sitting in this ancient hall, listening to battles of bleeding Bendigeidfran – Gods speed his blessed soul to Annwn.

I've never seen Arianrhod – and I'm curious, though most say she's mad. She's a few years older than me, and when I was just a tiny girl her reputation for learning reached even us over on Fôn. They said she could read the night sky as easy as her mother's face, that she went to bed wrapped in the downy mysteries of the Milky Way, and that her bedtime stories were the whispered secrets of the moon.

Then her mother died, and she was left in charge of her land, and she turned from the world. Though men said she was as beautiful as she was clever – some say she's more beautiful than me, when they think I can't hear – she would not allow any man to visit and made no secret of her contempt for that half of the human race. She kept herself to her own domains: the castle she soon built, perched above the sea, and the high moors above it.

Then, when she had lived in that solitary way for near a decade, it came out that, despite her scorn of men, she had a son of her own. And so her name was dragged through the mud, more or less. Folk tried to drag it quietly though, as they guessed that all that time in her castle was spent not quite alone, but rather with the mysteries of air and sea, and that she might wield these against her fellow country people, for whom she seemed to have little love to spare, if they provoked her.

On the whole, I like the sound of her, don't you? You can come with me to Caer Arianrhod – she called her castle after herself, of course – unless you mean to hurry home? Ah, good. I hear she has tolerated visitors of both sexes in recent years for the sake of her son, and, besides, if she summons the queen of Gwynedd so peremptorily she should expect I will bring with me who I like.

'Evan. Go saddle me the black, would you, and the dapple grey for this stranger. Put up provisions for the evening on the road for ourselves and Aneurin, and any other half-dozen who feel like a holiday. Tell Aneurin we are going to Caer Arianrhod . . . tell him we have just left, and he may catch us on the road.'

I'll carry on my story along the way.

GOEWIN

2

Half the village had come out to see King Math and the war party, and the other half came afterwards to stare at me. Perhaps because my mother was a stranger, I was often a little apart. When Mam left I felt it more. It was not always so – when there was urgent work, the bringing in of the berries or the cutting of the hay, I seemed to slip into a useful place well enough. But at other times, I felt a distance. And now the well known faces seemed newly strange – the awkward place I'd made for myself among them seemed to close behind me. No one spoke; not even the younger children, whom I had half expected might say a word in regret at the idea of my going. I was about to tell them all that I did not plan to budge an inch, when I saw my aunt pushing her way through the press.

She had her apron on, as ever; she often reminded me that she never got to take it off. It was always clean, but marked by work and worn by washing until it was neither white nor any other colour. It was frayed and pale like her face, and seemed as much a part of her person. Both gave the unchanging impression of scrupulous tiredness. But other parts of her could emphasise it. Her shoulders just now looked more bony, more burdened, even than usual, and her hair had been seized and knotted up particularly tight as she hurried out of the house.

'Well then. Never mind. You'll be wanting to be fine for

the court, I dare say. Well, it'll be a stretch to be ready in time, but I'll manage. Gaynor and Huw can go without supper if need be, though they do grow so fast since Imbolc, despite the odds, poor things. You thought someone else would come and tell me what had happened, I suppose, while you bask in your glory here? Never mind. As long as I find out somehow. Though there's enough for me to do. And I hope you'll not entirely forget your own relations, just because you're to be a lady of the court. But I'll go and buckle to getting your things ready for you now.'

'They're hardly gone a moment, auntie . . . but don't take any trouble – I'm not going! I can't spend my life sitting with an old king's feet in my lap.'

I had readied myself to argue my point, but I should have seen that was never the way it would be. My aunt merely raised her eyebrows, drew in her breath and lowered her eyes, as though the wisps of straw blowing about the ankles of the crowd were more likely to enter reasonably into her point of view than I.

'Well, you may make your own decision. Don't come seeking *my* advice! You know, in your heart, you would hardly heed it. Don't hold me responsible, that's all. You may do just as you like, as usual. Of course you may stay here; we'll manage. We will all do our best to suit your whims. Poor Huw can stay out longer with the goats . . . No one ever thought to offer him a place at court, and so he will never think himself above a day's work, young though he is. And I know you look down on your cousin Gaynor, but she never resents sharing the little we have with you. None of us do. You are very welcome to stay, of course.'

'I don't want anyone to go without or work harder because of me! I will work harder, to keep myself. You've never said before that Huw goes out with the goats because of me – and what would make you say I look down on Gaynor?'

She tucked her hands in her apron, raised her eyebrows again, pressed her lips together and smiled them at me, leaving only her eyes to openly pour scorn upon my words, as though her mouth could not condescend to quibble with such an implausible picture of past and future.

There was no arguing with that look. I knew it marked her mind as closed as her lips. I knew this game. And I knew that I could never win it. I knew I might make a thousand pledges of painful good behaviour, and though the failed attempt to keep to them might quite wreck my enjoyment of life, it would not move her certainty of my burdensome selfishness, and her own long-suffering generosity.

But now my stepfather Gryffydd stepped forward.

'Now now, Nan, don't be taking everything on yourself as usual. If Goewin is afraid to take this place offered to her at court, she need no longer be a burden to you. I'm getting old – I need someone to take care of me, and she is surely old enough to make herself useful now.'

I did not trust Gryffydd – and for good reason. He had not been good to my mother. I struggled to think how I might frame my resistance to this second threat.

And then old Buddug spoke up.

'Fifteen winters, from a squalling *baban* to a great hungry girl, Goewin has warmed herself at our fires. She's old enough by now to think on others 'sides herself. If she was in the court o' the high king over in Caer Dathyl, now, she could speak up for this village, couldn't she, ye? She could send good things our way – and it's high time we had any a good thing. You'd think good luck couldn't swim the Straits. We sheltered your mother, and now shelter you, *hogan*, all these weary years, despite your odd ways, and the way you keep yourself aloof. *Bobol bach*, it's my belief we have brought only bad fortune upon ourselves by doing it. Do you ever give a thought, now, to what we've done for you?'

There was a murmur of agreement from the crowd.

'She's a strange, wild creature, loving only her own company and that of dirty creatures, and it's little enough she cares for any of us, even those of us who *cwtched* her on our knees when she was a *baban*, and put food in her mouth after her mam left her,' said Annest. 'Now would be the time for her to show herself natural and grateful.'

'Aloof?' I tried to ask – but the lump in my throat was too hard. I would not cry, but my eyes swam so that I could not seek the faces where I might have hoped to find a contradiction of this picture of myself. I could only see the children at the front of the crowd, some of them my friends. I saw no surprise in any of them at this picture of me and my position. I knew that if this was not the way they had seen me before, it would be for the future.

Swallowing hard, I spoke.

'I'll go away from here, by myself – and take care of myself – and not bother any of you anymore.'

Buddug made a sound of derision.

'An' will you, ye? An' where will you go now, my fine girl? There's no bit of land without someone scratchin' a livelihood from it, which you'd be stealin'. You know you'd be found, ye, and taken for a thief, and brought back to us, bringin' new disgrace along of you. You think there are plenty other folk keen an' eager to take on the burden of an odd, wild orphan girl who's not learnt duty nor gratitude? You'll find we're no worse than others here after all – maybe a little kinder, that's all, ye – and too ready to indulge a youngster's selfish whims.'

I looked around again. The tears hanging in my eyes made me see double, with every careful blink – and I imagined those echoes of the figures before me were the villagers of other *cartrefi* where I might go – all just like these ones I knew, but stranger, and more resentful of the space I took up on the earth, and the awkward way I inhabited it.

And now the dogs jumped up against me once more. I felt the warmth of their blood under their soft coats; even their bony paws were warm. Again, a long velvet nose nestled against my neck, and I bent my head that way so the skin on the underside of my set jaw might feel the caress, and return it, while I still faced down the crowd. The dogs seemed to like me – I really believed they did. As one leapt higher than the rest, quite against my face, I took the chance to let my tears fall, and wiped my hot wet cheek upon her coat.

'There's no use reasoning with Goewin!' said my aunt. 'Save your breath to cool your porridge. She'll follow her own path, as usual. She won't learn respect for our opinion overnight. No doubt she thinks she judges best. She perhaps does not feel she owes us anything. And I and my children have managed to find her a place so far, and we can go on. It might not be as good a place as she'd like, but it's the best we can do, and she must learn to lower her sights a little. We'll find a way.'

You see it coming, do you, stranger? Can you explain it to me then? Why did I set out, the next day, obedient, as I was bid, to serve an endless term at the feet of the old bear king? Me, the wildest girl in the dark forest, who they struggled to get to the table for my meals, much less to sit them out once there – who had in my time pulled the beard of every venerable in the camp, and drawn the curse of every housewife?

Was it because the dogs lay down about me and watched

while I slept, cocked their ruby ears at my voice, and looked all confidence that I would always run with them? Because my heart was entangled in the horse's bright mane, my soul plunged deep into the well of her eyes?

I cannot tell you – I only know that I split myself in pieces, as I had done before in hard times. One part of me, a tough, acting part, decided, and acted, quite impassively. She took other, softer parts of myself hostage, and forced them to her will. And a third part still stood back, and watched appalled at this splitting, and the step I was about to take – watched, but could make no struggle or noise.

The tough part felt any sacrifice worthwhile to shatter the picture my aunt and the others had painted of me. And the soft part had lost all its will with the hope that someone in the crowd might leap to my defence. In that moment, I quite lost my belief in myself. If I was . . . headstrong, selfish . . . as the women of the village represented it, I would always be useless, unwanted and alone. I might find myself compelled by force to go – and would not that be, in all ways, far worse than to have chosen it?

There was a strong attraction, too, in my destination.

I had stared at the castle of Caer Dathyl in Tre'r Ceiri – the city of giants – for at least a thousand hours, throughout my life. From the beach, or from the upper branches of my favourite hilltop tree, I could see the well-known profile of the mountains. They stretched out – they ranged away – and spoke of every kind of experience in gigantic form. Some were heavy with peaceful contentment, and looked as though their backs would stay curved under sleep forever. Others rose and peaked in such an aerial sweep it seemed they could soar up into the blue on hollow bones, making light of stone. There were rough, brooding mounds, dark even in the sun, waiting long for their time to explode. There were rock faces that plunged as stark as fate.

Some peaks had partners that seemed to mirror their own particular grace or ruggedness, while others stood aloof or outcast, or loomed from behind the shoulders of the ranks ahead.

Calling each mountain by name seemed an incantation that would bring me closer to a life writ large: Elidir, Glyder and the Red Crest, the sharp beak of eagle Wyddfa; Moel Eilio Yr Aran and Mynydd Mawr, that crouching beast. The Hawk, the Horns, the graceful, sharp-pronged Forks, and Carreg y Llam plummeting headlong into the sea. Beyond that, the gently falling rhythm of Pen Llŷn tending towards the horizon, and Enlli floating all alone, the last gasp of land before the empty ocean.

I knew that some of the peaks I could see were half a hundred miles away, and I imagined the quiet lives that went on in the dozen valleys in the lee of each. But amongst the bare-headed peaks, one stood out. Yr Eifl wore a stony crown, and a lacy train of rock. I could not make out the exact shape of the castle of Caer Dathyl, or of the wide fort around it, but my imagination piled wood and stone dense and high, until the smell of tanneries and dirty streets, the dawn bark of masterless dogs and the chink of many hammers on horseshoe nails seemed to pierce the blue distance. I had not been amongst a throng of people since Da died. Since then, to imagine Tre'r Ceiri, as I swung soft in the arms of my favourite climbing tree, was to gaze into a past from which I had once glimpsed a wider future.

And so, a part of me wished to go, while yet another part knew well that this was a life that would be the death of me. I was used to kicking against all constraint, and here was I about to brick myself into a life of stillness, dusty inside air, and social rules more rigorous than either. But the part of me that had chosen heard all this quite unmoved by the vagaries of the other fluttering selves: it had pushed them backwards into an innermost space, and shot home the bolt.

I was a prisoner under escort of myself as I set off, on my true mare, the dogs coursing around us like chasing foam. When we got into the boat to cross the Straits, I kept my hand firm on the horse's neck that we might calm each other, and the dogs lay with their heads in my lap – and yet a part of myself seemed to lean against the opposite bow, and watch wonderingly that I never made a last bid for freedom, by plunging over the side. The grief at parting from my own fields and trees was hushed, and distant – nothing more than a cross-hatched, momentary ripple on the surface of the sea.

Once we reached the other bank, we kept near the sea, through the dunes of Dinlle – a bleached moon-waste from far off, but a carpet of flowers beneath my mare's light hooves; flowers of pale wax that I had never seen. Their upturned faces were so innocently strange that it seemed cruel – perhaps even dangerous – to crush them. Between them peeped heartsease and eyebright, and the sandy turf was so soft and lovely that it seemed we pressed a way across the delicate tissues of the earth's own spangled skin, and even Eponwen could hardly tread gently enough for me.

Then we worked along the mountains' flanks, just above the waves. I was not used to riding far, and the steady motion of the mare under me added to my sense of being carried along by something outside myself. The coast unwound with every bend. I was riding into the picture I had so often looked at. I had a clear view of the dark forest that had always been my home, now a swimming blot beyond the water.

We turned inland, and steeply up. The sun was blazing bronze just above the sea as we set our backs to it, and mist as softly dense as feathers from a pigeon's neck hung about the shoulders of the hills. A clatter of choughs wheeled above us, chawing as they kept our pace, and again my mind wheeled with them, somewhere far above my actions.

My mare climbed through the woods up to a dark, grey-rocked plain, starred with asphodel. Long drifts of ghost-grass fluttered and sunk in gusts that seemed to breathe from the stones themselves. April was too early for either flower – I found afterwards that both bloom there all year, under the same violet sky.

The castle, nowhere in sight as we crossed the plain, rose suddenly on its own summit, with the long stone walls of the fort skirting wide about it. Inside the walls were the bold goats butting the bars of cramped enclosures, the canny cats and wary dogs of the many people I didn't know. The folk hardly stopped to look as I passed, they were so busy about their intricate and alien works: fletching arrows, scouring vellum, spinning pots. The white hounds, who had stayed close by my side all the way, only trotting ahead to look back up in my face, now raced ahead. For the first time, I felt some of the fear at what I'd done, and leaned down against my true mare's neck for comfort. Her steady onward gait seemed to answer my caress as wisely as it might.

I was young. My heart is touched for that tender self as it might be for my own children. That remembered girl seems mine, but enough not-me that I can feel for her with a conviction that we can never muster for our present or recent selves.

What do you think? Do you care? Would some wine from the saddlebag help?

Many waiting hands helped me from my mare's back – I was right, I was always bound to come. All was perfectly ready. A small crowd parted for me towards the great hall, so that my path was clear. On the floor across the centre of the threshold lay a thick, pale wand, and I was about to stoop to pick it up, when I saw in the faces of those at the front of the gathering press that I should rather step over it. And in doing so, I crossed over into a new life.

I was made welcome in the long grey *neuadd*, and treated like a somebody, and given fine clothes to wear that did not fit, with seams which sorely itched tanned limbs used only to forest clothes. I looked down at my body dressed like that, and it seemed not mine.

The people might have thought me dumb. I had nothing to say which fitted the absurd occasion, and dared not speak a word for fear either of seeming to give myself undue importance, or to sink below the role that I had somehow set myself to play. Though I had never before been so attended, I had never felt so alone. Though many dogs, large and small, sleek and dirty, threaded the legs of the busy throng around me, look as I might I could not catch sight of the garnet velvet ears of those I counted my friends. And so at last it was almost with relief that I heard gathering commotion and saw Math enter the hall.

I had come here on the beautiful horse he had given me. I was dressed in the clothes of his foot-holder, embodied hours of painful work with brightest threads. If I would not now take his feet into my lap, the old bear king would die. I did not try to turn back. I had made this fate my own.

But there is Arianrhod's castle. I've never been closer than this – I've always given her a wide berth, as it seems to be what she wants – and look at those ravens up there! I know creatures set to carry tales when I set eyes upon them.

How could she build so close upon the swell? The towers look fit to shake down at the crash of every wave – and the sea thunders there even on the calmest day. Yet the highest towers in Gwynedd, they are. They say there is a cleft in the rock that runs below the castle, so that boats may sail in beneath the walls – and that Arianrhod herself used to bathe there, and swim out of the dark, right over to the sands of Dwynwen on Ynys Môn: the island of my childhood.

Ach – the sun slides so fast into the sea. But I always love to watch . . . to think there are only perhaps a thousand evenings in a lifetime, when the horizon is so clear that we may catch the ending of the day like that. And now here we are.

'I am Goewin of Ynys Môn – Arianrhod ferch Dôn expects me!'

Wait here, friend. I shall return.

GOEWIN

3

I'm sorry to have kept you so long, stranger – I hope you had enough to busy your thoughts. That view of the moon wandering over the sea would've been enough, I should think.

Well, I saw this lady of the silver wheel. I must admit, she daunted me. I found her in the topmost room of the highest tower, looking out at this same view. The door was open, and she did not turn to greet me. Her face was pale as the moon itself in its light, which picked out threads of silver in her hair, a dark mass melting out into the night.

She swirled and drank crowberry wine from a cup of lustrous shell. Her lips and gums were almost black with it. She looked at me with a hard cliff of a face, eyes narrow as a rock cleft – and said one word, pronounced one name.

'Gwydion . . .?'

Now that is the name I hate most in the whole world. If the name was supposed to be a question, I said nothing in reply, but she seemed to read an answer in my face. She tilted back her head and almost smiled, and it seemed, for a moment, as though a conspiracy of night-feathered birds beat out the fissure of her gaze and filled the room with the throb of wings, bewildering me.

'You share my feelings, do you?' she said, quite smiling now, her black smile. 'Then we may do business.' She pursed her lips and whistled, and in a moment there was indeed a bird – her hunched raven, discreetly folding his wings on the back of her chair.

She clasped her hand over his heavy beak, and half-whispered her instructions.

'Go to Arawn, now, and tell him we shall surely have the ally we need.' The bird hopped backwards to the sill, and plunged, upside down, into the night.

'Well, Goewin – hate will take us far. It is the black wellspring of human ingenuity. Walls and towers and citadels are built around it. And as any history will show you, there is no sounder footing for an alliance. I see we may trust each other on the bitter strength of it, though as a rule I have little trust or confidence in women – though I have less still in men.'

'And yet you think your hatred of that one particular excuse for a man good reason to order a queen to your draughty tower? At the end of a long hot day when most might expect to be left in lazy, half-drunk peace?'

'Indeed I do. And despite her incivility, I will deign also to persuade that little queen to concur with me wholeheartedly. There are many things to put in train, messengers to travel in anticipation of our agreement, and all things will be making ready while we speak. In the meanwhile let us learn each other's hate; let us gossip while we spin, as your country grandmother might have done – or perhaps knit something yet more intricate.'

She turned aside, towards a circular frame, across which were strung a concentric pattern of threads, so thin they barely caught the light. Amongst the threads hung tiny bodies that glimmered like stars just coming out. They might have been pearl beads – or the wings of flies bound up in silk might have caught the light just so.

Arianrhod took up the spare end of a silk floss hanging from the frame – a floss as airy as the Milky Way, that my sight could never have caught up in the darkness – and began to twirl it in her fingers. I saw her eyes narrow upon the feeling of the fibres between her finger tips, as she rolled and twisted them together into a thread. And then she filled a needle and began to stitch with it.

She spoke, sonorously at first, as though summoning something.

'For you, I will spin out a silver thread of hate, long and fine and strong. I will weave a web like a glistering wheel, to carry Gwydion down from his high place – to catch him fast, that we may twine him round with revenge's gauzy winding clothes, before we suck him dry.'

She looked in my face – for delight. I think she found it.

'Then I will go on. Let us be comfortable together. Sit down across from me. Here is wine. The longer the thread, and the more strands it has, the stronger. But mine is woven up with yours. I will tell, and then you, and then I again – over and under, warp and weft.

ARIANRHOD

4

I saw Gwydion first when I was nine years old. Though he was my mother's son, he had been brought up far in the south according to my uncle Math the king's distant oversight. How my mother came to let him go was never fully explained to me, and nor did I ever particularly wonder – she never cared very much for babies. Except for me, of course.

Certainly she did not seem glad to have him come to us, and rejected his awkward bids for intimacy. He had no talent whatsoever at winning hearts, though at that time he seemed keen enough to do so. He arrived, a gangling boy of twelve, ready to hold forth ponderously to any who would listen upon the many half-facts and misinterpreted truths of which he had made himself the tedious master.

He made few friends among the boys, who were far less impressed by the soporific murmur of his ever-purling fount of knowledge than he thought they ought to be. Instead of keeping to himself and his books, and working to acquire a deeper and more engaging knowledge, he fixed his wearisome attention upon me.

I was not so different at nine years of age from how you see me now. I never wanted to be a child. Even my mother, respected though she was, seemed to me to claim less dignity than I expected for myself. She told me how, at six months old, I would sit straight upright in my little silver driftwood chair, which I seemed to make my throne, and point imperiously at this and that thing that I wanted, as though it was beneath me to take the trouble to name them.

There was a price for the dignity, or course. Dignity is lonely. My mother was often away fighting, and I slept alone. Or rather I lay sleepless, as the darkness rushed in through my open eyes, and I shook through each nightly rehearsal for the final encounter with oblivion.

Perhaps I grew up as much at night as by day. By nine, I had learnt and mastered many things, and pitied the adults around me who were dull enough to judge my powers according to my size.

Most of them, of course, fell into this common mistake. But Gwydion took me at my own estimation. He followed me about, asking what I was learning, and telling me all the things he thought he knew, expecting, it seemed, that I would be quite awed. I was not – I pulled him down when he pretended to know a thing at which he only guessed, and argued when he overreached his gawky reasoning.

He seemed to like me none the less for that, and over the years that followed he boasted less and listened more, until for a while we were good friends enough, I will admit. My mother and I lived in the old *caer*, on the hill just above the shore from here, and Gwydion and I sat out on the beach at night together, under one warm, use-softened wolf skin, to study the phases of the moon and the movements of the stars. I found that teaching him, I learnt more myself, and that he had really learnt some things in the south that I had never heard about before.

He would have liked to have followed me everywhere, but my mother was still my favoured companion, and neither she nor I would let him share the rare time we spent together.

So it went on until I saw my thirteenth summer and a new priest, Uscia of Finias, came to us from Erin. She was quite young for a sage – perhaps thirty years old – but I saw at once that she knew more than any other bard I had ever seen and had a mind much larger than any I had ever known.

Her every motion spoke of knowledge possessed. Her eyes never had any need to dart, for they saw all within, and her lips, curving narrow as the new moon, seemed the close-clipped rim of the perfect truths that hung inside. Her hand, her foot, her cheek, had the inevitable compass and movement of the stars.

She made me feel – as I never had before – far less than I would like to be. My mind, my habits, my very body seemed at once an awkward, random mess. I found myself seized by the consuming desire to know all that she knew, and to learn to see as deeply as she did – to be close to her, and have wisdom drop down upon me from that firm mouth.

Gwydion, at first, seemed to share some of my excitement. But when I never came to search the tideline in the stirring dawn – instead rising early to take patties of laver bread fried with my own hand to Uscia, in hopes that she would tell the secrets of her dreams – he was chagrined. When I never huddled beneath the old skin on the pebbles of the sloping beach at night – instead creeping softly to Uscia's chamber, where she might tell me what truth leapt in the flames of her hearth fire, her palm resting gently on my head – he grew bitter.

My mother noticed it, and mocked him for his envy. At first I was rather sorry, and would have missed and pitied him had not my heart and mind been so astir with the new things there were to learn. However, as Gwydion grew more plaintive, and then sullen, liable to hold me by the arm and try to keep me with him at the times when I would most away, aversion for him crept upon me fast.

One day I had been swimming. The sun was hot, and I hauled myself out of the sea onto a jutting rock that stretched over the waves to dry myself.

I had been tempted into the sea by what Uscia had told me of the nature of the tide's pull, and now my sense of the outward world was dulled by my thoughts of that, the hushing of the waves close round me like a private cell.

However, I suddenly became aware of a tiny tugging upon my own person.

I rolled over, and saw Gwydion reaching over the margin of my rock, in the act of cutting off a wave of my hair.

It was strangely revulsive, to glimpse my secretly cut curl in his sweaty palm. I was almost ready to kick him, or stamp on his hands, so that he might fall down the jagged rocks up which he must have climbed to take me so by stealth. But instead I turned my anger to scorn, and ridiculed his weakness, especially when he began to cry. I said he should study how to be a man ahead of all these other abstract things, for which his mind, I feared, was too weak in any case. I said I could never care about a mere boy like him. And hot with my indignation, and wanting to be out – to wash myself clean – of his encroaching presence, without hearing any of the feeble whining he might make in his defences I jumped back into the water, and swam back towards the beach across the little bay there.

The sea cooled my anger. I was still disturbed by the impulse that might have made him steal a lock of my hair. I was unsure whether it meant some feeling quite unnatural in a brother for a sister, or some equally unnatural design to conjure intimacy or control against my will – and I was unsure which possibility was more disgusting. But as I climbed up the beach where we had spent so many happy hours together, I regretted the time gone by, and felt a new tenderness towards him, as one for whom I used to care. However, armed with my indignation, I felt no duty to ease the growing urgency of loneliness which I saw consumed him from within.

I did not see him for two days after that. I was freed from his eyes, and spent more time than ever with Uscia. In these last months she was coming to know me for who I really was, as even my mother had never done – and knowing me, she could guide me. She told me deeper secrets every day. She told me of strength and helplessness, and of pity and cruelty, and of the perpetual struggle of man with man, of man with woman, and of humankind with the earth itself. She told me how at some times the dead join with the living against the unborn, while at others they take the part of souls not yet alighted, and of the voiceless earth. This struggle, she said, is always there – a taut dark web behind our daily lives, on which those lives are woven, and without which no joy can bloom, no dream take flight. But from time to time, the struggle breaks through into the light, a blood-red toadstool, with warts as white as plague.

She told me of a prophecy only she had read, in the limbs of trees reflected in dark water, of such a time to come. In a war begun by the 'gilders of souls', earth would be set against its very self, and the dead would return, wrapped in the diaphane of time itself, to join the fray. One would be a man, gigantic in form and reputation, famous in song and legend; and the other a woman, all but nameless, her griefs unsung, and much too soon forgotten. And their floating armour of past years could not be pierced, and never could the strife be ended, until their names were guessed. Man's cruelty would be set against woman's pity, and the pity would not be overcome. All this, she said, was like a knot in the coming history of the land, which could never be untangled.

This mystery, and even one of the names to be guessed, she

shared with me, young and small as I was. Such tales of death and war, which should have made me shudder, only made my cheeks glow warmer.

As she tore a cake of bread with those pale hands, to give me half – and poured me out a fragrant steaming cup, the twin of her own, about which she now wrapped cold fingers, to look level at me through the steam – even my new-found diffidence could hardly leave me any doubt. I seemed to smell the growing intimacy of our thoughts in the very atmosphere that shook from the stiff salt-bloomed linen of her skirts, from the loosening knot of her hair. Her mind was opening to me, so that soon – soon – I trembled and turned almost faint at the thought – I would be able to swim right in, and strike out vigorously, or drift at peace under that enlarged horizon. When I closed my lids I seemed to see the patient depth of her watching eyes. I seemed to hear the chimes hidden in her voice whenever I was in silence. They promised everything.

On the third day, I woke at dawn to catch the low tide, and coaxed a dozen razor shells out of their burrows, to take to Uscia for her breakfast. I climbed the tower stairs with a soaring heart. As I saw the waves glitter in the rising sun through the window slits, I was even brighter and gladder than they were. I would soon comprehend the whole world, apprehend it in its lovely immanence, know it well enough at last to live a full dazzling, racing, plunging part of it.

I knocked gently at Uscia's door – no one else got such a reverential knock from me. But it was too respectful – she did not hear, she did not answer. Perhaps I had unreasonably expected her to sense that I was at her door.

I knocked more loudly. Still no answer. I felt a wave of disappointment – that she might have gone out, to the beach perhaps, in the morning light, and I missed her coming by a different way. I thought painfully of her quick foot on the stair, her fingers tracing down across the stones in the wall to steady her, and me not there to follow after.

She would have locked her door, if that were so, because she kept many herbs and other specifics there that must not be left open to the ignorant and curious.

I pressed the latch, and pushed at the door. It swung open.

I saw Uscia asleep, with her head on her arms, seated at her breakfast – a dish of laver bread, shaped just as I always made it – and by the side of it, a little string of bone-white moonshells, of the kind I always used as my personal token.

I had often left such a token on the threshold, at times when I had brought Uscia something and found her door locked, indeed that she might know it was me who had brought the morsel, or chart, or unusual specimen. But my hands had never touched that laver bread.

Trembling at my own temerity, I touched Uscia gently on the shoulder.

Then I grasped that shoulder and the other in my hands, clutched them hard with my fingers, and shook them – and yet she did not move.

Her body did not even yield to my touch as a sleeping body should yield. And yet I set myself against observing that: I would wake her, whatever it took.

I tried, and tried, and tried. And at last I knew that my cries were directed not at her pale sleeping ear but at the deaf world. My passionate grasp of her body no more hoped to stir it into movement, but only to keep myself from drowning in a new and terrifying loneliness.

She was dead. I would never again feel her hand on my hair, when I showed myself quick or deep in understanding. And – more bitter still – I would never know all she knew. If I ever found my way into that wider sea – and I doubted myself, for the first time – I would travel there weak and solitary.

I judged well. I have hardly ever – never, in fact – seen a mortal with an intelligence like hers, fit for me to look up to so – fit to be the intimate companion to my inmost mind. I had seen – and wholly understood – what intellectual companionship might be; such companionship as makes all other seem mere sham and makeshift. And it was snatched from me. Henceforth I would always be alone – and always know just how alone I was.

And I knew who had done this. I did not need proof – and a good thing, because there was none to find. Gwydion had provided himself, somehow, with alibis so numerous that they alone would have brought my suspicion down upon him.

No one else – not even my mother – would punish him for the deed merely on my say so. I blamed her for this. I thought it was because she felt motherly towards him, but now I doubt it was. She felt precious little of that for any of us – and he was hardest of all to love. She rather knew the excess of my feeling for Uscia, and suspected that my grief misled my judgement.

The fact that she could not follow me in my great pain caused the first ever distance between us. I spent more time upon the cliffs and headlands all alone, and we rarely smiled together. And, as though in natural consequence, before I knew it, just one short year after Uscia, she also was dead.

I thought that that, too, was Gwydion's doing. But it could have been the infection from the arrow's head it seemed to be. Perhaps the fault was my own – for not guarding her more constantly in my mind. Before long, I will make him tell me which it was.

She was grazed while hunting by the glancing shaft of one of her own men; a man who had served her since her childhood, whom even I could not distrust. She rode into the way when the arrow was already in flight. And the wound was nothing; not more than she had suffered, and healed, a dozen times in every year. At first the illness was not much either, so that at first she would not go to bed, and then would let no one wait upon her bedside – but it grew, instead of falling back, and ate away at her, over the weeks, until there was no way back. Then she let me come near her, but only me. Neither of us could speak of the parting we knew was coming.

If Gwydion's design was that he might be the only one left near to me, he was foiled in it by my mother, who had seen that we could never safely live together. In her final days, she gave orders that he should go to Caer Dathyl, the court of her brother Math at Tre'r Ceiri, and stay there with his uncle. He set out the morning before she died. I would not have wished him goodbye, but if I had not been unwilling to miss a single one of my mother's last minutes I might have come down to curse him. As it was however, I left my place by the side of her fading body and moved to the window just as he was mounting his horse to ride away. He could not have seen me, in the darkened room, and yet his eyes had found me out – found me, and my pain, and my last moments with my mother, and pried into them, with some uncanny power I had never before suspected in him. He looked up at the window, and his look was rage, ignited by humiliation into a simmering promise.

That is the first account against him. And now, Goewin Bach – let me hear something of you. What was it like to hold the old king's feet? I have reasons of my own to take an interest in the role, as you shall see.

GOEWIN

5

Before I took up my tale, I thought of you, stranger – in whose mind I had just tied off the start of it. I asked Arianrhod if I might fetch you, so that you might hear the rest, and perhaps hers too. She looked most doubtingly, but I told her: if we are weaving, between us, one the warp and the other the weft, it must be on a loom. Nothing better, I argued, than the mind of a stranger to serve for that.

She said nothing, but seemed to agree. And so – come with me now, up these winding stairs, to the room that looks out across the sea – and sit, quietly, in a corner, and listen. Watch the moon. It's my belief that Arianrhod has fixed it there, and that the dawn will not drain the ink from this night's sky until the double tale is told.

Well, Arianrhod ferch Dôn – here is my stranger with the open but unstocked and impressionable mind. We shall have a witness to all we say.

As you likely know, I was not taken by force from my home to hold the feet of the king. I chose to go with Math – though

I did not choose wholly. But sitting all day with feet in my lap, and nothing to do, there was time enough for shivered parts of myself to slide back into something like one whole. And then I knew what I had done.

All my life before that, if there was a narrow opening to be squeezed through, or a high fall to leap, a tree to climb, a thicket to be crept through, or cold water or mud to be traversed, I had been the girl for it. My skin had loved grass, and sand, loved to be rasped with bark and stroked by moss; loved river water and mud. I had loved to let my body follow my thoughts, almost wherever they might go.

And now it went nowhere. It sat, well weighted, while my thought seemed tethered within a not much greater range. And every day that the light crept in the high windows, the painful yearning to creep out again with it into the sun rose inside me. My muscles wasted, and my tan faded from my skin.

I was so still that I could not get the run I needed at any action to ease my captivity. As time went on, I was often bitter, and showed it. On such occasions Math would check me with a sharp 'Hey!' and a look or reprimand, that reminded me who he was and who I was and that my fate was quite sealed.

At other times I cried, and he was more sympathetic, and tried to cheer me. It wasn't so much that my days were empty – I sat below the high table and listened to the talk of the rise and fall and welfare of the rival tribes and *cartrefi*; even spoke up sometimes, as no other mere girl would have been indulged to do. I gained a reputation as a wise foot-holder for my years. Math was funny, too, a great storyteller – I loved to hear his tales of the heroic days of strife between my people of the forest and the warriors. I liked the way that we, the underdogs, were always the secret heroes of the tales. Even when they seemed written like propaganda by the folk who beat us, I could see that the hearts of the listeners were always on our side despite themselves. Every battle we fought and lost seemed a last stand of the magic of the trees and sea and stones against the dull effectiveness of metal arms.

Of course, Math himself had a little forest blood, bringing him his magic. He spoke to me of the deepest mysteries with which the magic arts dared meddle – of death and the journey of the soul. He told me of an Irish cauldron which could raise the bodies of the dead, but raised them dumb and hollow, the soul having been seared away in the process, like burning spirits. He told me other tales and prophecies of return from death – such as the story that, in times to come, a dark-hearted man would steal a hound and other creatures belonging to Arawn, king of Annwn, the fairy otherworld, and in this way gain the power to raise the dead. He showed how such reversals always stopped the turning of the wheel that might carry the soul onwards. Magic might sometimes steal a few brief days more of human life, but to steal so from death was to abandon the never-ending journey through earth's living forms.

I must admit I was distracted from the profound truth that he was unwinding for me, in telling this particular story, by his mention of the hounds of Annwn. I could not help asking what they looked like – and whether Arawn was a friend of his. He only winked at me. For he had a forest sense of fun, too, and would conjure me whatever I wished for: turtle doves to bill and coo and dance out lovely shapes between their rosy necks; a linnet to grip my finger and pour song into my ear; a pine marten to swing and leap from beam to beam and snatch scraps from under the noses of the feasting men – and, my favourite trick: a shrew and her seven babies, the tail of each in the mouth of the next, so that they wound their way across the flags like a dusky velvet rope moved by uncanny, many-souled life.

By the time I was sixteen years old, and had sat three years at Math's feet, I had seen each trick many times, and might see each any number of times again. Would my whole life be nothing but sitting and watching? Though Math was old, perhaps as old as the worn flags of the hall, he was a formidable magician, and, like the flags, likely to outlast me, even if my life were not cut short by the birthing of the children I would never have. My life was tolerable enough for today – but unbearable as a prospect.

I could not blame Math, when I reasoned it through. His very existence, after all, depended on *somebody* holding his feet. Quite apart from the natural inclination towards existence shared by everything that is, he had unselfish reasons too for feeling that his life was for the good of all his lands and people. His nephews, though active enough, were young and wild, with all the selfishness that that brings. Though already he had been forced to delegate the circuits of the *cartrefi* to them, they still had to defer to him in all great decisions, and answer to him when they messed up, as they often did. In the end, for Math's life, of so much advantage to so many, to continue, someone must play my role – and why not me?

But on the other hand – why me? I too had a natural inclination towards existence – and my life barely amounted to that. Math was mild – it might have been better for me if he'd been more tetchy – for he was rarely tempted into the many conflicts that a younger or more headstrong ruler might have got mixed up in. Spring might come round more than once without him going to war, when I would have had free use of my own lap for a while. I was shocked to find myself wishing for the murder and internecine bickering that might rile him up. But I tried to accept the idea that I would grow old, with no change at all, except that Math's feet might grow older still.

But one day I read a change that was coming to me on the

faces of the court. I knew those faces well. After all, I sat there all day with nothing to do but work out how to read them. Some of my time was spent in conversation with the ladies, or with the serving women. Neither fish nor fowl, me – women of all sorts, from princesses to scullery maids, talked to me easily enough, though never quite as though I were one of their own.

But the men, apart from Math himself, seldom spoke to me. They rarely even looked at me, in fact. Either they would let their gaze drift past me, as it might skim some wholly familiar piece of furniture, or they would avert it from me entirely. And no wonder. After all, to look too keenly at another man's wife is to challenge his honour. But to look too keenly at the virgin holding Math's feet – that was to challenge the high lord's very existence.

It is easiest to read faces that never turn a gaze back at you. Watching remains unwatched, and unabashed. I often thought how strange it was, that the more I talked with a person, the less I understood about them. In conversation I was distracted from the effort to understand by the effort to express myself, and I heard in what was said to me more about myself than about the speaker. If the words were not made to fit my ear, I made them fit.

But watching – as the walls watch – that's how you learn other people. I got better and better at it. Passively, without judgement, I let the faces of the court impress themselves on me, as though my mind were wet plaster.

Math's righthand man was named Aneurin – a man to get things done, rather than a councillor; to be out in the world, rather than whispering at the long boards. He had once had a wife, who had died in bearing his only child, now a ten-year-old girl. She lived with her mother's sister, in a village just below the town, but he saw her every day he was at Tre'r Ceiri, and was somewhat mocked for the tenderness of his regard for her.

He seemed to care little enough for that – or for most things.

I have said that few men dared to look my way. As time went on, Aneurin looked at me even less than not at all. Even when I spoke, he listened with his head aside. I was frequently frustrated by this, for he was one of the very few at court for whose judgement I had respect.

The faces I knew best were those which had flanked Math on that day he came for me – Gwydion and Gilfaethwy, the two sons of Math's sister Dôn – your mother's sons, my lady Arianrhod, though even I won't be rude enough call them your brothers. Your mother Dôn was my hero when I was a very little girl – I loved to hear how she led her people into battle, how every one of them, from swineherd to princeling, spoke of her with affectionate fear. I saw her just twice, but always remembered her mane of silver hair and the tattoos of flowers and wild beasts that trailed and chased up the muscles of her bare arms, as she announced her arrival in my village by hurling her hunting spear far ahead of her at the door of the great hall, hitting the very centre of the round of the great bronze knocker. It was said that Math was hardly needed on the circuit while Dôn lived. My father used to talk of her. He said she saved Math from the trouble of ever going to war by snuffing out each kindling dispute through the threat or reality of violence, or of the powerful magic that she was thought to use with terrifying unpredictability.

After her death, Dôn's sons at the court, Math's nephews, both commanded respect, or at least attention, in their turn, for different reasons. Gilfaethwy – Gilfa, as he was called, the younger – had the barrel chest, gangling arms and big feet that made up the best parts of a hero. He was untiring at his sword practice, and his physical size and restlessness made an impression in a room – though this was never quite matched by anything he said or did. He felt this, and was always loud and boastful, and occasionally cruel, in compensation.

He was in awe of his brother, Gwydion, who at only half his bulk, had a better claim to the space he took up in the world. Though I have said I knew both brothers well, Gwydion was in some ways still mysterious to me. His intelligence seemed broad and fast, and his temper playful and ironic. Both were animated by a stream of quiet energy. But I never could quite glimpse the spring of motivation behind the even but relentless zeal that drove him. He was always thinking, planning . . . to what end, or in what cause, I never could quite say. I only knew it was not love, or any liking for the common peace or good. He seemed to be almost fond of his brother, and yet to have contempt for him, which he often showed in quiet but public ridicule. It was clear that contempt came very easily to him. He was always polite to Math, as his king, of course, and sometimes looked at him with a warmth of respect that might almost have been genuine. But then Math would say something commonplace, and I would see the scorn creep back about Gwydion's mouth, and play there, and the momentary glow of affection I saw in his eyes would cool again to what I took for scheming. A liking for trouble was the only strong feeling I was sure he felt from one day to the next – that and a feeling for you, Arianrhod. Yes! I didn't need to wait to hear that from you. Your name was rarely mentioned, but when it was, Gwydion was absolutely silent. He would set his jaw so tight I saw it tremble with the force, and a little vein would beat, like a tiny heart, beneath the pale skin of his brow. Silent though he was, I saw no news could be told of you that was new to him – there was something close to an involuntary nod when there was mention of the impossible height of the towers you built – or even of smaller facts, such as your journey here or there. I saw, somehow, he knew it all already. But only once did he speak, when you were the subject. Math was entertaining a princeling from Powys – a good-humoured, handsome man with a well-oiled beard, benevolently intent on sharing his little stock of originality with the whole world. When the conversation turned to you – the rumours of your growing mastery of magic, and the way you barred the male sex from your door – he said he had hopes of winning an exception for himself, as a man of good conversation, and that magic was as good as any other hobby for a wife, and would keep you out of other mischief, and more ordinary men's beds, should he choose to take you in marriage.

As he spoke he reached for his cup of wine, but it was somehow knocked from his hand. It made a resounding crack upon the long board, and the wine burst, trickling across the furrowed oak, and the sudden silence. And Gwydion spoke.

'You will find,' he said, very slowly, his hand, outstretched low towards the guest across the table, with a tremor in it, 'that my sister . . . my sister . . . Arianrhod . . . is . . . not easy to impress.'

It was clear he had more to say, but instead he pressed his lips closed, and pressed his fist upon the table, and seemed to screw it down tightly there with the twist of his own forcibly lowered gaze. Those dozen words were the only ones I ever heard him speak of you, but the silence around them told me much indeed.

I learned also that Dôn had left two other sons, who shunned the court as carefully as Gwydion and Gilfa hung about it. Your brother Amaethon was said to hate polite company. I heard he managed a wide and fertile plain between Rhuddlan and the sea, and no one's harvest carts were half as heavily laden as were his. It was said he took up the plough, and sowed the seeds himself, and liked to work and eat and sleep beside the men who worked his land, as though he had been no more than the least one of them. Some admired him for his modesty in this – but others said that he could only bear to keep company in which he was always first, and where no one could hold him to account for the bursts of rage and viciousness he enjoyed. There were vague stories of men, and women too, murdered in anger at his hands – but these might have been no more than the snobbish rumours of an effete court for all I knew. No one seemed to know him, or what to make of him, and I could form no picture of him in my mind from what I heard. This was one thing I learnt from watching men, without throwing myself into my view: there are a few who, even in thousands of hours, we can never read – perhaps because they aren't stories at all, but brute facts, too plain for us to grasp.

Folk were too afraid to make idle gossip about your other brother, Gofannon. I heard it muttered that he too had killed more than one outside the rule of war, almost through the accident of the strength of his arm. I knew him as the finest smith in the land. Math told me he could make the best swords and the most beautiful jewellery for the body of man or beast; could make a man an arm out of silver if he found himself one short, and could craft birds and beasts that moved about from nothing but folded metal. Whatever the fancy could summon in air, Gofannon could beat out in glowing bronze. As well as such intricate workmanship, he could strike out the deadliest spearhead with three blows of his hammer. It was said that the force of his broad chest was ten times that of any of the youngest, fittest warriors. And yet he was short, with a face as hard and smeared as his leather apron, and he walked with a cane, as though his joints froze awkwardly away from the intense heat of his furnace. Gofannon of course kept himself to his famous forge in the cave under the Trysclwyn on Ynys Môn, never entering into politics or war, but was respected and feared by all, though Gilfa and the braggart youths affected to look down on him for his dirty trade and crooked foot. Sometimes when I was bored by the chatter of the court, I let my mind wander to the forge – the glowing heart of the ragged mountain. I thought of flames leaping in the dark, as dreams leap up – and of a furnace hot enough to fuse fancy and reality. My mind was wandering so, quite unaware that its presence would be required, when at last things began to happen.

Of course tales were told about Dôn's only daughter at this time too. You were respected and feared for unrivalled learning and beauty and pride while I was still an undistinguished girl. I would like to know how you passed those years while I sat at the king's feet.

ARIANRHOD

6

It was not at once I earned such a reputation. It took time for me to find my way. And no wonder. By the time you came to Caer Dathyl, Gwydion had been growing and studying in the court of Math for five years. And all that time, I studied alone, on the cliffs and under the sky. I nursed my hate for Gwydion even from the first, but he seemed far beyond my reach, under Math's protection. I nursed it like a changeling, which took and took, and ate and ate, until I was almost sucked dry. All I could do was learn. With Uscia and my mother both taken from me, the moon's was the face that I knew best, and the bosom of the ocean the only comfort I ever thought of.

And Gwydion had, it seemed, spoilt even the comfort I took from gazing out from my castle. To calm myself, I used to let my eye run quietly down the mountains of the Llŷn until they sank into the sea. They fell as softly as a note falls from the air, as the evening light falls from the sky. And yet, halfway along loomed the cliff called Carreg y Llam. It was dark, and plunged into the deep like a calamity. My eyes had always skimmed over its crouching back, but now – it was as though the shafts of light that shone down between the clouds directed my sight that way; as though the mist that hid the hem of the other mountains left it alone, crisp and close to my view. It seemed like my life. Abrupt, cut short in ugliness, aloof from all the other lives around that rose and fell in peace.

Yet on my own, alone with the moon, all was not changeless. I began to feel – surges – within myself. When I watched the tide rush through the strait with all that weight of water, growing slow and then breaking the contrary current and bearing down so suddenly, I recognised it. My anger and my desire for power ebbed and flowed inside me through the days, swelled greater, deeper, blacker as each month wore on. And for a time I was as full and satisfied by my hate as the sea sits against the strand at high tide.

But then the tide inside me would fall back again, and leave behind it a line of broken weed torn from the depths by the storm, tangled with branches and snapped rushes, and the bodies of crabs and birds. I smelt it like death, heard the alien buzz of the cloud of flies around it, and wondered that all that dark band of mess across the clean sand had been dragged up from my own depths.

It was unbearable to feel such shrinking dread of myself. I had to confront what was in me. And I knew where to do it – the ugly plunging cliff of Carreg y Llam.

And so I set off, one summer day, on foot, when the tide was at the lowest, that I might walk along the beach for much of my journey, and watch it coming in as I neared my destination. It would mean returning in the dark, but the moon was waxing towards the full, and with my lantern would give me light enough.

The day was warm; the sun throbbed somewhere behind a taut dun haze. I walked along the sands, the sea far out, and my destination far ahead. Both drew imperceptibly but steadily nearer as the brightness slid down the sky. At last I could hear the hiss of the sea, which crawled up across the beach in low, chaffing

waves. There was a chance it would overtake me here, and cut off my way forward. So I set off inland, where dune slacks stretched in a low-lying hollow.

As the hidden sun drew near the horizon, copper light leaked through the haze, making the sky and the sand and the skin of my hands all the same colour, while the sea was dark as lead. As I entered the valley, crushing the dry grey smell from the creeping willow, I noticed a softer scent floating above it. I saw ahead a host of tall wax-white flowers waving in the grass – and above them, a cloud of white moths, the soft shine of their wings fluttering free of the twilight. I sat down for a moment and lit my lantern, that I might look more closely.

They were albiflorous orchids. Each floret on the stem was like a flesh-pale insect, with a deeply hooded face, and a lap and wings spread wide, hungry for the clasp of the dusk. And they received the moths, which settled lightly and slid their tongues deep into the bodies of the flowers, where the nectar was.

It was one of those rare moments when day-time ordinary seemed illumined from beyond, or from within, as the waxy petals seemed to glow with a light that pulsed out to answer that of the sinking sun. Sometimes the loveliness of flowers seems a fleeting glimpse of some boundless ur-being which is nothing but beauty itself. Uscia told me it is Fairy that we sense in such moments. With her eyes on the surface of the twilight sea, she showed me how it swelled with revelation – of breath, and will, continuous with but far beyond what we can know. That is how things truly are, she said – beyond the dusty hanging we drape about our feeble minds for fear of too much light.

I stretched down on my elbow in the long grass, where the scent hung heaviest, to watch the coupling. My lantern drew the moths around me, and they alighted in my hair, as well as on the blades and flowers around it. I watched one flutter nervously in a shrinking circle, touching flowers only to float off again without tasting. At last it lighted on a spire just near my face.

Its feet reached for a flower – its wings were a diaphanous blur until it was still, when they at once crisped into folded satin. It unfurled the coiled length of its proboscis and drank long and deep of the flower.

But now I saw, furtively penetrating the moth's powdered fur, a translucent spike. On either side of its body, pale prongs stealthily extended. All around it, white needle limbs were slowly closing.

And now, suddenly, the embrace was complete. A bloated spider, pure white but for a blood-coloured death-head mark upon her back, had sunk her jaws into the neck of the moth. Her front legs hugged tight, buried deep in the pile of its body.

The spider did not notice me, as it sucked the life from the moth, and I did not disturb her at her meal. But the hollow eyes of the skull on its back seemed to search deep into me, and recognise me.

At last she let the dried and empty body fall. It drifted lightly to the ground. And looking down, I saw a little pile of white wings, like the pages of the twilight's book, scattered amongst the grass stems below the flower. Hungry spider.

Now another of the moths drawn by my lantern flame was fluttering near, ready to alight on her flower. The beat of its wings was intimately near my cheek. I might have wafted it away with my hand, or moved away my lantern, but the tide was drawing high, the moon was waxing full, and I had no mercy. I watched the consummation of another hungry embrace, and then picked up my lantern and went on my way.

I could see Carreg y Llam looming above the beach. Rough

grey tongues of sea were slowly lapping up the sand, taking more of it every minute. But still the foot of the crag was dry. I had to be there before the sea engulfed it.

I was flooded with fear of the place, but also drawn on. Shadow deepened behind outcrop and in fissures. I was drawn to the darkness, fathoming each pool of it, searching to see the hard rock behind. As I came to the outmost reach of the cliff, I saw another chasm, deeper than the others. I could not peer in without wading through the incoming tide, which licked hungrier than ever up the beach. The sun had dropped below the leaden horizon, and a night wind was rising, dragging the incoming waves faster with it. The roar of it came off the sea and back again at me from the facing stone. And from inside that chasm, another, deeper note echoed.

Still, I could not see all within without going through the waves. And I must. The sand was swept from under my feet, and the tide tore and sucked at my skirts higher and harder than I had expected. But I pressed on.

Inside the chasm the last light showed a narrow slope of sand, swallowed clean by the tide. I stepped out of the sea, and waited for my pupils to open wider that I might see into the dark, aware that I must hurry before the tide rose enough to bar my way out, leaving me pummelled against the rocks by the swell.

The stone was grooved by the pounding of the tide and the rushing of the wind, yet it was ragged still, falling in sharp angles into the sand. I searched it, seeing how far into it my eyes could still penetrate. Then the light of the moon shone directly in, leaving only one sliver of darkness at the very back of the cleft.

My eyes were fixed by it, so that the intensity of my focus almost made my vision swim. It seemed to me that the angles of the shadow moved.

Yes – I was not mistaken. A hard, angular fall of shadow was detaching itself from the back of the chasm. It was pure darkness, faceless – and yet it had a moving form, and slanting lines as expressive as a face and limbs. And now it seemed that the roar of the waves inside the chasm was its voice.

Suddenly it slid fast towards me, and darkness colder than the sea slipped beneath my hood and around my throat like a clutch. I heard a deafening whisper, not just close but deep within my ear, within that intimate hollow space between my mind itself and the booming black around me – and was forced back hard against the wall of the chasm.

'I knew you would come.'

The voice was a hissing roar, and the words seemed to be drawn out of the tide's sound inside my own head. The grip around my throat was as hard and cold as death – and yet I did not struggle.

'I am Llyr. You had to come. Your skin is as pale as the moon with wanting this. And look how I can draw out your hair into the darkness, until we are both awash in the ink of it. And in your eyes, and your open mouth, I see an ocean of it. The moon swells, and with it the tide, and your hate. And from tonight, your power may rise as full as the sea, as full as the wind that rushes off it.'

Now a wave surged in, and crashed off the back of the chasm and into my face. Outside the sea was only blacker for the moon picking out the crests of the rushing waves. Again, the wave surged in, higher, stronger than before, so that I was pushed back against the narrow angle in the deepest fold of the rock – though whether by the water itself or the grip of the dark I could not tell.

'Sun and moon are aligned tonight. They conspire to pull the sea high; the wind joins to push it higher still. Do not fight against yourself. Let that black tide come. All along the coast, the sea will rush higher than its rightful level. It will break its bonds. It will tear out the laced sea-campion that grows close along the strand, chew away the sand dunes, bring down slices of cliff. It will crack the boats left on the beach like walnuts. It will float away the eggs of the terns and the plover that nest upon the shore, and drown the chicks, drenching and tearing the downy balls to meagre skin and bones. You know you have such power in you. Call up the tide tonight – stay here to welcome it.'

'At what cost?' I cried, feeling that the moment of decision was upon me, as each wave surged higher than the next, and sucked harder at my clothes.

'What cost could be too much? Take it – it is yours. Stay here with me through this flood. You will not drown. And the sea and tides, as well as other nameless dwellers of the dark, shall be yours to command.'

I had moments to decide. I might still swim out of this black cleft, striving hard against the tide, swallowing stinging salt as the waves broke over my head, fighting the breakers, setting all my little strength against theirs just to reach the safety of the beach. Or I might stay here and let the tide and its darkness take me – take that crashing, breaching power for my own.

I did not move. And now the sea rose in over me, my head was pressed up into the darkness of the chasm, the water rushed in through my mouth and deep into my lungs, and I saw the narrow view over the sea no more.

Instead, I saw everything, far and wide. I saw the sea, spread dark over the curve of the earth, crawling with silver crests. I saw the water sucked towards its pale mother, and the lateral drag and bulge as the vast heaving weight of it lagged the steady turning of the world. I saw the winds coming, whirled out of the heart of a distant storm, driven by the warmth and cold of the churning deep. The clouds spun out and raced in towering ranges and shredded bars, pale and dark, through the sky above. I saw ships wrecked and trees torn down into the raging swell, the sea ravage hungrily along the coast, howl through the Straits and bore the throats of rivers deep.

I felt it, as part of my will. The lines the moon etched across the black ocean I could draw together or tease out wide like a skein of silver threads between my fingers. I might pull taut the whole wrinkled surface of the sea into a waiting calm, or, with one shake of my mind, rouse up an enormous swell. I had swallowed the lightless deep, and made it mine.

I was found below the cliff at low tide, a crumple of black cloth. The fisherman must have thought I had been drowned and broken by the storm. But his touch woke me, and as I shook it off I knew exactly where I was, and what I had done. I walked away, home along the sand, keeping the tide at bay but knowing I could summon it and all its weight and power whenever I pleased.

I began to build this castle, here, above the waves, without the help of sweating men and grunting beasts of burden. I found the dark eddies inside me could form themselves into solid rock, and as I built my towers higher and higher, I tried what else I might do.

BLODEUWEDD

7

They say I was a girl made of flowers. Another one of their stupid narrow human lies. How could you make a girl out of flowers? I've always been flowers. I was flowers forced into the mere form of a woman. So don't expect me to be some sweet pretty thing. Or expect it if you like, I don't care – but you'll be disappointed. Flowers don't care about you. I don't care about you. I don't care a damn for any of you, except the ones of you I hate.

It took one moment for me to fall into their trap – and it would take one moment to tell of it. What's harder to tell is what I was before.

I was everywhere. You've seen me in the flush of heather from sky to sky, from hill top to the heart of the hollow; that warm scoop in the moor, where moths meal their wings in my shaken pollen. Those violets nestling in the bend of the river bank, where the light ripples up off the water? They were me. The blossom bubbling out from the joints of the apple branches were mine too. And in the foam floss of the swell of kale at the cliff foot, binding back pebbles thrown by a million waves – there I was.

I drank the sun and wind, the parts you cannot even see, and made my own sweetness. Across the breeze I cast my coloured skeins of scent, and wove a gauze with hidden wefts of musk and rot, so memory might stitch tight into the very air. The energy I did not even need flashed out in colours bright enough to dazzle, and the reflected light alone, in glowing shades beyond your sight, was still enough to lure a billion wings, draw out a trillion tongues coiled tight like ferns in April. I made the gentle tilting of the earth about the sun a desperate plunge through brittle death, decay and back again, through all the bliss of birth and growth and fecund fruitfulness. I teemed, and blew, and blazed across the world.

But then, one day, men came and cut me up.

All seemed right under the sun. But then something gave, and the spangled network of my roots begin to tear. And underneath, as you might see the chopped layers of fat and muscle and bone in a deep wound, I caught a glimpse of time and place.

Dragged and clogged by silting hours and minutes below, like a cresting wave the instant broke. I was blasted by a shatter of sulphur splinters, my bark breached wide – my tassels of oak stripped, my meadowsweet ripped from the dance by the stream, my swarming broom blossoms struck out of air, and clamped up tight. A dark constriction crept through all the months, as you might feel a sepsis seep through every vein – it snatched my waxy daphne stars from underneath the winter sky, pinched out my June blue chicory flame, and quenched the bristling heat of knapweed in its fist. And yet the world that I had been was spinning still, a midsummer cyclone frothing sickly pale with elderflower and fairy's lace, and me the empty core.

And then the motion slowed – the spin skewed on its axis – the globe juddered to a dead stop, with just one final stutter of the sky. All that was left were piles of severed flowers: mild upturned primrose faces plucked, drifts of bluebells snapped and stacked, gouged daisies, all within a sour green circle on the back of a hill.

And within the circle there were men. They talked and laughed, and they were making . . . something. They handled the flowers; inspected them, touched them, smelt them.

And I began to understand – they were making a flower prison for me; a flower prison *of* me.

They chose petals of the rose to make my face – held each to their rough stubbled cheeks, casting aside any that were streaked or wrinkled or which a little insect had laced with holes. They sought the perfect blue for my eyes – knocking the pale-veined petals from the speedwell flowers, discarding and trampling forget-me-nots among the grass because their blue was bled with pink. They made my body of lilies, which they stroked with thick fingers as they fashioned its lines and curves to meet their wish. They placed bursting buds where it pleased them they should be, and squeezed them to make sure that they were firm. They made chains of daisies to bind about my ankles, secured them to the mushrooms that had made the sour ring, and left – me.

What was I – where was I – that I could so be left alone?

From strand to mountain top, everywhere, and always, I had been used to feel the gentle touch of the sun, and open to it. Now I stood on the hill – a stark figure in a narrow place, quite apart from the herbs that threaded through the turf to make it bright. I felt time pass, and was appalled.

And then the men returned, bringing another male the size of a man but with young awkward limbs; he was large, with yellow hair. And he touched and poked my blooms and looked into my flower eyes and ran his fingers through the broom flowers of my hair. Then he told me to lie on the ground. I hardly knew what he meant, let alone how to do it, so he gave me a push and I fluttered down among the grass.

Then he lay on top of me. I did not understand. These men had made me as I had never been – tight-closed and small and lonely, like a cockle on the lightless ocean bed. But now he tried to force a way inside, to bore a way through my new shell, though he was as alien as deep-sea darkness. The crushing pressure of not-me rushed in to crush the soft new self inside.

He tore and bruised those petals which the other men had been most at pains to make just as they liked. The perfect convex hearts now hung in shreds, quite grey.

He paused. But at a shout from the other men, he turned me over. And did the same again. And then he stood, and kicked me over onto my back.

I lay in the grass, and stared up at the wide, distant sky from my new, narrow eyes.

Then the yellow-haired man pulled me to my feet – he said I was his wife, and, harshly, that I should dress myself, in all modesty.

I only gaped my poppy mouth, and could neither speak nor do as he bid. But then one of the other men spoke to me, with a smile.

'Come, Blodeuwedd – make yourself a fitting wife for my handsome nephew. He's a lovely boy, isn't he, and deserves the softness of petals. He has a hard, frigid, unnatural mother that doesn't love him. She cursed him, and said no woman could be his wife, never thinking he would so soon have all the lovely tints and honey pleasures of the field and the bank to use as his own. I have made him a high lord, with a great name and the finest arms, and he's much more than you deserve – and you nothing but frail and wanton flowers. Do your duty – put on a decent gown of morning glory, that you may at least look innocent.'

He looked hard into me – and I found that I could do what

he commanded. I made myself a dress of convolvulus, that might have been silk; I made long bell sleeves to cover my arms and hands, and a funnel neck, so that only my face, and frightened flower-eyes, betrayed what I was. A chariot drove up, and they undid the chains of daisies, and made me climb inside.

It was a drive of horror. I felt what you might feel attending your own funeral, unable to touch or speak to any of those dearest left behind. We passed flowering meads, bright spangled with ragged robin and stitchwort stars, and I only knew they were not me. I saw trefoil and vetchling racing up the banks, and knew their vigour was no longer mine. We rode through the woods, and I knew I no more shared the secret of their flowers' luteal green.

I began to cry, and my tears fell as petals of larkspur. I cried so much that soon they flowed out of the cart into the road, so that it seemed a stream, and the chariot all but floated in it.

At this the man who had called me Blodeuwedd – flower face – and who now rode behind, his horse stepping high, up to the hocks in my misery, called a halt, and rode up alongside. He grasped the petals of my chin, and looked me in the face.

'Ah . . .' he said softly to himself, 'the summer is too much for her.' And then aloud, 'She must learn to . . . inhabit . . . her new form, somewhere she may be quite at peace. The crypt below Mur y Castell will do well. Let her stay there until after harvest. Of course, you can visit her to . . . brighten the darkness of her days . . . as often as you like, my radiant nephew.' At this he smiled knowingly at the big yellow boy, and they both laughed, and we set off again.

And so it was. We arrived, I suppose, though I was blinded by my tears – and I was led down into the darkness, and chained there. And there I stared into the gloom, which was coal black at night and grey as ashes in the day.

My husband came often, sometimes in the grey and sometimes in the black, to grunt on top of me. I could hear him snuffle my bruised petals, though in the gloom I could see nothing but the pale straw of his hair.

Then one day the other man, whose brow was set in shallow folds, and seemed just old enough to be his father, came with him. He stood aside, as if to let my husband do as he was used to with me, but today he did not. Instead, he undid my daisy fetters, and took my hand, as he had never done before, and led me up into the light again.

Before we got outside, both men stopped. They eyed me in disgust. My petals, though still bright, were creased and torn. The green had blanched from every calyx in my body, which gripped my petals now like pale claws. The older man, whom my husband called 'Uncle Gwydion', spoke to me angrily, or with an affectation of anger.

'Blodeuwedd . . . you shame every flower in the field with your slatternly appearance. Make yourself fresh and lovely!' Again, I found that I could do as he bid – my head hung, a water aven, and I made my body and clothes afresh of rue and spurge.

My husband dropped my arm when he smelt the new smell I made under his rough grasp, and I saw blisters rise on his palms where he had bruised my skin. I had not intended this, only formed the flowers I felt inclined to be, which happened to have these properties, but it was my first thread of comfort, that I had one power left.

The other man looked at me with some disgust; he seemed about to bid me change myself again, but with a look at his nephew let me be.

Autumn was in the rain that spat into the court. Horses were being made ready, and my husband sprang into the saddle of one. I was helped up to sit before him, and we rode out into the lanes,

Uncle Gwydion following behind. There were many flowers still, brazen flashes of hawkbit and ragwort among the waste of their long summer riot. An unreaped field of wheat, limp from months under the sun's eye, churned and heaved. The wind smelt of frost-driven birds. But September always killed me. The familiar loss was almost soothing.

The horse carried me about before my husband, and people came out to stare. Their looks were hard, and you would have been ashamed, but I was not. I felt only the gaze of the sun, softened by a grey veil. The dripping hedges seemed cast down to see me, and I was grateful for their dejection. When all the people had had their chance to stare, we rode back to the castle.

As we neared the gates, Uncle Gwydion slid from his saddle, and picked some of the little flowers that grew about the foot of the walls. I found that he was thrusting the bunch into my strange hands, which lay slack on the horse's neck. I looked at the sodden pincushions of mourning-bride, the lady's-mantle beaded with rain, and the crumbling spires of pale toadflax.

I held them, as . . . something other than myself . . . and the sting of severance was in their cold blue and yellow – the light that they cast back at things outside themselves. It grew into an ache, and a sob, as I recognised my new self: flowers, picked and fading. Gwydion watched, his gaze as piercing as the acid yellow of the blooms. His eyes probed like a wasp into every flower in my face. For a moment our glances met. He looked all satisfaction, and I knew that he had found the draught he hoped for in the hopeless sob of my blighted flower heart.

When we came into the court, they pulled me down from the horse, and they told me to walk around the muddy circle. I have seen an ungentled, unweaned foal straight off the marshes walked so, in preparation for halter breaking; panic in the whites of its eyes. I walked, and found the strange limbs they had made me carried me with only the occasional stumble.

'Walk like a lady,' said Uncle Gwydion, as I passed near – and I found I could do so. I walked like the ladies I had seen crossing the meadow, lifting their skirts as though they would never stoop to pick a blade of sorrel or a stalk of grass to chew in the heat, as if they did not pulse out fragrance stolen from the iris and the rose.

The people came from work to look at me, and I saw Gwydion and my husband smile with satisfaction. The regard of the narrow-eyed ramparts was like a weight on my shoulders. The lichened faces of the stones were dark with wet, but I noticed something pale stirring high above the entrance arch – a lone maiden pink, trembling on a stem too fine to see.

With my eyes cast up high, my feet caught, and I fell. I heard a gasp that might have come from the walls themselves. I pressed my cheek against the mud. It was soft, and cool. But Gwydion and my husband raised me hastily to my feet, and hurried me inside.

'Look at yourself!' hissed Gwydion. The flowers of my dress were muddied as though cattle had trampled me. 'Change! Put on a dress of womansbane, fit for the high hall.' I at once appeared in ruffles as deep as the night sky. Gwydion straightened with his hand the drooping stalk of my throat, took my arm, and walked me into the hall.

I was sat down, and food and drinks were placed, and men talked loudly, while my gaze tangled in the dry herbs strewn across the floor – a crust fell down, and a mouse darted from a hole to snatch it up and pull it back to safety in its hole. Gwydion sat by me, and told me to eat, and poured me wine. Both I swallowed.

After this my husband took my arm, raised me from my seat, and led me up the stairs to a chamber with windows through which the wind and rain of the dying year breathed gently. I thought perhaps he expected something of me – he never had before – but I only looked at the snow-in-harvest that scrambled so near the window. So he took my wrists, and pushed me down onto the bed, and did as usual, except this time he stripped me of my midnight ruffles before he began.

GOEWIN

8

I spent the last part of my tale telling you about your own family. I will fill my glass, if I may, and try to tell the harder part of my own tale – though I fear my relations, and yours, will intervene, as digression and diversion and deflections, as well as causes and explanations. Our own tale so often turns out not to be our own at all, when we look carefully into it. And once you're drunk enough, it can seem like the same story for all of us, over and over – of being loved, or not being loved; of affinity and strangeness, strength and weakness, neglect and care. But before you get there – before the wine has gone to the head – certain days come back, as rare and unforgettable as the first face we ever loved, and seem like the only place to start.

 It was the evening of the third Lughnasadh I had passed at Tre'r Ceiri – the ripest day of a hot summer. The bilberries were heaped like dark pearls along the boards for sorting. The women's fingers pinched out the leaves and flakes of bracken neatly, but the men only made fumbled gestures towards helping, their fingers fat and slow with flower wine. As their fingers got thicker the jokes got dirtier and the laughter louder. My attention was drawn to the one spot of silence in the racket.

 I was used to looking where I liked, confident that eyes would never be turned on me. But when I looked now at Gilfaethwy, I met the full rake of his gaze. He looked away in another moment, but not before I knew, as much as if he had bellowed it out loud enough to raise the rafters, exactly what he wanted to do to me.

No one had ever looked even the shadow of *that* at me before. The blood rushed into my face in two waves, first with guilty self-consciousness, and then with anger that I should feel any such thing. I found myself looking down intently at Math's feet, something I never chose to do. Now I was comforted by the familiar look of them; of the old blue veins in which the blood seemed to flow so calmly, and the cool pale skin, relaxed about the bones. I cradled my lap a little closer around them.

It was days before I dared to look at Gilfa again, but when I did, it was just the same. I tried to challenge him by holding my own gaze steady, but this time he outstared me, flicking his eyes down and up again across me and squaring his jaw in a way that shocked me into another blush, and another spell afraid to lift my eyes from Math's feet.

Now I knew in a manner what all this meant, but I had no idea how to spell it out, either to myself or to anyone else. I had never spoken about such things. Sometimes, looking down the boards, I saw the women whispering to each other, or a girl confiding in her mother, and I knew that they were fluent in a language I had never even heard spoken.

My mother had certainly never spoken it. She was hardly fluent even in the public language of Gwynedd. She was a stranger here – stranger even than you are. You could see it in her – her eyes, which might have belonged to some creature of the twilight rarely seen; her skin, which glowed like the lip of candle, and her bones and fibres, which seemed stolen from birds or hares or even frogs.

My father first saw her at twilight on the shore of the lake – she was singing, and all the birds and beasts of the forest had gathered round to listen. My father listened too, and then asked her to come home with him. Because he had listened so well she looked at him carefully – and loved him – and so agreed. But she warned him that if a mortal husband should strike her three times, she would have to come back to the lake, and walk into it, and return to the other world that was her home.

My father never thought of striking her – he cherished her like a song too sweet for any singing. They were very quiet together. They knew each other's hearts without the need of words. My father told me once that all things of this world have their counterpart in that below, like a reflection in dark water, and that she was his, and he hers.

And then Da was killed. If Mam was his reflection, it was as though a storm swept across the water – she was blown to pieces. For a week she wept by the banks of the lake, and I knew she would have liked to go home. She felt all alone in a strange world.

But after that I never heard her grieve at all. She spoke to me seldom, though all day the tension of her worry wrapped tight about me. And very soon she was married to Gryffydd, the foremost man of the village, who had always coveted her, but whom she had always shrunk from. I knew she did it for my sake. Though afterwards I thought perhaps there was another reason too.

I don't know if she told Gryffydd what would happen if he struck her. It would hardly have made a difference. He wouldn't have believed her, and he never acknowledged what she was. No doubt you've heard the stories of men who struck their fairy wives three times in playfulness or mere accident, and so lost them that way. This wasn't like that. Gryffydd hit her because he liked to hit things, especially women. And the third time he indulged himself this way she walked out of the village, wearing nothing but her smock and the bruises he had given her, and was never seen again.

No, I didn't say Math reminded me of my father. He was fatherly, but nothing like *my* father. My father was never an old man, and it was always *him* who carried *me*. Shall I tell you just one story about him? He was famed in war, but I know nothing about that – I only know that it was him who made me what I am, by giving me a store of regard for myself that has lasted to this day. Not for him, I'd be dead long since, or taking orders – not giving them to other people.

The day I best remember, Da had brought me with him on a journey through the mountains. I knew he would have brought me everywhere with him if he could, but often he had to ride far and fast. This was just a day's walk, over a pass too steep for horses. Nevertheless, by the time the sun was sinking my legs felt too short for the distance left to travel, and though Da was careful never to remind me of it, I was chivvied by the coming dark.

Emerging from a wood, we were all of a sudden on the verge of a lake. After the gloom of the trees, the brightness of the sky was lovely in itself, but that brightness was doubled by the water's honey skin. Each blade of marsh grass in the shallows tipped the surface into golden rings that might have fitted my little finger. The scent of sweet gale hung above the water, as warm as bedtime caudle.

My unease earlier in the darkening wood now produced an opposite reaction. I thought nothing could make me feel safer. And then I saw the one thing that could. A little island – so small that in ten bounds I could have crossed its length, even with my short legs. Its shore was mounded with peat moss, glowing green under bronze. Along its spine, a knot of birches flickered in the light, their shivered reflection crossing almost to my feet. A tiny island made for me. But I couldn't swim, and we had no coracle.

Da didn't need to look at me to know my thoughts. Instead, he lifted me on his back and strode out towards the island, as if the quavering reflection of the birches had been solid stone.

He did not walk on water, of course, and at first I expected he would soon be up to his chest, and my feet dabbling in the lake. But as the channel grew deeper he grew taller and taller, so that I felt myself on the shoulders of a giant. I was newly conscious of my chubby calves, as though, all along, they had been there to make my grip on towering shoulders safe and snug. He lifted me down from an immense height when we reached the shore, to set me down upon the roundest cushion of moss.

I rolled there like a kitten for a moment, enjoying the welcome of the squashy mounds, but I was soon up to inspect the rest of my kingdom. Following the shore in one direction I came to a range of angled rocks, cutting into the water; stepping out along them I saw ranked schools of young fish gathered to greet me. At the opposite end, the island trailed into marsh – there were orchids as tall as I was, which touched above me as I sunk ankle-deep into the moss. Each foot made its own dark pool, into which hopped tiny frogs, scaled to my island, smaller than my little toes. I watched them neatly scissor their perfect tiny breaststroke back to safety before I went back, afraid of crushing the mustered hordes hidden in the long grass.

I headed inland, pressing through the mesh of birch twigs, my arms before my face.

But then I was brought up short. On the other bank of the island was a man. I was about to shrink back into the birches, but became aware of Da standing behind me, near his normal size. He put a hand on my shoulder.

'Fishing?' he asked, and the man turned.

His face was still above the water, and I could not tell what were wrinkles and what the reflection of golden ripples in his face. He smiled – or the water smiled – and gestured towards a broad leaf of butterbur spread beside him on the bank.

The glitter of treasure – three little trout, so bold-spotted, fins clinging dark to their shining sides; hardly dead – animated by the light.

In silence the old man reached another leaf from a neat green stack, wrapping two of the fishes in it, as though he were swaddling a baby. He handed them to me, nodding acceptance of my thanks before I had the chance to make it, and turning back to choose from an array of gorgeous feather flies – shimmering water shades of jay and kingfisher, waxy earth colours of grouse and merganser, twisted into immaculate forms and lined up neat in a narrow box, but each seemingly ready to take flight on the next breath of air, their hooks curled innocuously like tails beneath them.

Da and I watched while he cast his line again. The invisible thread was caught in the falling light as it snaked high above the water. It hung there, golden – an instant caught in time as viscous as resin. A part of me will always stay there, on the margin of the lake, marooned in an amber moment on that island with Da.

And then the fly sank soft to the water, as mayflies will, and was taken by the pull of the glowing skin. The tip of the rod trembled, and then bent steady to the onward force. We crept away, back over the water, and sat down by a pale flat face of rock, and built a fire, and cooked the fishes on it. As well as my own fish, my father gave me all his fish's skin to eat, with all its bold spots.

GOEWIN

9

I told Math that story once. Sit near someone long enough and you'll tell them almost anything. But he took it from me like a gift, and seemed to weigh what he might share with me in return. When at last he came out with something, I could see he felt them to be the most precious words he had.

'You mind me of my sister, Dôn. Your face is something like her girl face. Hers fades and ages in my mind these days, and I'm grateful to you for freshening it. Like putting a flower in water. You have some of her ways about you, too – though she'd have sliced my throat before now, in your place, rather than be so long sitting still. A wilder animal altogether was my sister. She had her freedom, and she liked it – all her liking was for the men's world, from a girl. She played with the boys, and learnt to fight; rode with the men, and slept among them, lying each night between her chariot wheels. And so one spring, when I was away in Erin, my father sent a guard of men to fetch her by force, and take her to be married to a match he'd chosen – a yellow-haired boy, heir to more land than sense or strength. Dôn killed three of the guard before they managed to take her. And truth be told, her new husband died, too, in circumstances that were never fully understood. But not before he had put children in her belly, callow as he seemed.

She carried twins, and birthed them – Gofannon and

Amaethon. Dôn shunned them both, Gofannon especially, because of what she reckoned a deformity in his limbs, it was thought. When he was born with a twisted foot, folk said it was because she had put him out of shape with all her hunting and sparring, which, after her husband's sudden death, she never gave over from the time he was a soft tiny chick inside her to the day he pecked his way out. She hated them for saying it, and never believed it – and yet she was awkward enough still with the baby. I could see clear in her face, when she sat near me while nursing – she had feelings for it that she never could make sit easy. Most girls ready themselves for the like with their dolls. She never had. 'I didn't twist his foot, brother,' she said to me one day, 'but I did bring a thing that's nothing but need and weakness into the world – and the very sight of his helpless body twists me up inside.' She was mighty glad when he was old enough to toddle off from her on his uneven little legs, poor thing – though I could see the sight of him always working on her, despite herself. And didn't he grow stronger and more able to stand to himself than any other man in Wales, at last? He maybe got that strength from her wanting it for him so bad. For saving that, it was not so overmuch she did for him.

But she must be doing something, and so she set her hand to helping – well! directing me, more like, it should be said – in the managing of all things in the country. Ach, she was canny, and wide awake to the movings of those about her, as women are – but with a temper on her like a man's, to make those pay sore who she caught in any chancing. The folk were more afraid of her than of me, by far and away – for she executed her judgements, as well as passing them. She was a finer shot with a spear or an arrow than any man in Wales, and she moved faster with a sword than ever I could do. It used to seem to me surely enough the flickering of her blade was like the speed of her mind, the sureness of her aim matched to the sharpness of her judgement.

And so when I lie awake sometimes at night, and the past comes drifting up against me like mist out of the valley, I can seize on no excuse to cloak me from the curses she should have heaped on me for not listening to her – at once – when he came. She warned me and I didn't listen, and that's a fact I can never call back.

You never, Goewin, lay out on the ground on campaign, past Calan Gaeaf, and felt how the cold is sliding in through every place the clothes are not wrapped snug; sliding in, and creeping along, until at last you find it's everywhere. So it is when that time comes back upon my mind.

One Beltane – nine midsummers before you were born, just as the greenfly were curling the leaves and the slugs were fattening on them – this fat-necked youth comes to the court from out of the south, with enough brag about him to fill up the whole of the year's longest day, and make it feel longer and stickier still, like sundown would never come. Marak, he called himself.'

Here Math gathered the mucus from the back of his throat, and spat onto the floor.

'He had . . . gotten a name for himself. Down there they play at fighting as sport. He'd won every game, and never tired he was of speaking of it. His small triumphs were sweeter to him on his lips than any woman's mouth ever was, you could see that. It was as if he got his cock out to play with before the whole court, when he started talking on his deeds – and seldom enough it was that he put it away.

Though we have enough of real war in these parts not to make a sport of it that way in the usual course of things, he would always be challenging this man and that to a contest or a trial of some sort. You know men. They couldn't say no, though they were half-ashamed to be indulging in such stupid child's play.

One night, he was boasting again how he had out-shot every one of them. Every man and boy in court was tired and ashamed of the business, yet none enough master of himself to rise higher. Then Aneurin – who was but a boy at the time – called out, quite loud for a quiet lad like him, that for all his bragging, Marak could hardly hope to hit his mark at half the distance Dôn could do with both eyes closed.

Marak gave Aneurin a long look. And then he laughed. Long and hard. And said nothing. But the next day, when the target was set up outside the caer, he said he would shoot only against those who had never lowered themselves to pitch their skills against a woman's. The word 'woman' spat out of his mouth like a dirty word.

There was a silence, for not one there had not shared a target with Dôn in their time, and seen their aim look sorely wide compared to hers. And yet these men, for all they were a swaggering lot, had not one the courage to come out and say so.

And then, through the silence, there came a thrum in the air, and the cap flew from Owain Meredith's head. And then another cap went the same way, and another, and another, 'til each man clutched at his head with both hands, looking for the cause, Marak amongst the rest.

He stood near the outer stockade. His hat was safe enough, but there came another thrum, and he found himself pinned back against the wall. An arrow stuck out from between his legs, sticking his tunic fast to the logs behind.

Marak turned an ugly colour, and wrenched the arrow out, tearing a jagged rent in the wool. And then he saw Dôn.

She kicked her horse quietly forward, paying no mind to what had happened, neither owning nor denying what they all knew – that such a masterful volley could only have come from the bow now slung across her back – and she only coming as if it were to share news.

'A white hart was seen yesterday, lying on the bank of the Ogwen near the falls of the *tylwydd teg*. One of King Arawn's own, I'm thinking – but if it's so, the fairy king should take better care of his herds, for the creature is now in our land, and mine to hunt. I will find that beast and bring it down, as no man has ever done. I will wait until tomorrow, so that I make no advantage of my early knowledge, and anyone who thinks he has a better chance may leave in the same hour with myself. Marak! You are a stranger here, and do not know the ways towards that part of the river. I will show you, if you wish, and then we each may do what we can to bring down the beast, and we may see how well your faith in yourself is earned. At this spot, at daybreak, any who wish to hunt the stag shall meet, and set off together.'

Marak did not speak to her. He did not look about him. He only snapped the arrow between his hands into smaller and smaller pieces. But the next day, there he was in the green dawn.

And so he and Dôn rode into the forest together. And when they reached its shady heart, Marak took out his bow, and nocked an arrow, and with all the strength of his arm bent the stave until the pale sapwood was stretched fit to snap, and the red heartwood was pressed tight to bursting – and loosed the shaft straight through the heart of Dôn's grey mare.

I know this not because she ever told it, but because afterwards, at every table he sat down, he turned the stomachs of his hosts by getting out this tale to play with. He told how he shot her horse, and it fell, and she falling with it, the mare's dead weight bearing down on her – ach, but it turns me too sick, to be thinking that such details as those can only have come to my ear through his sewer mouth.

She would have wanted me only to tell you this. She was the strongest woman, and the fiercest, in all the land. Her skill with bow and spear and sword knew no rivals – she had the inborn aptness, the will, and the long hard training of the warriors of the tales. And yet, unhorsed, unarmed . . . Marak stood a head and a half taller than she, his thighs were thicker than her waist, his shoulders as thick from front to back as hers were broad across. Alone on the forest floor, in the falling shade, the greatest skill and courage could count for nothing after all.

She crept out of the forest torn and bloodied, with bruises blooming out like violets on her face and arms, and dried bramble stems twisted in her hair so tight it must be all cut off.'

Math looked aside, gathering his beard into his fist. I saw something rise in his throat – and rise again, as he seemed to force it down with a slow shake of his head.

'I should have been there – though she would have thought it treacherous in me, and resented it. Better yet, I should have shot him in the back long before that time. He deserved no more.

Can you ask? I couldn't wait, even to see my sister safe, before I was off after him, with the dream of his death boiling black in my stomach, but lifting my heels and clearing my mind to ice. What he thought would happen I can hardly think. He must really have believed his own boasts of the strength of his arm. But though his barrel chest might save him alone with a disarmed woman in the forest shade, if he'd ribs of iron I'd yet have torn his heart out from betwixt them.

He was off, of course, before she came out of the forest – galloped out the south side he did, like a rat from a hole in a barn with the dogs after it. And his horse took him fifty miles away before we knew his crime. He must have been sure he'd be back home amongst his own people, and safe from me, before I could get close.

But he made it easy enough to track him, by the way he crowed everywhere he stopped of the pleasure he had taken of my sister, and the hard fight she had given all in vain. It was a long way back to his home, and I might have caught him even without the use of any spell. But I made sure he wandered three times round about each heath, each wood, he came to, and always without seeing how he was led out of the straight path. He was like a fish swimming between my fingers, taking them for weeds in the current. I closed around his sides, and was soon ready to clutch him in my fist, and beat his brains out on the nearest stone.

At last I got ahead of him in a beech wood, and I thought his life was surely mine. The trees grew tall and open over the swelling hills, and I sat myself in the sand of a badger sett below the crest of a rise, and had him clearly in my sight below me as he passed, with no underbrush to lag the flight of vengeance from my arm.

I never saw a woman I wanted come into my sight with half the eagerness I felt when I saw Marak moving to me through the trees. His mare stepped with easy freedom under him. I thought how I would make her my own favourite in gratitude for bringing my desire to me so sweetly.

I thought to have seen him fearful and shifty, his conscience warning of vengeance behind every holly bush, in every ditch. But wonderfully unaware he did seem of the doom hanging over him. There he rode, his chest puffed out like a pigeon. My mouth watered all the more to bring death smash-down upon him, to wring his fat neck and shred that deep-piled cockiness in a shower of bloody down.

He came closer still. I blessed the sunlight as it lit him, turning the curls on his neck to treasure, warming him, ready for me. At last he was within my reach – the ache of want passed into action in my muscles as I levelled all my strength into my spear's flight. And I smiled and sighed in contentment, in that moment, as I saw it wing its way towards his heart, like a thrushle to its nest.

It struck true – or I thought so – and Marak fell from the saddle like a stone. And lay . . . quite still.

I knew surely that this wasn't right. My spear had cut through the body of many a man, neat between the shoulder blades like that, and it was never this way death looked as it came to them – floating silent as the gnats in the slanting light. I drew my sword, and came on him warily.

He lay flat on his back. It was only when I was stood right over him that I could see his face.

His eyes were staring wide – and surely they saw nothing.

They were like no eyes at all. They were a clear blank, without iris or pupil. They had a pearly rose and lilac glow within, and red veins wormed away beneath their milky skin.

I could make no more sense of them than they could make of me. And yet . . . I see that pink, not-seeing stare still . . . It was all I could do to wrest my own eyes back again.

I thought at first his tongue was stuck out, as often happens some time after death. But that thick pipe . . . lolling from his lips, with the skin sagging around it, bagging loose about the tip . . . was . . . not a tongue.

I saw a dark spot in the hollow made in his cheek by his slack-hanging jaw. A dark, splinted spot, like a patch of denser stubble – the end of an arrow, broken off close to the skin. There was another on the other side. The wooden shaft held that new tongue in place.

I looked down Marak's body – his legs were splayed as he had fallen.

And now I saw, all down their inner sides, a dark, caked stain. And I knew, at last and surely, how just an end she had given him.

I joyed for her – but I was sorely baulked of vengeance, and my only way of making up.

I could have cried like a child whose toy is lost. I thought of kicking the body – but it was no one. She had blanked him, in what she'd done, while my vengeance would have made the ugly fact he ever lived ring loud, somehow. Now that thing lying there was surely not a man. He had never, truly, been any more than this.

I sat down on a rise, and rocked myself, thinking of how she had enjoyed what I had missed. I soothed myself in thinking how it must have been.

I saw now arrow holes in his clothes and skin – two tiny twin mouths in the flesh of his throat, where she had passed an arrow in and out again without cutting windpipe or artery – a thing which could only be done by design, and with great skill. She must have brought him from his horse with a spear, and pinned down his limbs where he lay with arrows through the flesh, without one mortal wound, and set to work, with his screams like music in her ears.

I thought of her hunting knife – recurved like a hart's tongue fern. I thought of her hands – her fingers neat and sure – busy about their work. I wondered if she'd sliced off the bag whole, or just slit it open, snicked through the roots, and pulled them out, like a little pickpocket.

And then, to harvest his new tongue; like cutting through a leek, it must have been. Her knife was always sharp. Only the skin at the back, pulled tight in her fingers, would have resisted at all. She'd have liked that – the spring of it, the touch of hasty force she'd have needed to cut it free.

Of course, she'd have emptied his eyes, and cut out his tongue, only after he'd seen it all, and she'd heard him cry like a baby for his bat and balls. I remembered, suddenly, how she had told me once that a man's bollocks are the same size as short-sighted eyeballs. I wondered, with a chill on me, whether this is a thing all women know. And I wondered . . . had she left the sack swinging where it was after all, and were his eyes rolling there now, cold and glassy? I hoped they were, and that somehow they could see.

She must have meant his horse to carry him back home like that, that his own people might see his true face. She might have guessed I would cut him off long before that time. She might have thought so, and liked me to see what she could do for herself, after all, without any of my help, so late.

So I smoothed the nose of Marak's waiting mare, and hauled him back up again onto her back, with the stripped hazel sapling up his back, as Dôn had placed it, to keep him upright in the saddle. I was sure the horse was happier to carry him like that than living. She seemed to know her way home. I was glad for her, that she might play her right part in showing his own people what he was.

So Dôn had her vengeance without any need of me. But it was never the same she was, from that time. Before, she was strong and tough. After, she was hard. Hard, though her body was swelling again with the soft lines that come to women when children grow inside them. I could see the shame she felt at her own belly. She saw it for a traitor. I watched her many a time, sitting in this hall, bite her lip hard and raise her eyes, so that she might not see it, even on the edge of her gaze. Yet it swelled beyond the usual scope, as if to spite her. She carried two sons, the midwives told me, though she would not let them lay a hand on her. Would not let it be spoken of – the event, or the result either.

One night, as we sat here together talking of war, she rose suddenly to her feet, and moved towards the door. She staggered, and gripped the long board halfway down, but found her feet and raised her head and never looked behind. 'Don't follow me,' I heard her say, in such a voice I could not think to disobey.

The next morning she was in the hall again. Her great belly was gone, as was her woman's gown. 'Brother,' she said, her voice shaking only as the spear does as it bites the target, 'have your people look in the hollow of the cankered ash above the fall in the *nant*. There are two male infants inside. They are out of the reach of creatures of prey – save maybe the stoats or polecats – but they cannot last long unless someone should take pity on them.'

I tried not to stare too hard at her set face. I got up, and myself stumbled down to the ash tree. There I found as she had said, lying in the charred dark inside the trunk, two little babes – Gilfaethwy and Gwydion, as I named them, then and there.

They moved feebly, and the bones of their limbs were so small, and showed so through the flesh, that I shuddered to see their elbows and knees jar against the walls of that hard nest. It hurt me to look at them – or to look away. They seemed waiting to be killed by spite or mistake, eaten or crushed or drowned or bruised to inward bleeding. That they should be so weak – it was seeming to turn my stomach and win my heart, both at once.

At their navels were the stumps of the rope that had bound them to their mother. That weird colour, that only such chains between life and nothingness do show – neither green nor mauve nor blue nor white nor grey either; unearthly shadow of such colours, as rainbows might have in the world before light. They seemed to blanch and shrivel in the air before my eyes.

The stumps had been sliced cleanly with the sharpest knife,

and tied off good and tight. I thought again on Dôn's careful hands, Dôn's hunting knife, so near those small swollen bellies, paring away the cord.

I wrapped their bodies in the soft of my cloak, away from my sight, as quick as I could. Gilfa slept, but Gwydion was wide awake, and over the silver fur his eyes watched me – slate-grave babies' eyes. It seemed they were surely looking on me from somewhere far beyond what I knew. I touched him with a finger, as though it were to stop his judging me. He never took those eyes from my face, gripping my finger with his own; tiny fingers, so fine the light seemed to shine right through. I thought of the size of the bones inside – just strings of little beads, they must have been, under the flesh; more like the brittle trophies wee lads tease out from the pellets of the owl than anything human. The thought made me sick and tender all at once.

And so it has been, ever since. I have no children of my own, but have been something in the way of a father to those twins, never sure if I did it for Dôn's sake, or despite her – for my own sake, or despite myself. And still I love them, and yet sometimes feel them strange to myself – though that feeling comes now from their strength, rather than their weakness. I set out meaning nothing but that they should survive, and grow strong enough that neither I nor their mother might crush their bones to splinters if the will happened to take us. I felt – still feel – for them in their weaknesses. Gilfa because he had so little behind those cow eyes of his. And Gwydion because I could see his very sharpness made him lonely. When he was a little fellow that loneliness sometimes made him turn to me again, and take another tight grip on my hand. He would ask me sometimes – with eyes his face struggled hard to keep from spreading wide and dark, like dropped ink – why he had to sleep alone. Even years later, when he came here after my sister's death, I would hear him crying out with nightmares. I still hear it sometimes, and don't know what more it is I can do. I never was clear in any duty except to keep their little bodies safe from harm.

That's never the worry now, sure. They ride with me, and I see them crush, and maim, and rape with the others. Gilfa does it so gross it turns my stomach, and Gwydion so calm and subtle it turns it worse. But I never taught them not. I have done such things in war myself. Such is the world. And still we love one another, and pant for vengeance as though it might make all fair again at last. It's little better I can do. And yet I try quite blindly – and it sometimes seems I do it for her sake – as though a twist from my guts could ever make me fair. You know the story now, Goewin. Perhaps someday you might teach me what I ought to learn from it.

Free again, and back amongst the world of men, my sister at last took lovers, in sport, as a man might be doing – men she liked, who it pleased her to keep company with. The folk tried to make her ashamed, but she never was, and so they gave over trying and let her be. She had her punishment at last, when she fell pregnant yet again – I think she really had it in her mind that since she spent so much time in the training ground, she could take no harm there. But her last child, Arianrhod, was to her a symbol of her freedom, as well as a child after her own heart. She loved her, and respected her, as she never could her other children.'

This, I think, my lady Arianrhod, tallies with the picture you have given me of your mother's love for you.

I saw Math, and his court, with a little less puzzlement after hearing this. I watched on, still. I tried harder to be grateful for the safety which came with the stillness. And before I managed it, it was broken. But while I sat there with feet in my lap, did you inhabit your new powers in perfect calm, my lady, even with that raging sea so close beneath you?

ARIANRHOD

10

As for my powers – I felt, at once, that the time would come when I might need them. But for that reason I was never inclined to squander strength on trifles, but rather focused on learning to extend and control them. And yet – one thing occurred during that time, despite me – you are a woman, Goewin, and no mere girl, and so I will tell you even that which I once hardly dared to speak of to myself.

One hot day in summer, not long after I had embraced the power of the tide at Carreg y Llam, and as I was testing how far my new skill and knowledge might be extended, I set off to spend the long hours of light in study of the contours of the mountains. I was still hardly used to my strength, and sometimes felt agitated and impatient that I had not yet made use of it. I almost dreaded contemplating the things I might gain power to do. But I was soothed by walking, and by the sense of my own smallness amongst the great limbs of the hills. I stopped at last to bathe in the *nant* that tumbles down the back of great Wyddfa; somersaults, like the young stream that it is, new sprung from the sponge of peat and sphagnum on the mountain top.

Here was a ladder of tiered pools, each as round as the moon; the water gushed and plunged from one into the next. Harebells danced down the slopes, and mountain cranberries clustered on the banks, their red and white beads dropping into the water, where they span and sunk and floated again, before the current plunged them on.

The headlong tumble of the stream – the strong forms of its flowing motion, the folding and moulding and pleating and pilling of light-flooded water, over and into itself – compelled me. I wanted to drink it up and to be drunk by it all at once.

It was cold enough to numb my feet as I undressed in the shallows, but I was hot from the climb, and could hardly wait. I plunged, and heard my heart race, and felt the cold run through me bright as sunshine. The shadows about my heart were at once dispelled.

I swam the few strokes to the inner side of the circle, towards the bottom of the fall above, where the water was white and airy as swan's down. It was soft on my skin – almost warm after the dark water in the centre, and I closed my eyes as though I had just tucked myself in bed.

In one minute I gained as much in energy from the foam as from a sound night's sleep, and pulled into the full force of the current, beneath the twisting liquid bars that plummeted from the pool above.

The current pressed my muscles and worked my limbs. Its fluid force incited every inch of skin. I gave up myself to rushing cold and light and water, and gasping, closed my eyes.

I breathed there, alone, in the blank behind my eyelids, which seem the peaty red of the water's depth. I was nothing but my own sensation.

But then – a conviction grew upon me from out of that tawny dark. I began to feel I was no longer alone.

Not that some stranger stood upon the bank, watching me bathing naked.

Much worse than that.

This force that gripped my arms and rushed around my

waist and stung my nipples and pummelled at my thighs was . . . becoming . . . more than the just the force of water.

I opened my eyes and saw it plainly. Those smooth swells of current beneath the fall were biceps and triceps. And now the dark heaving centre of the pool rose as gleaming shoulders.

It caught me from behind, as I turned and tried to run in the clinging water. At once I was pulled down below the surface, and saw the light above me beaten into foam. It bubbled at my lips and filled my mouth. I felt the crushing weight along me, as jets and rills and spreading eddies rifled my body, and a clutching current held me down and took me for its own.

Desperation summoned all my might. I felt my elbows grasped, my ankles hauled, but I fought out and upward.

The energy of the water was enormous, and it took all my strength to strike for the pool's edge, and drag myself panting onto the rocks. And yet something in the creaming froth, lapping and falling back from the rocks, told me it had been content at last to let me go.

My body shook uncontrollably with cold. I could not bear to have it so far out of my control. I forced my arms through sleeves that clung to my wet skin, and wrapped my skirts about me tight.

And when I was dressed, I decided nothing had happened.

BLODEUWEDD

II

Life faded from the year. Mine faded to a sequence of repetitions of some part of that first day above the ground again. I rode out sometimes before my husband, and each time fewer flowers remained to wring my heart. I walked about the court, or sat in the hall, or lay in my chamber, where I watched the snow-in-harvest pile in drifts.

When winter came at last I was merely frozen, and was numb enough to walk in the gardens, where I met other lonely flowers, quite out of season – buds on the rose bushes that would not have time to open before nipped back by the frost, solitary daisies waiting to be crushed under boots. I was less alone. I liked also to walk in a little copse, where the bare branches told only of the wind that had shaped them into one hunkered form.

But one day a splinter stung the corner of my eye. I looked down, and met the full strength of the sun glancing from the petals of the year's first celandine.

I covered my face and tried to move away, but the roots of the trees grasped at my feet, which still I hardly knew rightly how to use. I fell amongst the dead leaves – thought it was over – until from amongst the steadying smell of death I caught a dangerous breath of honey.

Opening my eyes, I found myself lying amongst coltsfoot, jabbing leafless from the ground. At first I saw one, two – and then a whole host. The flowers were like coins flung in my face, kicks along my limbs, flames amongst tinder that would lick me up.

I screamed, but no sound came – gold flowed from my mouth – more coltsfoot, and celandines too, which flourished as they fell. My body heaved, and out came a stream of crocuses and aconite. The flowers found their roots around me as I tried to raise myself and run away, until the floor or the copse was as bright as the sky behind the branches. Every sob and gasp brought up more flowers, and so I forced myself to lie quiet and still.

I concentrated all my will into an effort to disperse myself – back into the earth, that the flowers might drink me in through their white roots, and I might blow with them in the breeze again.

But my lids would not dissolve, and though my limbs diffused a little, becoming rows of trembling snowdrops, I could not be more than my new woman-self. I must be somewhere, and a narrow where at that. My body could not drink new life from the earth and the sun and the air. I could not feel the tide of spring flow in and through me, but just watch it flow past – or worse – flow into me with no way out, so that it might scour my insides with all the fury of white water.

After that, I dared not leave the castle. I hid in my chamber. Even there I was pained by the irises and heartsease that some cramped hand had picked out in wool upon the hangings. And soon, beneath the dust and must of the tapestries, the springtime penetrated – I smelt the tender yellow of the primroses, the pure white sugar of the blackthorn hedge.

So, in my chamber, I drank; as that, I learnt, is how a woman dulls the spring – spirits of grapes and grains, and not the mead or flower wine which would have sent me spinning. The strength of that was enough to burn away the gentle scent of March.

But April! That wild smell shook the hangings, and green spears shot through me at every breath. I felt grass and nettles rising like a tide, heard tree buds crack their scales and burst out into light.

Despairing of doing the same, I made my arms the sea-blue stems of sleeping poppy. I took a knife and made a long slit across my wrist. The severed fibres pearled into a bracelet. I lapped and sucked my own pale blood until my senses drowned.

And there I lay, as near to nothing as I well could be. I did not note when my husband came to me in my chamber, and when at last he went away from home, and ceased to come.

But one day, the west wind blew straight from the bluebell wood. From out of the darkness, I saw the swimming sky on the woodland floor and the young lime leaves flicker above like swarming bees.

I could bear no more. I flew out into the court and out the gate, dreaming of burning wings, determined to feed the green leaping flame of spring with my own body. I heard a hunting horn, and I dreamed that the spring was running me to ground. I longed to be caught, to be torn to shreds, to bloom bloody across the brakes.

But I saw men, on prancing horses, and a pack of hounds. I would have hurried by, for they could have nothing to do with me. But at once, in a shaft of sunlight that broke through the thickening lace of leaves, I saw a face I knew.

I recognised him, though every other man and woman seemed as strange to me as moonbeams are to noon. I remembered how, as a boy, he had always taken himself to the oak wood when tired of his companions – and there climbed amongst my green may garlands, and nestled close to my shaded heart. He had hidden himself in my haze of broom, while his friends, jeering after him, tramped past unaware. He had stretched his growing length each summer under my foam of meadowsweet – I could still almost feel his weight, the way my stems bent close about his frame.

I knew then that if I might feel that weight again as a woman, I could be something of myself even within that bonded form.

GOEWIN

12

When the first day of autumn came, the sunlight sighed in slants through the windows, and the air trembled under the remembered freight of every fall that had ever passed. It was an hour after the early meal, and the hall was almost empty. Math's feet, like the rest of him, were asleep. I longed, as I had done a hundred times, to lift them gently from my lap, and run outside into the air. Another year had passed me by.

One of the few left in the hall with myself and Math was Gwydion. He sat apart at the bottom of one of the boards, lost in a task. He had, in a basket near him, a pile of fungi – mostly the hard white razorstrops that grow like cakes of bread on the trunks of dying birch. From these he was whittling neat little figures with his knife; I saw him try to stand one on its four legs, and watched his satisfaction when, by trimming a sliver from one foot, he made it steady. He made a whole pile of these, and put them back into the basket.

He then took out a pile of smaller, darker mushrooms, which at first at my distance I could not make out. And then I recognised them, unmistakable. Morels – neat, crumpled, dimpled spheres; little brains.

Gwydion sorted through them, as though looking for one to suit him. He took what seemed to be the biggest, and cupped it between his hands.

He pressed his nose to the gap between his thumbs, and breathed in deep. His eyes were open, and I watched them flicker with intelligence, as though he were seeing – learning – calculating. Then he closed his eyes, and breathed in again, drinking deep the mushroom's smell of flowery earth. He was reading these little minds – and the wider ones he made them represent.

When he opened his eyes, his face bore the expression of amused, serene mastery that was singular to it. His temple was fixedly inclined towards the sleeping Math, so that his eyes looked anywhere but in his direction. He placed the morel on one palm, and looked at it. And then he took a pine needle from the basket, and, with his head tilted judiciously, poked it into the tiny brain. He took another needle, and another, and did the same, giving the last the subtle twist that each such needle naturally has.

He then took up a smaller morel, and began the same process from the beginning. This time, he smiled, almost laughed to himself as he pressed the pad of his finger to the end of the dry needle and pushed it through the resisting surface of the meandering sulci.

When he was done with that, he began efficiently to pierce each of the remaining morels with one needle each, without taking the trouble to smell them first, but giving each an efficient, tiny twist. Then he put them back into his basket and, taking up a song to hum, carried them with him out of the hall.

The next evening I sat as usual at my place. It was dim, and had been so all day – cloud had blotted up so much of the light that there was little left to creep inside the windows, and the smoke from fire and torches burning all the day made the evening darker still. But the feast had been all the merrier to make up for that, and the fog of wine made the hazy air seem quite as clear as needed.

Gwydion sat in his usual place, by Math's side.

He had two different voices for use in the great hall. One was smooth and politic, and clear enough to be heard all down the boards. The other was a fluent undertone – a tone that, even while Gwydion looked straight before him down the board, carried the sense of a sidelong glance, a wink, a knowing arch of the brow. It was in that tone that he now began.

'So what, my lord, do you think Pryderi would be at?'

Math was in his contented after-dinner state, and blinked a little in protest at the notion of anyone being at anything. Gwydion's speculation often met with such wary welcome. And yet he was always heard.

'At? Straightforward fellow, is Pryderi. And a friend, though it's eighty years or more since we spent much time together.'

'Ah, so you'll be able to read him. They say he's changed, however, in that time. Straightforward he may have been – but who would say the same of Arawn?'

'Arawn King of Annwn! It's hardly for a fairy king to set up as a plain man. What has he to do with the matter? He keeps himself to himself. He took an interest, as you know, in the matter of Goewin here, but that was for reasons of his own which I'm sure were good enough: he could see, somehow, that she would play an important part for the good in the fate of both our realms. Certainly the result was much to my advantage. He has not meddled in Wales since before I was king.'

'He has not, indeed – not since he grew so close with Pryderi's own father, Pwyll – a loyalty they say that came before any owed by mortal man to man.'

'Ach, it's too late for a history lesson, Gwydion, I know all this! What is it you imply?'

'No doubt you also know that, just days since, Arawn sent to Pryderi a gift. A herd of creatures that in the other world are known as pigs, or swine – they say they are wondrous good eating, and make your finest ribeye taste as weak and bland as a water sop.'

Now Gwydion inclined himself very slightly closer to the king.

'What is more, they taste even better, it's said, when they have feasted on the bodies of dead men. Some say – though you and I need hardly credit it – that the bones of those they have so feasted on spring up again like green corn, and take up arms for any that own the beast that devoured their flesh.'

Math looked sceptically at Gwydion, but did not stop him. 'And?'

'Oh, I would not presume to impugn the intentions of your old friend. But, being an anxious and suspicious fellow myself, I would always rather try than trust, if trial is easily in my power. Don't you think it would be neighbourly in your old friend now to send a few of these beasts up north to Gwynedd? Pryderi is well known for his hospitality and the deal he makes of honouring his guests. He would surely give me such a prosaic gift without a thought, if I paid a visit and asked him for it. Unless he had some special reason not to grant it.'

Math threw his big head back a little on his shoulders, as though in avoidance of some flying object.

'You want to go all the way down south, through the heart of the mountains, just to ask Pryderi to give you some fantastical beasts supposedly capable of raising a fairy army?'

'Oh, the beasts are real enough, though talk of their strange powers and appetites may be idle. And the deer are not as plentiful as once they were around Ffestiniog, and there's nothing like the lack of a good steak to breed discontent and even insubordination amongst a people.'

'Oh, the people know me – little enough danger they'd kick against old Math – though I would give each a good dinner of the flesh of fairy swine for love alone, if it were in my power.'

Now I saw Aneurin catch Math's glance. His brow contracted slightly, often his most eloquent contribution to any debate. Math pressed his lips together in acknowledgement.

'Come now, Gwydion, what is your true motive in this? I might as well ask the reason of the stream or the storm and expect the true answer, I know, yet let me look at you and read it . . .'

Math's eyes flickered blue in their wrinkled caverns for an instant – but then it was as though a high haze of cloud crept across their sky, and his expression turned bland.

'Well then . . . you may give Pryderi my best. No doubt he'll give you the pigs at once, for he was always more than generous, and less than prudent. I look forward to savouring their flesh. Go speak to Dewi now, and see whether he has learnt any of the songs that that young stroller brought to us from Erin . . .'

'I will take my own men with me, and perhaps Gilfa too; he would be glad of a holiday. But as to those new airs, I'm afraid Dewi is a slow learner . . .'

And so the next day, Gwydion, Gilfa and the rest set out. You both know the story – No, stranger? Well, the details hardly matter. Pryderi would have given his guests what they asked for willingly enough, had he not vowed to his people never to sell or gift the beasts away until they had bred their first litter. Gwydion, however, convinced him that to *trade* the beasts away would not go against his pledge, and turned the toadstools he had whittled at this very board into a pack of richly caparisoned greyhounds, as lovely as the dogs of Arawn himself, which would have tempted any folk into a foolish bargain. Pryderi's court urged him to do that deal. But no sooner had Gwydion and Gilfa ridden out of easy reach with their newly acquired pigs, but the hounds became toadstools again, Pryderi's kingdom was up in arms, and the great war between the north and south began.

I was worried, as I knew what war meant. But it also meant

freedom from the feet, for the first time in the three years since I had been at Tre'r Ceiri, and so part of me could not help but be glad. With Math at war, I was free. I had so many places I longed to go, confidences I longed to share in private, games I wished to play, and cartwheels I wished to turn in the high meadows. They must have made me dizzy, that I didn't see the next thing coming.

BLODEUWEDD

13

I watched him as he rode, slipping behind the smooth trunks of the beeches, and back into my sight. I must not let him slip away. But the dogs were bloody – they had just brought down a hart – and they had as yet no new scent to follow. More than one of the huntsmen noticed me, a pale lily in the green – he noticed me – and I saw he knew me too.

I asked them whether they would be my guests – I spoke to all, but my words were only for one, and he knew that too. And so, as we rode into the stony court, the dull space shrank away like morning shade, and the distance closed between us of itself. Formalities were on our lips, of straw and meat and stabling, while our looks spoke of the bursting of the buds in May. I think I bid him stay the night, with all his men, and learnt in turn his name: Gronw Pebr, prince of Pen Llŷn. He looked into my eyes, which became the sweet violets he had so often laid his cheek upon the moss to look into – and now, as then, I felt him draw the fragrance from me.

I would have wound up about him as pink possession vine

then and there, clung tight around his body as woodbine. But there were cold eyes everywhere, and I would not bring him any harm.

And so, for all that long afternoon, while his men stabled their horses and hooded their hawks, I was decorous, steel sea holly. But as the guests assembled in the hall and the warmth faded from the day, it grew within me, so that I feared the jasmine scent of dreams of what must come might tell my tale at any turn.

I tore myself away from his presence while there was still much food and some drink upon the boards. Once alone, with my doors bolted, I became a cloud of flowering crambe, drifted out the window and floated down outside the hall. I could see Gronw seated at the board, and under his lids, his eyes seeking me. I made my face a musk rose and peeped right in between the mullions.

He jumped from his seat as he saw me there, and I knew he would be after me.

Beneath the castle cliff there was a shallow cave. I started towards the path that left the garden and threaded down that way. I soon heard his fast tread – my heart kept pace with it, but I dared not look behind. I was all pale flowers, gloaming forward in the dim only to melt back again into its warmth, that he might see me far ahead even in the fading light, and follow.

The mouth of the cave faced west, and the last light of the sky still shone in. For a moment I gazed into the deeper dark, and then, as I heard his step almost at my heel, I turned to face him.

I saw he wanted to take hold of me, but hardly quite knew how. I reached towards him myself, the petals of my fingers fluttering as though a breeze shook them, and in an instant his hand was gentle beneath my chin, on the harebell stem of my face, which he turned towards him. He stroked the apple blossom of my cheek, and fathomed the gentians of my eyes.

His eyes to me were summer skies, prising my petals apart with all the force of the ascending sun. His mouth was rain, quenching my parched roots, making me shoots and sprouts and crisp stems full of juice, where before there had been only hollow straw.

And then he was a growing gust shaking the flowered edges of the wood. He was a bee plunging the depth of the foxglove of my lips. He was a hawk with strong wings beating between the arching briars to my heart. He was both the field mouse and the grass snake in hot pursuit, darting amongst my milky stems of meadowsweet, shaking the crumpled petals of the poppies until they fell.

He reaped me to the ground.

And now I was only crushed and scattered flowers on the clay, and could not have pulled myself together if I would.

He was still, as though dismayed at what he'd done. But then he gathered me up, spray by spray, into a single sheath to fill his arms. I felt him breathe my scent deep into his lungs, and I was something like a woman by his side once more.

GOEWIN

14

Math had been at war a full week. I was alone in the hall – I'd been helping sort and wrap in dry ferns and lady's bed the apples we'd gathered in the woods, but the other working women had been called away – somewhere. I had heard hooves and the sound of hounds outside. I doubted it could be Math, arriving without greater commotion, but if it should be I would not go out to meet my renewed sentence of time with the feet. Instead I enjoyed the freedom to pace the hall. The apples smelt fresh as eglantine, though there was such a promise of autumn in their skins that I seemed to smell the season change as I counted the glowing piles.

I was startled by the slam of the great hall's doors behind me.

There was Gilfa, and behind him Gwydion, lowering the heavy beam to fasten the doors. I was immediately afraid.

Outside I heard the sound of jeering, and of dogs barking – and cutting through it, the liquid, otherworldly snarling of a cornered brock. Badger baiting would fasten the attention of everyone – even the women who didn't like to watch would be busy checking rising trouble amongst the men. Already the din was growing. Even if I could reach the window, there was no chance anyone would hear me call for help.

I measured my enemies. Gilfa looked confused – his cheeks were red blocks, dry as sand, his fists clenched by his sides. But

Gwydion smiled with what almost seemed like sympathy at me, and advanced.

'A fine day to bait a badger. The men and hounds who rode with us will be happy to change their role of quarry for that of hunter. Running away puts a chill in the blood that needs something to warm it away. And enough trouble we've had in stealing these fairy swine. You'll likely guess for whose sake. Yes: this war was always getting at one skinny little bitch, not a handful of fat sows.'

He smiled again. I stood at the end of the hall, with nothing between myself and the two brothers.

Now I darted behind the long board that ran all down the south side, leaving my shoes behind me so they wouldn't slow me down. I thought of hares. I knew I had my own turn of speed, and had worked on how to use it. The hall was long enough for me to bolt from them, but small enough that my more nimble size and explosive pace might give them a run for their money. I danced on my toes, ready.

Gwydion looked back at his brother with a performance of wonder. Gilfa looked back. And then he looked at me – the way he had the last year past.

He sprinted for one end of the long board. I was out from behind it and across the hall before he had halfway gathered speed.

Gwydion stood at the bottom of the hall, still as a tree. He didn't seem set to intervene.

Behind the boards along the north wall, I grabbed apples in both hands and threw them as hard as I could at Gilfa's head. I hit his shoulders – he grunted; they must have hurt – I smelt clean juice.

I threw another volley, hitting him in his face, which got redder still, his eyes watering with pain. I thought there might somewhere be a knife amongst the piles, and sent my eyes racing in search of it, but then saw Gilfa move again.

He ran round the top of the hall, and I ran down the side, still so far ahead that I stopped to pelt apples back at him with all my might. I bruised his pride as well as his body; his face twisted, and I thought I heard him growl – though it might have been the dogs outside. Anger froze him, and then moved him on with a new force, but I was still far too quick for him, keeping almost the whole breadth of the hall between us, and keeping up my hail.

Now Gwydion laughed – Gilfa heard it, and looked back at his brother without checking his pace. He smashed into the end of the table, so that the pyramids of unwrapped apples shook and then bounced down across the floor. Outside I heard the hissing gurgle of the badger at bay, and the crowd's shouted encouragement to the dogs.

Groaning from the collision with the hard oak boards, Gilfa lurched after me again. But now his big-booted feet tripped and slid and turned amongst the apples, while I danced among them easily, chipping them up at him with my bare toes. For a moment he was on hands and knees, and then up again and after me. I ran straight down the hall again full speed, and as he sprinted after me the momentum made his next fall a hard one – he slipped on an apple and flew down on his face. I turned, and heaving up a sack of lady's bed, swung it at his head. It was soft, but certainly served to further bewilder him, as I darted back to the other side of the hall and looked about me once again for a knife. I could not see how he was ever likely to catch me, and was not without hope that I might finally beat the small sense he had out of his head with my continual rain of apples, even if no knife came to hand. I shied a full basket of wrapped windfalls at him, and almost laughed to see how the scores of them rebounded off his body, as the basket span around his ears and came to rest on his shoulders, covering his head.

'What chaos – what a shame to bruise so many good apples!' Gwydion now moved down the middle of the hall, selecting one and biting into it.

'Little brother – this, you know, you really must do for yourself. I cannot drink for you to slake your thirst, or take a piss for you when you are near to burst, and neither can I rape a woman for you. I thought traipsing the length of Wales, and swindling dear old Pryderi out of those delicious brutes of his, and starting a war on your behalf might be enough. But still I must do more for you, must I?'

Gilfa raised his hands to lift the basket from his head. But then he paused. I watched, as a tremor seemed to pass through his body. I glanced at Gwydion – he had set down his apple, and made a pointed gable with his fingers, which he was rubbing against his chin. His eyes were closed, his eyebrows raised, as though in peaceful thought. Then he blew across his fingertips.

I looked back at Gilfa. His head had sunken forward under the weight of the basket, his shoulders hunched up behind, thick and broad. He made as if to raise himself, pressing his knuckles on the floor and locking his elbows. Again, a tremor – and looking at his hands, I saw his bent fingers fuse into two dark blocks of nail, his thumbs into a third. Dense hair sprouted from his bare arms, and his spine rose into a high sharp ridge. His legs shrunk up into his body, narrowing and shortening, while thickening his trunk. He gave his head a shake, and the basket flew from him.

Instead of Gilfa's familiar face, I saw a long snout, pointed ears and red eyes smouldering under a narrow, protruding brow. His leathery upper lip was curled upwards on each side by yellow tusks. As he looked at me, knotted muscles bulged along his neck.

He arched his ridged back, and his clothes split along the seams and fell. His form sloped upwards from a brush of a tail to a vaulted mound of thick-haired brawn – a brindled wedge of force.

And now he sprang towards me like a rock from a catapult. I ran to get the board between us, but he was under it, overturning it with the ridge of his spine. I dared not look back, but I knew he was only bounds away from catching me. I felt him at my heel. Outside I heard a guttural screech and frenzied cheering.

Hooves on my back knocked the air from my lungs, and then I was down on the floor amongst the apples and dried fern, with a terrible weight on top of me. On each side of my head was a dark hoof, a bony bristled bar of foreleg. Hooves scrabbled at my skirts, and coarse hair scratched the skin of my thighs.

I could feel my pelvis pressed so hard into the floor I thought that it might crack – I could not hope to wriggle away. But my arms were free, and I punched out sideways with the bones of my arms against the jointed forelegs with all my might.

One of them gave, so that the beast kneeled on that side – and my whole body echoed with a deep grunt of pain and rage, reverberating through my ribs and chest so that it almost seemed my own.

Now wet heat was on my nape, breath through my hair, and long tusks closed against my skin. The jaws were wide and strong enough to crush my neck in one snarl, but instead they grasped it, irresistibly. Further down, something hard and blind was rooting.

Now that there was nothing else to be done, I started to scream, and screamed on, above the frantic growling from the badger nearing its end, and the excited yelping of the hounds.

Why look at me like that? Do you think I ought not to tell it? Should I swoon at the very thought, perhaps – or turn my eyes down in shame as I stammer out evasive, incoherent fragments? Well, I don't feel guilty or tainted. The only reason I can imagine that I shouldn't tell is if my listeners are like to enjoy the thought of my degradation – to wish me to lose. You don't, do you?

I resolved right there, still pinned by the beast's weight, my teeth clacking as it ripped and pounded into me, that I would not let shame or horror inside myself. *That*, at least, I was nimble and strong enough to resist. It felt suddenly that the rasping screams tearing from my throat only guided him the way to hurt me deeper. So I stopped, and steadied my gaze on the hall and the apples and the dancing motes in the beam from the window, even as my body was jolted by the desperate thrusts of the animal on top of me.

At last he shuddered to a stop, and was still. I knew he must see the same long hall about us that I saw, the same rosy apples, the same beam from the narrow window. Nothing was changed. I was not changed. He could not change me. I heard the life rattle out of the badger outside, and the noisy triumph of the hounds. I had no intention of dying.

But now there was a sandaled foot and ankle between me and the apples and the dancing motes. Gwydion stood, head on one side, looking down on us with some amusement.

'They tell me boar stay locked inside the females they have taken for some long while afterwards by the excess of their own inflammation, even after it is more than satisfied. It gives them time to think on what they've done, I suppose. But I imagine you two have had more than enough of each other already.'

He steepled his fingers before his chin again, and pursing his lips, sucked in air. The beast shrank out and away from me, and instead there was Gilfa, grovelling on his hands and knees, naked and sweating. I kicked furiously backwards at him – he grabbed my heel, wrenching my leg around, but I pushed myself up and kneed him in the face with all my might.

He dropped my foot, and I saw blood from his nose gush out from between his fingers as he still kneeled there, and I stood over him. I watched his blood spread and pool in the hollows of the flags; flood over and hide the stain made by my own. But then I heard Gwydion's laugh again.

'Get up, little brother, before she spoils your good looks any further. You've not got the talent for rape, it seems, and might want to give charm a try next time.'

And then – he looked from his grovelling brother to me. I sprang for the nearest window, which was on the side from which I'd heard the badger baiting. I could reach the frame with my hands, and my bare feet found crannies to propel myself upwards. I screeched for help with all the searing shrillness of feminine panic, screamed, 'Rape! RAPE!' that all the world might hear me. But I felt myself pulled backwards by my dress – into Gwydion's arms. His hand was clamped over my mouth, and as he pushed my face against the wall, and I saw, from the crushed corner of my eye, Gilfa rising with a new smile to join his brother, fear overwhelmed me at last.

And then a rattling of the great oak beam that closed the entrance – the sound of spear hilts hammering the doors, angry men and anxious women's voices. Gwydion let go of me, with a shrug of resignation. I saw no sign of frustrated desire in him – I thought perhaps he had only meant to shut me up, whatever that might take.

'That badger died before his time. Not you though. Think a bit, before you sow trouble between me and my uncle over this, will you, girl? You know you'll be despised if you tell it all. They'll pity you and laugh at you by turns. Say nothing and you may yet keep your place.'

I looked away from him, and he proceeded to the door, where he lifted the great bar, and let the people in.

I am not quite like you, Arianrhod. I must admit that at first I thought only of my own survival, on almost any terms. Though I would have liked to run away and hide, I knew such a course might be fatal. I could feel sympathy and protective anger raised on my behalf amongst the crowd. I knew I must accept it warmly now on its own terms in case it should be soon withdrawn.

Perhaps you think I should not have been able to think about survival in such a moment. I heard it whispered at the time that a true-feeling woman should have been more broken. But I'd rather not depend on love and respect that relies on my injury and weakness; I find such kindness tends to raise and drop the pitied victim according to convenience. As I told you: I had determined not to let this kill me; that it should be others who would pay. I was resolved to win recognition of my wrong, which was still wrong even if I had survived it. I was galvanised to make it so.

And so when the people came in, I let those I trusted most come close, and comfort me. I was surprised by some of the faces in which I found the truest sympathy. Many a woman I thought had never liked me now conveyed, through a shake of the head or a pressure on my hand, a profound sympathy that was new to me. When I saw the anger of some of the men – even, or especially, of some of those most quiet and meek by habit – I was glad to find, for their sake, that Gwydion and Gilfa had somehow made themselves scarce. There would be a surer path to truer vengeance than the rashness of their plans, which seemed to soothe their feelings most when they made least practical sense.

I told what had happened in the plainest words to any who would listen, without leaving anything out. I hoped that the sheer honesty of my account would make folk believe me. The part about the boar, it's true, was hard to swallow. Some thought I exaggerated, or was deranged by the terror of the moment; others thought I lied. On one level, even *I* thought I lied. But when I let some of the women undress me, and put me, shivering, into a warm bath, they saw my bruises and found bristles from the boar still in my hair and stuck to my body. With my permission they showed these last and told everyone who would listen what they had seen.

By the time I was dry and newly dressed and somewhat steady again, I was confident that the best part of Tre'r Ceiri was firmly on my side. I was even confident enough to ask for help in the plan which had started forming in my mind.

I knew too well that Math, on his return, would dwindle quickly if no one suitable was at hand to hold his feet. And with Math gone, what would be my position? And what of the people?

The answer to this question was not absolutely clear. Math had four nephews, and a niece also, who had a reputation as a powerful sorceress, despite her youth. And there were others, too, who might hope to succeed him as king of Gwynedd. But it was certain that Gwydion would seek the role for himself. He would have studied his chances far better than I had. If he thought himself unlikely to succeed, he would find a new footholder to prolong Math's life – a footholder chosen in one way or another to his own advantage.

Whether Math should live or die, the worst possible

outcome was that he would dwindle many days in weakness under Gwydion's influence. I had to stop this at all costs. And I wished, too, that Math might live – I was fond of him, and he was a better ruler than those I had met who were likely to replace him.

I cared, also, for her who might be the next footholder, if there was to be another. Many times I had heard Gwydion tell his uncle that that role must be a role for life; that to change one virgin for another might risk falling under the curse. I now strongly doubted the truth of any of this. If Math could change once – as my rape would compel him to – he could change again.

And the horror of the role of footholder came only from its permanence. I thought I might find not one, but several women for whom a spell of a year or less in the high hall of Gwynedd, hearing and even joining in the council of the powerful of the land, might not seem an unwelcome prospect. But I had to make clear the reality of such a life truly and fully, as no one else could do, before tempting any other to accept it.

If I could find someone – the right person – to take on the role, and have her ready at hand by Math's return – to be brought forward only if it were offered to them on the limited and temporary terms that I conceived – I thought that I might extend my influence over Math for the present and future both, and help to secure myself and the country against Gwydion.

At first I made enquiries in the village. And then, seeing, as I had anticipated, that my task would not be as easy as all that, I asked that Eponwen might be saddled and made ready for a journey, laden with all I might need for many days upon the road, and perhaps some nights under the stars.

It was very difficult to dissuade some of the men, many of whom were still flushed with defensive fury on my behalf, from coming with me – but I knew this was a task for me alone, and reminded them that no harm could come to me on the back of my true mare.

I found great comfort in having a thing immediately to set about, and was almost happy as I hurried to find Eponwen at the stable gate. It was only when I saw the remains of the baited badger – abandoned there, since the moment my cries for help had made themselves heard – that I felt my weakness.

The margins of the lines of black and white along its nose were still uncannily pure. The curve of its back under the gently graded brindle of its fur was soft and limber. But hanks of coat were missing, and there were long tears in the skin showing layers of fat and flesh and muscle, in such an obscene diversity of textures and tones of red and pink and pale as never should be seen. I saw torn and bleeding teats, and feared she might have been a mother. I saw the strong paws – such tough and well-made little padded shovels to shift a ton of earth – and the neatly curved claws – now matted with tufts of fur of many colours from her fight against the dogs. She had fought hard. At the centre of the white shield of her forehead was a crimson star.

I retched against the stones of the great hall. Then I cried for the badger, and a little for myself. And that ache, which was in my heart, was dull and wearisome in my back as well. Too heavy an ache to stand under. I sat down in the dirt, as the walls around me quivered as though reflected in water, and the blue sky seemed to flare up through violet to a bright white too strong for my eyes.

I sat there, eyes half closed, while the time passed at a pace I could not measure. At last there was a hand on my shoulder.

Geraint, who tended the stables when his rheumatism and his love of drink allowed it, looked down on me with bleary sympathy.

'I'm afraid . . . I need help . . . again,' I said, hardly able to explain my trouble, but the old man knelt and got his arms under

me, and lifted me. He staggered a little under my weight and last night's whisky, and then set off plodding steadily back towards the hall. I was soothed to be gathered up in the smell of spirits on his breath.

He hollered to a knot of urchins at the corner that they should fetch Owena, the wise woman, and fetch her quick, and by the time we reached the hall there she was. Owena was always ready.

Her brusqueness recalled me to myself a little. She daunted me by being so busy, but she called me *cariad* too, in her gruff way. She asked me to tell her where it hurt – tapped the place on my back gently with her thorn-stuck, leaf-stained fingers – and shook her head and clicked her tongue when she saw my wince. And then I saw tears in her eyes, methodically blinked back.

'Bechod. This is bad fortune, *cariad bechan*. It is an infection – not caught from the beast himself, but only from him treating you so roughly, as no woman was made to be treated. But I'll look after you. No fuss now, ye? Get you back in the bath, that's the best place for you. I've all of the help from the forest and field, new gathered on midsummer's day just past, to carry you through it. We'll get through together won't we, ye? Look at me, *cariad*. It'll get worse before it gets better, but we'll get through.'

I let her put me in a tepid bath, and watched quiet while she cast in herbs, dry ghosts of their summer selves. In the water they came alive again. The marigolds smelt brassy like their petals. The nettles, whose hair-fine needles had been gentled down by age, became green and sharp once more. The couch grass unfurled its tangle. I thought of blind white roots thrusting scentless through the soil. The crumpled mallow sprang into pink love hearts with purple veins. What was this strange life I floated in?

Suddenly shivering, I tuck myself into the warm water, and my eyes close themselves. I slip, boneless, down through the tiered branches of a tall tree. I am a raindrop sliding slowly criss-cross down a glossy leaf, my coherence quivering with tension as I hang plumping on the tip.

And fall.

And the falling drop is caught in a copper pot.

There I grow aware that the pan is set upon the fire, the water is slowly coming to the boil, and yet I cannot rouse myself to clamber out.

At last someone comes and overturns the vessel, and I dream I am splashed out sprawling, a stack of hot bones under skin.

I know that he is coming and I must hurry to get away.

But I cannot go naked: I rub myself dry and try to pull on my clothes, but my limbs are still sticky with heat, so the clothes cling on my arms and legs. I pull harder, coaxing them on to me, but they twist and stick, and I am merciless and pull off the skin as I drag them on, leaving the softest places raw.

I run helter-skelter into the great hall, but there are other rats fleeing ahead of me. The great door is barred, and so they squeeze their bodies through the narrow chink under the oak. Their hides tug at the parched splinters of the grain as I wait my turn, dancing from foot to foot, until at last I know that it is too late and he will be there before I am safe away.

I am in bed, with an ember of pain between my legs. Whenever I breathe, it fans it to a glow, so I hold my breath. But at last I gasp up air, and it burns hotter, redder, until at last I tumble out of bed and search frantically for the piss pot.

The swirl around the walls of the pot is red as rubies. But it is such relief I want to keep on pissing, to piss myself away. When I am finished, though, I find that the stream has not put the ember out. It still winks wicked in my dark inside, ready to feed off my breath. It will not let me rest – it pries my lids apart; I cannot sleep, and cannot forget it, even for one moment.

And I reach blindly for the pot again. But all the while the dull pain in my back and beneath my pubic bone watches stolid, and the ember waits to leap back into flame. Soon even this relief is gone, and it feels as though all that flows out of me is molten rock. At least the burn keeps sleep and dreams away – until I can resist no longer and the very heat fuses pain and sleep together.

I crawl back into bed, and curl myself into a ball around the hurt. I feel my kneecaps hard under my palms, and hug them close for comfort, but as I shiver beneath the sheets and lose myself, I know that he will come again, and this time I cannot fight or run.

I shrink smaller and tighter, my only hope to snuff myself away.

Am . . . I . . . gone? Hands reach out. Something recoils. A name called. Something feebly resists the claim.

It limps and flutters away, along the ashy banks of a dry river bed, towards a dead and sunken sea.

But at last it hears a name that might be mine, and I am aware of something out beyond the pain.

I see Owena, calm and quiet, looking me judiciously in the face, and I smell lavender, cleaner than the sky, in the cloth she holds to my brow.

'You stay here now, *cariad*, ye? That was close, we nearly lost you. But I got fast hold of you now.'

At last – at last – the lava seems to cool a little . . . and then to harden and to shatter, and I feel I am full of shards of flint. But I am cooling . . . and Owena helps me into the bath again.

The mallow and the horsetail makes the water slippery, and I feel my skin slide over itself. I feel tears seep softly from wet lashes. My lungs sponge up moisture from the very air. I bless the water and the gentle herbs that floating brush my shoulders. I bless Owena, and my tears drop down faster and sweeter with the blessing. I will the water to heal me, and I can almost feel rips knit and scabs dissolve away.

And so I got better, and turned my thoughts back to my journey – though full of a sinking feeling that my body had lost me too much time. Soon, I would be leaving Caer Dathyl behind for the first time in many years, still clinging to the hope that I might find someone to take my place before Math's return.

ARIANRHOD

15

All through the years, I kept myself apart from all the petty struggles and wars which my mother had spent her time in winding up to the advantage of our family. I considered them beneath me. I never sent out men to fight when I could help it, even when the great war arrived against the southern king Pryderi, though Math sent asking for my help. Pryderi, my mother always told me, was a good man, and besides that, a close ally of Arawn, king of the other world of Annwn, whose life Pryderi's father Pwyll had once saved. That seemed a mad cause.

In time, however, I heard that Pryderi was killed. I sensed, in the air as it were, that there was black magic in the killing, and somehow connected it with the thought of my brother Gwydion, though nothing I had seen in him as a pathetic boy suggested he could be capable of such a momentous act. In any case, now the war was at an end – and I received a summons to Math's court, such as I had never received before. The messenger gave no explanation, though he urged the utmost haste, and I gathered that the king was ill.

My mother always loved her brother, and so I set out without dispute for her sake, and rode inland towards Tre'r Ceiri. I knew enough now to gauge the magic about the place – it was in the wind that swept the rocky field of asphodels which we crossed below the citadel, and as we approached the castle walls, I felt

magic in strife, as though more than one there had the power to wield it, and not all in the same cause.

Many eyes seemed waiting for my arrival. Many hands helped me down from my horse, though the faces around seemed closed. I knew that my reputation as one aloof, and strange, and learned, had spread far by that time – none of these qualities likely to win a crowd – and I never studied how to carry myself to win popularity through gracious smiles and gestures of modesty. I was not here to win friends, but only to help my uncle, and I returned cold glances with chilly interest and hurried into the hall.

I found it thronged with guests, as though on the occasion of some great feast, instead of what I had understood to be something like a deathbed scene.

And there was the king, old and grey – grey with more than the grey of years. He was supported by young men on either side, upon whose shoulders he leaned. The crisp black substance of their garments showed in contrast that Math was . . . less than substantial. His face, his hands, his clothes, his very being, were something less than there; he seemed made of dusty cloth, with the light shining through it.

He saw me, but it appeared only with half his attention. And now I looked around at the men at his side – and knew one of them for Gwydion.

In the eight years since I had seen him, his face had grown longer, harder, much more self-possessed than I had known it. He was a man indeed at last, and not such a young one. He did not look at me – and I had hardly ever seen his face before without it being turned full on me, and me alone. I saw, almost for the first time, the straight lines of his profile, and saw him pour a fluent stream of quiet words into his uncle's ear. Now the old king spoke.

'Dôn – I mean, Arianrhod, my dear – so like your mother – you see it's a sorry state I'm in here, and your brother has told me so much about you. He thinks perhaps you might save an old man . . .' but here he broke off, and seemed to stare over my shoulder at something near the door. I heard him mutter to himself.

'She comes! But it's all right, nothing to fear – she's only getting her babes to sleep. Ah! "Suo Gân", their favourite lullaby . . . it always was my favourite . . . as Mam rocks us at night. Mam! Sing "Suo Gân" again – I cannot get to sleep . . .' and here the old man began to sing, in a low voice only half lifted by the tune.

'Do not fear, it's but a leaf
That rustles, whispers at the door
Do not fear, it's but a wavelet
Moaning, murmuring on the shore . . .'
Now he leapt suddenly to his feet.

'Mam! *Mae gen i ofn!* I *am* frightened! I'm not brave, I can't, I can't be – don't ask it, please, Mam! Make them go away! . . . Ugh . . . It's them, outside the door, all bloody, it is, sure – and – and – I can't call to mind where I put their heads . . . they're likely rotted by now! Their mother, she'll be after me. Did she tell you what I did, Mam? Did she? Did she tell? I never meant it, only rock me and forgive me, Mam, and don't look like that . . . O – Mam – don't! – don't look like *her*.'

The king's eyes were wide with horror, and he whimpered and tried to hide himself behind his companions like a child. I saw Gwydion pour out another stream of whispered words, and pour a vial of something white into the king's cup and swirl it round and put it to his lips.

Old Math drank like an obedient baby fed with a cup, and almost at once was calm again, though his eyes looked glazed, and more than ever he seemed a concentration of grey mist, rather than a solid being.

'I am . . . bad . . . and you may help me, Arianrhod. My nephew tells me I can trust you. It need not be for life, but for a time – my need is so pressing. I beg you, my child, as I am your mother's brother . . .'

I was very sorry for him, and said I'd help in any way I could, though I had no idea what was being asked of me.

Now there was fast movement in the hall – a space was cleared in the centre, before the throne, and in the bustle I tried to make some sense of what was happening. It occurred to me that I had always heard that Math must, on account of a *tynged* cast against him, always keep his feet in the lap of a virgin. And no virgin was at his feet. What had happened to her? I recalled Math's words, 'it need not be for life' – they gained significance because I had always thought with horror of how that role, of foot holder, seemed indeed to be a life sentence. Could that role be meant for me? I determined I would speak to the king in private, would certainly do so before I went anywhere near his feet. But what was all this?

The people were still and silent now, standing or seated around the clearing before the throne, and I saw Gwydion once again pour words into the ear of the king.

'First, you know, there is a mere formality. Gwydion tells me it is safest – safest, you know, to go through the motions – the customary procedure – even though of course it can mean nothing in this case, my dear, and it will only show us all what we are all already quite sure of. Of course, you are . . . what you seem . . . my dear?' I nodded, though confused by what he was saying, and he, apparently equally uncertain, looked at Gwydion. And then he half-stood, and made a painful effort to pull something from his belt. Seeing him failing, and looking like to fall, both his nephews rummaged amongst the clothes about his waist to find what it was he sought.

At last, with their help, he pulled out a thick wand of elder, plain and smooth. Trying to rise, and then falling back, he handed it to Gwydion.

'You do it. Get it over with, by Annwn, before I expire.'

Gwydion's gaze now met mine for the first time in eight years. Our faces were so much changed in that time, the intimacy we once shared long burnt down to ash and scattered on the wind, and yet our eyes knew each other. Despite me, our gazes seemed for a moment to dance together in the air between us, as flighted insects will, sizing and smelling and reading each other. I hastily broke off the look, which was disgusting to me, but already I had sensed that there were powers in my brother now that I had not known before. As our eyes parted his lips were freed to speak to me, and he greeted me in words that any might have heard without guessing what we were to each other. In his voice, as well as his gaze, I sensed a self-possession, even an inward satisfaction, which I had never known in him before for one moment since first we met. And now he raised a serious face to the crowd about.

'By my dear uncle's bidding, I will perform the ceremony of the trail, to prove the worth of my dear sister here.' He stood up, and pacing slowly round before the guests, drew a circle in the air low to the ground with the wand. He then placed it on the floor in the centre, between myself and the throne.

He made a gesture of welcome towards the wand, while he looked at me.

'Step forward, towards your king,' he said.

My mind fanned out in desperate effort to find what all this meant. The king's feet were still safely below the board – my danger there, if there was any, did not seem imminent. But there was something in the confident movement of Gwydion – and a sense of tension now in his immobility – that made me feel something was at stake.

I thought I grasped it at last, the nature of this test, and stepped forward with new confidence. If it meant *that*, it was no matter, and I could hardly hesitate further without bringing derision upon myself. I strode towards the wand.

But even as my momentum was enough to carry me over it, there was a sickly chill about my heart. It was a chill I had felt before. I had to force myself to find the cause; I had tried so hard never to think of it since the day at the moon pools.

Since that time I had not felt wholly well, not quite myself, and I put it down to phantoms of the mind that must be driven away. I had been frightened by the power of the river, my brain perhaps a little turned by too long in the cold. There could be nothing in the river – no one – let alone any person I might know.

And so I told myself again as I stepped over Math's wand within the magic circle.

And nothing happened. Nothing at all.

Except that I sensed a strange taste in my mouth, as though I sucked a rusty nail.

Or as though someone else sucked it, with my mouth – or I sucked it, with a mouth that was not quite mine. I noticed that my breasts felt tender and my nipples hurt in my tight gown, but that was a sensation that at least seemed *mine.*

In other ways, the sense of the inside of myself was strangely unfamiliar – like a home that one returns to after a long absence, to find none of the spaces or relations quite as you remember.

I was struck by the smell of the feast that must have been eaten in the hall earlier that day. I was distracted by unravelling the different scents, tracing them back – guessing the age of the cheese, the colour of the plums, the fat the cakes were fried in. I thought I smelt a rat nearby, and chickens, but nevertheless thought I would like very much to eat a great quantity of the roasted, salted hazelnuts in honey that I smelt so close. Perhaps with some of that roasted grouse concealed somewhere at hand – I would be prepared to suck its bones, if that were all that were left.

I was about to ask for these as fortification for the interrogation of Math that was now in order, when it struck me that I did not want nuts, or grouse, at all.

The shades of the skein of scents that I had just been following with so much relish turned sickly, became each moment more noxious as they invaded my nostrils.

I turned hot, and faint, and was about to rush for the door where the air might be clean and cool, when nausea overwhelmed me. My palms and the back of my neck beaded with cold sweat.

I fell to my knees and vomited violently, splashing the feet of the front of the crowd.

I heaved, and wretched, and heaved again, and felt as if I had swallowed and must disgorge every scrap that had been eaten in the hall, and the dust on the rafters, and the strewing herbs, the woodsmoke-drenched boards themselves, down to the last rat and chicken. But my stomach was almost empty, and soon the waves of retching brought up not even yellow bitter bile, and it was as if my body would expel my very self.

At last the swell seemed to flatten a little, and I struggled to my feet. But now I was crushed beneath an overwhelming weight of weariness. My back ached as though I had carried twice my weight a hundred miles. I looked down at the cold flags of the hall, and longed to stretch out my length on them and close my eyes.

But that thought, too, was interrupted. Silently, and it seemed very far inside myself, came a flutter. And then I doubted I had felt it. But again it came – faint as a burr from a moth at a night-time flower that I might sense as I passed through the garden.

And then less faint, as I might feel that moth in my palm, if it strayed inside in foolish wooing of the candle, and I caught it in my hands to return it to the safety of the dark. For a moment I thought of nothing but that moth, and the secret velvet colours of its wings.

But the more I thought of it, the more it seemed to change – until the wings were the feathered gills of a young tadpole. And then those slowly shrank away, and the tadpole was strong and lithe as a young trout, leaping and somersaulting after flies at dusk. And then it had kicking legs, as strong as a young colt – and then fists too.

And I felt fists, and feet, inside my skin. Movement and intent inside me that was not mine.

And now my stomach grew, faster and faster. My clothes bit into my skin and would have cut it, if I had not torn them off me. And there I looked down and saw my naked stomach, rounding like the moon, and writhing from within, marks like little gleaming rivers flowing along its sides towards my hips.

I remembered where I was, and looked up. The faces around me were transfixed – revolted. I was struck, and horrified, to think that these eyes knew my new body better than I knew it myself. To be simply naked would be shelter and secrecy by comparison. In this swelling flesh of mine there was a concentration of exposure that should have been enough to suck into itself all the clothes of those who watched about me, and leave them stark and fleshy too. And I saw they felt this themselves as they watched, and were affronted and appalled.

Now came a rumble through my body like far-distant thunder.

I could hardly call it pain. But the next crack seemed a little nearer – hurt a little more. I looked around me again, desperate, frantic to be alone – I darted towards the margin of the circle, spurred by longings for a dark mouse hole or a form amongst dense brush.

But the blank faces there did not stir to let me through.

And then it was as though I saw the bruised sky and the ragged clouds of storm bear down upon me. A wall of pain hit me like a rising gale. It gathered itself from the depths of nowhere. The strongest howling gust tore through my back, stripped my thighs and hollowed my belly. Not a fibre of my body was not flattened and pinned.

Each rumble of the thunder was closer, shook me deeper, hurt me more, until I shrieked as if to shout it down, and sank to my knees again. I was squeezed by the unseen fist of the thunder, tighter and tighter – thunder inside me, and not mine.

I could not understand how a clenched fist could yet close harder, and harder yet – how was I not already ground to dust? How was it such a storm did not blow itself out – how was there energy enough in all the atmosphere for this?

I heaved and retched again, but I hardly noticed it, for now I sensed – a change.

The sky seemed to draw in its breath. My body, I knew, was gathering itself for something desperate.

The clenching of the fist was now instead a pull – my body, without leave of me, was hitching itself up. It was about to open me.

There was a moment's lull, and I again became aware of the watchers round me. Lost in the storm, there was only so much I could care that they should see me naked and vomiting on my knees before them. But that my body should be rent – that *I should rend myself open* before so many prying eyes, seemed more than I could bear. I was a hind run to ground before a baying pack of dogs.

But there was no escape – with a searing crack, the storm was on me again, and I knew that I must force it out of me, towering and dark and wild as it was, or be killed by it. I knew the struggle was hopelessly unequal, but I unclenched my teeth to howl back defiance at it. I roared to the empty bottom of every breath, to sound bigger than I was.

I was feeling a new pain – this time in one place – in a part of my body that I never knew I had. Where, between my legs, there had been a narrow private gully, there was now an open plain, and I seemed to watch from above as the grass around its circular margins burst into flames. I closed my eyes, as if that might put the fire out – and saw on the inside of my lids a dark circle of shadow moving across a glowing ball . . . an eclipse, as I had watched when I was seven years old. As the visible margin of the glowing orb narrowed, it seemed to burn brighter, and hotter, and I heard myself, somewhere small and far below, wail in agony. I was transfixed as the two circles moved towards alignment – tense and terrified to see it achieved. It seemed impossible that one should happen to fit the other, or that their paths should cross exactly.

But they did – and at last the black disk was superimposed upon the golden one, which was nothing but a searing circumference, a branded line. From three dimensions, to two, to one, to – none? I pushed oblivion outside myself with all my might.

My body tore wide open, and something slid from me.

And the storm was over.

I looked down and back between my legs, and there, on the herbs, was a milky bubble, as large as my belly had been before. It had the shine of the inside of a shell, and living lights inside it like a baby squid.

As I stared, it moved with a liquid motion. And as I looked closer I saw... underwater eyes – eyes like my own – blink at me.

I saw tiny hands raised as if to clear the pearly liquid from before a face, that it might see me better.

My eyes were locked to the gaze of that stranger in its underwater world.

And then hands closed around it, and it was lifted away. I saw it placed on the long board just near at hand, as though it were a joint of meat, and a hand, holding a knife, raised over it.

Before I could move, I saw the knife cut through a twisting vivid lilac cord that stretched, I now observed, from the bubble, down between my legs. And then bodies intervened, and I could see it no more, and was surrounded by a crowd.

I leapt to my feet, and sprang towards the long board, but was stopped by unfriendly hands and faces, as hard as any wall. I tried hopelessly to squeeze between them, begging to be let near my child. But the ranks only closed tighter, and the noise began. A low murmur of condemnation. And then something like a jeer. Hissing. 'Get out,' I heard, and 'Shame on you.' There was a kick to my backside. Someone pulled my hair, in the direction of the door outside. Many hands and feet pushed at me that way, until I fell, could not crawl fast enough to evade them, and was afraid I would be trampled or kicked to death. My head swimming at the frantic beating of my heart, I just managed to push back up to my feet, only to feel my shoulders pushed, and showers of spit on my face.

I was suddenly terribly afraid of this mob, which I could not believe was made up of men and women like myself. I longed to go back and find my baby, but could now see it nowhere, and despaired of wresting it from this hostile force, which seemed as invincible as any giant in its united hatred. I had no hold of myself, and could only hope to run somewhere out of their sight, to piece together again the woman I had once been, who might be capable of action. I rushed headlong towards the door.

As I neared it, I felt an echo of the former storm – one more wave of pain ran through my body. And something – the afterbirth – slid out of me and clushed heavy to the floor.

I stepped free of it, and of the purple rope that had dragged, stiffening, from me as I ran, and at last burst outside.

Ah, Goewin. For god's sake tell me of revenge.

GOEWIN

16

And that I will! Revenge that, if it did not quite satisfy me, gave me an appetite for more that might almost match your own. You might very fairly wish vengeance on the best part of Tre'r Ceiri – the same crowd that spared me in my trouble. But pity and cruelty, beyond the personal, simmers in every crowd, and our gratitude or hatred is best spent on those who throw the big log on the fire, which makes it overboil at last.

Strange to think our stories almost touched so long ago – that first you, and then I, stood on one spot, so that it seems our shades must have touched each other. I even glimpsed you – but not as a fellow woman for whom I should care, and whose mutual help might more than double my strength. Ach, how many lives brush against each other in this way; how many shades touch, and even hug, only to have the busy bodies that cast them drag them mercilessly onwards, past and away, to a future more lonely than needs be.

Before you hear of my revenge, you must hear first how I won it – though the progress of my search for a new footholder is hardly worth relating. For six weeks I went from hamlet to hillfort, from village to hall, in search of someone who might benefit from my proposal. I found virgins common enough. But when I privately explained the business to them, I found that not many of those who called themselves so would take the risk that the *tynged* might not recognise them as such. Virginity is more complex than men would like to think. I hoped there might be older women who would gain most and risk least in such a role, but amongst them, too, I found that the notion of chastity was used rather more loosely than it was likely to figure in the Irish magic.

Most nights I was offered shelter by the women to whom I came to speak, but I was in great haste and sometimes it suited me best to sleep by the road. Then I would stand at Eponwen's shoulder, and coax her to lie down, after her long day of carrying me. Though she was, by what I heard, older than any horse of this world, she always seemed young, and would lie down for the four darkest hours with me at night as though she were a mere foal.

I loved to lie near her. While we were both awake, I would stare into her sad eyes, and tell her how my search went on – I was sure that she felt my troubles and wished me strength. And then it was a mighty comfort to be lulled by the deep, large movement of her breathing, and feel her warmth as the chill of night crept in.

Sometimes I heard her murmur unconsciously, like a sleeping child – and I noticed, as the days passed by, that such murmurs grew more frequent, and more distressed. Some nights her hooves would twitch, as though in sleep she galloped somewhere urgently – so that at last I thought it couldn't be safe to lie on that side of her. Eventually I was kept from sleep myself by the sad querulousness of her dreams. Watching her dark lashes flutter like a moth in a spider web, seeing her velvet lip tense and draw back in fear, I was forced more than once to wake her from her dream. When she woke, she looked around bewildered, the wells of her eyes drained even of their sadness.

I now heard rumours that the war was all but over, and that Math was victorious – I became more fearful than ever that he might return before I did. But thankfully, I thought I had found what I needed: three sisters, too plain and too formidable in their intelligence to be very hard pressed by the men, who lived holed up with their father in a farm high on the moors, with barely enough to eat between them and their many younger brothers. They worked like slaves up there – if Math could send their family help, they would be more than glad to expand their world and minds, and might perhaps share the role of footholder between the three of them at once. I had, however, left them to think on it for seven days, while I searched on for other candidates whom I might perhaps place in line to succeed them, or take their place if they should after all refuse. I found no one else however, and Eponwen and I now returned into the high mountains to fetch the sisters, if they were willing.

One night we had to spend on the open moor. The wind had dropped down, and the moon was round and high, so that my eye was carried far on the solemn swell of the land ebbing dark away around us. I was glad I was not alone.

I coaxed my horse to lie down and made myself a bed of the thick moss that grew beneath the heather close by her side. I was too weary to tell her tales that night, and within moments I sensed our breathing slow together as we slid into the shallows of sleep.

I was started awake by a groan that shook the springy peat on which I slept.

I put my arm over Eponwen, but she groaned again, more deeply – and suddenly I found myself thrown aside as she leapt to her feet, and screamed.

With her head back, she shrieked into the night. It was as though the scream came from outside her, and the agony it expressed was more than hers. I saw her closed eyes, her pale forehead furrowed with pain, and her mouth like an upturned spout through which black pain flowed.

Though winded by my fall I sprang to my feet, and to her side, but she seemed quite unaware of me – and abruptly the scream choked off, and she hung her head.

The moon was very bright on her pale neck, now bent low, and more than ever like another moon itself. I saw her dark lashes lowered upon her cheek, and saw a tear slowly slip out from under them.

It did not shine silver in the moonlight. Neither did its twin, that glided out from her other eye. They stole darkly down across her cheeks – darker than drops of lead, darker than the death-watch beetle creeps across the sanded hearth at night. And they left behind a dark and slender trail.

I pressed my forehead to my true mare's brow, and held her as she cried, all through the night – and as the sky cracked crimson with the dawn, I saw that she was weeping tears of dark heart's blood.

I spent several days on that open stretch of moor, while my mare recovered something of herself. At last she was calm again, though the pail of tears that I saw in her eyes seemed constantly to overflow, and the stars that shone there seemed deeper drowned than ever. At first, instead of riding on her back, I walked at her side, my cheek pressed to hers. I would have liked to continue so – but I began to fear greatly that Gwydion and Math might return before me, so that all my efforts might be in vain.

I got hold of three more fast horses along the way in the name of King Math, and, when I reached the cottage of the three sisters, found them quite impatient to come with me. However, when at last they and I approached Caer Dathyl, I found that my fears of being late were well founded.

There was such a stir and chaos around Tre'r Ceiri as only a returned war party makes. The fields around were full of knackered horses, and a stream of carts flowed up the road brimming with food and forage. I could only hope they had not been there long, and that Math still lived: I was given hope by the fact that I saw nowhere the look of confusion I might have expected in the faces of those whose leader of many generations had passed away.

But as we neared the village, I saw the streets emptier than I would have expected. I heard a sound of hooting, and a throng of harsh voices raised together from the direction of the hall. And then I saw something I could not understand – from a low sheep gate on the far side of the fortress I saw something crawl – not a sheep. At first I thought it was a roe deer, but its motion was limping, and it was milky pale in the bright sunshine. And then it seemed to me it stood on its hind legs and ran. It looked for all the world like a naked woman – but soon it was out of sight, and I was in too much fear of delay to follow what seemed most likely to be a trick of my eye or exhausted mind. The thought of that pale sight turns me sick, now, my lady – I wish I could have sought you out, to give you the help you so sorely wanted. We could have been friends – or allies – before now.

As I entered the village I found that I had arrived in the very moment of crisis. I gathered that Gwydion had indeed attempted to set up a footholder of his own, that the attempt had somehow gone awry, and that the old king's life was fading fast.

It seemed to me that the moment for bargaining and diplomacy had passed me by. I explained the emergency to the three sisters, and we agreed to hurry at once together into the hall.

People were streaming out, hurried in their departure by followers of Math and Gwydion. I saw it might be difficult to make my way inside – I was not certain that Gwydion's men would not try to stop me once I was observed – and so, instead of dismounting, I trotted towards the great door, calling the sisters to follow me. As I had hoped, the crowd parted for us, and ducking our heads we rode into the hall together.

All turned at the sound of our horses' hooves on the flags. With a deep shudder, I saw Gwydion and Gilfa turn from their business towards me, in obvious surprise.

What was that they had been busy about? It seemed a moving heap of gossamer cloth, or a cloud of dust. And then I saw it was the king.

I gave a word to Ystwyth, the oldest sister, and she kicked her horse forward, right up before the king – jumped down, and lifted something that drifted where the king's legs should have been, whole into her lap.

At once she held there the substantial war boots of Math, and his feet and legs within them. I looked immediately to Gwydion, and was relieved to see shock – even panic – in his face, sitting so unexpectedly there that he seemed a man I had never seen before. I called an order to bar the door in the name of the king.

I looked behind me and saw the followers of Math about to lower the great bar, but look to him for confirmation of my command. His bulk was now as dense and heavy as a hill once more, and I could see in his face that he was making a strong effort to gather his faculties in the moment. He had fought many wars, seen his people through many unexpected disasters, and was calm and decisive under the greatest pressure, even while acting on mere shreds of understanding. He looked at me – and trusted me – and loudly called for the 'tardy dogs' to 'shift themselves and do as Goewin says at once, by Annwn!'

I jumped down from Eponwen's back, and strode towards the throne, my eyes fixed on Gwydion, who seemed for a moment frozen. He took a hold of the king's arm, as though he had been an invalid still, and began to speak softly in his ear – but Math shrugged him off with rising vigour and some impatience. Now Gwydion – and following him, Gilfa too – stepped forward and blocked my way towards the king. I took another chance.

'Men – in the name of Math, seize these brothers both. They have dishonoured their king and endangered his life.'

No one moved.

'As every man and woman of Tre'r Ceiri can bear witness, Gwydion and Gilfaethwy, who dishonour the name of Dôn their mother, took me, the footholder of the king, by force, here in their lord's own hall. Here, under the herbs, you may still find the stain of my blood, and that of Gilfa too, which I spilt for him as I tried to defend and avenge myself.'

Even as I spoke, I saw Gwydion turn to the king, and begin to pour scorn on my words. There were yet servants in the hall who had been in the village while the war party was away. I now looked from one to the next of them, as though confident of their support.

'Was it not so, Dewi? Gwyn?'

Both men hesitated but a moment before giving their 'aye' in confirmation of my words. I saw Math look past the eager-talking Gwydion, into my face. He gave a nod.

'By the Pale Hounds of Arawn, do as she says! Seize these insolent young whelps and bind them fast. Do it now! Gods rot you, must I do it myself?'

With this, and without further warning, he stopped the flow of Gwydion's eager words with a punch in his mouth, and drawing his sword, directed it at the heart of Gilfaethwy. In another moment both brothers were dragged from his side, though Gwydion still attempted to shout some defence, which no one could make out.

'Shut your mouth, Gwydion, or I'll feed your tongue to the kite!' cried Math. 'I have been addled with your words quite long enough. Stuff his craw with spoiled meat, one of you – give him something to chew over. And get him out of my sight – throw him and his brother in with those precious "pigs" of theirs, and set a guard over them. If the swine happen to be hungry and have a taste for some over-cosseted flesh, I doubt there are many with cause to miss them.'

And now Math, leaning back in his chair again, his heaves of exasperation quieting a little, looked to me.

I hurried to his side. I told him all that had happened in the hall. I told him what I had done since, and my reasoning – introduced him first to Ystwyth and then to her sisters, told him the plan I proposed, and argued strongly that no information or advice that Gwydion had ever given him, recently or in times long past, should be taken at face value.

When I had said all I had to say, Math took my hands, just as he had done the first day that we met at home on Ynys Môn.

'You saved my life today. And you saved our people, I do believe, from a lying dog of a tyrant. And – and this is the thought to take hold of, as a terrier might a rat – you did these things through courage and energy and wisdom, qualities I have always seen in you and should have taken better notice of.

You have seen, just now, how frail my hold on this life is. I am a thin defence to stand between you, and my people, and such a determined man as Gwydion. While weakened by the curse, I cannot even recall what I was party to. This is the second time I have good cause to beg for your help. I know I am old enough to be your great-grandfather's father – and I would expect nothing from you in . . . that line – you might be quite free to please yourself with more fitting companions – by Annwn, I've kept you from that too long already. But will you, Goewin, marry me and be my queen? I would pass to you all my power and authority, and when I die, the succession will be clear. With my blessing, the people would transfer all their loyalty to you, without question.'

I hesitated – but not for the reason he thought. In truth I thought I would make a good queen, and I wished nothing more than to see things done well, and better, around me. In the past years I had seen a hundred ways it might be so. But there was yet one thing I had not told the king, for I was not sure of its meaning, and dared hardly contemplate it. There was nothing for it now but to out with it.

'I would be honoured, King, to accept such an offer, on the terms you suggest. I would try to do the job. But I must tell you – in case it makes a difference – that since . . . it happened . . . I – I have not bled.'

He looked very long and seriously at me, as if to read my face. He gently touched both of my cheeks, and sighed.

'Goewin – *bechan bach* – I can see that you do indeed have new life growing within you – not one child, indeed, but three.'

My heart paused. I looked down at the grey boards.

'But, *fy nghariad* – such children cannot live. They have too much of black magic in them.'

And now it lurched.

'I would not have you bear, in pain and suffering, the children got with such violence. Would you?'

'No . . . but . . . neither would I have them . . . die.'

As I spoke, I remembered that if I was Math's wife, I might never be that of another man – might perhaps never have children of my own. And I pressed my hand to the place where I knew my womb must be. I thought of sparks in that darkness. I thought of potentiality. And I thought of death.

And then a band of pain flashed under my hand. There was a gush of something warm on my thighs.

I snatched at Math's shoulders. 'I *would not have them die*! Help me!'

Math now tried to leap to his feet, forgetting that Ystwyth held them – he sat back and bellowed out his orders like an angry bull.

'Gweno! Arwen! Fetch things to make a bed for my wife, here in the hall – fetch cool water, and lots of it, if you please. Call Owena. Gwyn! Make a chamber for her of the great screen, there near the window. Huw, Hywel, fetch my nephews from the sty – but make sure they're well-bound – and gagged too, gods rot them. Be quick about it, you sheep-brained fools!'

He looked me in the face.

'I will do my best. All may yet be well.'

The women – my friends – helped me to the bed they quickly made, close under the wall, handed me clean linen to staunch the flow of blood, then left me alone behind the screen. I hardly dared move lest I should shake free the feeble clutch of the new lives within me. Even the movement of my mind might be enough to dislodge them. To care so much, and to have so little I might do . . . I tried to become a blank, another piece of furniture in the hall.

Soon I heard a jostling, and mumbled curses, and knew that the prisoners had been brought before the king.

'You two, I can hardly bear to have near me, even in my pigsty. And I will not. That forest below shall be your home now. And you shall inhabit it as beasts. Goewin – my friend – my wife – is deeply wronged by you, and you shall bear the brunt of it. She carries new life within her, but you have entangled it about with your own evil. She shall never risk her life to bring it into the world. No – I'll tell you what – *you will.* You shall feel the other side of your brutality.'

There was a silence – and then I heard the muttering that I knew was the sound of Math working magic. I turned my head, and peered through a narrow crack in the screen.

On the ground lay two large, bound bodies – a stag and a hind. The brothers were nowhere to be seen.

'Cut them loose!' cried Math, and Dewi took a knife to their bonds, and the deer sprang to their feet, their ankles trembling.

'You, Gilfa, shall feel all the desire that ever demented a rutting stag for this hind here, that is at once your brother, Gwydion. You shall lust all day after Gwydion, in the shape of that gentle hind. And you, Gwydion, shall feel what it is to fear, and to get fucked against your will whenever Gilfa can get hold of you. And then, in the course of that coupling, one of the new lives that lives in Goewin – the good part, the part of it that is hers, stripped of all dark magic – shall grow inside you, and you will bear the heavy weight of it, and then birth her son, in pain and suffering – though, being only a deer, and not a true woman, not as much of it as I would like. And then you shall bring him here.

Oh you think you've got off relatively light, do you, Gilfa? Think being a randy stag happy to shag anything, man or beast, even your own brother, is not so much of a change for the worse, eh? Ha! I'm only just getting fucking started.

On your return, I shall turn you, Gwydion, into a boar, and you, Gilfa, into a sow. And Gwydion, in his turn, shall be consumed with lust for his own brother, and you, Gilfa, shall feel what it is to have another force themselves inside you. As often as Gwydion can manage it. For a year. And your body shall plim, and your teats shall swell painfully and drag on the ground as he pursues you, until at last the second son that Goewin carries inside her may rip his way out of you. And you shall bring him to me.

And then you, Gwydion, shall become a wolf bitch, and suffer another year in which your brother, a dog wolf, may take you by force whenever he can, as no true wolf ever takes another – for you will be much less than true wolves. And you shall birth Goewin's third son, and bring him to me.

And then I'll see what shall be done with you – but as long as I let you live, you shall carry the marks of those rapes and those pregnancies and those births on your men's bodies. At night you shall be haunted by the memory of the consuming, wasting lust you felt for your own brother's cunt, and the monstrous beast you made yourself in taking it by force. Now. Get out!'

In one fluid movement, Math seized the earthen piss pot that he kept beneath his chair, and flung it at the turning deer. It burst on the floor between them, drenching their legs as they clattered from the hall – the doe ahead at first – and then the stag in hot pursuit of her.

I felt at once that my pain had gone, and the bleeding stopped. And I laughed.

BLODEUWEDD

17

Three days Gronw stayed at Mur y Castell, and three nights the springtime coursed through me in his arms. On the fourth day he must return to Pen Llŷn, and I resolved to follow him. Of course, I had to take my people with me, as though on a formal visit – but he promised he knew a hidden cove where no one went but him. He longed, he said, to see me blooming in the honest light of day.

Pen Llŷn – where the range of mountains tapers soft towards the horizon, as an asphodel towards the sky, while on either side the land plunges steeply, so that the long heartwood of oak and birch is fringed by turf alight with all the flowers that love the sea. We took the road along the coast, and it was as though Gronw had spread all the riches of his realm beneath my feet to welcome me. Milkwort, trefoil, eyebright and a hundred others of my kind – they ranged and danced between land and sea and sky.

But when we reached his hall, perched high above a sweep of sandy bay, he was not there. My cheeks, which had been rich as orchids, paled to scurvy grass, and I thought I could not live another minute from his side. Though in my natural state I cared no more for days and hours than the sun itself, I was panting after moments with a mortal man.

I feared my people might mark the sudden excess of my distress and tell my husband, or worse still, Gwydion, of it. So I hurried off, alone, along a path that led precipitately down towards the sea.

And there, at a bend in the way, he caught me unawares. I learnt at once I loved the limits of his arms, as he caught and pressed and held me tight. There was a narrow overhang of turf, midway down the plummet of the cliff. He laid me down under the full gaze of the sun, and he made stars of scilla of my eyes, mounds of cliff rose of my breasts, and blowing campion of my thighs. I brimmed and spilled over the margins of the ledge, hanging over the churning sea, clinging to him above the void. I knew my sol-flower roots were anchored deep enough in him that I could swing there safely, and flourish in the face of any drought.

He was no mere sluice, as I had vainly thought, through which the current of my being might escape its bounds to join the universal flood. Together we were a rushing part of that, for sure, but just as I could not drink the sunlight without a resonance of excitement between coupled particles within my cells, I knew now that if I were all dispersed again, each piece of me would call to part of him across the world, so that to be nowhere, but without him, would be a new and bitter loneliness.

On the cliffs and in the woods of Llŷn I was so happy. To be with him was all, as once I had been all unto myself. We sailed into the spring, the may and cherry creaming away before us. Ours seemed to be too small a craft to brave such depths. But to feel each pulse of the season right through my new slight frame, hear the liquid murmur of the great tide of spring so close at hand – be carried to the crest of every swell, run down into the emerald heart of every valley, trail my wrist in the race of bluebells – the very danger of being overturned seemed part of the bliss of floating, sailing on. The days waxed with our joy, and by midsummer we seemed adrift in an ocean all our own.

But I must go home. My husband had returned from his long stay at Tre'r Ceiri, and had sent a messenger to call me back.

I hoped the parting need not be long. Gronw, I thought, might easily follow me, and stay at Mur y Castell as my husband's guest, and it would be easy enough for us to find our moments. My husband would never guess me capable of any of this. And I might come back to Pen Llŷn when he was next away.

But Gronw was not so easily satisfied. He could not bear, he said, the thought of how my husband came to lie amongst my flowers. I told him he might as well be troubled that Lleu should walk out in the meadows amongst the saxifrage and lady's smock; it never made them his, and nor did lying with me make me any part of himself. How could I be, when he had nothing, knew nothing of my nature? But Gronw was tormented: he spoke of how my scent must rise from petals pressed beneath Lleu's body, and could not bear that anyone but him should breathe it in.

His sadness passed over me like the shadow of a cloud. My colours dimmed, and I shivered in a breath of cold. And though I made myself all the brightest dancing flowers, I could never keep the thought at bay for long, and would soon find myself trembling in shade again. I turned my mind on how I might dispel it.

ARIANRHOD

18

This part of the tale I can hardly bear to tell, for I was weak, and behaved like a desperate thing.

The sun blazed down without mercy. I had been in the hall a very little time, and yet everything was changed beyond all recognition, and I was hardly sure that I could yet breathe the air, or that my eyes could bear the light.

Instead of looking for clothes to cover me, or the horse that had brought me to Caer Dathyl, I ran. Naked and torn and bleeding, I ran for cover like an animal, though no one followed me, and no private shelter of any kind was close at hand.

Once outside the village I thought of curling up behind a stone, but they were too small to act as any shield. Their lichen-crusted sides seemed to shrink into the peat sooner than give me sanctuary.

The wind whipped out dry from behind them to bite me, and whined away across the high plain. My only thought was of a place to hide. I set my eyes upon the nearest strip of forest, and made straight for that.

Those hard grey rocks. The blood that flowed down the inside of my thighs got under my feet and made me slip in the moor grass, and often I would fall against them. They seemed bladed on purpose to slice me up. My strength flowed out with the blood, and my knees shook under me, but I fixed my eyes on the hard face of the next stone in my path, and aimed for that no matter how roughly it faced me down. The sky span and darkened above my head, and each breath hurt my throat, but at last I made the trees.

The dimmer light in the wood was my first comfort. I thirsted for the shade of the tall ferns that clustered there almost as much as the water of the brook that bubbled close at hand.

On my knees I quenched my thirst, and then crept in under the ferns, where the moss was soft, and curled up tight, and knew no more.

I woke to find the light gentle green with twilight in the wood. And over my shoulders was spread a blanket as fine as spiders' web. I sat up, clutching it about me, to raise my head above the ferns and look around.

From the branch of the nearest tree hung a green dress and a grey cloak. And at some distance, I saw a man standing in the greenest of the shade.

I shrank back at the sight – and was inclined to stay tight and quiet under the ferns, like just another brown-downed uncurled frond, but the clothes so close at hand were irresistible. I longed not to be naked, and I saw I could twitch them from their twig without leaving cover.

I crept towards them, kneeled up and gave them a tug, so that they crumpled softly down on me, while my eyes were fixed upon the man. His back was towards me still, and he did not turn around, but, though I had been as quiet as a rabbit, I thought I saw in the movement of his head that he sensed my own actions and my gaze upon him.

With added haste I knelt low among the ferns to dress myself. He knew I was there, it was clear, and I would rather approach him than have him come to me.

My movements opened crusting lacerations all over me,

stinging across the ache of my muscles. Through all the hatchwork of cuts and grazes, I noticed how my body was stretched, and how the skin hung slack around my stomach, but the dress fitted perfectly, and the cloak was warm and soft as the blanket – the softest thing I had ever felt against my skin.

I stood up, and now the figure in the green shade looked my way.

As he did so, it was as if I saw his face form itself out of the moving dapples of the shadow.

He walked through the ferns as if the wood were his own smooth-paved hall, and, stopping at a little distance, bowed deeply to me with studied formality. I bowed to him in turn – relieved to find that I could do as much, for still I was little more than a frightened animal – but with no sense in the world of any words that I might speak.

He saw all this, and took the burden from me.

'Arianrhod ferch Dôn, if I am not mistaken. A great privilege, my lady. Your learning and your character are spoken of more widely than you dream.'

I bowed again, and would have asked his name – but I still felt the animal shrieks that had torn my throat so recently, and could hardly trust myself. Again he seemed to read all this.

'You must be tired, and I will not keep you in empty talk. I will say only what I must, for your sake. I – am a stranger. But I know that you have a son.'

My head span again at these last words, but still I did not speak. My interest in what he had to say was almost painful, and I would have liked to throw my dignity aside and hang upon him pleading for another word. Yet I was now too much myself again for that.

'An effort was made to keep the child from you. But I arranged to have him stolen away and taken to safety in the night. No! I don't have him here. He is no babe of the wood. You will find him . . . in his own element. My messengers have brought me word of him, and he is safe enough, but wants his mother. If you will come with me, I will show you where you may find him.'

He held out his arm to me as if I were a queen – I took it, I am rather afraid, more like an eager child, still speechless, and let him lead me to the farther margin of the wood. There stood his horse, grey as mist. Very gently, as though his touch might offend me, he helped me mount, and climbed up behind me.

The sun had set now, and I could not have seen my way, for the moon was very low in the sky, and hidden behind the hills. He, however, set the horse in swift though even motion, and it never stumbled. We rode on, and soon I lost my sense of where I was, and slipped away into the dark again.

I awoke to find myself once more covered in the airy blanket – but now I was all alone, and lay on the sand of a little cove, facing out towards Ynys Môn. The warm light from the sun just below the horizon was melting back the dark, and the morning star hung a watch light over the water. I heard patient lapping, very near at hand. The high tide was slack, and little glossy waves slid and pearled, glissed and pleated over one another.

As I sat up I felt my body again. The bruises, and the torn edges still raw between my legs. I knew I must get up to seek my son, and yet my bones ached too much to carry my weight. The salve of that silken water would bring me the strength that I needed.

And so I folded the dress, cloak and blanket, and put a round pebble upon them that they should not be carried away by any breeze that might rise. And stepped into the water, which was warmer than I had ever known the sea, and let the ripples lead me out.

When the water rose above my knees, I slipped myself whole between the waves, and felt all the comfort I had longed for there. It lifted me gently, took my whole weight, and rocked me in its arms. The salt stung my wounds only for a moment; the water was like balm on my broken skin, and it seemed to heal and knit and smooth again as I floated there.

My thoughts, however, were only for my baby, and I set to wonder where I might find him.

I looked about, and my eye was caught by a cave at the side of the beach. Its ceiling was as high as the roof of the greatest hall. The sun had risen, and shone deep and bright into the water at its mouth, but the depth inside looked all the blacker for that. I thought of the chasm where I had met Llyr, but trusted somehow that this place could not harbour dark violence like that. I took a deep breath, and swam in between the towering walls.

Now that I was close to them, I saw that the hard rock was not black at all, but pink and crimson. It was mapped with spongy coralline, velvet with sea moss dark as wine, and blossomed with the soft red mouths of sea anemones. As the sea breathed, it lifted me against the walls – the rock seemed so strong in stillness, and the sea so strong in fluid movement, that I felt I must be crushed between two modes of force. But as I was sucked against the walls, I found the sea had smoothed away all edges that might have hurt me, and the cushion of weed made a soft passage for me between the forces of rock and wave.

Still I went in deeper, surrendering to the swell as it lifted me. Once I crossed the threshold into shadow it lost its edge, and instead it slowed my pulse. I swam on, pushing the water behind me with each breath, feeling it let me pass, bear me on.

The swell was now no more than the ripple of my breathing, which bore me on deeper to the back of the cave.

Since my eyes had yielded to the darkness, I saw perfectly without light. There, where the cave closed itself, was a silver crescent of sand, without a single print. The water nudged at it, and at the margin was something, tumbled to and fro.

My feet touched shingle, and my bones hardened, weighted by flesh again as I crawled from the water towards the bundle.

A wide ribbon of kelp was loosely wrapped around something soft and pale. I thought it was the swell that animated it, but as I held it up, it moved of itself. As I unwound the weed, I found soft limbs, a silky head, and a sweet face – with a sucking mouth. My son.

I sat on the little secret beach with the baby in my arms and put him to my breast. He squirmed with eagerness, but his mouth was no good fit, and he breathed in air, his sucking uncoordinated.

The swell lapped at my feet, warm as milk now. I pulled myself back down the beach into the shallows with the muscles of my calves, until the breathing of the sea – my breathing – lifted and rocked me, and the child in my arms. And now he sucked, and as he floated free, the rhythm of his suckling was the rhythm of the waves, and my milk flowed out, as a wave rushes out between rocks with the suck of the swell.

I floated freely now, with the baby suckling from my breast like a whale calf. My face was turned upwards to the dark air, but he needed that no more now than when he swum inside my womb. I knew him certainly for my own – knew that he who brought me to him had been a true and powerful friend. I saw both myself and the water in the baby's nature. Though I now suspected, from the recollection of the familiar malevolence of that moment, that my cursed brother had played some role in his fathering, it was the stream, whose embrace I had returned so willingly, that he took after.

The sea drew us back out of the darkness. I spread my limbs like a starfish, and we floated together under the dome of the sky.

Floating there like that, I learned for the first time how to exercise all that I knew. The miracle of my son's birth showed me how easily I could spill over every limit I had ever thought was set for me. I named him Dylan.

We floated together for a year, sometimes crawling out onto the beach at the back of the cave, where my boy learned to sit and to crawl and to smile at me.

Once he could walk, we swam together to the wide beaches of Sir Fôn, where the golden sands stretch on as far as the eye can see, and the shallow waters swirl silver with sand eels.

He delighted in playing on the edge of the land as human children do at the margin of the sea. I would set the tiny waves going for him, and he would chase their rolling ripples across the beach, trying to catch them by stamping his little heels upon them. He would return to me to nurse in the shallow water, and as my milk pulsed out strongly with every wave, it leaked from the corners of his mouth, and foamed and bubbled and made rainbows all along the high tide line.

When he was older, we would swim together over the sandbank, and I would help him marshal the shoals of mullet and herring and bass, who would file over and under and past each other like neat battalions of toy soldiers. He wrestled daily with an octopus as though it were his dog – it changed colour every time my son pressed him to the sand, and squirted ink to hide his shame when he knew Dylan had got the better of him. I found him a leather-backed turtle to ride upon, and together they hunted jellyfish as big as chariot wheels. At night we chased the lights of little sea gooseberries, and sometimes swam by the point of Penmon where we set the waves themselves ablaze with colours stolen from the northern lights, so that the breaking of each wave was an azure cymbal clash. In the small-pebbled coves of the love goddess Dwynwen, he would gather tiny cowrie shells, and string them into bracelets for my ankles, while the seals sung lullabies at my bidding.

GOEWIN

19

I was soon more than well, and very busy. Math had made it clear that all power and authority was mine – he let it be known in public and in private, in no uncertain terms. And yet I was glad that I would know always where to find his counsel, untainted now by the whisperings of Gwydion, and instead refined and clarified by his constant and close conference with Ystwyth, who proved as clever as ever I had thought her, though by no means as even-tempered as myself. The sharp quarrels between herself and Math, in which she almost always got the better of him, became the entertainment of the court. I did hear that once, in sheer frustration at his stubbornness, she took up his foot and almost bit off the big toe – but of course this sounds most unlikely.

I was not there when this incredible event was said to have taken place. The war had hurt the land, and many a family had lost some lynch pin, needed to bring the food to their children's mouths. Before I could help them, I must learn, and I set off in circuit about the *cartrefi*.

I loved this journeying. It recalled the times my father had taken me on missions with him – the pleasure of seeing new places, and of unpredictable encounters with strangers – and the warm welcome that was almost always given to one who they knew meant well and would work hard to do them good. I knew I was keen and sharp at finding a course of mutual advantage, and close alliances and new bonds of trust sprang up around me wherever I went.

I rode always on Eponwen, of course, and lay down near her at night. And now I understood her better. Since my return to Caer Dathyl, I had made sense of her wild grief on our last journey.

I remembered how Math had on that first day – I thought in jest – told me that Eponwen was the sister of a king. And I put this together with the tales of the birth of Pryderi, king of the south, that I had been told as a child.

It was said that Teirnyon of Gwent Is Coed owned the most beautiful mare in Wales. And on the first of May, every year, for six years, she bore a filly foal still more beautiful than herself. But every year, this lovely creature vanished from the stable during the first night of its life.

When the first of May came round the seventh time, Teirnyon was standing under an old hawthorn tree that foamed above the meadow as profuse as clotted cream. He wondered to himself how he might keep the lovely foal when it was born. So lost in thought was he that he was quite surprised to look up to find that he was not alone. There stood a tall man, with a sword in his hand, and features that, as he began to speak, seemed to form themselves from the shadows of the moving bees in the blossom above.

He asked Teirnyon what troubled him that he should brood so grimly under the blossom on such a lovely day as that, while the very hares and squirrels raced exultant, and the bluebells rang with joy. When he heard Teirnyon's story, he gave him the sword that was in his hand, and told him to take it with him that night to the stable, and there set himself to watch.

Just at the darkest hour of the night, he saw a great claw come through the window of the stable, and grasp the foal. With his sword, he severed the claw, and heard a mighty scream, and the sound of a huge beast retreating through the wood. When he came out of the stable, he found on the threshold a lovely baby, who in time was found to be Pryderi, the lost son of Rhiannon and her husband King Pwyll, closest friend of Arawn the fairy king, who perhaps had been the stranger met by Teirnyon beneath the fairy may. In his joy in being reunited with his son, Pwyll bought the foal from Teirnyon for a handsome sum, and sent it as a gift to Arawn, while Pryderi stayed with Teirnyon and his wife, who had no children of their own, as a foster child.

Could Eponwen be the seventh filly of Teirnyon's beautiful mare – and in this sense the foster sister of Pryderi, brought into the world of men and women together with him? I learned that on the same night that my true mare cried those tears of blood, Pryderi's life had been taken from him by Gwydion, who had challenged him to meet in single combat as honest man to man, only to use the blackest of magic arts against him. I could doubt the relation between the unlucky king and my poor little mare no longer.

Eponwen was shaken, still, by that dark night, and it was hardly safe for me to sleep near her, so often did she roll and kick in her sleep. And yet I hated to sleep alone; to feel the chill of the night on all sides. And I had bad dreams of my own.

I thought sometimes of the licence Math had given me, when asking me to become his queen. I wondered whether any man would want to touch what had been touched so by a beast. I longed for another to erase that ugly act, which in my dreams still sometimes seemed to have become a part of my darkest self.

I know it is quite unseemly for me to tell you of this – but around this time I found there was a man I wanted.

I have told you of Math's lieutenant, Aneurin. He now was mine. Most days I had some commission for him, and always found him as competent and energetic in carrying it out as Math had ever done. I found great attraction in such competence and energy, and the strong intelligence I glimpsed flowing deep beneath.

I told you, also, that he would never look at me. And now, since he had become my own lieutenant, he seemed to look at me less still. He would stand with both hands on the hilt of the long sword before him, his head bowed, nodding in acknowledgement of my orders, but never looking up into my face.

Mostly I put this down to his general character, which was reserved and taciturn enough. But sometimes I wondered if he thought of what had happened to me, and saw some part of the darkness of it in my face, and turned his eyes away from that. Such a thought made me feel lonely.

One night I lay as usual, in a clearing of my own a little way from the main camp. Eponwen would not lie down, but stood motionless, and asleep, with her head towards the heart of the forest. I had been still a long while but was half awake – the cold crept underneath my wrappings, yet I could not bear to move and let a gush of the chilly air around my half-sleeping limbs.

I could hear the tread of the sentries in the leaves at a distance, and was grateful that they kept me safe. I only wished that they could patrol the boundaries of my dreams.

And then I heard, very soft, another tread: the dead leaves gently powdering under a careful foot. I heard slow, tentative breathing – and a longer, deeper crunch of the forest floor, as though someone knelt by me. I smelt wood smoke and long riding. And then the breathing paused – there was a soft weight on my shoulder, which could only be heavy velvet; I felt it dropped carefully over my bent arm, my waist, my flank. Another body had lent the cloak warmth, and at once the silver beads of cold along my spine crept away as silently as they had come.

I heard another breath – and another pause.

And then the softest touch upon a curling lock of hair that lay behind my ear, its spring compressed a shade, before it loosed against my skin.

The hand was still there, but I knew it would be almost instantly withdrawn. And yet I longed for him to touch me. There was only one who could have covered me with such ineffable gentleness, and I needed more of that.

I lay with one hand beneath my cheek and the other resting around the back of my neck, for warmth. My finger trembled as I raised it towards the silent place from where that touch of my curl had come.

Skin, thicker than my own, a finger twice the span of mine, and yet more restrained – and a breath caught up, in uncertainty. I touched the callous made by the reins, and slipped my fingertip across the cool surface of the nail.

And at once our hands were clasped. Mine covered, and pressed – a pressure that relieved some lasting smart inside. I felt warm breath in my hair again, and wanted it.

I did not turn around, because I trusted him – his kisses on my neck were gentle promises. His hands crossing my skin seemed to leave silken paths behind them, as though scales or fur or feathers rubbed the wrong way and tingling were now smoothed down. I had looked trustingly at those hands so many times, knowing their adept strength and skill brought calm and order everywhere they moved. Now I longed for them to touch every inch of me.

As he touched me I heard him listen, rapt, to my breathing, intent on catching my pleasure. It fluttered up inside me; something I never knew was there, of vivid colours I had never even dreamed. It was ready to be startled and float away again ... but his fingers moved more gently.

I willed it to hold still, wings spread full open to the sun – blood warming, sucking nectar deep. Slowly his hands closed around it, cupped, careful not to raise the pile of velvet scales.

And it was caught, and fluttered violent against his palms – fluttered strong, beat there until I could hardly bear it—

And then he let it go, and it sailed up and out between my lips, with a sound too soft ever to have been mine.

It did not fly far – it sank down close at hand, waiting to be caught again.

For hours of the night, I felt his pleasure in coaxing mine, until that butterfly lost all its flightiness, and drank eagerly from his very lips. Sometimes I felt him hard, and yet it did not feel like a threat – though I was grateful that he never pressed it upon me, that first time.

BLODEUWEDD

20

At first I hoped to make my husband turn away from me. Instead of soft clover and downy willowherb, I made myself a blue-green dress of spear thistles, the mauve fur about the throat the only part that welcomed touch. But Lleu was nothing daunted – he seemed to take pleasure in the difficulty of stripping me of my sharp spines, and the hurts he got in doing so, and only to enjoy the more the pale down he found hidden inside.

When Gronw learned that this plan had failed – and why – it was all I could do to restrain him from rushing to Lleu with some incoherent, violent intent. The thought of such an encounter made me sick with fear. My straw-haired husband was known for his skill with the sword, and I could never have borne to have Gronw's sweet life come within its swinging heft.

But worse than that – it was well known that Lleu's uncle the magician had given him all the protection from death that a man might have. He could be killed, it was said, neither when riding nor on foot, neither indoors nor out, neither naked nor clothed, neither on dry land nor afloat – and with no human weapon made under the light of this world.

I thought of all this deeply. And then I smiled, to think how easily Gwydion's puny obstacles might be overcome when I had in view the hope of basking in the full light of my love.

And so, I told Gronw to fetch copper smelted from the ore that crumbles from beneath the green fairy mound at Tresclwyn, and to cut himself a staff of alder from the fairy fearn at Dwyran on Ynys Môn. Working only on a Friday, and only in the light that lasted in the sky after the sun had left our land for another, he must make himself a strong and heavy spear – and have it ready by the year's shortest day.

Meanwhile I set myself to work upon my husband.

When Lleu lay with me, I was used to turning my thoughts and eyes elsewhere – to gaze at any patch of sky if I might see it from the window, or, if he came at night, to look within myself at dreams of past summers. But now I turned my eyes on him – swimming doll's eyes, full of tears and promise.

The petals of my mouth used to droop open and slack as he went about his will. Now I curled them gently to, crisp and soft as the close cups of a candy rose.

My body – resistless until now as a drift of fallen petals – I gave the gentle spring of an arching briar, the coil of vetch tendrils, the melting curve of a lily's stem.

And soon, as I hoped, he longed for me to bend to him, like a sunflower towards the light; longed for me to cling to him, like briony about the bough; longed for me to open for him, as a full bloom opens for the bee. He longed, and yearned, and sickened to have it so. And I was glad to see it. He came less often to my chamber – then not at all – but met me in the woods when I walked out, and crept closer to my side as we sat together at the head of the long board.

I never encouraged his nearing, but one day I asked him what it was that made him look so sad.

He took my tulip hands in his, awkwardly, creasing the petals.

'Blodeuwedd, you don't . . . *want* me, or really care at all about me, do you? . . . Ah – you make me feel like a boy who's never had a woman and can't get the only one he wants.' His grip on my hand tightened, crushing my outer petals to translucency. I only widened my blue eyes.

'I want to tell you to love me as your duty, as I have a right! But . . . that will never be enough for me now. I dream every night that you give yourself to me freely; that you love me; that all the beauty and life of the spring that is in you rises to my touch . . . I need that to be more than a dream.'

At this he blinked a fat tear from his strawy lashes, and I hugged myself within. But outwardly, I only let the petal of my lower lip tremble, as though his tear had fallen on it like a bead of dew, and cast my doll's eyes down towards the floor.

'How can I make you – love me, as I love you? – I suppose that's what it is. How can I make your spirit mine, as your petals have been for all these months?'

And now I looked up at him, with eyes as full as April skies.

'I was flowers, and they took me from my dance by the river and my swing amongst the high boughs of the trees and my gambols in the meadow; took my freedom and my wide life from me that I might be the wife of a mortal man. I was boundless and I was placed in bonds, for you.

But still . . . I hoped that I might love in you something I had never known: a man's courage to face the limits of his life and strength. The bravest thing in life – the bravery of a soft body that must die. A true man's strength, beyond that of the mountains or the sea, springs from his very weakness. Only a brave man can do without hope of comfort or protection, and still look deep into the pale eye of death, and face him down, never daunted.

Oh – in the arms of such bravery, I would throb as a blooming cherry tree alive with bees. To the hand of such courage I would bend as a full rose, heavy with her own scent. And yet, now I learn that you are no such man – not really a man at all. Your uncle the magician, I hear, wrapped you around with protective spells, like so many swaddling bands . . . You cower from death behind the full skirts of his magic.'

Ah – I had not missed the mark. Lleu gnawed his lip, and became indeed the irked child I had painted him, despite his pompous height.

'Are you calling me a coward, wife? I never asked for such protections – they were given me when I was no more than a baby.'

'. . . and have kept you no more than that ever since. A man would never suffer himself to be stripped so of his manhood.'

'You know full well, Blodeuwedd,' he said, his face as pale and blotched as rendered fat, 'that such *tynghedau* once cast, cannot be recalled – they are anchored in a future beyond our reach.'

My penstemon lips curled. He snatched me and crushed me to him, sending petals flying, but I gazed aside, past his shoulder, at the racing clouds.

He quickly let me go.

'What do you expect me to do?'

'I expect nothing. Leave things be. Why take the trouble to persuade me to give you that which you can take whenever you want?'

'But it's your very giving that I want, and must have. What can I do?'

'Well. There is a way – if you really care about it.

On the shortest day of the year, when death is closest – I

will arrange it so that you may brave him, armed only with your courage, as every true man braves death every day he lives.

When you have passed, for the first time, through his sights – oh, then I will unfurl myself for you, my petals warm as August, although it is the depths of wintertime. Nectar will well within me at the thought of your touch, and you may drink it as your own.'

And now I gazed full at him, and the azure snake-flowers of my eyes swam with the haze of summer heat. They watched him, even as he plunged deep into their mirage. I seemed to see the last stray straws of his hair float, bob – and then sink beneath the glistening blue, gulped down by my spring.

GOEWIN

21

I had other times with Aneurin – but my hours were full of business. I had taken in hand the realms seized by Gwydion and Gilfaethwy in the south, and much needed to be done there. I loved to see things done well, and it was an added satisfaction to know I managed much better than the native lords who had lost out in the war. But I knew that any direct rule that sought to straddle the mighty mountains in the heart of Wales would always stretch too thin not to break. So I sought allies amongst folk of the south, who might forgive the unjust war so recently waged on them, and whose rule might be both wise and popular. However, resentments were strong, and did not breed honesty – and it was a long time before I was confident who it was safe to trust.

After a year, however, I had things well in hand. And now, maybe because the excitement of fast learning and action was over, I was slowed by a leaden tiredness I had never known before. Suddenly I felt like an old woman instead of a girl. I thought I might need rest, and settled myself to a month's stay at Caer Dathyl.

But still I was listless, and at last couldn't drag myself from my bed in the mornings. I slept late, and only got up to wander aimlessly around the chamber.

On the wall is inset a huge piece of obsidian stone, which Math brought from the land of the Scots as a gift for me, cleaved into one smooth gleaming face. I looked at the reflection of my naked body swimming in the dark stone. It seemed strange to me – and I tried to trace the strangeness.

My eyes flowed along the lines of my hips, the curve of my waist like a river bend; the hollows of shade rippling between and beside the muscles towards my navel. Turning, I saw the long arc of the valley of my spine, and the twin dimples that sat above the rounds of my backside.

It was in these curves that the difference lay. Their meaning had changed. I turned again to look at the reflection of my breasts – so full, fuller than usual. They spoke softly of . . . comfort. Safety. Nourishment.

I looked down at them – and saw each nipple beaded with what might have been a drop of golden honey.

I tilted one breast upwards, and bent my head to lick.

The amber bead on my tongue was too salt for honey – almost as salt as the sea – and another shade of sweet. It told no story of the heather or the clover and the busy wings of bees. Of what did it tell?

I heard the angry barking of the dogs below, and instinctively pulled a wrapping about myself, scattering the second golden bead. I went to the window.

There before the gates stood a ragged-necked stag, with one antler broken, and by his side a meagre-ribbed doe. A few paces behind them quivered a newborn fawn.

That tremor shot like an arrow straight through the narrow window to my heart. I gasped, confused, at the sudden, mortal sting of it, but taking another breath rushed down the stairs half-naked as I was and to the gate, shouting for it to be unlocked before me.

I burst out through the gate, and scattering the stag and doe aside, ran and knelt beside the fawn. I opened my arms, and she came: trembling, her slender legs still half-furled, crying out for me.

She crept under my arm. Her soft spotted back was so small that I could feel the heart beating beneath the wicker of her ribs, and dare not let the weight of my arm or of my love fall full upon her.

And now the smooth dark nose was nuzzling at my breast – I lifted my nipple to her mouth, and it closed on it, and she closed her eyes, and sucked.

There seemed ten times more power in that suck than in all the rest of her little body. The force of it took my breath away – a deep, pulsing throb; a tug as steady and purposeful as any motion in the world.

Inside me, a secret spring burst and flowed into spreading trees of conduits and acequia I never knew were there. I felt my body running like a brook; I heard its murmur and saw it slake the tiny, velvet, swallowing throat. I heard the eddies and gurgles of my life flowing into hers.

We knelt there, together, in the dust a long while. At last I took her in my arms, and imperceptibly her velvet melted to skin smooth as butter and smelling of sweet curds, and her long nose into a pink button as sweet as apple blossom, though her eyes were still the dark, thick-lashed eyes of a wild deer. And when I rose up with her, to show her to Math, her helpless limbs became long and soft again, and she slipped from my arms, and tottered by my side, a little fawn once more. And so, as she grew, she slipped from deer to girl, and back again, without ever losing every trace of one in the other.

I brought her to Math, who seemed almost as struck with her as I thought he should be. We named her Hyddwen – bright doe.

My first day with her was like a lifetime, and it extended out into the days beyond, as the hourless rhythms of her body melted ordinary time away. We stared into each other's eyes, and hardly blinked – her gaze thirsty, wide and knowing. When she nursed, she made a music without consonant or vowel, sweeter than any turtledove. And when she slept, I marvelled at her tiny hands curling like pink spring leaves, her eyelids like new moons, the dark fringe of lashes resting as quiet as falling twilight on her cheeks. At night, my breathing was her lullaby, and I curled myself around her like a nest, until we breathed as one. She woke often, so that night melted into day, but always I woke into the sweet meadow of her breath, strange and silver with moonlight or warm with gently slanting sun.

And now I was glad that I had chosen, so carefully, capable allies to govern in every part of the realm – for I must admit, I could hardly raise any interest in it any more. I cared more, in those first months, for each of Hyddwen's smiles than for all the harvest of the south. Her every cry wrung my heart more than the news of the mortal hardship of many hundreds. And as for the constant jockeying of men – their quarrels and complaints, their pride and complacency, their envies and resentments – these things seemed such pathetic child's play that I could hardly hear of them without laughing.

To nurse and soothe and teach a growing baby – it brought home the need to get things done. And so I would only listen to petitioners who had some definite scheme of practical action in view, focused on some particular end. Even then, they sometimes found I failed to pay attention, was ready to forget they were there and lose myself again in the deep pools of Hyddwen's eyes, or to catch up her smile, to toss it back to her and wait breathless for the next.

Each day with her was different, and posed challenges more demanding than all the juggling of the affairs of the realm. The year seemed like an era, and by the time September came round again, I had grown and changed as much as she had. I, also, had made progress just as fast in competence, and skill, and strength. The stakes of life felt higher, while what used to seem large challenges now seemed easy, in comparison to the creation and rearing of a new human being.

One day she sat on a thick sheepskin on the floor of my chamber, a mostly human child, talking to me fluently without words, when suddenly she stopped silent. Her eyes, which had been locked in mine, now scanned the room and shot towards the table, and she stuck out her tongue, and began to pant.

'Yes . . . dogs! It is the dogs!' I said. Indeed, there was barking at the gate.

I lifted Hyddwen in my arms and we looked down together. She pointed a damp pink finger at two ragged boar, and a tiny hogling who stood behind them, furry and striped as a little bee.

'Your brother!'

We ran down to the gates, which the guards were just opening to let through the little one, who trotted forward, knowing the way home. He gave a tiny squeak of contentment, and pressed his ears back as I gathered him up off his four short legs and pressed him tight. Hyddwen, standing by my side as a little deer, nuzzled her brother. And now we were three.

I looked up for a moment, but soon looked away, as I saw the big black boar attempt to mount the smaller sow, who did her best to shake him off, turning back to the forest and starting towards it with a wearied limp, her mate at her very heels. She must still be sore from the birth, I thought . . . Gilfa must be sore from the birth of my son.

Hyddwen would have liked to play with her brother, but he was hungry. I picked him up to suckle, and found him very different to nurse than his sister had been. He was much less adept, swallowing air, and butting his spongy snout into the pink halo round my nipples to make the milk flow faster. His little trotters pushed against the muscles of my stomach.

Hyddwen was soon impatient at all this, but I gave her the other breast, and soon the two lay quiet in my arms, looking at each other earnestly as they swallowed in synchrony the sweet milk that flowed steady as a stream in spate.

When he was a mostly human baby, small and helpless, Hyddwen had no patience with her brother, but when they were both their little four-legged selves, he loved to caper after her in the mossy glade that we made ours, and she loved to have a tiny follower. He learnt everything from her, and soon she learnt some things from him that I had never taught her. When she and I had played together in the wood, I told her the names of the flowers that I loved while she listened wide-eyed, or we stared together up into the depths of the leaves above. Now her brother taught her how to kick and butt, jump over branches and splash in the shallows of the brook. We called him Hychddwn.

My love for Hyddwen had been so single-minded, I sought to make her world perfect. Now everything was a compromise – a weighing and a balancing and a cheerful resignation to the facts of limited time, and strength, and attention, and hands. Once again, when my son wished to suckle, I could not run when I wanted to – and when Hyddwen asked me to run with her, amongst the spears of the daffodils just coming up through the dead beech leaves – to roll with her down the mossy slope above the stream – I felt it more than ever I had with Math's feet in my lap. But when I looked at Hychddwn's closed eyes as he lay in my lap – closed, while time crept upon him steadily, equally regardless of his sweet oblivion and my vigilance – I thought about the future time to come, when I might be free again to use my body as I liked, with impatience and regret hanging trembling in balance.

Hyddwen had been my own perfect dream. Hers, it had

seemed to me, was the only way to be born, and to be a baby. But I loved Hychddwn rather because, like his nursing, he was himself before he was any dream of mine. They were so different from each other – and so I knew that perfection was not the singular thing I had always thought, but the very function of mess and unpredictability.

Poor lad! That year was hardly a tenth as long as the one that went before. My world could not arrange itself neatly around him alone, as it had around his sister. With two young creatures and a realm to keep out of trouble, I learnt to care nothing for the small disasters. As long as no one was killed or maimed by the end of it, I counted each day a success, and I relaxed into the chaos of love around me.

As the summer drew towards autumn again, and I watched the bees gather busily the dregs of nectar from the latest flowers, I knew what was coming. Another child, another beginning – and also the beginning of an end. My last child – I was sure I would never have another – would hardly even wish for more. And this child would bring with him the return of Gwydion and Gilfaethwy.

It was the break of dawn when we heard the barking of the dogs at the gates, fiercer and more alarmed than before.

There in the grey light stood two wolves, their hair hanging in matted locks, their ribs lean and hungry. And there behind them was a tiny velvet pup. His eyes seemed almost blind, and his little paws were blunt and soft and unsteady under him. But his mouth was pink and wide, and he tilted back his head unsteadily and let out a tiny howl – for me.

I ran out through the gates and caught him in my arms – and shuddered a little as the two wolves followed me back within.

'Take these beasts to the kennels, and chain them,' I told the guards. 'I must get to know my son, and will not be troubled with them for some days.' I saw the way that the wolf was eyeing the bitch. 'But chain them close together, mind,' I said.

This last little one we named Bleiddwn. He was the most high-spirited and playful of my children. He gambolled all day long, blindly at first, and then with an agility and strength that I delighted to marvel at.

I felt, soon, and vividly, that he was not only my baby, but also my son. I had my reasons to distrust men, and all the ways that they marked out as especially theirs. Yet, in him, I loved the marks of swaggering strength and daring that would make him a name for being a man amongst men. I doubted myself a little in this feeling, but I could never doubt him. When, in time, I saw the other boys of the village follow him, and imitate the way he skimmed a stone, or wore his hat – following him in his madcap ventures, always venturesome almost to the point of stupidity, but not beyond – I trusted, for no reason I could have told, but which nevertheless compelled me, that he might be gentle as well as strong, careful as well as capable, merciful as well as brave. It is hard to love your sons and not have hope.

He was loyal, like all wolves, and justice was the only thing that made him scrupulous. I often saw his boy's cheeks flush, and his eyes fill with angry tears, just before he leapt into some desperate measure to correct a real or imagined injustice. I loved to see how, when he was not teasing her, he still listened to and learnt from his elder sister, acknowledging that she was always two steps ahead of him. His love was as open as his spirits, and he would curl up beside me, his soft eyes closed, perfectly at peace, so that all seemed simple in the world.

Yet – all was not so simple. When I had spent two weeks in gazing at my last-born son, I knew I must turn my mind to the fate of Gwydion and Gilfaethwy.

I found Math and Ystwyth in the hall, of course, and ordered everyone else away. Math knew what this meant, and took my hand.

'This is hard on you, Goewin bach. But, as I have said before: whatever you decide, I will think right. Yours was the wrong, and you understand best the crime. I have had my – fun – with them, and now they are yours. There are many swords more than ready to take their heads this very evening, if you wish it.'

I would have preferred he had not framed the decision in that way. My hands shook, to feel they held lives.

'I wish this might not be about myself, and the price I would exact. Can we not reflect on their just desert – or on the good of the realm? Is it good to let such men live?'

I saw that Math hesitated to give his opinion. And yet I was determined to have it.

'Tell me what you would do – we both agree I have the right to set aside your counsel.'

'They are my closest kin. I loved their mother more than anyone that lived, and have loved them in turn. In Gwydion, as a boy, I saw glimpses of good – a loving heart, and a tendency to thirst for the best company. I've had no glimpse that I could read as easily since he learned to counterfeit like a man, but I fear that may be in part my fault. He was lonely, and never had a mother's love, or a friend his equal to talk with, and I fear I failed to fill the chasm. My ties, and my guilt, are likely to twist my judgement. This is how I see it, but I warrant you'll judge more keenly.

Some men wrong women. Either because they think of them too little as full fellow beings – as I think Gilfa does – or, as may be the case for Gwydion, because they think of them too much, and feel themselves unmanned by the thought of women worth ten of themselves. Now – we have taught these devils a long, hard lesson on this score. It is not impossible that they have learnt it. And – in truth – I never saw in either outright evil towards man, or beast, before this crime, beyond what is expected of a strong man, the like of which I have committed myself. If their lesson is learnt, they may be now no worse than most of their neighbours – who, granted, are for the most part bad enough.'

'And yet – by wronging me, they also threw two kingdoms into unjust war, so that thousands were killed outright, and all our people's work for the year was burnt in the fields and rotted on the trees. Homes were burnt, children orphaned, safety forever destroyed.'

'This is true. But was not it all for your sake – to get at you?'

'Was it? I'm not so sure. I'm sure Gilfa thought so, but Gwydion . . . do you never think his chief aim was not my body but your life, and the power that might come to him with your death?'

Math ran the fingers of one hand upwards through his beard, and tugged at a shaggy eyebrow with the other.

'It might have been so. They came close enough, by the face of Arawn, and would be screwing the realm at this very moment if you were not such a formidable woman. But all this – was my fault. By making no plans for the succession, and allowing such untrustworthy shits into positions of so much trust, I placed temptation in their path that perhaps many would have struggled to resist. There would never be such temptation again. The realm is yours; you are young and clever and loved. We have three children, all yours, likely to inherit all your strengths. At least one of them will turn out competent. And I still live – and, though I have been taking life easily, anyone who even thought of threatening you or them must have very little imagination in turning over the likely fate of such a traitor at my hands.'

'Ystwyth, what do you think?'

She thought for a moment.

'It seems to me that there is little love for these brothers at the court, or beyond. Not to put a tooth in it – people know them for the scum they are. Without affection, without dignity – and with all their retinue and land stripped from them – they can be little threat. If they were to leave the court, they would starve on the land – the people would piss on them sooner than feed them. You could let them stay in court awhile, and see how they have taken their amusing lesson – and kill them only if, as I suspect, they have failed to learn it. Though personally I would prefer to watch a kick-around with their heads this very evening.'

She spat. And I felt a little better. And a little more merciful.

'Let's give them until Beltane,' I said, 'and I'll see whether I can bear to share an earth with such *cachiau*. If it looks like they're much the same as before, Ystwyth and I can use the time in planning something truly special for their final day.'

And so I again got used to the sight of Gwydion and his brother at the long boards. I saw much less of them than before, as I was mostly upstairs with the children, or in business counsel, from which I made sure they were always banished. I could see, however, that both were changed. Gilfa did not look at the women of the court as he used to. And Gwydion had lost all his blandness. His gaze was withdrawn, his cheeks hollow; he had the look of a wolf who has got used to hunger at the end of a long winter, which in another would hardly have inspired trust, but in him seemed a reassuring sign of human weakness. He made no effort to seem humble, or to ingratiate himself – which was lucky enough for him, as that might have brought forward Ystwyth's mooted football match quite considerably.

I watched him when I could, and had him watched. But he spent no time in building new alliances, or even in winning back the allegiance of those men at court who had previously been his followers, as had been my chief fear. Instead he spent most of the day shut up alone. Eventually Gilfa was more frequently taken into his company, and I thought this perhaps a sign that he was opening himself to natural comradeship and affection. On the whole my mind was quite at ease: I could think of no natural path in which he could ever become a threat to me again.

 I have told quite enough for now. My lady Arianrhod – though that moon hangs still so high in the sky, and still shines in my face while yours is nothing but shadows – it is your turn.

ARIANRHOD

22

Dylan grew like the waves of the tide, motion onwards hard to mark with the naked eye. One day he would be full of independence, only to retreat the next in fright at his own forwardness, and be all the more my baby again. And yet, as surely as the tide comes in, he did grow. Soon he would swim across the Straits by himself, and go out alone to play amongst the pods of whales in the Irish Sea. I missed him when he was away, and sometimes made it hard for him to go. I was amazed to find myself lonely with only the sky and the sea – and to have my mind always drift off with the waves towards my son.

In my castle built with magic, right on the rocks above the sea, Dylan could feel himself in two elements at once. The booming of the waves in the rocky chasm below haunted the chambers to the highest towers, and in those rooms I fed my thought on earth, sky and water all at once.

I was conscious, however, that the parts of my mind which had no relation to my son were barnacled and dragged with weed, like ships long in port. When I tried to send out thoughts away from him they moved with resistance. And so when unexpected visitors were announced, I hardly even listened, and I found myself quite stunned to find Gwydion in my presence.

I sprang up to push him out of my sight bodily; words would hardly come fast enough.

'How dare you? *I know what you did . . . all* you did . . . Get out of my sight!'

'Good sister – I have only come to bring you your son.'

This word was the only thing that could have stopped me from launching him down the stairs. Dylan had that morning gambolled off with his blunt friends, the porpoises, whom I generally consider safe company . . . but perhaps he had been gone too long.

I looked around Gwydion, hoping to see Dylan somewhere behind.

Instead I saw rooted to my flags a thick-built, straw-haired boy, around seven perhaps – Dylan's age, but in no other way like him. His glance was dusty blue with unconcern.

I thought of my Dylan, quick and sleek as an eel, and almost smiled with scorn and relief.

'This is not my son, assuredly.'

'But, sister, I promise you he is your son . . . at least . . . he grew inside that weakly guarded body that I'm looking at right now . . . first slipped into the world through that slick cunt of yours, so near at hand, that magic lets me see.'

I darted at him again with murder in my teeth and nails, but was again brought up short.

He held out before him a wand much like that over which I had stepped on the day of the trial.

'Don't interrupt me, dear sister. It is to everyone's advantage that you should hear me out.'

There was almost nothing I would not rather have done. And yet, that pale wand, through association with my moment of greatest weakness, or some other influence Gwydion wielded through it, effectively sealed my mouth, though I sickened and gagged inwardly on his words.

'How could you forget your own little child! Who shared a

womb with your other spoiled son! I have looked after him, with all a mother's tender care, since you dropped him like a spoiled haggis amongst the straw and dirt of the hall, and scurried off to save your own silky skin. You deserted him there, leaving nothing for him but your shame. But I saw him – and my heart, tender as it is, at once took pity on him. Indeed at the time he would have made a spoiled haggis look promising – for he was an ugly sack of adulterated meat, with scraps of the shredded inside of your body still hanging from him – yet I saw promise in him; I knew I could make something of him – and as you see I have!'

My gaze fell again on the stolid boy, and found no anchor whatever there. And yet my mind's eye saw through Gwydion's words something I had not recalled before.

As I ran from the kicks and hooting in the great hall of Math, there had been that final, lonely rumble of the storm. It had wrung out my womb, closed it tight as a fist again, and something heavy had slipped easily out of me, to clush down amongst the herbs.

I had felt the doors of my body burst wide for Dylan, with a fanfare of pain, as I screamed loud as any bugle, and all drew back in awe at his bold arrival. That was how to start a life.

If any other being had begun that day, it must have snuck out of me like a rat through a tattered sacking screen, matted with straw and lice and darkness.

My eyes could still find nothing of mine in the boy's yellow hair.

'He's your son . . . or perhaps I should rather say, you are his mother. When I squirted him into the dark of you – oh yes, we both know I did do that, that day in the moon pools of the river – I sent him with instructions. He became my little deathwatch – are you sure you never heard him tick?

Such a little deathwatch infests every woman when she bears

a child, and the secret second burthen, the afterthought of birth, grows inside her alongside the baby, full of the energy of the man who set her swelling – full of a life that cares nothing for hers, but as an end to its own.

Let me tell you how it happens.

Inside the walls of your womb there are five thousand lovely scarlet spirals, that bear your blood. They are fine as spider's silk, and as strong. They are lined with sheets of smooth, toned muscles, which contract and relax with perfect modulation, that your blood may flow soft and even like a meandering lowland river without angry spate. A dull state of affairs. Too dull for you, I thought.

So I told my little maggot to chew and gnaw his way inside these little filaments, to digest a secret bore through which he might penetrate each one. From within, it was an easy matter to spoil those muscle walls. He injected them with one of my specifics, which brought on a slow but complete paralysis, so they could no longer close themselves. And then he stretched them mercilessly, to ten times their proper gauge, until they hung thin and slack and powerless against him, so that the blood flowed through unresisted in a gushing angry torrent, bursting dams and carrying the banks away, flooding the meadows where he waded deep in gore. Now, he might have gorged himself on you at will. He might have sucked you dry, if he wanted to. I own, I did encourage it.

But he did more than take! I also gave him gifts to give, and these he forced into your ravaged vessels quite without your will. His secret cypher was carried all around your body, telling it how to grow, and your mind how to think, and your heart how to feel. Oh, your body tried its best to fight him – suffusing your blood with gallant warriors, little orbs as round and pale as tiny moons. But I told him what to do in that case. He polluted the rushing stream of your blood with a potion of anxiety, which made it flow faster still, your heart beat frantically and your mind race and gouge deep memories that would never leave you.

And now from the sullied stream rose a miasma, which made the moony knights who lived on the river banks strangely slow in combat and hard to wake of a morning. They pined and languished and lost all their vigour.

And then, under cover of darkness, this little one of mine started an enormous fire behind your womb, so intense that it melted the flesh. Thousands died helpless and unprotected, and none were left to bury the dead. Such was the scale of the putrefaction that all around sickened and fevered with foul contagion. Your poor chivalrous moon knights, weakened as they were, had enough to do to save your life.

You were quite at his mercy then. His business was to take all he could. He grew pale fingers, blunt and sticky – so long and so many that if they had been joined into only five, they might each have reached from here to Ynys Môn. With these he rummaged your depths, and grasped everything he wanted. He stole the air you breathed, the best of all you ate, and robbed your teeth and nails of their strength.

Best of all, I bid him leave behind, in your liver and your lungs and your brain, tiny parts of himself – parts of me. He, and I, are *everywhere* in you. Since then you have never been yourself. You are now a chimera. You may deny that he is your son, but you cannot say that you are not his mother: he has branded every organ of your body with an owner's mark. Oh, you are his mother, and no mistake. The mother of *my son*.

And as he left your womb, I told him not to bother to close the door, as every other decent creature does but man. He left all of those raped arteries gaping open. You'll remember how the blood flowed down your thighs, and didn't stop for days . . . so that you might have been left quite white, and dry, and dead, as millions of your kind have been, losing their frail lives to create another? Ah, that was our doing too! We might have killed you, but my son was wise to let you live that we might track the trail of blood for some more sport.

Look at him, is he not a fine fellow?'

The boy seemed to swell with pride at Gwydion's picture of his deeds. His skin looked thick and powdery, like the shell of a dead egg. I thought of Dylan's brown limbs, shining in the sun.

Gwydion seemed to read my thoughts.

'That other brat of yours has nothing of me in him – my share I gave over to the stream whose form I took in getting him. And so it was that he so quickly found his way into the sea. But this other, human son is truly mine. I made quite sure of that.

When I saw how his own mother had abandoned him so cruelly, I took him, and wrapped him tenderly in silk, and had him placed in a little chest by my own bed. Unfortunately, I was then – detained – for some time, by some petty spite from my uncle, and he was, it's true, more than a little rotted by the time of my return. But then I wove magic around him, that I might build a true life from such a scrap of offal as he was. And I made sure that all that was in him of mine might thrive and blossom, and grow faster and taller than a normal child, and all that was in him of you might wither away.

To be sure, one might say that has left him only half a man; but it is the better half, and I like him all the more for that. For a year, it's true, I had to give him over to a wench that he might suck the milk from her body, but when that tiresome business was over I took him back again, made sure he forgot her, and made him more my own than ever.

As he grew, I taught him who he was. What men are. And what women are. You can imagine what I taught him about you. And now I bring him to you, that you may own him as your own, and love him, and give him a man's name. A man must get his name from his mother, and every natural mother is proud to bestow it. You may thank me as you will.'

I looked at the boy once more. I did now believe that he was a windfall of my body. But he was cankered and worm-eaten in my eye – by Gwydion's words, or in himself, I could hardly tell, but it made no matter.

I found my voice again at last, though the deep and bitter sound of it seemed hardly mine.

'By the waxing of the moon, and the scarred side of her we never see, that bone puppet behind you shall never be a man! You shall never have a son. As you say that he is mine, he may never have a man's name unless I give it him. I swear it!'

I summoned all my powers, reached up behind Gwydion's head, and caught on my finger a spider web that hung there. I had watched the spider, gravid with eggs, weave her perfect web, only to have it destroyed when the wind from the window whipped up the hanging against the doorway. I had fastened down the hanging, that the same might not happen again – but my raven, wheeling in the narrow space, had caught it with his wings, so that she must begin again. I had been sad to see it – winter was coming, and she could not live long.

Now she had but half a web, but in it were silver bundles, crisp and dry. These now hung from my finger, while the spider lowered herself upon an invisible thread. I caught her on my other hand.

And now I ate the web – crunched the desiccated carapaces, and rolled the silk into a ball on my tongue, before I swallowed it.

The spider lowered herself faster towards the ground, but I caught her unravelling thread with my other finger, and raised it so that she hung above my face. It must be her free choice.

She alighted just above my chin, and at once, as I had hoped, crawled forward between my open lips. I closed my eyes, and felt her creep across my tongue, then down my throat. Opening them again, I saw that it was Gwydion's turn to stand dumb. The child also gawped at me.

There was a tickle in my throat, and I let go the shriek of fury that had been rising in me for so long. A thousand venomous spiders sailed from my mouth, each trailing a filament of silk, onto Gwydion and his little doll.

They turned to flee – too afraid, I saw, to brush the spiders off, in case they should bite.

'My curse on you!' I growled at their backs.

Gwydion was never one to give up the last word. I heard his whining as he vanished from my sight.

'By Annwn, you are a spiteful bitch, to punish an innocent child merely in vengeance. But the boy shall have a name in spite of you.'

Despite myself, Gwydion's words had struck me as so many blows, and I could hardly stand. I went to the window to watch for the return of Dylan.

Soon I saw the sun catch his bronze back, and ran down to where the sea beat up below the castle, and was ready to welcome him in my arms. He felt cool and strong as a wave. I held him tight for a moment, guilty that for the first time I sought comfort from him instead of giving it.

BLODEUWEDD

23

I looked in sympathy at the flowers now run to seed, and dragged to earth by the autumn wind that harried the margins of the meadow. To maintain the act I had adopted for my husband was harder than I had thought. I had grown used to his use of me, but to hold out the pretence that it might ever become something I would wish and enjoy – that felt a degradation.

Gronw was often at Mur y Castell from the turn of the year, and though I found my way to his arms often, yet the shadows lengthened. He was forced to feign friendship with my husband, and I hated to see it. He entered with Lleu into all the stupid sports of men. My husband excelled Gronw at these various ways of tormenting and despoiling living things – the subtle variations played out with such ingenuity around such a mean conception. I could not persuade Gronw that this did not injure his standing in my eyes. Lleu, I had heard, was named for the dexterity of his hand when raised against a helpless little fellow creature, and it was true that I could not see him thread the eye of a rabbit with his arrow or bring down a running hart with his spear without sickening at the thought of the danger to Gronw in the case of discovery.

And the hours apart from Gronw grew colder, and darker – I could hardly open my petals in the morning without the hope of seeing him to swell my cells, and I hardly knew how to hold up my head, or where to turn, when he was not within my sky. And in my unhappiness I was less bright, and feared he would miss the comfort of my summer warmth. A tiny piece of my happiness fell softly with each leaf from the trees, and at times I longed to go and hide myself in the mounds of sear waste that each wind gathered in the hollows of the wood. I felt the fist of the closing darkness tighten around me.

So I fixed my thoughts on the new life that would begin on the shortest day – of the green shoots that would burst through the frozen earth, split the sheath and tear to lovely birth in that blessed moment when Gronw should pierce Lleu's heart. And at last, I willed on the darkness, and buried myself in it like a crocus corm, in preparations for the day. And when it came, I was ready.

When I met him in the court at dawn, Lleu smiled at me in a way that I could hardly bear. But my longing for another made my role easy to play. My impatience was real enough, as we hastened down towards the river. I had explained to him that I had found a way that we might be together outside his uncle's spells – a way, and a place, he might take me, neither naked nor clothed, neither on foot nor on horseback, neither in open water nor on dry land.

I could hardly believe that Lleu could plunge so unsuspecting towards his doom through all the omens of death. The air of the valley bloomed with freezing fog. Branches dislimbed ahead. The path floated up before our very feet to join the ghosts of water. Yet in his impatience Lleu kept before me, and at times was nothing more than a moving blot.

I searched the mist for the first glimpse of my handiwork.

On the margins of the river I had built a canopy, framed in fresh-hewn alder and thatched with rushes. The cut ends of the wood, which had been milky pale under the carpenter's axe, now oozed crimson, according to its nature. The eaves were decked with thickly beaded holly. At each corner was a bunch of mistletoe, strung with viscous plasma pearls.

Under the canopy was a huge cauldron, big enough for a man to swim in, filled with water from the river, around which a fire had burnt all night, so that the water was warm, and steam eddied and span up from its surface to weave itself with the shroud of mist above.

And there hung the net I had spun for my husband, from the finest threads of piskie flax – almost as sheer as the mist itself.

He was arrested at the sight of my preparations – I thought he might be disconcerted. And so I turned to him and, gazing in his face with deep blue impatiens eyes, I felt my way along the inside of the belt that held his sword, and unhasped it. Now I busied my pale-petalled fingers with the fastenings of his clothes, as I had never done before. He trembled under my touch. Garment by garment, I stripped him bare, until he stood pale and stark and ready before me. Indeed, for once I thirsted truly enough to see him so. Almost tenderly, I wrapped the net around his bare shoulders, tight about his hips.

And now I made appear in my hand a bunch of June hay, honey-sweet with clover and foaming maiden's hair, whose scent sang out summer into the grey air.

And they heard it. Out of the mist loomed dark, forked branches; and then the long, wild heads that carried them – the valley's two strongest stags.

'Follow me, and make me yours,' I whispered soft into my husband's ear – and using my fragrant bundle to entice one of the stags to draw near and be still, I quickly climbed onto its back, coaxed him to the very margin of the high brim of the cauldron, and then slipped off down into the water, becoming half opened water lilies as I floated there.

Lleu panted at the very sight of me, and sprung astride a stag, bringing it to the margin of the bath. I panted too, knowing that the moment was at hand.

He saw the impatience of my desire clearly enough, and hastened to set his foot upon the brimming rim, where I had promised I would show him my true passion.

In that one pulse of my heart, he stood erect above me – neither riding nor on foot, neither indoors nor out, neither naked nor clothed, neither on dry land nor afloat.

And I heard a deep thrum like a prayer in the air, and out of the mist shot the dark shaft of Gronw's spear, with all the strange force of the twilight in it.

The stag reared, and I heard a thud as of a drum abruptly muffled. Lleu fell forward, and blood showered my face and shoulders as warm as summer rain. He slid down the inside of the bath, and beneath the swirling surface. Red flowers, as bright as any of my own, blossomed to the surface – fast-unfurling petals, and darker uncoiling tendrils, which I felt might take a hold of me and drag me under. I heaved myself out of the water, up onto the folded rim of the cauldron, and leapt down to the river bank.

A rumble of running feet through the ground beneath me – and Gronw caught me tight.

And, for the longest moment, that was all. Our lips were

pressed together, not for parting any more. All the time was ours. There was time, and plenty, for me to feel the coming and going of his breath in my arms, and feel him catch and hold each one of mine. I stroked that cheek of his that I had always known, and leant mine against it, and all that moved was my warmth into him and his into mine, through that melting film of skin that seemed no longer to divide us but just to make our fusion tangible. I was sure I would never be alone again.

And then, looking in each other's eyes, it was as if we tumbled into the longest, warmest day of June, and sunk into its endless sky. His love made me one dancing flame, and melted the snow around us, and the frozen ground beneath, until we moved and clasped each other in a bed of poppies, bloody cranesbill and love-lies-bleeding, a scarlet bullseye in the snowy bow of the river bend.

As I arched the eglantine of my body, my eyes wide wild succory at such excess of bliss, I gazed back beyond the cauldron at the ashy sky.

There broke into it a beating shade, that bent the air beneath and slipped away into the mist.

But I was drunk on Gronw's longed-for light, and cared nothing for shadows.

BOOK TWO
SEED

ARIANRHOD

24

The tide of Dylan's youth continued to creep quietly up the beach, so slow that I could never see which way it flowed. All I knew was that the tide could not be slack – even when our life ran smooth, I feared the race below. Gwydion's intrusion into my life had had the intended effect: he had disconcerted me, and set me against myself. He had made me fearful – for myself and for my son. More than ever, I wished to cling to Dylan closer just as he strove for wider independent compass. He gently resisted me, as he had never done before, which only made me all the more desperate to keep him close.

As he started to grow faster, again, in body and mind, as he had in the first year of his life, I tried to trust him with some of my magic. I thought hard about how to do so – I did not want him to feel patronised or slighted, though in truth I feared he was too young and wild still to understand fully what I told him. I need not have feared – every lesson I taught, he thought he could improve upon, by devising a more direct method or a more worthwhile object.

One morning he planned to go hunting on his turtle, and I went down to the bay to see him off. I watched him out of sight, afraid to be alone with my thoughts.

I noticed a boat I did not know tied up amongst the other traders at the *glanfa*. Each month brought some unknown corner of the world into my own neighbourhood in this way: glass, in fanciful forms of frosted frozen motion; pottery and metal worked to fashions that told of lives lived according to lilts and rhythms that I would never see; dyes vivid enough to have stained the water of the bay to every colour of the summer meadow. Now the smoky scent of new leather warmed and filled my nostrils, and I saw that the craft was laden with it – leather from Córdoba, with the scent of orange blossom still breathing from it. It was the colour of caramel, and soft and pliant as butter even to the eye.

In the boat sat an old man hard at work stitching a shoe, and a young boy, dirty from his soles up to his pale hair, amusing himself with a little bow and arrow.

The man looked up at my approach, and rearranged his wrinkles for me in a smile.

'Lady! They speak of the grace of your foot as far away as Al-Andalus, from where we bought this lovely leather. We have come this way with no hope other than that we might have the honour of fitting it. Will you not let me take its measure, that I may make you a shoe? I have here leaves of pure gold for the gilding of it.'

He unhasped a great wooden box, carved deep with hunting scenes, and I saw within the flakes of airy gold move and lift on the breeze as though alive. He held up a full-made shoe, and I saw how its toe was striped with gold like spreading shafts of light at dawn, and its heel studded with shining dots like stars.

In mere distraction, I set my foot upon the gunwale of the boat where the old man indicated, that he might trace its outline.

As he held my ankle and I waited for him to be done, a wren pealed out from the gorse that tumbled down the slope towards the pebbles of the beach. At first I could not see the source of the stream of liquid sound, but then I picked out the emphatic little body alighted on the highest bough of prickles, still laden with nut-scented blossoms.

Now the old man gave a whistle between his teeth as loud as the bird's, and to my surprise the brown stranger fluttered to the rail of his craft. At such close quarters I admired the bars neatly marked on its tiny wings and the acute angles of its beak and tail. Wrens were ever my favourite bird.

There was a thrum in the air, and at once the small brown rebel fluttered violently against the rail, pinned there by a fine arrow slipped between the sinew and the bone at the back of her foot.

Hearing a whoop, I turned to see the boy contorted with delight. He crossed to the bird and wrung her neck happily, pulling out the arrow and letting the body fall into the water that slopped in the bottom of the boat.

The perfect fans of its tiny feathers were quickly darkened by wet and entangled with the weeds and scraps of leather and other scum that bobbed there. Sickened, I took my foot from the gunwale. I expected some reprimand from the old man to his grandson, and hearing none I could not but insinuate some such myself.

'He clearly pledges to be a true man, that kills with such a steady hand.'

'Ha! The clear pledge with a steady hand, "Lleu Llaw Gyffes"!' I knew you'd find a name for him somewhere in that dark heart of yours.'

As he spoke, the old man's wrinkles filled and lifted and paled, and I found myself looking into the hawk face of Gwydion. He leapt onto the landing stage beside me, and the leather and gold and the boat and her masts all tumbled down into the water, where they became only driftwood, broken sedge and flotsam. The boy, who had been left on board, plodded through the water for the shore, and I recognised at once his sturdy, stolid limbs.

Gwydion was already marching him away, but I could not let this pass.

'A name alone does not make a man. I have plenty more curses in me. By all the power of the ocean swell, and the depth of dawnless dark that lies beneath, that familiar of yours shall never carry arms until I invest him with them!'

I sucked in my breath, and there arose out of the sea a high licking wave that broke ranks with its fellows and chased my brother up the beach. He ran, holding his little favourite up by the scruff as he threatened to trip over the pale logs of his own legs. The wave caught them, and carried them away like scum to somewhere far away from me. Once they had gone, another wave washed clean the place where they had been.

GOEWIN

25

And so Beltane came round again. Math had gone in a chariot with Ystwyth, at her insistence, to visit her father up on the high moors. She said that if she could give him and her childhood home so few days, one of them had better be a high feast.

I had been in the forest all day with the children. They all three, as their little furry selves, loved to play hide-and-seek in the bluebells, until their coats were dusty with pollen. As human children Hyddwen and Hychddwn climbed up inside the heady clouds of may, while Bleiddwn stood beneath and yapped. Hyddwen knew the names of every flower in the wood by now, and Hychddwn could repeat them after her. She showed her little brothers which leaves were good to eat, laughing to see their noses wrinkled by the sour of the wood sorrel and their eyes pop at the buzz of the daisy buds. They lay down, something very close to still for several moments at a time, to watch the kingfisher's blue burr up and down the river. They tried to make friends with an otter, who, however, smelt that they were half human and kept the river well between herself and them.

I went home happy, with some cheerful anticipation of the bonfires that would mark the night, and of the feast that would come before. Many perch had been caught for the occasion, and dumplings made of ramsons, which were in their pungent prime. But first I must get the children to bed – they might be up again later to enjoy the riot, but they must go to sleep with the sun as usual.

I lay flat on the bed as they clambered gently over my body, Hychddwn and Bleiddwn nursing avidly, occasionally swapping breasts for reasons best known to themselves. I enjoyed the mess of milk and fur and relaxing limbs, and almost dozed myself as I saw the tiny eyelids close, the nursing ease and slow, and the tiny mouths slide, still quivering with the reflexive echo of their suckling, off my nipples.

I did not mean to sleep, but the nursing always sent warm honey through my blood that made my lids heavy. And now, there seemed something more – a drowsy influence in the room that I could hardly resist. But the very consciousness of this had the contrary effect – I felt, with alarm, that if I slept now, I would not wake in time to take my part in the feasting.

Yet, I needed to lie very still awhile not to make any of the three little ones stir, and seek more milk. I heard the preparations for the feast below, and some sounds that I could not make sense of.

At first I thought that someone was driving in a stake above the fire in preparation for a roast. But the hammering went on – it seemed like music, but with no tune. And it grew steadier, louder; the sound of not one instrument but many. I smelt burning too – not the usual mellow drift of the fire from the hall, but the acrid smell of an outdoor blaze of fast green wood and bones. Yet the Beltane fires should not have been lit without my orders.

Soon I was impatient to leap up and look, but Bleiddwn stirred, and I was afraid that the combination of my movement and the racket below would wake him enough that he would lay claim to my breast again just when I least felt like giving it to him. So I lay still and tried again to read the noise.

I began to understand its source. Whenever there was need for a rousing racket, some youth or other would pull out a crowdy-crawn, or skin-tray – those corn-riddles, made by stretching goat skin across a wooden frame, for sifting, measuring and storing grain. Now I heard the beating of a hundred, as though each house in the village had hastily tipped out the miscellaneous mess that was always stored in such instruments when not in use, and began to beat on them, as one.

This made up no part of the Beltane celebrations as they were usually marked, or as I had ordered them. And yet – there seemed orchestration here. I was at first annoyed that the row would wake the children, but then became quite puzzled that it did not seem to do so. All three slept quiet, breathing steadily, but hardly stirring at all.

As I lay there thinking what this might mean, the dark suddenly seemed to come down deep and heavy, and I slipped from the bed. It was very cold, all of a sudden, in the room, and I covered the children softly with a fleece, and pulled on some clothes myself.

The window of my chamber looked out towards the main gate, and over the mountains. The sound, I was sure, came from the stable yard behind. But when I looked down I was surprised to see no guards at the gate.

I ran down the stairs, determined to have the guards back in post immediately, and to know how all this commotion had come about without my knowledge. Once I was far enough from my door not to wake the children, I called the orders that I knew would set dozens moving to serve my will.

Nothing happened. No one came. I knew, somehow, that they had not even heard. All sound was entrained to the beating rhythm from the yard outside.

I reached the bottom of the tower stairs, and looked out through the barred window into the court, thinking to catch the guard who should have stood there unawares, and shame him back into proper diligence.

The yard would have been very dark, but for a large fire that burnt in the centre – it was leaping higher every moment, and from it streamed dense, choking smoke of damp wood and burning rubbish. Through the double obscurity of smoke and darkness I could see nothing, at first, but the fire itself. Then I made out the hall's largest cauldron, in which we would sometimes take a bath, set on the margins of the fire. It added its steam to the turbid atmosphere, and I smelt in it rue and gallwood and other bitter herbs.

The fire itself seemed to leap to the rhythm of the bodhrans, and I could see now that the yard was quite crowded with people. They seemed to me one mass, juddering in the circle of the beating light, like the grains of corn winnowed in those skin-trays that now beat so loud.

And now there was another light – a flaming torch, carried high. The bearer stepped into the aura of the fire. And through the smoke, I saw . . . Gwydion . . . but so unlike himself that I could hardly associate him with the figure before my eyes.

He was naked. I had never dreamed before that he had real flesh beneath those clothes. But his body was oiled, and muscle and sinews shone ochre in the leaping light. And holding the torch high, his body moved with a powerful confidence I had never seen in him before. And – though my pupils tried to shut against it – I saw a part of him I could only ever have thought of soft and bloodless, now oiled like the rest of him, and rigidly erect. With a rousing gesture, he raised a low cheer from the crowd.

And now I saw dark figures moving around him – Gilfa's gross shape, I thought, and others – and a crown of bones, woven with ears of corn, was placed on his head.

The tempo of the drums was slowly rising, and the crowd murmured louder in rising anticipation.

Gwydion stepped forward, towards – what? – a grey mound before the fire; smooth, ridged; gently, beautifully curved. As the fire leapt higher, I saw that it was white, not grey.

I pulled at the door, but it would not open – it was locked or barred on the outside. Desperately I reached my arm between the bars of the window in the door, feeling for what it was on the outside that secured it, finding nothing, my gaze still transfixed by the spectacle outside.

Gwydion moved towards what I now saw was a horse – my horse? my true mare? – and as his torchlight illumined her, I saw that her neck and head and legs were pinioned to a beam, so that she could not move them. And yet now her body writhed powerfully, and I heard her scream again, as I had heard it on the night of Pryderi's death. As it echoed round the yard, it seemed to echo back to me as my own screams from the hall, as the screams of the dying badger baited there.

My mind was dinted and battered by the hammer of stretched skins. Something came loose there. I knew my hands tore on the rusty bars of the window, my lids blinked dust, from my rattling at the door, across my eyeballs – and I recognised my own scream. Still no one heard me, and I had no hope that they would, as what was around me seemed to be unwinding from a turning spool of its own accord, beyond any will that might tug it out.

My heartbeat felt chained to the rhythmic chanting from the crowd, forced to beat slower than I needed, so that there was a sick crush in my chest. Gwydion knelt down behind the horse. I knew now *that* would happen. And then it was happening, and the speeding tempo of the beating drum, his thrusts and my own heart were all reaming off the spool. For a moment I thought that it was all my dream, and I might cut it off by clipping shut my lids.

But the sound still poured out – poured into another scream from Eponwen – which was then snatched unnaturally from the air. There was an instant of blank silence, which threatened for a moment to crush all who heard it, until it was filled again by a wild cheer from the crowd, louder and more desperate than ever.

I looked again – and saw a black fountain arc and fall to dim the true mare's back. Knife blades like sparks in the dark.

She was . . . butchered there, but not as any butcher might have undertaken such a task. I saw her legs, her rib cage – still covered in her lovely, soft-bloomed coat, so terribly sullied – her whole body, segmented by a dozen knives, and carried to the cauldron by the fire, until I smelt her on the air, transformed to nothing more than meat. All that was left of her for my eyes was the spined, recursive chain of her vertebrae, a pale blood-shredded character which I read too clearly.

Time passed. I looked inwards at that image of Gwydion kneeling, and of the blades flashing in the dark. Once I became conscious again of what was before my eyes, the fire was dying down, but I saw deeper into the darkness for all that. I hung dull by my hands, watching through the bars – and saw steaming cups of broth filled from the cauldron and handed round the crowd.

Yet no one drank. I saw Gwydion raised aloft on dark heaving shoulders. He wore one trailing scrap of hide from Eponwen's belly on his back, and another around his hips. His greased skin was now dulled with ash and blood, but still he wore the pale crown of bones and corn.

They carried him to the cauldron.

I saw him pause on the brink.

And then with a fierce yell he plunged upright into it, his projecting hips spraying a steaming splash into the faces near him.

I saw his eyes close as his shoulders lowered into the water.

Covered as he sank deeper still. The crown floated, and his hair was pulled below to the last lock.

Then a roar from the crowd, and I saw he stood erect again, the crown snatched back, his naked body reglazed in the blaze, and a hunk of flesh seized between his teeth. I saw his eyes wild as he gnashed at it, like no animal.

And heard his name ring with triumph from wall to wall. And now the crowd was seething – getting to business.

ARIANRHOD

26

Gwydion never said a word in threat against Dylan, and yet I knew that my love for him was a terrible vulnerability in me, something Gwydion could hardly feel for his mannequin. I would have liked to have shut myself up with my boy, day and night, with walls of magic spun around us and my hand on his chest while he slept, to make sure he lived and breathed.

I now greatly feared Gwydion's powers – all the more because I could not help thinking of him still as the hapless boy I had condescended to at nine years old. There was something almost uncanny in the power I saw he now could wield. Perhaps, I thought, it was founded not in powers of mind equal to my own, but rather in the very vehemence and endurance of his hatred of me. I saw now that he had kept me in his thoughts, as the object of all his dark designs, all through the years. I had underestimated him already, greatly to my cost, and must not do so again at cost to my son.

I knew that the best thing I could do to keep us both safe was to cultivate my own power – to feed and widen my knowledge and my mind, that the magic I wove about us might be strong enough to defy any enemy. I knew now many of the sea's greatest secrets. I must resume my study of the land and sky.

And so I took myself inland, when Dylan was away. All my life I had inclined towards the sea; now I turned my back on it, and set my eyes on the mountains rolling off towards the heart of Wales. I walked up to the top of the moors in all weathers. And there I struggled to keep my thoughts from my son – from the many dangers my love conjured from beneath the crushing green weight of the ocean.

I took this walk one day when the hills were stark and brown under the March sun. I kept my eyes upon the sky and the ranges of the clouds, higher and deeper even than sharp Wyddfa and all her court of lesser mountains.

The sky above the moor held few birds, beside the larks that poured their silver trickle into my ears from out of sight. But now I saw a new incursion – a flock of lapwings, flying high.

As they came, their nature wavered in a mutual metamorphosis. Now they were a race of breasting waves glinting white in the sinking sun – and now, at once, obscure motes between the light and my eyes. And now they were bright rollers again, and now again shadows, after-images; inversions of themselves. Their wings made the slack-tide ripples I knew so well – the very essence of waves – an oscillation around an equilibrium, peace and energy lapped up together.

Then I heard their voices. An uncanny sound – a high baby cry; warped, as a straight reed seems bent and displaced when seen through water – and indeed there was water, as well as sky, in the sound. It was the cry of a changeling, catching at the heartstrings, only to twist them out of tune.

As the sound reached me, it seemed muffled almost at once; and I saw sheer cloud seep across the sky at the lapwings' back, and overtake them, so that soon pale breasts and dark wings alike were lost in milky air.

A wind came with the cloud, and soon it reached me, hanging the dun haze of moor grass with crystal beads, and streaming out my hair in wet cords. Before long I could see only a stone's throw about me, and as I dipped in and out of the hollows, I found I had no sense of east or west, or even of the incline of the land beneath me.

There was a smudged shape against the blank grey ahead, and as I grew closer I saw it was a thorn tree, its shape speaking of a thousand winds like this one. I found it was truly speaking – singing in the wind – or the wind was singing it.

I listened more carefully – and heard that each tussock of moor grass sung in its own tune, in such close harmony with those around it that it seemed one song. I stood still, and found that the wind was singing me, too – my hair, the clothes wrapped and flapping about me, my very bones. I strained to hear what my own song might say.

Listening still, I looked down, and saw at my feet a scrape in the grass, within it a pale halo of straw, and inside that four umber-blotched eggs, their pointed ends all meeting together, so that all four formed a perfect fragile quatrefoil, lying there quite open to the sky.

I looked up from the eggs, and watched for some time a new spectacle. Among the golden, bending swells of grass, there moved silver waves – waves that seemed to bend under the wind just like the grass, but then to bound onwards. And as the grass was tufted here and there with russet spikes of faded coltsfoot, so these silver waves were tufted with bright red.

By the time I had observed all this, they straightened and stilled themselves into a pack of pale hounds with scarlet ears, formed into a wide ring around me. They eyed, I thought, the eggs near my feet.

Raising my eyes again, I saw another shadow in the mist; a looming, shifting shadow.

A man on horseback – bone-pale horseback – with a cloak that seemed a denser swirl of mist, and a face, under his hood, that seemed to condense itself from out of silver vapour before my eyes, only just in time for him to speak.

'This hill is mine. Those eggs . . . are mine. Did you mean to take them?'

'I did not – heaven forbid! Lovely, undefended things. Though, as far as I'm aware, I walk within a domain as much my own as moors so high can ever be said to have an owner.'

'Ah! Arianrhod ferch Dôn. Forgive me. Perhaps these moors are the more yours because they are spread so near the sky; I know of your influence over the moon and her orbit. And yet, I was sure they were mine. Still – I will not let my dogs eat the eggs today, as I see you wouldn't like it.'

I thought, as he spoke, that perhaps I knew him – though I had never seen such a face of mist before. And yet it made me think of forest shade. But I was distracted from his words by noticing, beyond the ring of dogs, a movement among the grass.

A crouching lapwing, its shimmering green and purple drowned by the mist, all dismal black now; one wing was hanging, half-spread, at an unnatural angle at its side. It began to hop and flutter faintly across the tussocks towards the brow of the hill.

'Follow the bird! She knows the way, even in the mist,' said the horseman. I was already doing so – not because an abrupt stranger told me to, but rather feeling anxious to help the broken creature if I could. I found myself strangely weak and sympathetic at that time.

The lapwing flew and limped by turns, always keeping the same distance ahead of us on the slope. It was one of those moorland rises which, even on a clear day, promises that you are almost at the top many times before you find yourself there. The bird, the field of vision and the seeming summit – all kept pace just beyond me, so that although I walked on fast it was just as though I never moved at all.

At last the bird gave a stronger beat of its good wing – and the broken one miraculously snapped back into grace and power. It scooped up the wind and plunged deep into the mist.

But now the air was clearing too – and this was, at last, the summit of the hill.

I thought at first that I knew the place – the heather and the moor grass, the bilberries and harebells; I felt I had seen all a hundred times before. I looked about to get my bearings, but though the mist had cleared here, it was still thick on the slope around us, so that we seemed to be standing on an island in a milky sea.

The sky was brightening, and the sun, halfway down the sky in the west, now showed as a crisp blank disk. Slowly, its margins began to melt, as though it had been a round of pale butter on a skillet, and light flowed out golden across the sky.

The bell heather sprang into magenta fire, and I could almost hear the harebells ring in welcome of the returning sun.

And yet, this could not be – for it was March, when the lapwings start to lay. I crushed my eyelids shut, ready to look again, less incoherently. But when I did, the flowers still blazed, and the mist below had melted to reveal sea close around us – *all* around us – a sparkling summer sea, with flying breakers and a glitter path that stretched away to meet the sun.

I glanced quickly around, and there was the horseman still. Behind him stretched a tapered line of mountains, reaching out into the sea towards us, but falling long short, their margins blurred by the distance of sea spray, and their summits hidden in cloud. We were indeed on a little island.

The horseman shared none of my surprise, it was clear. He looked at me with amused interest, which I was loath to gratify with a question. And yet –

'Where are we? How did we come here?'

'Some call it Enlli.'

'Ynys Enlli? The island? And does the heather and the harebell flower here all year? And how could we have reached this place by walking from my home?'

'If you had taken a boat of strong men from Mynydd Mawr, and had them row you over towards Enlli – supposing you had not been tipped into the sea and drowned on the way, as you most likely would – you would have found the island, when you came ashore, just as bare in March as any other moor in Gwynedd. And yet – it always blooms when I am here. And you came . . . with me.'

'I came to try to help the bird – and not with you. Did I fall, and break my head – did you dare to carry me here, across the water?'

His quiet smile beneath his furrowed brow was hard to bear. 'I did not. You came here of your own free choice, just as it seemed, I swear. But – you are now in my domain, and cannot deny it. You need not look at me as though I were some errant ploughboy, barely worth the effort of questioning even when you find yourself so far at a loss.'

He looked little enough like a ploughboy. The lines in his face spoke nothing of decline, but they did speak of sadness that had passed only to come again; of change and loss and resolutions ever and again new-cast. His eyes seemed to read me – but not just me. He seemed to place and measure me in relation to all the other things that he had ever seen.

'Well! I will tell you the truth of it, without giving you the trouble to ask, as that seems more than you can wring from yourself. I call this place Ynys Afallon, the isle of apples, and it is just one lovely slice of the land of Annwn. The land is not really mine – I said so only in hopes of cheating some respect out of you. It belongs to no one. But it is my duty to take care of it. I am Arawn, he who men and women – who in truth know nothing of the matter – call the king of Fairy.'

He sprang from his horse, and drew closer towards me. 'The moon and the sea and the winds, and the very rocks themselves, have told me of you. It is a privilege to have you as my guest.'

My hands were clasped behind me, so that he had no chance of reinforcing this seeming politeness with any gesture. I have a deep suspicion of all such words. And yet, I never saw a gaze more earnest and direct – and despite myself, I half believed the flattering sentiment. Besides – I knew that I had met this man before, knew that he remembered me, and yet, with remarkable delicacy, would not allude to an occasion when he had seen me so vulnerable, and done me so great a good. He continued to speak as though it was our first meeting.

'I once had good friends amongst you mortals. Pwyll of Dyfed saved my life by killing Hafgan, my greatest enemy, and ruled fairy land for a year in a guise so like my own that all took him for myself; even my own wife, of whom, however, he never took any advantage. And then Pwyll's son Pryderi was a closer ally still, for I knew him from a boy. Were it not for me, he would have been snatched from this world while still an infant by the beast that harboured Hafgan's soul. I helped to save the little fellow for a long life – though it might have been longer if not cut short by his own trusting generosity, and the shameful treachery of a brother of yours.'

'Do you mean Gwydion? I must tell you, in case there is any misapprehension, that though we shared a mother it is all we ever shared. No one has a greater loathing for the sins of Gwydion than I.'

'My lady, this I know. I tell you, I know well who you are.'

Again, I was almost persuaded by the intense gravity of

his manner to believe his words, though none will ever truly know me.

'Perhaps – as you have come so far – you would do me the honour of sitting down, to rest and eat and drink, and to talk with me. Here is a pleasant spot at hand.'

He gestured to a circle of close-cropped turf, enamelled with eyebright and lady's bed, and jewelled with sapphire milkwort and orchids rich as rubies. Two stones, low and flat-topped, damasked with lichen, stood at a little distance from each other. Between the two now appeared, spread right on the grass, two crystal vessels of rich-coloured wine, tiny cakes adorned with violets, bowls of soft-bloomed dewberries, a shell dish of hop shoots swimming in butter, and a dainty pot, from whose spout coiled steam heady with the scent of gorse and heather.

I never care much for food and drink. I can go days without food, and never think of it. But these dishes in the sun tempted me, and made me aware of my appetites. For a moment, in that bright sun and sea breeze, the thought of the yellow crumb of cake was irresistible.

My host, for such I tacitly consented that he was, gestured formally to one of the stones as though it were a throne at the head of the longest board.

'I have, of course, a hall below, with a hundred fairies to wait, and food much finer than this. But I would like to talk, and there is no better place than this, if it will suit you?'

I sat down, and he on the other stone, not far from me.

And there we ate and drank, and talked. He spoke with the fluency of knowledge and conviction, of many things I did not know. And yet, he never wound up what he said, instead leaving it open to what I might add. He listened to me, his eyes anxious to catch the soul of my meaning before the breeze should carry it away. And his mind ran out to meet mine, and often we rode down the apt conclusion between the two of us, when one or the other alone would have let it slip away. And so our talk flowed on, until, where the strongest currents of our minds met, and it ran deepest, there were still stretches of limpid mutual silence.

We talked . . . of a thousand things . . . and though time felt light as air, I thought I must have sat there very long. But the pot of tea was still warm under my palm when I went to pour us each another cup, and the sun still hung halfway down the sky, above its dazzling path.

And so we talked on for as long again, until the glow of satisfaction that warmed my intellect told me plainly how completely I had indulged myself. It was a feeling I was unused to, and it pricked my conscience, somehow.

'I must go. I may be needed. My son will come home soon.'

I hardly knew how to address him. We had only so recently become acquainted – and yet . . .

'You will come again. We will speak again, soon. It need not be here, if your duties make it difficult for you to get away. But we must speak soon.'

I nodded the assent he presumed.

'But how may I get home?'

As I spoke, the air thickened and chilled – became so thick that I could no longer see his face, or even his form – and I found myself alone amongst dark heather. I had no sense of where I was, but sensed the slope of the ground, and followed it down.

In moments I found myself just above the path to the castle, and now the mist cleared as suddenly as it had come down.

As I entered the courtyard, I was greeted with eager cries of welcome.

'Ah, it's good to have you back, my lady – all has been quite well, however, while you were away.'

And then I saw Dylan. Or – was it Dylan? It was himself in air, and his own carefree, confident, open smile. But he was much taller than I. He had always walked with a swagger, and now he had the breadth of shoulder and length of leg of which it had always seemed the anticipation. His face was lean, and the line of his jaw and cheek had a new determination. This could not be my boy Dylan.

And then he spoke.

'Mam! You're back! It's so good to see you. I missed you more than you know! I have so much to talk to you about. Can we go and sit by the fire, and I'll tell you all you've missed?'

His voice was full and rich – a new timbre, but a well-loved tune.

'Missed? . . . How long, Dylan, do you think I've been away?'

'Oh, *almost* too long, Mam *cariad*, for I was just about to miss you sorely. But I have been very well! And you'll be pleased with all I have to tell.'

I followed him, too shocked for speech, into the hall, where we sat down before the fire. And there he truly pleased me with his tales – stories of whales and horses and winter gales, all of which told of his new skills, new strengths, new daring. I was pleased too, beyond measure, with the warmth of his pleasure in seeing me – I recognised in his eye the expression of joyful welcome I had seen in it when he was a baby after he had for a moment lost sight of me behind a rock.

I went to bed still staring in bewilderment, and let sleep overtake me in that state. But when I woke I sprang up, determined to find the truth of this.

I wrapped my cloak around me, and going down into the courtyard called for a horse. And then I cantered up onto the brown back of the hill.

'Arawn!'

I was quite alone, and let the hills ring with his name. I need hardly have done so. In the corner of my eye I saw a movement, and there he was, quite close at hand, sitting with his back against an edge of peat filigreed with silver lichen and cushioned with velvet moss, and now just folding up his long legs to stand and greet me.

'I expected to see you. I am glad not to be disappointed.'

I leapt from my horse.

'What does this mean? What enchantment is this? Why is all so changed, as though I were away for many months, or years – is it you that has done this to my home?'

His face was filled with trouble, his eyes – to my surprise – with tears.

'I have done nothing to your home, I swear it. If it seems changed, it is because you were indeed away. Did you think all our talk – all our deep acquaintance – unfurled itself in brief minutes and hours? Time, in Annwn, passes differently. Remember, you came, as you reminded me, of your own will, and not at my instigation. You stayed only until you chose to go.'

The tears in his eyes bred a mirror in my own, and it was all I could do to hold them back.

'But Dylan – he is so changed! I have missed the boy he was, last week, last month, last year!'

'My dear friend – so you always would have done. Each of those lovely boys would have fled out of your reach before you had time to hug them as close to your heart as you would – they would have slipped, laughing, away from you, and within a week you would not have been able to recall their faces distinctly enough to say to which week or month they rightly belonged. Did not Dylan welcome you, more your son than ever? And didn't you know him? And were you not both happy in being together? Was anything broken between you?'

Part of me knew, in truth, that far from breaking anything, my absence had rather mended matters between myself and my son, and brought us closer. And yet, the thought of the days I had lost still choked me.

'In this world, days pass. Every moment is a moment to mourn. Moments are defined by loss. And yet you have still your son.'

As my anger began to slip away from me, I grew more inclined to show it.

'You knew, and you never asked me! What right had you, to decoy me so?'

'You are right. I had none. But if you knew how long I had waited to talk so with another . . . so many years, that they make the few months you have lost seem less than a sliver of a moment by comparison . . . you might forgive me. I told myself I was only following your will. I knew if I showed you the truth, you would have been away after mere minutes or hours – worse than nothing for the meeting of such minds as ours. I told myself it was for your fulfilment, and happiness, as well as mine, and that I only let you follow your inclination, without calling it back to the cruel human clock. Forgive me. Though I know much of the hearts of mortals, I know less of those of mothers. Pwyll left his kingdom and his family for a year without a second thought. Until I saw the shining of your eyes, I never knew quite what it was I let you do.'

Still regret surged in me like a nagging pain. And yet, I had traded the days I might have spent looking after Dylan as he grew and changed for those hours – days, months, perhaps – of exchange of mind with Arawn. My haemorrhage of regret – for so I felt it, pulsing out strong enough to sap all my other forces – would not be staunched by throwing another irrevocable loss after the first.

'Never presume to know my mind for me again. If you don't know me as a mother, you know nothing of me at all.'

'You will forgive me then – if not today, at last?'

His face had the anxiety of a boy's, which was touching amongst the lines of ancient and well-used care that marked it. He took my hand, and pressed it – kissed it – and I did not snatch it from him. And after that, we met not infrequently on the moors, and in the wood, by the bend of the river and where it flowed into the sea, and I forgot for a time the wrong he had done me.

GOEWIN

27

I had thought my mind broken by horror, but now it clicked into fluent action. Instead of shrieking inarticulately at the bars, I began to call out the names of those I trusted most, with all my authority. But still no one came. Some part of me grasped rationally that every heart and mind was caught by Gwydion's magic, and by the glamour that he had built for himself out of it.

I was sure I was alone in the tower, but methodically cautious, I ran back up to check the children. They slept on, lulled by the beating of the drums. The rising moon peered in the window, and I looked out at her as though she might counsel me.

I asked to be noticed by the night. The hills around were hollowed by unanswering dark, and the stars were very far away. But still, I claimed help for my babies, and for myself. I begged that somewhere, somehow, there might be a mind with space to feel my trouble as if it were its own, and come to me out of the night.

There, riding towards the gate, I saw a horseman. He was hooded, and at first I could not tell who it was, but as he approached the gate he threw back his hood that the guards, who should have stood there, might know him.

It was Aneurin. My heart surprised me by the way it leapt into my mouth, but that did not stop me calling out to him; shrill, but not more than loud enough for him to hear. As he looked up at me, I saw a little less surprise than I had expected, but more concern.

He dismounted, and I saw him creep through the gate as quietly as he could in speed. I hissed to him that Gwydion had raised a coup, and the door of the tower below was locked. He held up a hand in acknowledgement – and I saw him move towards the smithy.

He was out again in a moment, and I saw tools glint in the moonlight, before he slipped them underneath his cloak, and pulled up his hood again.

And now he vanished from sight, and I knew he was making his way into the court, and to the bottom of the tower. I looked at the sleeping children. And I knew I must act, now, without a moment's further reflection, though to wake sleeping children never seems less than a desperate measure.

I willed them to be their forest selves, and so they were, and so woke quickly and completely. I lifted all three in my arms, and carried them to the window.

'Hyddwen . . .?'

She knew me, and understood at once, as I had known she would. She blinked at me only for half a moment, and then opened her mouth and shrieked into the night.

It was a grating, piercing sound such as I had hardly ever heard her make – and it quickly gathered force.

And now Hychddwn joined in with a squeal so piercing it seemed likely to bring the walls of the tower down.

And then, from his small mouth, louder than all the others, Bleiddwn let out a heart-rending howl. He howled and howled, until I was sure even the moon must hear him.

In her light, I saw a dark stream pour from the forest. At first it seemed one smooth flow, and then it was broken by choppy waves – a thousand moving backs. Moving fast. Running towards the castle.

At that pace, they would soon be here. I slung a knotted scarf over my shoulder, tucked the children into it behind my back, and threw my longest cloak over my head and them. Then I crept down the stairs, to see Aneurin just sliding through the unfastened door.

With a finger to his lips, he beckoned me to follow him outside, keeping in his shadow. We slipped out, and moved in the dark of the wall back the way he had come. The people in the court were drinking, but also busy assembling arms; they all moved with a strange automaticity, as though it were not only I who felt this as a dream.

They did not notice me, and soon I was outside the court, near the gates.

'I will find you a fast horse,' whispered Aneurin. 'We can get far, far from here before they notice you have gone. Perhaps we may find shelter in Erin, or we might ride up north to the land of the Picts.'

'Get me the tallest horse in the stable,' I said, 'speed does not matter. I do not mean to run away tonight.'

And now I could hear the sound of many thousands of feet beating the hollow turf. Aneurin heard it too, and it drove back the remonstrance he was about to make.

He brought me out a mighty plough horse, and helped me scramble onto his back. I told him to open the big doors at the rear of the smithy that led into the yard. I brought the horse to the outer gate, and feeling the babies wriggle against me, pulled off my cloak. They clung and peered around my body at the army they had summoned.

At the front were five red deer stag, the antlers spread like banners above the heaving ridges of the backs around them.

The sharp horns of the roe were raised like halberds. The forward force of the heavy shoulders of the boars seemed barely restrained. Wolves raced silently around the flanks, keeping them in rank, and now ran forward, like a dividing stream, around the two sides of the curtain wall, and sat back on their heels in a ring around it.

The drumming in the court had lost its music, and was drowned now by the sound of voices and the clank of weapons. I heard an angry exclamation – my own name – the open door of my tower had been discovered at last.

Without giving myself another moment to hesitate, I rode through the smithy, and, ducking low on my tall horse, through the doors into the yard. I murmured encouragement to my horse, and to the children, who all set up again their separate cries.

From all around the castle, the wolves began to howl. And now the red deer and the fleet roe and the heavy boars all rushed in around me. And between my horses' legs slipped the five largest of the wolves – to take their place before me with teeth bared.

As the howl of the wolves fell out of the darkness, I found that all was silent. The faces of the people were blank and empty. This was my chance.

And yet no time for speeches.

'Here I am! Do you know me? Do you know these children? Or has the dark magic woven here tonight from death and blood blinded your eyes? These creatures around me mean you no harm. They are not monsters. You know who the monsters are, though they have used the fear and glamour of death to make you bow down to them. With the bloody dawn you'll see the horror of it. Bring me Gwydion and Gilfaethwy, and no one else need die here tonight.'

My words were drowned now by the snarling of the wolves before me, and another howl from those outside the walls, and all inside the court was seething chaos. The gathered weapons were all caught up – I could not at once be sure whether in my cause or against it. I caught sight of Gwydion surrounded by a knot of followers, who I saw meant to defend him.

If there must be a fight, I hoped it would be a short and decisive one. I leant down and whispered to the wolves and boars, and they shot into the throng.

Quickly I saw one group – almost half – fall back towards the further wall, around Gwydion and Gilfaethwy; I recognised their ploughman brother, Amaethon, with them too. I saw the wolves snarling at their heels, the tusks of the boars harrowing their backsides. I saw they were already bent upon retreat.

Faces I knew were thick around me now, and seemed to see me and know me again as they had not before.

Now all was a mess of snarls and ash, blood and weapons – a violence so sickening that it was only bearable because it was everywhere at once. Tools used to plough and reap and harrow the earth cut up the flesh and guts of men. Be thankful you have never seen it.

This was my first time, and I was no natural. I was so mesmerised by the sight and the sound and the vivid, varied smell of the gouging and ripping and tearing that I had to wrench my mind back to strategy.

'Where are their horses? I saw none that might have been Amaethon's in the stable. They mean to get away. Stop them.'

I heard Aneurin shouting orders, and there was a seething of the crowd and fiercer fighting near the gates out of the court on the other side. The half of the crowd fighting for me moved to block the way towards the stable, hacked at and hacking as they went. But the seething went on, unbearably: the courtyard was a bucket full of eels.

A terrible balance trembled in the chaos of motion: it seemed that each life claimed saw one taken back; each limb maimed was paid for with equal butchery on the other side, so that they might go on, wasting and spoiling, until all were dead or mutilated. The fulfilment of my order had descended into a melee that seemed perfectly blind, and I saw only horrors against the horror. I saw a flying forge-hammer cave the ribs of a young lad, all on one side from the collarbone down, so that his human shape was spoilt – I didn't know if he fought for me or against me. I saw one of Gwydion's men gaping from his mouth to his waist, from a lateral blow from a sword or a scythe, wielded to block his rush towards the stable gates. I saw the jaws of wolves streaming with bouncing strands of blood and saliva, and another running whimpering with the flesh hanging from her thigh like a rolled stocking. How much more of this, if I stopped my enemy's flight, and forced them to fight on?

This death of men. I told myself it was the way of things. And yet – now I knew that I myself was pulling the thread of the moment from off the skein, hand over hand, and could hardly bear to see the tangled lengths of horror I was piling up. I seized on the sight of the animals. I had been happy for these creatures to fight for me, and for my children, who were half their kind. Suddenly I was not sure it could be right to let them die for me.

'Fall back from the east gate there! Drive them out! Let them go! See them on their way with something to remember!'

Almost instantly I saw Gwydion rush through the gate with a dense press of men behind him. I heard the sound of horses whickering without, and then the sound of their hooves on the cobbles. The crowd parted for me as I crossed to the east gate.

They were already spurring away, many two to a horse. The waiting sentry wolves streamed after them, leaping up and biting their heels. The deer and boars behind me surged forward, and then pulled up at a sound from the children, the stags stretching out their sweating necks to bellow after them. The air was full of the power and the fury and the threat we sent behind them. And then the hatred fell back down across the high plain like dew, lost amongst the rocks. They were out of our sight, and only the moon watched them.

ARIANRHOD

28

Arawn little thought what challenges he had set for me at home. My boy, overnight, had grown into the right to have his independence considered. I am imperious in my habits. I had, naturally, not been less so in my demeanour as a mother. In truth, few had managed to impress upon me any advantage they or anyone else might possibly gain from exercising a judgement independent, let alone contrary, to mine. If I knew best, what place was there for other wills? And yet now, watching Dylan's pleasure in his exercise of judgement, which mirrored his pride in the new powers of strength of his tanned limbs, I saw that the freedom to err was worth fighting for. And I did not want Dylan to have to fight me for it.

He must now be more than just my son. If he were, in time, to follow my ways and my judgement, he must choose those freely, in the knowledge of other paths.

Years passed slowly – Dylan making new friends of his own, and I, despite myself, turning to none other but Arawn to talk over my unease at the growing mutual independence between myself and Dylan which my meeting with Arawn seemed itself to have begun. For Dylan's sake I attempted to adapt my long-established habit of barring the world from my castle. If he was to tangle with the world of men, I would rather he did it with me at hand. And so I let visitors into my hall if it seemed they might amuse him – though still I turned away all but those who had come far and would take themselves on further after they left me.

One evening in the heart of winter two such came our way. Youths of Dylan's age, they were caught out in the storm as they walked the coast, and begged the shelter of the castle. They said they were from Erin, and I always took an interest in the people of that country, and the tales they told so well.

One of the youths seemed light-brained enough, but the other took the world sadly, and his conversation suited me. He told me he was from the land of Connaught, which had been the home of Uscia, and he soothed my heart with tales of those who lived along the cliffs that faced out even further west than mine, while Dylan drank with his merry companion.

It was very quiet in the hall, for it was a feast day, and I had marked it, as was my habit, by giving almost all the people a holiday, so that only Olwen the cook remained to wait on us, and one old man, Gareth, to mind the animals.

To my great surprise, Gareth now came trembling into the hall, to tell me that he saw three barks sailing not far off the shore, and seemingly making for the castle.

This seemed a most unlikely tale, as the storm blew fit to swamp any boat, crack any mast, carry any sail away. Besides, the coast here was notoriously treacherous, and while ships might blow ashore by accident, no captain would be mad enough to chart a course that way. However, I would not do Gareth the disrespect of dismissing his words as mere rambling, and could not discount the chance that some unfortunate wreck was driven our way before the wind, and that when it inevitably came to smash there might be survivors able to profit from our help. And so I went with him at once into one of the seaward towers.

The clouds were racing across the moon, and the rain across the sea, so that all I saw was in snatches. But there, beyond doubt, were three large crafts – with sails full set. They seemed made themselves of storm, and drove before the gale as though it was raised on purpose to fill their canvas, which showed when lighting flashed across the dark to be the livid colour of thunder clouds.

I knew at once that these could be no natural ships, and thought immediately of Gwydion. I could hardly imagine what he could mean to do, but who else but he could set three ghost ships to raid my castle in the middle of a storm?

I had magic of my own however, and did not despair: working with the waves, I might conjure defences too powerful for Gwydion's spells to breach. But I must work alone.

I hurried back to the hall.

'Dylan, friends – it seems black magic has been worked against us this night. There are indeed three ships, spun unnaturally from the very sinews of the storm, heading this way. But I am sure I may repel them. You must excuse me, however: I must retreat above, where I have a clear view over the sea. You would do well to arm yourselves as best you can in case I should fail.' I took a key, which I had in my own possession while the people were away, and unlocked the armoury, handing out a bronze trident to Dylan and the tarnished battle axes and mildewed leather armour that languished there to my guests.

The sombre young man of Connaught took the arms from me with an earnest look.

'Thank you. You do us greater benefit than you know,' he said.

Turning, I saw his friend donning the armour I had passed him. In it he looked, I thought, sturdy enough to vanquish any army of mist and rain sent by Gwydion. And yet something in his substantial appearance raised in me some insubstantial shrinking.

I turned back to his companion in time to see exactly what I feared: the gentle, straight-lined profile resolved into the aspect of a hawk, the young skin lined with curves of guile. Gwydion's face was before me.

'Thank you, kind sister! You see, you are a natural mother to my dear – your dear! – Lleu, after all. There he is, your own bright-haired son; you have armed him bravely, and now he is a man in fact!'

I now saw indeed the stolid limbs of Lleu, clad in my own armour. I could not bear to look at him, and my gaze flashed to Dylan's face, fearing Gwydion's own eyes had beaten mine.

Dylan's hands tightened on the trident, and I saw the blood slip from his cheeks behind his tan. My greatest hope was that he was for the moment frozen by surprise.

I was appalled that Dylan and Gwydion should be in one place. My instincts were so much in conflict that I could not trust myself to act with the decisiveness I needed. I could hardly bear that Gwydion should so bait me in my own home yet again – I would have liked to seize him and destroy him then and there. And yet my mind turned faint at the thought of any exchange of blows or words between himself and Dylan – I knew that the untempered strength and anger of my son could hardly be proof against the poison with which Gwydion would surely tip his weapons. And I recalled the sight of those tall ships of howling storm. Even if, as I now believed, they were only insubstantial spectres, I could not conceal from myself the fact that, in the years I had spent in studying the ways to love my son, Gwydion had made great advances in the artifices of hate.

I wanted only for him to be gone. I darted to the window and leaned out – the wind whipped my hair away, so cold around my throat. I threw back my head and invited in the storm.

First a single swirling gust, which plucked at clothing and rattled the furniture. But this was just a feint – so close behind, just as that little gust seemed dwindling, there came at once the wind's whole massive throng.

It howled and tore into the room, which seemed fit to burst; the mortar between the great stones seemed stretched like stitches, the granite shaking like a tapestry.

Dylan knew well how to ride a sea-storm, but Gwydion and his son were ridden by it, pressed inexorably towards the door, their hair and clothes strung tight by the wind, the skin stretched across their skulls, their breath snatched on its way to their lungs.

The same wind, however, seemed to swell out my own voice.

'Lleu is a pitiful toy soldier of base metal, and shall never make any other being subject to his manhood. No woman shall ever be his wife, I swear it!'

Gwydion had shaken me. Even as the gale snatched fiercely at the flesh of his face, it seemed to me merely to winnow out the smile of mastery that had chilled me before. But that could hardly be. As the storm hurled them from the room, he had to scream over the wind that almost tore his hateful voice away.

'You're proud of your mastery over the sea – but the scope of my powers will soon rival yours, as I make the earth itself my slave. My son shall have a wife. And she will be a pure woman – that is, good for nothing but to serve him with beauty and pleasure.'

Now, as father and son were forced into the passage, the concentrated power of the wind lifted them from their feet and carried them backwards and away from us. I heard them bundled bodily down the stair, like sacks of fire wood. I knew they would be blown from the castle mount, and back inland, far away.

And now Dylan and I were left together, in the lull at the back of the storm.

The wind, and my anger, passed over; I was slack and useless as an empty sail. For the first time I was afraid of my own son.

I had built, as his mother, a new integrity – stronger than that which had been cracked in the river, and shattered in the great hall, as I retched on my knees and my body opened itself before all those eyes to give birth. My mother-self was strong and controlled her own destiny, and Dylan's, both. Her body was her own to give in nurture, and he had relied for his very life upon its resources. He had come to me with seal's eyes, so big in his little head they seemed still to see another world. I had stopped him from slipping back into that other world; held him in this one, and made him substantial enough to inhabit it. I had watched his baby's body grow and fatten, almost from day to day, on cream and sugar meted from my own body's store. And as he drank less milk from me, he drank truth, instead, from the same well. I had watched his mind grow as quickly from day to day as his body had done, getting stronger, and moving away from that infant fragility that makes a mother's heart so yearn and tremble. Just as he had swallowed that nourishment, mixed of a thousand different elements that welled for him in my breasts, adapted from hour to hour to suit his size and health and mood, so he had drunk knowledge.

And now Gwydion had forced himself into my hall, between myself and my son, and as much as told my Dylan that neither his mother's body nor her truth were whole and her own, as he had relied upon them to be. I felt myself naked and soft again, as when I caught my skin in running between the razored rocks on the plain below Tre'r Ceiri. I might have been a periwinkle pried from its shell. I was hardly ready for Dylan when he spoke.

'Mam! Tell me what this means!'

'That man is my mother's son – your uncle, Gwydion. He now lives with his brothers as an outcast, shunned by the world because of his foul and unnatural practices. He is a traitor, a deviant and a dark magician, and he is my enemy. But as you see, I am more than able to deal with him. He need give us no concern.'

'Mother – he called that lad your son, and you did not contradict it.'

'Ach, I scorned to do so, Dylan – would you have me lower myself to argle-bargle with such scum as that? Isn't it obvious that such a lump of tallow could have nothing to do with me or you? There is nothing of me in him, I swear it.'

'Mam, tell me true, for when I look into your face . . . I think you lie.'

I reeled inwardly at this as from a heavy blow, but would not let him see it.

'How *dare* you, Dylan, speak to your mother like that? How can you – my own son – doubt me? Would you accuse me of dishonesty, and of having some part in the ugly lump of boyhood that stood here just now? I have given you everything, and reserved nothing to myself – do I not deserve your respect?'

I saw, with equal pangs of relief and guilt, Dylan's stern conviction crumble from his face. There I recognised the same boy's trust that had looked out from his eyes since he was born. I saw he longed for nothing more than to lean and depend on me, to let me hush away his fears. Surely it was my place to do that for him. As I saw the tears in his eyes, I could not truly doubt it.

'Oh, Mam . . . forgive me.'

His head was on my shoulder, and I held him tight, as though he shook from a nightmare. I locked my fingers in his hair, and breathed deeply of its smell of sweat and sea. I held him tighter to me, that over his shoulder I might look as I would in safety from his gaze; that I might let the shame and fear flow from my eyes out into the night, so he might find only warmth and comfort and confidence in his mother.

BLODEUWEDD

29

When all was done by the river, and done again, Gronw gathered me up like a garland in his arms and about his neck, and carried me to the castle.

There I made myself magnificent as all the richest flowers of the garden bed, and told the people that Lleu was dead, and that Gronw now was lord of all. They stared, but hardly could resist the glow of summer through their hard-chilled winter bones.

And so we went up to the stony chamber where I had been used so long as Lleu's bride.

There I thought our passion, now growing rampant as bine, might tear up the walls, and make the tower and all the ramparts fall. But at last too much became enough, and we lay at peace, while the once-bare walls of the tower room clustered with the tiny stars of breakstone, rock-crop and love-links all around us.

Now Gronw was happy – he loved his new position, and his new castle – he was a man yet – and he loved that we might love where and when we liked without concealing it. When I rode out with him, some, indeed, looked very hard at us – once a young woman spat, and it was all I could do to dissuade Gronw from some retaliation. I persuaded him that such things meant less than nothing to me, reassured him that I cared nothing that his mother and his sisters would not welcome me, as long as I might have him, and have him happy.

And so, while the snow still fell, and the earth in the meadows churned and splintered with the hoarfrost, it was a short-dayed summer within the castle walls. The winter mud in the court grew to a velvet, daisy-spangled sward, the stone walls became a hanging garden, and the thatch itself bloomed with all the flowers of the green cornfield.

Some came to marvel at the spectacle of our unseasonable happiness, and for Gronw's sake I tried my best to take an almost human notice of them, but for the most part our visitors were very few. And so it was with surprise that I heard a mighty clamour at the gate one evening, just as the sun was bulging red on the rim of the land.

It was a visitor of some importance, in a dark cloak on a black horse, and with a train of discreetly armed followers around him. I heard him ask the people for Blodeuwedd, in a clear bland tone.

I was dressing myself in respectable alkanet in order to go down to the great hall to meet my visitor, when I heard a brisk tread on the stair.

There was something in the unchecked confidence of the tread – which rang on the steps every bit as loud as seemed natural, and no more so – that I could not help but recognise. There was a knock at the door at once decorous and peremptory. And I found, not for the first time, that I could not help but obey it.

I called to Gwydion that he might enter, and in he came.

ARIANRHOD

30

I had told Dylan, when he was a little boy, that his father, if he ever had one, was the stream that runs down great Wyddfa's spine, and that was why he was of the sea. He had never questioned this, and truly I believed it. I remembered that moment of pleasure and freedom, in myself and the water, that had come before the horror, and it seemed of a piece with my son. But now I saw his mind had space for only questions.

That I was his mother had been his emotional axiom. Now, though he still believed it, he questioned what it meant – and who his mother was. I saw that anything that made me less than just his mother pained him, but at the same time that uncomplicated conception of me could no longer hold. To confess anything of the entanglements of my life would destroy the simple image of me to which he clung, and worse – it would make him sorry for me, and I was not yet ready for that. But to deny that things were more confounded than they had seemed was to challenge his credulity too far. And so now, I feared to come too close to him, and he sought answers elsewhere.

He went further out to sea than ever before, sometimes swimming far with a pod of humpback whales in competition for a cow. I was once with him in the water when he set out on such an expedition, and rapidly felt it no place for me. I had an affinity for the sea, but was not of it, as he was. I swam to shore and watched from my high tower.

The bull whales surged close together in their pursuit, until, swimming closer and faster, they drove a giant bore of silver through the ocean's heart. The cow at the centre of the pod pulled them together in the very urgency of their competition. As they swam the bulls launched sheer bulk at each other. They swallowed tons of water, and used the borrowed weight to ram each other's sides, until the silver bore was threaded with their blood. When they swam up to the surface their spouts filled the air with angry rain, and their flukes slapped the water to a white fury. I feared, and marvelled, and hardly could believe that I saw my own son's arm bent above the frenzied water, ready to pull him deep again into the heart of the fray.

At last the cow would slip away again, and the bulls would drive their immense combined force back down deep into the ocean in pursuit, and I would see Dylan's back arch above the swell as he dived down to a place I had never been. And so it would go on for days, until the cow took her final, deepest dive, so deep that even my imagination could not follow her. I could not conceive how it ended, down there in the deep dark.

Later the pod would float up from the depths, breaking the surface one by one, like stars at evening. When Dylan came back to me, it was with something of the strangeness and the distance of the depth of the night sky.

He went out hunting with the orca, taking the trident I had given him from the castle armoury. He told me once how he had made a kill of a young seal, and he and the whales had sported long with its broken body, tossing it in the air between them. I had to look straight into his eyes to believe that he was still my son, as he told me this. I smothered revulsion, and anger, and bewilderment that he would tell this to my face. But I saw he could not understand that I could not recognise any shade of these impulses in myself. And I knew that half my shrinking was not for the sake of the poor seal, but from the recognition of an impulse in him that he never got from me – as though he had toddled home to me one day at three years old, speaking the accent of men of another land.

And I knew that if he wished to go abroad and learn another tongue, I had no cause whatever to hinder him. I might not converse with him in it, only admire his fluency when I could, and regret its cruelty when I must.

And so he went in search of others to whom he might recount his hunting prowess. He spent much time in the small halls of the villages nearby, always having a place near the top of the board. I hardly knew whom he met there.

But when he came home, he was Dylan still – and, when we looked at the midnight sky together, he saw new things in the stars; things I had never told him. He told me of these things, as a wind soft with salt blew off the velvet sea, and I was proud of him.

One morning he came into my chamber earlier than I was used to, and I could see he had been driven from his bed by the force of some unusual determination. He looked hesitant as he sat down on the bench around the wall, his back straight up against the cold stone. When he began to speak, his voice was quieter and more steady than usual, with none of the plunging lilt of enthusiasm and energy that was natural to him.

'I have thought, Mam, that the battered trident I take out hunting is no good.'

'Well? Then choose another.'

'But none of the weapons in the armoury are ... what I ought to have.'

'The castles of your ancestors have been defended with those weapons – the blood of their enemies spilt, and your own blood preserved – for time out of mind, Dylan. Is there not one amongst them good enough for you?'

'But they were not too good for you to offer them to strangers. To ... that boy, who you say is not my brother. Does your true son not deserve better?'

All of a sudden, I saw that much was at stake here. I was inclined to argue with him, but immediately felt that I would not like to articulate or defend my reasons – and I could ill-bear Dylan to expand further upon his own. More than the weapon, he wanted a certain reaction from me. And I would do that much for him.

'Very well. There is only one man who can forge a weapon fit for a true son of mine. My eldest brother, Gofannon, lives under the hill at Trysclwyn, on the side of Ynys Môn nearest to the fairy realm of Annwn. From the ores and deposits left there by fiery eruptions in Fairy itself, and with the great powers he inherited from my mother, he forges weapons the like of which have never been cast in this world before. His swords hold and edge fine enough to cut a clear path through mist. His axes are so forged that they multiply a man's strength until he may split an adamantine crag in two, as easily as dry tinder. I will take you there, and beg him, for the sake of blood, to make you a trident like none the world has ever seen – with tines sharp enough to catch the silver sand eels as they pass, and strong enough to pierce the hide of a bull whale.'

My knowledge of weapons was limited, but I tried to enter into the subject as worthy of interest, and Dylan seemed satisfied.

'Well. Thank you, Mother. That would please me, and be very fitting.'

I had not seen my brother for many years. My mother had never done anything to make us friends, and we disliked each other, with respect. I knew that Gofannon was my mother's son in his strength of arm and mind, and in his more-than-mortal talents. Yet it was almost part of my esteem for him, and for my mother, and the relation we each bore to the other, to regard him with great wariness. My mother had been briefly subjected to his father – the only period of such subjection in her life – and she had hated, and perhaps killed her husband for that fact. She had pried the twisted body of Gofannon from her own, like a thing grown in and extracted from her womb by force, and kept him at arm's length from then on. I knew she had tried to despise him for his malformation and his dirty trade, and I knew she had failed, in the face of his manifest strength and genius. I was sure he knew of the attempt, not sure he knew of the failure, and certain it was not for me to enlighten him further.

The sun was low as we approached the forge, and the faces of the worked rock were double dyed: with the choleric shades that marked their fiery subterranean birth, and the dying blaze of the distant sun. Dylan strode ahead of me, and I watched his supple onward movement from stone to stone against the frozen flows of sulphur, rose and carmine, hacked at and exposed by the miners to glean the copper, lead, silver and gold which my brother worked into his metal wonders. Occasionally I saw his fluent motion paused as he found himself suddenly on the verge of a deep pit – he would peer into it a moment, and then step round and move on just as hastily, so that I bit my tongue not to bid him take care.

He saw the entrance to the forge before I did – a dark mouth in the mountainside, breathing smoke – and I saw him check the instinct to pause until I came up. Instead, he moved on, and by the time I reached the mouth of the cave he and his uncle were already eyeing each other silently.

Gofannon was ever silent, as though the bellows of his lungs, which visibly swelled the vast barrel cage of his ribs, were always refilling themselves from his last successful contest with fire and metal. I had a moment to take him in, and saw he was not changed – unless the lines of his face were deeper folded, blacker, from another decade of staring into his furnace, and facing down volcanic heat. His beard and his leather apron were as crude, rough and dirty as I remembered them, and the muscles of his arms, deeply scarred by flying embers, bulged and knotted beneath their veil of soot just as they had when, as a girl, I had resolved never to let him frighten me.

The forge was at the mouth of the mountain's deepest working, and darker, narrower passages opened from the wide-blasted chamber in which my brother worked. There were many fires, and many furnaces, and billows of fiery light chasing ragged shreds of shadow back into the inner voids. Every form, from the anvils and racks of new-forged weapons to my brother himself, cast many moving shadows – now rearing and lowering, now shrivelling and shrinking against the blasted walls. Somewhat to my surprise, I noticed that behind Gofannon worked bronze automata in female form, their gleaming bodies fashioned with outrageous perfection, rather to please man's gaze, or touch, it seemed, than to fit the hard labour of the forge. I saw Dylan's eyes also travel that way, catch there a little longer than he meant, and flash back anxiously to my face. I, however, gathered some of the confidence of disdain from the sight, and spoke to my brother.

'Greetings, brother. This is your nephew, Dylan, whose deeds, as one of the princes of the ocean, you must have heard of. We come to ask you to fashion a weapon for him, worthy of, and fitting to, his birth and his own native powers.'

Under his bristling eyebrows, Gofannon's black eyes, which had met mine while I spoke, now flicked back towards Dylan, whom he regarded for some moments without any speech or motion.

'You wish him to have such a weapon as *I* may forge – before he has a beard?' he asked me at last, but with his eyes still fixed on Dylan, so that he must have seen the added flush that crept up to his temples, visible even in the crimson glow of the furnace and its reflection from the golden weapons on the walls. There was another moment's silence, before Dylan spoke.

'*I* wish to try the best trident you can make. With that weapon . . . I am good . . .Unbeatable. The whole sea admits it. Your skill in craft and manufacture are as well-known as mine in action and war. My mother comes with me here to introduce me, but I would have come without her even if she didn't like it.'

My brother puffed air through the bristles of his nostrils, and then a billowing flare of laughter burst from his chest. It lit up Dylan's eyes, just as fiery – I saw my son set to speak again, but no words would come.

Without that bellows, my brother's laughter now only flickered within him. He spoke barely audibly to me, his eyes still on Dylan's.

'He has a boy's delicate temper I see, too. Can he expect me to believe that he *defies* such a mother as you are?'

I saw Dylan's face gather as much darkness from the sink at the back of the cave as it had gathered flush from the fires before, and so I answered very hastily.

'You mistake me, and my son,' I said, moving quickly forward, flinching from the sight of Dylan's mortification. 'He is a man now and I would judge it fitting for him to have the best of weapons, even were it still my place or power to decide for him, which it is not.'

Close to Gofannon now, I gave him a look that I would not quite have my son see, though I was afraid he suspected it. Abruptly, my brother shrugged his barrow shoulders, and turned away towards a rack of rough metal ingots in the shape of axe heads which hung against the cave wall. He took the smallest of these and handed it to Dylan.

'How does that handle for you?' he said.

Dylan handed it back as hastily as if it had burnt his fingers.

'I can do nothing,' he said, with great stiffness, 'with a weapon as light as that. I hope you jest, uncle.'

Now Gofannon took up with one hand the largest of the ingots and handed it to my son. From my brother's handling of it, it might have been made of the lightest tinder, but I saw the veins in my son's hands stand out as soon as it was in them, and the smooth muscles of his arm tighten with the effort of holding it exactly as high as it had been handed him.

'Well,' said Gofannon, 'strength may build to earn the weapon. Let me watch how you wield a polearm.'

Dylan was still holding the heavy ingot, and I saw his forehead shine with sweat as he glanced sideways at the automata at work around him. One passed close by, bearing a heavy pail of water, the furnace glow catching bronze nipples like cherries. Another was on all fours, working the bellows at a small furnace for the smelting of gold, the painstakingly sculpted and smoothed contours of its brazen buttocks shining, the cleft between as dark as the inmost recesses of the cave. I felt another impulse of contempt, that this should be the fruits of my brother's great talent, and Dylan, passing the ingot back to his uncle, said, more angrily than ever, 'Have you no place more fitting for my mother than this dirty forge?'

'I doubt my sister minds my soot and smut,' said Gofannon, with half a smile 'but certainly, she might prefer to wait in the upper gallery away from the sweat. I will have her escorted there.'

At this, he caught one of the automata by the waist, turning it away from him and bending it forward, so that he could turn a dial at the small of the back. His hands, which always looked remarkably neat and adept on such burly arms, made minute adjustments. Then the thing straightened, and, gesturing with a beautifully curved and tapered arm, made to escort me from the forge.

After a moment's hesitation, I followed the metal hips, swaying as mechanically as a pendulum, up a narrow path in the hillside, which led to a disused working revealing rock in all the colours of a dusky underworld rainbow. The shelf looked out across the valley, and was deep enough to provide shelter on some gorgeously wrought benches around a brazen stove in the shape of a goat's horn. I sat down to wait, the automaton standing rigid by my side, the light of the sinking sun rippling on its lissom abdomen. This, I thought, must be where all my brother's illustrious customers waited while he devised their commissions – they and he both dreaming how barren scars might be made to yield lovely pliant metal; to be cast and twisted and beaten into heavy and substantial manifestations of shining human dreams – dreams of action, beauty and destruction.

I would much have preferred to stay and watch what might occur between my brother and my son, but I was certain that Dylan would rather I did not see. I thought perhaps Gofannon's baiting of him might be less, or feel less, out of my presence. But my hands twisted in my lap, and my own face flushed as I imagined what tests of strength or skill my brother might set him to fail, and how his hot boy's responses would shatter in the cool of Gofannon's confidence. I almost thought I could just make out grunts, yells of effort, gasps of pain – and was sure I heard great billows of deep laughter.

It felt a long time, but the red light was not out of the sky before I heard voices louder below, and sprung to my feet. I could see Dylan standing outside the forge, and hastened down to him.

Dust caked his sweating arms, and I saw trails of blood on his legs, trickling down from clenched fists. I could not say whether it was his own. His face glowed – it could have been with the sunset light, or heat, or exercise, or mortification. He could not meet my eye, as he bade his uncle farewell.

'I'll look forward to having it. I thank you. I'm glad to have seen my uncle, and what he is.' He turned away and made towards where we had left the horses, and I stepped back to speak to Gofannon with some relief.

'My thanks also, brother. My son, as you see, is well on his way towards a man, and I'm grateful that you help him along in your fashion.'

Another quiet lick of laughter from Gofannon.

'My privilege to arm such a brave and noble youth. Perhaps I'll get my mention in the myths through him at last.'

Now he laughed outright, but I looked at him hard enough to make it stop. He shrugged, and went on in his natural tone.

'He may do well enough by the time he's thirty, if he can

handle himself through to that age. But I'd watch him. Goodbye, sister.'

I noticed that the automaton had followed me, and now stood behind. I could not resist saying, in an undertone, 'And so the legendary strength of your arm and ingenuity of your brain goes into fashioning such toys as these for yourself now?'

'Not for myself. They are for our brother Amaethon. He has plenty of wealth to buy, and is a lonely man. Lonelier even than me, as his brain does not teem as mine does. No – he wants them for their labour I believe as well as . . . company . . . and I am only . . . testing every function . . . trying everything he might want to do with them . . . seeing if there is any greater use or charm or perfection I can add to them before I send them to him. As a good craftsman should.'

I thought he smiled, but now his beard shielded his face from my eyes as effectively as from the heat of his furnace. But he is no taller than I am, and his black eyes now levelled again with mine under the twisted thickets of his brows. Our gaze locked a moment, as though riveted by the levers of love and hatred, debt and envy, secrets and knowledge that makes up kinship of the blood.

I thought of Amaethon. I had never met his eyes in that way. He was a man you could look at, but never into, and whose actions never gave any clue to inner currents. For an instant I imagined him . . . using . . . the automata. They were fit partners for him – I was sure his action would be as mechanical, and as silent, as theirs, as he put them to his purposes. But there is no sex without drive. Amaethon was a man, and so, unlike them, purposes he had. Sometimes I imagined that his self-containment was precisely a matter of placing that purpose under pressure, so that one day he might seize the wheels of fate and drive its cart onward in his own direction with one singular outward surge of his private will.

I was happy to be on my way. Dylan gave me a hard enquiring look, and when I had nothing to tell him, was cold with me that night, and on our journey home the next day, and never told me any more of what had passed between himself and his uncle. However, as the days went by, all seemed well again, and by the time he had his new trident in his hand – its tines with a liquid ripple on them like the first wave licking the sand, and the barbs like the curl when it breaks; the weight and balance so perfect that it seemed an extension of his living arm, and the whole thing adorned with inlaid scenes in silver and gold of lovely, ingenious, exuberant slaughter – he seemed, truly, more a man than ever.

BLODEUWEDD

31

Gwydion smiled ruefully at me, and looked me up and down in a way intended to remind me how he had fashioned every inch of me to meet the taste of my husband – that the body through which I felt Gronw's love was of his making.

Shamed despite myself, I paled and flushed as a medlar blossom, and waited for what he might say to me.

'Well, my dear. So you've been enjoying yourself. The tongues of all Gwynedd have been kept warm with tales of the summer heat of your bed. There's not one unbearded stripling this side of Powys who doesn't think of your breaking buds and petals when he takes his cock in hand. Never blush at that! – it's only natural after all.

I myself have not been joining in the fun. No. I hardly ever have the time to think of the things I mean to do to you. Shall I tell you how I have been busied instead? I have been searching for my son. At length, and at great trouble. I have been all through Gwynedd and Powys, and Dyfed too, until even my steady patience was beginning to wear thin. But then one night

I came to Maenawr Penardd, where an insignificant vassal of my family lives, who was only too happy to parade the paltry state of his establishment before me.

As I sat at the long board, I noticed a stir near the door, and in came a dirty common fellow with a string of yellow teeth around his neck, the shape of which told me he must be the swineherd. He grabbed rudely at any meat and drink he could get near him, and I heard him whining that he hadn't had a proper feed all month.

I took a roasted lark from my own trencher, and a dish of mushrooms – went and sat beside the oaf, offering him these delicacies. He was pathetically grateful, of course. Such men will be so when their appetites are gratified, and he opened his tale to me with touching, tedious comprehensiveness. I had to hear much rambling besides the point – of the ugly bitch his wife, of whom he seemed inexplicably fond, but who I would bet is regularly nailed by his best friend the carpenter – and of the teeming progeny of bastard brats he imagines his, all as useless as their cuckold father no doubt, and likely to rob him for want of the brains to make a living of their own.

At length, however, I sifted from this conversational scum the matter of the case. 'I have this sow aye,' says he, 'an' every mornin' before I've a chance to shake the sleep from off of me, I hear her roarin' an squealin' fit to wake the bloody dead. So I goes down there, aye, an as soon as I turn the latch of the sty door, she's off, out o' there, scarpering along the valley like the tallow of her ass was set alight. And then I don't see hide nor hair of her all day, 'til she comes home dead late, fat as the sinkin' sun, and with a stench on her breath like a witch's cunt – and by the time I have her penned up again aye, the bloody food in the hall's all gone, and I'm stuck with eatin' crusts of bread an suppin' the dregs of other men's *cwrw*.'

I offered, if he would show me the sty, to take on his duty with regards to the sow on the following day, so that he could fill his belly properly for once. Again, he was disgustingly grateful to me – a fine lord to take on such a dirty job! But he showed me the sty, and next day I was there at dawn, on my horse.'

As ever, when Gwydion was talking, I felt at first that I could not speak for all the world, but then at last that I couldn't bear to remain silent.

'Your words come as many and as relentlessly as blasted leaves in an October storm – sticking in my hair and scratching at my face – but they are quite as dry and useless and as dead . . . '

'Oh – they are not dead. They live, like the spores of contagion – they will drift past the whole and healthy without harm, but find out every flaw and weakness, every unclean cranny and hidden wound, and stick fast and breed there. If my words hurt, the fault is in you.

I will resume my story.

When I opened the sty next morning, the sow bolted out. Truly, she was uglier and fatter than the swineherd's wife, with her rows of teats dragging low beneath her like the edges of a ragged wound. And so it was not hard for my horse to keep up, as she ran along the river, until she came to a *nant* that sprang up beneath a spreading oak. There she began to gorge herself on something in the long grass.

My horse picked its way closer, and I looked down on the sow. She was consuming a stinking pile of meat. Rats, with their guts spilling out of them in violet coils; dead birds rotted to eyeless skull, their feathers clotted with gore; half-dried carcasses of frogs and toads, their sinews brittle while their skins and bellies were plimmed and mottled with decay – all mixed among strips and shreds of rotting, feathered flesh, which crawled with maggots and bloomed with many-coloured mould.

As I looked with great interest at this sight, my horse shied – another strip of dark flesh fell past her shoulder out of the tree. I looked up, and made out among the topmost branches a great eagle. Its wings were folded broad behind its back, but its breast hung in tatters, so that I could see the breast bone pale beneath the feathers and the skin. The branches of the tree were laden with beasts that must have been the prey of the bird, impaled on twigs, as you might see venison and chickens in a butcher's shop. And as I watched, the eagle tried to swallow a plump rat – only to disgorge it violently, so that it fell down to join the heap on the forest floor.

Do you know, Blodeuwedd, how that wretched creature came to sit there, like that, in such a disgusting state? I knew at once. This foul fate was the consequence of the fouler treachery planned against him – this unnatural sight was the result of the evil plotting of a wife to take her noble husband's life. I recognised my nephew Lleu, and, in his suffering, the depth of your aberrant, abhorrent crime.

Ah, you don't want to believe it. Or you hope that is the end of the story. And now you tremble – like an Eryri lily alone in its crevice in the rock, so helpless, and so beautiful. Poor Blodeuwedd.

I sung soothingly to my poor nephew, and soon he came down from the tree to my lap, and it was then a simple matter to change him back into a man – though you have reduced him to a sorry state indeed, mere skin and bone, and his flesh eaten away by death in many places, so that it may be a year before he regains his full strength.'

I had wilted down into a chair, and yet my eyes were fixed on Gwydion – I knew he was a liar, and prayed to the sun and air that he lied now.

'If my husband is alive, as you say – why would you give me

any warning of it? The train you have brought with you is not large enough to seize me here today.'

'Blodeuwedd, *del*. If your husband finds you, he will kill you – and your lover. Do you think I wish to see my lovely handiwork destroyed?'

I thought he did.

'And besides, Lleu would like to take revenge himself – shred your petals with his own hands, perhaps repay the insult you have given his trust in other, fitting ways too, as a man should. And it will be a long time before he has the strength to do that. In the meantime . . .' and here he almost paled as he looked at me, and for the first time I quite believed him, 'it pains me to think of your happiness – to hear the valleys ring out with tales and songs of the unnatural pleasures you enjoy in my son's corrupted marriage bed. I much prefer to think of the tender petals of your little heart a-flutter with fear than with love.'

He looked at me and, observing just the tremor that he desired shake through my frame, seemed satisfied, and smiled, getting up to go. In the doorway he turned again.

'You know besides: my nephew – my son – can take no pleasure in bringing down his quarry unless it is in flight. Let the chase begin!'

ARIANRHOD

32

I woke one morning with an oppressive anxiety for my son. He was on land that day, and I had come to fear the dangers there even more than those of the green unfathomed depths. I feared myself, also, when he was on land – feared that I would hang about him in thought, if not in person, and raise in him that resistance against my care that I feared so much.

And so I set off up into the hills, to try to think of something else, and climbed fast until I was alone under the sky.

Not quite alone. I saw the lapwings coming – seven of them, mere spans apart. As they drew closer, I could just hear the united beat of their wings, like the pulse of the sky.

Suddenly the foremost plunged earthward. It crumpled – white, black, white, in a disordered, weighty tumble – like the dream of life, I thought, falling back into the chaos of the dark.

A six-fold keen slit the sky as the single bird fell from the flock. My heart turned over with every fold of the creature through the air, sickening at the approach of the earth.

But the instant the blunt tip of its wing touched the heather, the bird lost all its weight, and floated upwards on the dying breeze towards the back of the sky. Its brothers were there to catch it up on their unseen skein: they pulled it tight, and all seven tacked silently away, stitching up the rent clouds.

I was not relieved, as I might have been. I saw a puckered scar where they had flown. I had been left alone on the dark face of the moor with death.

I turned hastily for home, cutting through the heather towards the *nant* which threaded the crease of the land down into the wooded valley. There it joined the river, which I must follow half a mile to reach the ford.

As I neared the ford, I looked narrowly at the tumbling water. I seemed to hear in it a new sound – a note sustained and steady under the gush and murmur, until modulated to a pitch so unexpected that it gave the former note, still echoing in my ears, a ring of sorrow I had not known how to recognise, and which seemed all the more poignant for that. I dreaded the next note, fearing it would make the slow-unfurling song sadder and sadder still.

And indeed, the third note, and what it made of those gone before, was enough to break my heart.

And now I saw that they were sung by a hooded figure stooping at the ford, washing linen and wailing at her work.

I drew closer, hoping I might know her, and wanting more than all the world to give some comfort that might stop her cry, which seemed to sing among the rushes, and echo from the alder trunks bent dim towards the stream.

As I approached, I saw that the water, which flowed clear and bright towards her hands, was strangely darkened as it slipped downstream. The stones in the river bed, I thought, must have been rusty as haws just there, for there seemed curls and coils of rich colour glowing in the water.

With her hands working deep in the water, its surface was quite smooth, and I looked for, but could not see, the reflection of her face.

And then she raised it.

It was – no face at all, seemed nothing but the reflection of the water. It was a dark stream, singing; flowing so steadily that it almost seemed at rest.

And in that seeming stillness I saw – despite my struggle not to see – a reflection of my own eyes, wide with a pain I did not yet know.

I looked down at her hands – were they mine too? They twisted pale linen in the water, and from out of it unfurled fronds of blood. As the song wrung my heart, the shirt was wrung tight in the icy water – and I recognised it for my son's.

At this time I would expect to find Dylan at home – now I ran frantically that way, knowing I would not. Fear was a smooth knot of drenched linen in my throat. I ran so fast down the narrow track that cut down the ramparts behind the caer that I almost left my feet behind, and fell headfirst into the agony ahead.

BLODEUWEDD

33

I did not tell Gronw of Gwydion's visit. I knew he could hardly take better care of himself than I would take of him. And I longed to foil Gwydion in his purpose.

He had meant, by threatening me, to rob me of the whole year of happiness while Lleu built up his strength. With the shadow of a word, he sought to rob me of the courage of the spear-armed snowdrops, sharp against the winter – of the ventures of the first bumblebee queen, nudging and spilling warm sun from overbrimming crocus cups – the March balm of primroses – the hope of the cowslips pealing in the April grass – all May's milky constellations – the calm of the buttercups floating over still-lush hay – the pure fire of the bugloss in the haze of July heat – and all the clinging, twining sweetness of the softly, gently, slowly dying summer. Each week, each month, is but a little time, like the cloud-blossoms of the breaking dawn, and the violet of the evening falling swift in silence – and only the more lovely for that. I meant to bind to every branching pleasure of this year, as the tendrils of a vetch about a bramble, or a passion flower about a spreading bough. I would love Gronw still, but never let him know how dead a frost might come with the next winter.

And yet we could not sit at home, like birds on the nest, inviting the shafts of Lleu and Gwydion. We began a wandering life, going from hall to hall, or often sleeping, or staying awake, under the stars. There our love hung heavy in the air, as rich as phlox and tuberose, and words could cast no shadow across it.

As a new year blossomed, at last whispers reached Gronw that Lleu was still – or again – alive. My own anxiety had only grown with time, and so I determined that I would find our love a mossy hollow between the day and the long night. We agreed that we should hide ourselves in the alder fearn at Dwyran.

It was a safe place – the trees leaned silently in the marsh, and the surface of the water was oiled with colour above its peaty shallows. We made ourselves a soft bed amongst the rushes and the ferns, and pressed each other tight.

ARIANRHOD

34

I shouted to be let in, and the doors were open for me – I rushed to my chamber where Dylan would have waited for me.

And there he was, lounging near the window, his eyes upon the sea.

I snatched him to me, as tight as though he was a child again and had crept into my bed shaking from a dream – tighter, knowing his man's body would not be crushed even by the full violence of my concern.

Crushed he was not, but he hardly liked it. He placed a hand on each of my shoulders, and pried me gently off as though he were breaking a seal, and afraid he might tear me and leave some part of me hanging from him if he moved too quick.

'Hey . . . Mam . . .? What is it? *Paid nawr.* Don't. Has something happened?'

'Has it?!' I search his chest with eyes and hands, more than half expecting to find the great rent there that had let out blood enough to stain the wandering of the stream. I tried to hold him again – there was a sickening emptiness in my arms without him there – but he held me back.

'What has happened?' he demanded.

'Nothing – nothing has happened *yet*. But I have seen what will come to pass. By the Gods, I beg you – trust me, Dylan – and change your course . . . whatever it may be!'

'And if I change it, that changed course will be the future you have seen. This is mere nonsense, Mother. Give over now, will you? I know you have powers greater than any man or woman alive, and yet no one can see the future, as it has not yet come to be. Let me fetch myself a cup of wine.'

He made to go, but I could not bear it. And yet I saw that I would drive him away if I did not gather myself, and that was a sickly thought.

'I will fetch you one. You stay here, and keep your eyes upon the sea.'

I stepped down into the hall, where the great jugs of wine were set upon the boards. The dark stream wavered on its way into the belly of the shell cup as I poured, but I managed not to spill a drop. I was beginning to collect myself. I had to think clearly on what I had seen, what it really meant, and how best to advise and influence my son, if needs must.

I returned bearing my dignity as steady as the wine, determined to speak with him, and to watch and listen if I might not find some seed in his present intentions that might grow and bear such deadly fruit. I handed him the cup, as though in treaty.

He took it, his eyes upon my face, and I saw his relief and returning respect at the sight of my regained calm. Satisfied, he looked down into the cup as he raised it to his lips.

His eyes sprang wide, and he flung the contents of the cup out of the window – a banner of crimson unfurled in the air, then shattered and sparkled and fell onto the rocks below, to slide into their crevices.

'Mam! What do you mean by this? Do you mean to unman me? By all the souls in Annwn, that was a foul trick.'

I looked all the bewilderment and dismay I felt, but, finding questioning looks received no answer, I grasped his arm and asked him bluntly what he meant.

'You *know*! To fill my cup with blood – did you tap the throat of some unlucky passing goat? – when I had asked for wine. To add force, I suppose, to the crazy visions you would impress on me.'

'*Cariad*, I filled your cup only with blackberry wine – look, you may smell and taste it still, on the sides of the cup! Perhaps I unsettled you with my concern... Let me fetch you another to calm your nerves.'

And I went back down to the hall, and this time could not help but spill as I poured – it sank into the grain of the boards, as wine should do. I smelt it, in case it should be soured; tasted it. It was rich and strong, as wine should be.

I took it to my son. I would not for all the world have seemed timid before him, and yet I trembled at the shadow of his anger, fearing it might come between us when I was most desperate to stay near. Still, I forced the tremor back within, and handed him the cup with some asperity –

'You drink that now, or I will know which of the two of us is crazy with wild visions.'

He gazed into the shell – and I saw, with horror, anger gather up behind his eyes. He looked bitterly at me, and holding his hand out of the window, slowly inverted the cup. The wine fell in one sudden mass, like guts.

'I will not be teased so like a child. Whether this is some twisted magic of yours, or just some domestic trick you've hatched up with the cook, it is equally insulting, and mean and sly of you to play with me so. I am no boy now, Mam – can't you treat me with respect?'

The fear within me undermined my authority. I fought hard to keep it down, yet I found myself pleading with him.

'Dylan, I fetched you only wine, by all the oceans of this world, and those of Annwn too...'

'Mam! Fetch. Me. Wine. And fetch it now. Then we may talk, and I may try to understand what has brought you to this sorry pass, and I dare say I may forgive you, or understand you. But I cannot bear you treat me like a child.'

For all our tender closeness, I had always spoken to him with authority. This was something quite new. I tried to kindle the anger that would have licked up had any other treated me so. But I was haunted still by the sight of his dear heart's blood unfurling in the water.

I let my tears fall as I went down the steps to the hall, hoping to shed my weakness with them. But it seemed I had not; I could not lift the jug, my hands shook so. I tilted it, and tilted the shell cup low, so that the dark wine flowed in slow and sullen, never touched by light. I spilled plenty and never cared, was almost glad, as if such a release might help me – for one moment I leant my arms upon the board, and let my tears fall into the dark pool that I had made. I saw my face tremble there. Then I raised my head and set my jaw and armoured myself.

'Here, Dylan, is a cup of wine I just now poured from the great jug in the hall. Don't *dare* accuse me of disrespecting you, but think rather of your duty to me, your mother, before you set up delusions as reality against me.'

He stared at me – and I could see him waver between the wish to maintain his anger and his wish to love me and to trust me and to let me be again the bulwark between him and the hard world. He took the cup.

He only glanced into it.

His face was impassive. And he spoke one word.

'*Dare?*'

And then he threw it in my face.

I tried to blink clear, and rushed for the door – rushed on to the stairs, calling his name – fell, and picked myself up at the bottom, and burst into the court in time to see him kick his horse away, and out through the gate.

I thundered at the empty court to bring me a horse, any horse! and hurried to look after him. I saw him mount the ramparts by the shortest way, and disappear from sight.

Meirion brought the black mare into the court. As though he had been no more than a dead tree, I used his body to scramble into the half-buckled saddle, and cantered to the top of the rampart.

I could see Dylan – nowhere. And I sobbed, for a part of me argued that all was lost. And yet I kicked the poor mare, and we set off to seek my son until we should find him. The front of my gown was stiffened, and there was a tight, cracking band across my forehead and down my cheeks. I bit my lip, and spat out drying blood.

BLODEUWEDD

35

There were no petalled flowers in the fearn. There were only the cones and catkins of the alders, the secret spores of the ferns, and the tassels of the sedges. I might have been happy to let the slow fuse of this green flame run down my life, but Gronw could not bear it.

And there was still no definite word of Lleu. Perhaps he could not recover himself, or perhaps Gwydion had lied, from first to last. I began to believe so.

And so we moved again from one of the great halls in our possession to the next, and sometimes returned to Mur y Castell for a little time. We were always happiest there, the place of our first meeting, and the only place, now, where we did not feel ourselves in flight.

Yet often Gronw would start from sleep, and sit up straight and cold with fear. One night he awoke just so, while the dark was still deep and silent, convinced morning had come early, and he heard the sound of trumpets join the chorus of the birds at dawn. But I assured him it was not the morning cock or the jay he heard, but only the owl and the jar and the loving nightingale, still about their darkling business. I wanted so to comfort him.

I made myself the softest flowers – full-blowing roses, spiced pinks and tender muskmallows – and wrapped him in the scent of my lily arms. He turned to me, holding me tight, as I loved him to hold me, though I would have hated anyone or anything but him to hold me so, and gently kissed the peony of my mouth. It was a kiss as perfect as the peony bud itself – a little perfect round world, full and entire unto itself – and I wished he might never take his lips away from mine. But men must sleep, and at last he turned away again, but nestled close to me, and I wrapped myself as jasmine around his waist, and breathed the scent of orange flowers to lull us back to sleep.

When we awoke Lleu's men were standing at our feet – and he close behind them.

'Gronw Pebr! What an honour! How do you like my bed? And how do you like my sheets? And how do you like my wife of flowers, lying in your arms so sweet – as though she'd never heard of thorns?'

Lleu snatched the sheets from over us, and I shrank back into stonecrop on the bed, and grew clinging over Gronw – but he sat up.

'I like your bed and your sheets very well, though I like your wife better.'

'Get up, put on – I'll not have it said I killed a naked man. I have two swords here by my side, and you can have the best of them, but we'll settle this before the sun is another hand closer to the earth.'

I knew that this was nothing more than an offer of willing

death – the bores of the court talked of nothing but Lleu's swordsmanship, and no one had ever beaten him. My Gronw had had better things to do, in the meadow and the wood, than to practise thrashing about him with a sword – and I never regretted it until now.

Slowly my love got up, and slowly he put on his clothes – slowly, with heavy limbs, thinking he'd be slain.

I hung as creeping-seefer about him.

'Husband! Take back all your lands and castle, and Gronw's too – they are nothing to us. And I am nothing to you! Let me go – let us go, into the forest, and melt away, and you will know nothing of us – the whole world may think you killed Gronw here today, and we will never let ourselves be seen to contradict it.'

Lleu only smiled. I tried for a smaller stake.

'You may give Gronw the finer sword, but it is still cowardly to challenge him with your own choice of weapon – a weapon you are known for the skill of. Let him choose the weapon.'

'You imagine this a battle, do you? In my mind it is an execution, as you both deserve for laying such an embroidered plot to murder me. We may use spears, instead of swords – but Gronw must let me cast mine first. We'll go down to the river, and he may stand on the spot where I stood when his spear struck me, and I will cast mine from the spot he chose.'

A sweet thought sprang into my mind.

'I will stand between you! As it is I who has caused the strife between you, who once were friends, you cannot prevent me from doing so.'

'Indeed we will have no women sullying the business further. Yet it is true that it is your witchery that has come between us, and so Gronw may place whatever he likes, in your place, between my spear and himself.'

My heart leapt up at this – for I remembered that, at the place where I had set the cauldron, stood upright one flat stone, as thick as my arm, and wide and tall enough to hide a crouching man. Even Lleu's famous marksmanship could never hit a man who placed such a shield between his enemy and himself.

ARIANRHOD

36

Nothing so wearisome to relate or hear than the details of a fruitless search. I looked in every one of Dylan's usual haunts, and nowhere could I find him, or anyone who could give me any clue as to where he might be. I saw almost no one on the road, but at last I came out on the straight track that runs past Clynnog, and saw a black figure of a man ahead, his cloak flapping in the crosswind. I knew it could not be Dylan, and yet I seemed to recognise the figure – somehow I felt that under that hood, there might be news.

I cantered to overtake him, and drew up as I levelled, looking back into his face.

It was Gwydion's. I was about to spur my horse away from him, when, with that cursed knack of his, he said the one thing to still me.

'Darling sister! You seek your handsome son no doubt. I saw him only now, and can tell you exactly where he is.'

'If you can tell me indeed, tell me now, in the name of the mother that bore us both!'

'Ha, you would conjure me with the name of our dear mother, would you? Tender as she was to me. Well, I will: it would be my pleasure to ease your heart of all uncertainty. But you must let me tell you not only where he is, but how he came to be there. I know your tendency to shirk a mother's duties, but you know you ought to take an interest in your sons, and how they spend their time. So let me tell you how Dylan has been spending his.'

I was almost choked with anxiety and impatience, but I knew of old Gwydion's love of the sound of his own voice. To let him speak would be the quickest way to whatever answer he might mean to give me. I froze my face, fixed my gaze on the floor, and set myself to listen.

'A month since, I met him in the mead hall at Clynnog Fawr, and in a sorry state I found him, much in need of a sympathetic ear. Oh, I did not appear in my own guise – nor Lleu neither – we were another pair of likely companions, such as you welcomed into your hall that night you turned us out so rudely into the storm – but a little rougher, and a little fonder of wine.

He was eager to learn, from any source he could, more of the ways of men and women. Ha! We helped him there. We told him every dirty joke and lewd tale that is current this side of Cadair Idris. We told him how to bait and catch a woman. And, relaxing to our company, and reeling a little from the strong wine I had given him – something stronger than that maiden's piss you serve in your hall, sister – he begged me to tell him, if I could, more of his own parentage and birth than he could glean from you. Shame on you for keeping him so in the dark! Fortunately I was able to tell him something that satisfied his curiosity.'

My eyes had leapt up into Gwydion's face, and I had to wrestle them down again with all my strength – I would not delay him with any argument or rejoinder, even of look – but oh, the agony and hatred with which I heard that he had spoken to my son of me.

'He asked me, was he indeed your son? I told him, of course he was! And he asked me, had he a brother? Now, I could not deny it, dear sister, could I? He was quite shocked to learn he had a brother, and very eager to hear how this had come about. And yet, you may perhaps be glad to hear, I did not tell him the true story of your humiliation at the court of Math, or of the role I had the honour to play in seeding him and his dear brother Lleu – I mentioned nothing at all of the pleasure we took together that day, in the moon pools round the back of the mountain, before I let you slip from me, like the tease you are – though as a rule I love to dwell on every moment of it.

No. I told him quite a different story. A story that I took the trouble wholly to invent. See if you like my fairy tale.

I told him – broke it to him very gently and kindly, you understand – that it was well-known through the country that from the time you were a girl, your own much older brother, the hunchback Gofannon – dirty and hot and strong from his forge – took his pleasure of your body against your will. And that it was he who fathered my lovely, radiant Lleu, his hair glowing with the white-hot flame of the furnace, and the violent struggle of his conception.

And was this not a pretty story to divert him from the shame of the truth – the truth that you *enjoyed* that unnatural moment, with your own brother and a wanton brook, that started Lleu and Dylan both? Enjoyed it and then concealed it, and set yourself up in false virginity?

Well, but this was not the limit of my invention. I told him further that it was whispered that Gofannon had recently come in disguise into your hall, open as you had recently laid its doors for Dylan's sake. I told him that seeing you there, he found you not so very ravaged by time and motherhood but that he had a mind to try you again – try whether the birthing of such a hefty son as Lleu had not quite spoilt the pleasures of your cunt.

And finally – and I hope you have taken all this in – I told him that Gofannon, fearing that Dylan, as your son, might offer resistance to his enjoyment of you, was plotting his murder – plotting to get the son out of the way that he might more freely enjoy his mother.

Oh no! not a shred of truth in any of it – except that when I had, before this, told my brother Gofannon in his turn that Dylan had treacherous designs against *his* life, he did not take it kindly, and looked murderous enough indeed. He was at first loath to believe it – cleverer than he is handsome, is my brother – and so I told him that I would show him the very trident, forged by him for Dylan, and now ungratefully designed to be the weapon of his own murder, hidden in the rock in a certain hollow in preparation for an ambush, if he would meet me there at a given time. I then told Dylan that he might catch his uncle unawares if he hid in that same crevice in the rock within the hollow at that same hour.

Oh, you would have been so proud of your boy! So pale at imagining you in this new light, and thinking of your sufferings. So full of bitter anger for the wrongs you had endured. So full of regret that you had opened up your hall for his sake, and so determined to protect you in times to come! He raged and swore almost like a man, poor child. So fond of his mammy. Is he weaned yet? He still shits as yellow as daffodils, I'll bet.

Dylan would have liked to fight Gofannon fairly, man to man – but I presented to him that the strength of Gofannon's arm is unequalled in the kingdom, so that in an open fight he would surely kill Dylan and so have you entirely at his beastly mercy. I told Dylan he should not, in mere pride and vanity, take such a doomed course. I said Gofannon had forfeited all right to such honourable treatment through his unnatural behaviour towards you, and treacherous designs upon Dylan himself.

Well! And was not today the day fixed for the meeting. And did I not see Dylan, trembling pale, and pretending to be a man, on his way towards the spot not three hours since?'

'What spot?' I cried, ready to tear the words out of him.

'I think I mentioned to them both the granite-ribbed hollow above Carreg y Llam.'

Hope died within me as he named the place. And yet I reared my horse around, and kicked it mercilessly into a gallop.

BLODEUWEDD

37

Although I was not to be allowed to sully the business, no one tried to stop me following the men down towards the river. First we went towards Bryn Cyfergyr, the hill which I had so carefully chosen for Gronw's place of ambush. There my poor love showed Lleu the tree behind which he had hidden himself, where he had taken aim so many times in practice at the mark I had set up for him.

Lleu's hair blazed golden in the sunlight, and, as I looked back, I thought I had never seen him more confident and happy, as he leaned himself at ease, spear in hand, beneath the trunk of the beech tree, smooth as bare young skin, and watched us escorted onwards by his followers.

I knew there could be no immediate danger – and yet as we approached the fateful place, and I saw the grey stone beneath which my love must cower for his life, I feared so much that I became no more than ghost grass shivered on the wind, and pressed a cheek whiter than death itself against his, in too much terror even to weep. Lleu's followers tore me from him, though

I clung with a hundred slender tendrils that they had to snap to part us.

I feared that my distress might distract Gronw, and turned away until he should be safely hidden behind the stone. When I looked back, I could see him no more, and was comforted that it did so well in shielding him.

I looked up now at the *bryn*, and saw Lleu's bright head catch the sun – and the bright tip of his spear glint as it was drawn back. And then I watched it winging, heard it singing through the air in an inexorable arc.

It drew my eye down with it towards the stone, and I saw in imagination how it would snap or bounce aside on impact with the rock, heard a fore-echo of the ring of stone defying steel.

But there was no ringing sound. The spear passed through rock as soft as flesh and I heard a familiar hollow thud as it was stopped by – something.

The slope of the ground carried me to the spot in an instant, and there I pulled the spear back through the stone with all my might, as if I might thread its flight back through time and make it never done.

But his sweet body, without the spear to hold it, now tumbled to the ground, and I heard my own desperate calling of his name echoed from the empty valley as I gathered him in my arms and pressed my mouth to his in desperate hope of some return.

I saw Lleu looking down at me, and at his work, and turning away to go, satisfied that he had snuffed the joy from the world.

O, my love, my love, my love – I crept as woundwort under his body, wrapping him in my downy leaves; I was a mat of self-healing over the gash in his chest, as though closing and hiding it might make him live again.

And yet he was too still – in desperation I became honey-suckle, and bound him tight and lifted him in my arms, pressing every inch of him to me with all my toughest fibres, pouring scent into his nostrils sweet enough to reach the gates of death.

Still no answer. I looked in his face – at that chin that I had shone golden light upon when he was a lonely boy and I a buttercup; at that cheek, which turned to tan while he slept in the grass and I watched him and watched out for him with every one of my moon daisy eyes. There was a terrible burning in that narrow place they made my heart, and I knew that it must burst.

My scream was a stream of helleborine as dark as garnets, exploding with all the force of a ruptured artery, and flowing around our bodies as though it would drown us both – I wished it could! But still I was – I felt the pressure in the place they made my brain, and my temples shattered into a shower of white rose petals.

For a blessed while, I was only petals, covering his body and the pain as softly and deeply as a drift of snow. I thought we were alone, and fit to sail together at peace into the white heart of blank despair.

But at last I became aware that the round hole in the rock left by the spear – that hole that let out my dear love's life, and black misery in – was an eye.

It blinked. Pitilessly, it blinked again.

The pupil was narrow and steady. The iris a fixed slatey ring. The white was veinless. It was drier than the rock itself.

Gwydion arose from behind the treacherous rock, and as he looked down on me he smiled, and conjured me back into the form of a woman – a woman with petal skin paler than death, and eyes and mouth of flowers dark as wine.

This coherence was too much to bear. I ran into the woods, not by the path but straight into the thicket, hoping the thorns might tear me up – but I was weak now, and Gwydion's magic strong, and though scarlet pimpernels bloomed where the thorns bit deepest into my breast and arms and legs, I could not dislimb myself. All I could do was cower among the briars, like the sick and wounded animal I was. I heard the magician come after me, but soon give up the search – he knew I could not get far, and nothing he could do could make me suffer more than I did then.

Instead he returned, alone, to the dear body, and dug a long grave to lay it in. He used magic to peel back the sod, and raise a pile of earth, rich and black there in the cradle of the river. And then he pulled Gronw by the arms – those arms that should have been only mine, only for holding me – dragged my darling by the arms until he lay beside the grave, and with a kick of his boot rolled him in.

I could not bear it, but as I jumped up to go back to him, I found that the briars formed a cage around me – what twisted, evil magic, to turn a part of me against myself! I dissolved in helpless tears, was a pool of speedwell and forget-me-not on the dry floor, and knew no more.

I must have lost myself a long while, for when I woke the season had turned round, and the last yellow leaves trembled on the birches. But my pain was fresh as ever – I was aggrieved, to have been cheated by sleep into placing so many hours between my living love and myself.

The bramble stems were brittle now, and could not hold me – in moments I was back on the spot where Gronw lay. For an instant, my love overcame my pain – I made myself the fairest flower of the spring, to make his grave as bright and young as he had been: daffodils and pasqueflower, anemones and columbine.

But as the wind tossed my brightness, as though there was nothing wrong at all, I found it would not do.

I sent my roots down, deeper and deeper, and made them churn the soil; churn it and displace it, until beside the grave there was a pile of dark earth as high as Gwydion's magic had built it.

And there was my love . . . so changed . . . but still the substance I had clasped, and which had held me as I had never wanted to be enclosed by any other force.

His eyes were gone, and so I grew through them. I grew between his lips, and through the chambers of his heart. I was every parasitic plant – dodder, sending my clinging red threads about his limbs to hold them together, sliding into his capillaries and through his veins; toothwort, growing from his mouth like a new tongue; broomrape thrusting from the hollow of his pelvis – and I sucked him through my roots, thirsting for all the spring that was in him still. I mated myself with and in and through him again, with all the fire of the October woods.

And when it was over, I pulled the dark earth down over us, and hoped it was the end.

ARIANRHOD

38

I don't remember how I galloped along the road, and up through the heather towards the sea-facing summit of Carreg y Llam – that dark plunging cliff that I had always recognised for the shape of my fate; a shape I had embraced when I went there to take on my powers. I was about to learn the cost. I knew that high hollow above the cliff well – and I pushed away from myself the comfort that tried to come from the familiar sight of its rising margin, which swept clear and innocent against the sky. I knew I could not see within until I was quite upon it. I marvelled, for an instant, at the way my mind guarded itself against meeting unprepared by utmost dread a blow that must in any case be fatal – as though I had raised a hand to shield my head from the slip of a towering mountain face. All of life is one such useless cowering.

I toiled desperately as the land rose towards the lip of the hollow. And at last I saw over the heather.

A spear pinned Dylan's body to the ground. And he was dead and stark.

I tried to leave, and come back again, and see differently. And then, in despair of that, I quarrelled with death, and refused to see that he was really there. And then I lost myself awhile, and cannot tell you what I did.

At last I found that I had made my arms a cradle again. He

weighed there just as though he lived. I had somehow pulled the spear from his body, and if I looked away from the hole through which his life had passed I might have thought he lived. His eyes were closed, and his cheek was brown and true as a hazelnut, and promised a sweet kernel. The lines of his mouth and jaw were bold, untouched by the shadow of death. It was impossible that it should have fallen upon him with his sun so high, and the path ahead so open.

And yet – I knew that it was so.

Now the hollow was a cradle, and I craved for it to rock me still, for this was too much for me to bear. I nuzzled for comfort in the memory of his mouth at my breast – the tiny recurved pump of his lip, drawing love from me with fathomless capacity, the crescent of lashes on the moon curve of his baby cheek. I wailed and whimpered, small and helpless, when the succour would not flow.

I thought how the first question and then the first smile broke like a clear day in his face, and seemed to answer all I ever craved to know – of the small fingers that took one of mine so surely that I never doubted a moment where he led.

I saw him growing fast as corn, the sun gold on his arm drawn back to skim a stone, and how he careless turned to smile at me. His limbs, that I had made just so, flowed smooth as water when he ran.

And now I found I could no more ring his first laugh within my ear, could not feel the first soft Ms of my new name, and could not see his eyes look up at me in trust.

Here lay a hundred dead, all mine – every darling boy he had ever been, on his path to this bloody hollow – each child I had let go from me. I should have seized and held every one wolfishly, and bared and gnashed my teeth at time, and never let him take a single one.

Once again I crushed him, ground him in my arms, as though I could reverse his growth and drive his life back to its source within myself again.

And yet there was not a tear on his cheeks for me to kiss away, and even his wound ran dry, and could not slake my heart.

My body bore more heavy to earth than his, and I begged the sky to weigh down heavier on me still.

At last it pressed me numb, and I dragged Dylan's lovely body towards the outer side of the hollow. As though he'd fallen into sleep in some awkward pose, and I would settle him in comfort, I moved him softly in my arms, onward close towards the plummet.

I looked into the face of my sleeping child once more, to tuck him snuggly into bed, to make sure he might rest easy. I kissed his soft-closed lids, and then his mouth, and rolled him over gently into air.

And – he fell so fast away from me.

His body plunged into the shining swell as deep and quiet as a tern.

The invitation of the sea, which seemed so still, so far below, was the sweetest I had ever known. I only stopped to bless the silence for promising to calm my life's storm.

And yet – within, I heard breakers crashing in the caverns of my heart. A sea wind wailed, and I heard sorrow rushing through the rocks.

The row was now without, as well as within. The sea grieved with me; he was her son too.

The storm came tearing off the sea, and beat itself white against the cliffs. There was no quiet death below for me.

The rising gale gave me a voice, and I howled and shrieked in its hold. The swell was a rising moan, and the wet rocks wept. The waves clutched groaning at the cliff, and I outsung them all – sung them all my sorrow.

And when I had done, I gathered again my last step.

But something struck me in the keening of the waves.

The groan was now a growl, the howl a hiss, the shriek a snarl, the plaint of sorrow and regret a roar of rage and vengeance.

My soul set itself eagerly to the tune, and I became at once far too bitter for death. I knew that I might jump, and that though I plunged deep down towards the quiet depths, my hate would buoy me rushing up, to burst back into this seething storm.

I could no longer live, that much was certain. But surer still was that Gwydion must die first.

BLODEUWEDD

39

It might have been the end, if it hadn't been for Gwydion – but he was inveterate. I don't know whether he really thought I could still make his son a wife, or whether he enjoyed kicking at dirty, rotting petals for its own sake, but he would not let me lie. In the winter, he returned to the bare dark mound where I lay with my love, and began to cast a spell. He conjured a coverlet of toadstools for our bed – blanched destroying angel, death cap, fool's funnel and funeral bells.

The mushrooms are no kin of mine – their kingdom of the dark is as alien to me as that of men, and Gwydion, a night creature himself, had no difficulty in conjuring them to work against me.

The first I knew was something coming between my love and me – a mesh or net, whose strictures spun tight again my hated woman's form.

The mycelia of the fungi bound me up and tore me from my love's arms, dragging me back to the living world, into the air.

My only pleasure was to see the shock in Gwydion's face

when he saw me. I was the flowers of death – jaundiced henbane, densely webbed with blood-black veins. I made myself a flaunting bridal robe of hemlock lace, and stood before him on the desecrated mound. The pleasure I felt in seeing his face waver from its cunning serenity was greater than I had ever thought to feel again. It helped me find my human voice.

'Gwydion! Am I the beautiful bride of flowers, the most lovely woman in the world, designed by you for your nephew? All he ever had of me was poison, and rot, and death – while, despite all your hate, I opened for pure love all the tender pleasures of bursting summer buds. In the form you gave me, I have known not only the cruel grip of winter frost, but also the gush and melt of spring – not only what it is to be a closed and lonely seed, but also the ecstasy of unfurling double joy, grafted with another, our sap rising together. Though you have stolen this joy from me, snapped off my other half, yet I rejoice to know it is a joy you have never known, and can never know. Look at me – deep into the poison tunnels of my eyes – and see into your own heart.'

For a moment he was still, and looked at me indeed, appalled. I was delighted to feel the twist of rage that made him seize the blotched stems of my arms. He grasped my throat, crushing the petals, and I breathed on him my smell of rot and death from every flower.

At once, the poison in the air began to numb his mind. I brought my face close to his, and breathed again. He reeled – his pupils dilated, his eyes black mirrors of my own. Now he was in my power, at last. My arms were briony now, and bound him tight against me, that my poison might seep into him at every pore.

When pupils dilate so far that the iris disappears, eyes see beyond and through this world to another – or they see inside the dark globes of themselves. I could see that Gwydion saw me no more.

Ah – I panted with joy at the sight of the next symptom on the road to flowery death. His skin flushed, as I had never seen it, and I felt him both stiffen and melt with the desire that he had always seemed the master of.

'Arianrhod . . . is it you? At last? I have been so lonely for you, so long. And wanted you so badly.'

'Yes, brother. Hold me close. Let us be brother and sister once more.'

I pressed my purple belladonna lips to his, sliding my pistil into his mouth, and felt his tongue circle and lick the poison from it.

Almost at once his heart began to race, and I saw terror in his eyes, as his mouth gaped under mine.

'Stay with me, under the wolf skin, Arianrhod? Don't leave me – I'm so afraid. The boars and . . . the wolves . . . are coming for me. They hunt me when I'm all alone.'

At once I turned myself to blackthorn and gorse and thistle, so that he loosed his hold on me with a shriek of pain. And now I spat at him.

'I will not stay. I will leave you alone – I will take away even my hate, which is all I have . . . Look into the dark!'

His eyes rolled back, and he began to convulse. I let his body fall at my feet, and kicked him where he lay, the froth from his mouth pale as the uprooted toadstools on the dark earth of the burial mound.

'This is pain and death, brother . . . and loneliness . . . and I wish it on you with every part of the soul that you have blighted.'

And so I left him, and returned to the meagre fibres of my love's enfolding arms that decay had yet left me, hoping never to leave them again.

GOEWIN AND ARIANRHOD

40

I have never been sure whether I did right to let Gwydion and his brothers go that awful night of the attempted coup, or whether I could have caught and killed them. They retreated to Amaethon's lands, and there made themselves quite secure. Amaethon's people were well-fed and happy, and had no reason to drive out their familiar master or his brothers, and though their lands were surrounded by mine, they were more or less sufficient to themselves for all that they might want.

And so, for fifteen years, they sat at Rhuddlan, and I hesitated to move against them. They have given me no provocation. I have my spies, and they have reported nothing to give me concern. I could not know, Arianrhod, that during this time Gwydion's hate and wiles were focused all on you. I wish I had known it: such power as he showed, in his efforts to make you recognise his son as a man, are a constant danger to all of us when coupled with animus like his.

Then one day this winter, as trees and hillsides waited still and hushed under a silent fall of snow, I was brought word that Gwydion was dead. I could get no convincing account of the manner of his death, or of his resting place – and couldn't help fearing some trick. I will not underestimate him again. And indeed, as the snow melted, and spears and fists of green thrust through the earth, I heard rumours, equally incoherent and inconclusive, that he lived again. This too, certainly, could be a lie put about by his brothers, who I heard were quite at a loss to keep up their position without his brains to guide them. Arianrhod, you of all people must be able to tell me.

I regret to say that I can.

Every day, in the long months since I lost Dylan, I have been out walking, to plot my revenge with the land and sea and sky. I knew I must wait for my brain to cool a little before I could lay my plan, but I was sure it would freeze into a dark glass that might be split to take the sharpest edge – an edge to slice through skin and flesh and brain and bone equally without resistance.

Winter helped the freeze – the cold pulling the skin taut over my bones, and making ice stilettos of my whitening fingers – and when spring came the roots of determination spread and branched beneath the surface, and my growing hate lengthened with the days, ramping over my whole mind with the returning briars and nettles.

Just days ago, I was walking high on the moors when I spied the lapwings once more. I almost laughed to see them, though they made me shudder. There was no fate for me to hear in their whistle that might fill me with dread now, for the worst had already come. And I saw they knew this – they bore not directly for me, but a little aside. And now I watched the dance, and knew it was not for me.

I watched their flight, like a pulse between the darkness and the light. I saw the moment when the thread which joined them into one being seemed to snap, and a single dim, shining bead plummeted earthward. Again, I almost felt the ground rush up to meet the bird, yet I knew that unlike my boy, or me, it would somehow save itself at the final moment. It seemed cruel, to act out before my eyes the reprieve that all believe in, but for us had never come.

And yet now this miming of the plunge of death struck a new chord of recognition. Brightness folded into dark. Confident flight, crumpled and broken. It was too much – I blinked my eyes at the moment when impact would have come, and opened them to see the bird soar upward again. But the air over the heather was empty. And when I looked up, I saw the other lapwings wheeling in disorder, and I heard their mew – that heart-twisting cry of the abandoned changing child. And now I saw a bent figure fleeing fast away across the moor, something clutched to his body.

The lapwings keened more plaintively than ever, reproach and warning in their chorus. I became aware of another sound altogether – the beating of hooves through the turf below me. I turned to see a grey horse and rider, mane and cloak flowing wild, breasting the summit of the hill – and racing ahead of them, six pale hounds with blood-red ears, careering down towards me. The eyes of the hounds flashed red, as though already suffused with the blood they meant to spill.

Arawn pulled up his horse beside me.

'Where did he go? By the moon, tell me quickly!'

I had done everything to shun Arawn since the death of my son, and bitterly regretted the almost daily meetings we had had in the months before. I knew he knew that I did not want to see him ever again. I could not now forgive those months, and days, and hours of my boy's company he had enticed me to miss. I sometimes grieved for them as though they had been everything, and that it was Arawn who had done me the greatest wrong of all. And so I paused to answer.

'I beg you tell me, for the good of many more than myself!' he cried.

I had little enough to say, and it seemed absurd to pretend I had useful information to withhold.

'I saw some person sink there into the valley just below, but I could not tell you, or any man, which way he went. The river branches up stream, and widens down, so that there are many paths he might have taken. I could not guess which.'

He jumped from his horse, and ran his hand through his hair, pushing back his hood in doing so. His eyes seemed to comb the heather for some solution or relief. And then he turned to me, catching up my hands.

'I grieve, with all my heart – bitterly grieve, every minute of the day – for the heavy fate that has fallen upon you. And I repent, with all my heart, that for which you blame me. And yet – for the sake of this land, and of my own – for the sake even of your son – you must let me tell you what has happened.'

I could never forgive him, but yet I knew he would not conjure with the name of Dylan without the gravest reasons. I withdrew my hands from his, and bent my eyes aside and low, as though I had tears to hide, but I did not stop him.

'I must speak of Gwydion. His name should be blotted from the memory of man before ever you should be forced to hear it. And yet – you are not the only one who hates him, and with good reason. What he did to you, as a mother, was the utmost crime and cruelty against all that is human. But he has sinned just as deeply against the other, not-human world, of which I am guardian. When, some years ago, you laid your last curse upon Lleu, Gwydion determined to make his son a wife despite you. He shackled and enslaved the flowers, made them into the form of a woman, bound them in darkness and forced them to serve man's basest pleasures. The power of the dark magic he used was great enough to conceal from me this vicious meddling in my kingdom all this while. But his cruelty and arrogance are a weakness, as well as a great strength. Not long after you lost Dylan, this tormented creature, crushed into form by him from ravaged, pillaged blossoms, revenged herself at last. She took aim at his life – and he died, in agony, with the thought of you, and the wrongs he had done you, and the hatred you bore him, in his mind. As soon as his life slipped away, the trees, whose whispering branches had been bound up by his spells, told me all about it, and about the flowers he had tortured.'

I was bewildered – I would have rejoiced at this news, but all my thoughts and energies were centred on the prospect of wielding this revenge myself. However, while my mind yet reeled, Arawn spoke on.

'Ah. But it is not over. Hear me out, before you rejoice at this. Gwydion's brothers learnt of his death – themselves found and brought home his body. And they were fast to conceal it, for they knew that if it was widely known that he was dead, their own position would hardly be secure. While Gwydion lived, those three conniving sons of Dôn were something like a match for Goewin, rightful queen of Gwynedd. But with him, his ingenuity and magic gone, Goewin's brains, and her well-founded enmity, would be more than enough to overcome the long resistance of Gilfaethwy and Amaethon.

Amaethon is a man that few understand. I never did so. And he has surprised me with his audacious ingenuity. The first warning I had was a report of roebuck missing from the great birch wood that lies in the east of Annwn, around the lake of tears. You would never notice such a thing, but we fairies count every faun and hare, every wolf and weasel as they weave the shade between the silver trunks. And one was missing – a fine strong roebuck who had lived there for three hundred years or more, and before he came to Fairy wandered the woods of Pwyll's realm in Powys, and gave many a noble lord the slip.

At first I did not know what to make of this. But soon it became all too clear. Another day, I went with my hounds along the boundary between your world and Fairy that is formed by the spray of the river as it flows through the oak wood of Felinrhyd. There lies the body of my friend Pryderi, another killed by Gwydion, and I wanted to visit his resting place. I myself, as a memorial, had caused a great oak, hung more luxuriantly with moss even than the others that grew in that valley, to spring up above his body, and express something of his soul.

I was thinking deeply of my friend, as the limbs of the great tree twisted strong above me, when my hounds, who had been exploring by themselves, came whimpering to me across the river.

Their coats shone silver from running beneath the waterfall, and their eyes also were wet – and their red ears drooped as I had seldom seen them.

And then I noticed that there were only six. The youngest, Mai, was missing. She was young and slight, and inclined to wander separately from the rest. And yet hounds do not stray far from their pack. I saw at once that the others had tried in vain to find her.

And though I searched until the mossy trunks were softened further by the falling light, I myself had no better luck.

There is a prophecy I once told you of, and which you said you had heard from your Druid teacher. It tells that he who steals a roebuck, a hound and a lapwing of the land of Annwn may take back one whom death has claimed, and that he who holds the stolen beasts may vie with the king of Annwn himself for all the powers over earth and trees. When I heard of Dylan's death, I thought of this prophecy – for of all those I have loved who have lost their lives, there is not one I would wish more to see brought back from death. And though I greatly fear to see such power in the hands of almost any other, I would gladly share my powers over earth and trees with you.

And yet, when I thought of it – you could not steal from me that which I would have so gladly given you. The words of the prophecy could not be twisted so. And now I see that it will be fulfilled in quite another way. You just now saw Amaethon steal one of my lapwings. He has now all three of the pieces he needs for his next move. He may bring Gwydion back. And, when he does, the sons of Dôn will have command over the forests and the field, the fens and fearns. They will be formidable enemies, even for Goewin, the queen of Gwynedd. Even for you. Even for me.

Come – you have good cause for anger with me. But you have far, far better cause for hatred against them. Unless we combine together, we can have no chance. I would not take it as forgiveness if you consent to trust me in this. Let us build our alliances, and be ready.'

For a moment I felt something like joy at the prospect before me. To set all my energies against Gwydion in such a cause was all my mind and body needed. And yet – looking at Arawn, I could not see beyond my loss, and the part he had played in it. I could hardly bring myself to speak to him.

I saw now however a reflection of my own pain in his face so vivid that I knew no reconciliation could relieve it. And on those terms we could turn to business.

And so here I am, Goewin – warning you of the danger to come, and asking you to combine with myself and Arawn against it. And to join in wreaking with me a bloody vengeance on my brothers. I will leave you to think of all I said, and take counsel with this stranger here, whom I can only think you brought with you for such purpose. I trust the way of hate is clear.

GOEWIN

41

What do you think of this then, stranger? I must say, I have no hesitation. Even if I did not hate Gwydion almost as much as does Arianrhod, my clear duty is to protect the realm against any possibility of expansion by the sons of Dôn.

But in truth, I fear Arianrhod is mad. I might be too, in her place. If any were to take one of my children from me, I can't think how there would be space in me for pain and rage and reason all at once. And she had only one. And, again and again, to have to stand and bear the twisted spite of Gwydion – spat, as it were, into her face – and never have a chance to strike back – ach, I could never bear it.

She trusts me, I know. And I trust her, though she frightens me. But I didn't watch like the walls for all those years and learn nothing. There was something I know she didn't – couldn't – tell me. It may be nothing that matters, but it's best to know.

Yes – I have a little magic of my own, which again I learnt by watching. Almost my only trick, but a useful one. These morels were grown in the dunes at Dinas Dinlle, and I never pass in March without having some gathered for moments like this. These are a little dry and hard – but so is Arianrhod's bitter brain. I have watched Gwydion read thoughts this way often. Place one of the little fragrant, furrowed balls – the one that most reminds you of the mind that you would read – in the warmth of your palm, and breath in the thoughts, like this.

Ah. I see why she said nothing. Poor heart.

It's unlikely to be of consequence. I would tell no one but you, but you will soon be gone, and have no one to tell. Arianrhod loves the king of Annwn. And she trusts that he loves her. But he has a queen in Annwn, and duties there. Certainly his wife does not rely on his absolute devotion – he has waylaid many a girl in a forest glade and won her to a tumble in the long grass. But that will not do for Arianrhod. She tries to make it enough for her heart that she shares his counsel. Good luck to her with that.

War and death may swell her pierced soul, and buoy her a little longer. War it shall be! Get you home in safety, stranger. No doubt you will hear what happens next. No secret woman's story this, but one set to echo down the great halls. Our bards will sing it; it shall be made to bounce along in lines, and maybe set to music. One day it will be as hackneyed as the Battles of Bendigeidfran. And I shall be in it – as tall as a hero, with all sorts of unlikely powers.

Or if you wish to hear it from my own sun-chapped lips, in my own plain words, find me out again once I have won: I will always be pleased to see one who does such a good impression of patient listening – and I do believe, though it may be the wine that keeps you here, that you listen to at least one word in every four. Some battles drag on for years, but this one will burn out fast – by Gŵyl Awst I will have good news for you, or no more words at all.

BOOK THREE

WAR

GOEWIN

42

'Who goes there? Guards! But . . . what? It cannot be you, stranger? Come all the way across the sea and the wide warren to hear the story's bitter end? And now wandering in the dark in hopes of tripping over the thread of it? That was a daft risk to take – all other hazards aside, the story was well enough laid down as it was. You know the close always disappoints. When we break off the thread, it's either after an ugly knot best tucked out of sight, or we leave it loose so it's likely to let the parts already neatly sewn up come apart again. What is an ending after all, but the final pothole that jerks the wheel off the cart, so that past actions seem to fly forwards like turnips, and land in a mess in the dusty, empty road.

It's a dark night, and I can hardly gather what's left of my turnips without moonshine, though I must be on the spot to do it by dawn, and so I hurry. But I'll tell you what has gone by along the road, if you can keep my pace. Be warned though – any triumphs I have to glean from this mess will be so dirty and bruised with war you'll shrink from taking them up.

We laid our war plans hastily, Arianrhod, Arawn and I, and soon all was ready for the battle to come. We were not sure what powers Gwydion and his brothers had gained with the theft of the lapwing, but we knew the fight would come quickly, and that we must meet him here, on my own Ynys Môn. There was a race on both sides to muster men and arms, and to transport them here. We did not cross the Straits until all our forces were already sent across in ships, as Arawn and Arianrhod had mystic preparations to make.

The sea seemed to mean no good, as we crossed the water – I felt the sandbanks shift in uneasy sleep beneath us, and the boat was rocked by brooding eddies despite the care of the ferryman. He looked grim, as the wind clawed his dirty beard and his cloak slapped from its knot.

'You're not the first I've took across today,' he said, 'though like you'll be the last. Here comes a storm. All the talk's of massive ships – they yours? – that carry men and horses past Malltraeth and up the river through the marsh.'

I told him some were ours – though inwardly feared the greater part were not. I warned him that as well as a storm there would be a battle – told him to get home and fetch his folk and beasts inside. Told him, with feeling, to look after himself. In war, when you know you're bringing so much random death, it helps to care randomly, too – for any dirty beard that comes your way, and for his goats and unwashed children into the bargain, though you spit on yourself for a hypocrite, and spit on the ground for refusing to provide a level place where the moral scales might balance.

I feared my own home beach, Traeth Gwyllt – wild beach, maddened beach – would earn its name at last, through me. As we walked up the shore, and the black tidal mud sucked at my feet, and the wrack tangled my ankles, I seemed to see a dirty beard, and folded goat limbs, and unwashed chubby arms tangled there too, sucked at by death. At last I stepped up onto the crumbling edge of the meadow and moved easily again, but part of my mind stayed snarled there.

Our way led up Siencyn's hill, past the village of my birth. I waded through the moon daisies of the home fields, where I used to hide through long summer days, when they reached almost to my shoulders. My loyal men followed after, and crushed a great swathe through their midst – crushed so much red campion, so many buttercups. What was this, brought home? My aunt always said . . . the whole village always knew . . . I would end in trouble. But she wasn't alive now, to be pleased how well I sunk to her expectations.

On the far side of my own hill, we crossed the river Braint at a bridge. Beyond it lay the territory Arawn had marked out as the focus of our campaign. Though our war bands would engage with Gwydion's right across the island, he would use other weapons of war, which he could only muster from the right place. Beyond the fort at Caer Lêb, where we saw our men mustering, we went on to the dolmen, the hollow hill, of Bodowyr. From here, Arawn explained, he could summon powers direct from fairy land, which he hoped would help us win the day.

On one side, spread below and to the west, was the level valley of the Cefni marsh, and on the other, across the ribbon of sea, the mountains rose up: Carneddau, Wyddfa, Glyderau and the Llŷn, ranged out like guards on parade. The mountains seemed frozen in the stillness of blue distance, glazed with silent light – and I longed to be back there, serene, far from the ugly mess that was to be waged down here. But as I tried to steady myself by drinking in their massive calm, I blinked at what I saw.

Movement. The horizon shuddered. The summits seemed to shiver, and then to shift, and shale began to slide, and heather set itself alight into a purple blaze – a flame not eclipsed even by the sunshine – brighter because the distance hushed its crackle.

'Ah,' said Arawn. 'It has begun. I thought I had control of those high hills, but steal a lapwing and you steal a part of the soul of the wild land. Damn your bastard brothers, Arianrhod. Don't look. We have enough to do here, and it's here the struggle will be lost or won.'

Though I saw Arianrhod riveted by the sight of the shifting contours of mountains she counted as her own, I followed Arawn's advice willingly. My own mind flew to my children, who had each their own warband in a different quarter of the island. And with my mind flew out a swift, flying a mile in every minute.

Soon it returned, and swooped in arcs far high above our heads. We all three watched it, watched it joined by another, and another. The curved blades of their wings seemed to shear through the cloud that floated above us, and through it, instead of the blue of the sky, we saw a distant scene.

Bleiddwn, my youngest son, standing on a cliff above the sea – a cliff I knew well, crowned by another hollow hill called Barclodiad y Gawres, the giantess's apronful. I knew the cliff well, but I knew my son better. I saw the wind ruffle the starry tuft of paler hair on the crown of his head, which I had noticed when my fingers first traced the silken swirl over his fluttering fontanel.

I turned sick, and weak . . . I myself had sent my baby there. One thing to send your son away to war, and quite another to watch death approach him, as though you have invited it.

And there it came. My vision followed his, down across the marshy valley. The bog was ringed by forest, and now the crisp crimped dark of its margin began to fray. One broke, then three, then ten, then more than anyone could count – enemies teemed out across the rushes, like mice across a stubble field.

I hope you never know, stranger, the horror of seeing your child run towards death, exactly as you could have wished him to if only he had not been your own. You feel you might as well have prayed for his death as raised him to show courage like that. His valour was a black well from which I had insanely hoped to draw up pride, and seemed now instead a place I should throw myself headlong down. I longed more than anything to expose my life instead of his. But though he was minutes from me by the swift's flight, he was hours away on horseback.

I heard my son rally his men, call them to follow him down across the *cors*. Twenty to one, he must have seen, but judged it better to meet them on the plain than to be driven back over the cliff by force of numbers. And now I heard his young man's voice – deep now but clear as a bell, clear as his rational orders – drift towards his wolf's howl. He threw his head back and howled long, and longer.

All the marshal command of a war-horn was in the cry, but also the plangency of animal need, sounding quivering bonds of birth and blood and suffering. Such a cry could hardly go unanswered, and now from the woods streamed weaving shadows of his cousin wolves. The dark skeins caught at the ragged margins of Gwydion's army, and formed little knots – when a wolf brought down a man, and tore his throat out – which then pulled out straight again with the onward tug of the pack. Harrying the forces towards those of my son, the wolves reduced them – but still they thronged, and soon Gwydion's men turned back, in twos and threes, to butcher the oncoming wolves, and turn again to advance.

As I had stood transfixed by the sight spread out above me, I was dimly aware that Arawn and Arianrhod were not so still. Standing opposite to one another on the brow of the dolmen, they had clasped hands, and bowed their heads towards the hollow earth. I saw great effort in their shoulders, in the set of jaws and cheekbones. But my attention only flickered towards them before it was back in the field with my son.

There now I saw that the motion of his enemies was changing.

The centre of the force had been running smoothly, unstoppably towards my son, like peas through a wide-meshed sieve, and the foremost were about to hit Bleiddwn and his vanguard. But now the motion became clogged, as though many of the peas were a little too large for the mesh.

My stomach lurched, as the swift whose view I shared swooped suddenly nearer to the ground. I felt its speed, as my brain stumbled on itself to take in the sights flying by so fast. I saw feet sinking into bog, legs trying to shake free, knees over-extended, boots breaking loose at last as men stumbled forward only to plunge another foot too deep. At last I saw the vanguards meet, and the blades of my son's friends cut up enemies fixed and unbalanced by the sucking of the bog.

Now the swift looped dizzyingly, and flew back over the marsh. I saw those of Gwydion's men still on drier ground surge forward yet, killing as they went, and bellowing with confidence – a band of six of them pursuing Owen, one of my son's men, their weapons and sweating faces blinking bright in the sun's hard glare. I saw Owen's desperate eyes reach out for help – saw it was my son whose eyes he caught for his life. I sickened to see Bleiddwn turn readily to answer the deadly plea, levelling his blade – and the change in his face as blood bloomed the hollow of Owen's collar bone. A spear had passed through his nape.

Time stuttered over Owen's ending, and when it flowed again it seemed more slowly. The swift regained height, and I saw a strange change across the bogland's spongy skin. It reddened and crawled as though breaking out in hives. The swift swooped low, and I saw that the peat crept with what looked like thousands of scarlet spiders, bright with winking sticky orbs.

I recognised the little flesh-eating plants called moor-gloom, now freed from roots by magic, growing beyond their natural size, and set upon prey larger than the tiny creatures that usually made their meals. Fast then slow then fast again they scuttled, on blood-red outstretched arms and plate-shaped stomach-hands with sticky wiggling fingers, catching what they could. They clung and wrapped round toes and then round ankles, cloying movements with little balls of honey that swelled and burst with growing hunger.

Now, as the swift passed again, I saw the drier places shuffling with yellow-green star-shaped pads, as pale as tallow. Tacky white-rot, another flower thirsty for blood, large and growing, and now moving like starfish across the bog, and shimmying up the chasing, fleeing, juicy armoured legs. And once they touched they clung, some wrapping and clinging at the groin, and others slipping further up under breastplates, felling Gwydion's men with waxy weight, and bathing their wounds tenderly in their secretions.

Overcome as much by horror as by force, they abandoned themselves to the clammy folds, to the honeyed embrace of hairy crimson limbs. The plants crawled over them and covered them, and sucked up every drop of goodness through their pores, until at last every one of Gwydion's men was reabsorbed into the bog's black heart.

I had been mesmerised, but now saw that Bleiddwn had become a wolf, and ran in triumphant circles with the bloody packs until they filtered back into the trees. And then I saw him stride back out into the sunlight – a man again – more a man than ever. He had done all too well without me. He turned back to his comrades that were left alive, and I saw them hug each other close while shaking hard, their hands and eyes searching each other wincingly for wounds. And then the picture faded back to the blue of the sky.

'That magic is not all mine!' cried Arawn. 'I have the ally I hoped for – Gwydion's other victim – she rises from her despair and calls her cousin flowers to wreak a second revenge, and we may work closely together now. The best that Arianrhod and I could do just there was to find her out through the roots and beg her help.' But he hardly seemed to feel relief. 'The bogs and marshes answer to us – but boglands lie closer to Fairy than to human realms always. They are never fully yours. I'm afraid I feel a counter-influence in the woods. While Gwydion holds hostage my little roe, he will find green shades to fight with him.'

As soon as my mind was released from its terror for Bleiddwn, it followed my other children. Arianrhod was ahead of me. I saw a goshawk soaring above us, and instantly knew it was her spy. This phantom of the forest only breaks cover when it wishes to be seen. I watched it wheel higher and higher, until the centre of the spiral became a spyglass, through which I could see across the island to the camp of my firstborn son, Hychddwn.

I saw his men, resting in a forest ride, leap to their feet and circle back-to-back, quite sure they'd heard an enemy at hand. But nothing moved. The hawk had clearly watched them from a perch, and all in the forest was still. I knew it for the forest at Llanfaes, for its deep green, and the enchanter's nightshade that carpeted the floor. Even the breeze could not find this place in the heart of that forest. There were only rising trunks weighed down by heavy falls of ivy, which hung limp and heavy. I had never seen such heavy ivy. I shuddered – and the ivy seemed to shudder into movement. Almost imperceptibly, its downward drag became muscular, and I saw it drape and grow and slowly reach for Hychddwn and his men. Suddenly seeming to take momentum from its weight, it caught one, and in an instant twisted him into pieces, and the ride burst into war.

The men slashed with their swords, but the ivy stems were flexible and thick as arms, and their writhing grip was irresistible. It coiled round limbs and wrenched them free of sockets and pulled them up into the canopy, until veins hung down like aerial roots in search of anchor, and parts of men were hung like bright garlands of gore across the twining, writhing cover of hungry green.

My anxious eyes saw that while Hychddwn slashed at the stems that dismembered his comrades, he had so far escaped their grip – he stood alone in the centre of the glade, and tendrils reached searchingly towards his shoulders. But now at once he crouched, and was a boar – and roared.

Almost instantly there was a thunderous crackle in the undergrowth, as the heavy shoulders of his barrel-browed brothers smashed through the scrub. A hundred came, their speed and weight carrying them clear through the curtain of ivy. Even as the tendrils grasped at their hind quarters, with their tusks and heavy jaws they began to dig.

They rifled through the earth, uprooting the thick roots of the vines, nosing the heaviest rocks aside as if they were light as feather pillows. The ivy slackened and shrivelled as it lost its anchor in the earth. Before my eyes, the green glade was transformed into a waste of clay and clods and mud, and the vines all wilted, slack and dead.

I saw Hychddwn bury his boar's head in the churned earth in despair. His heavy boar's shoulders shook. At last he rose up as a man again, his hair full of leaves, his face black with loam and channelled with the pale tracks of tears, as he looked around to see his comrades so broken up like stones and earth; and the forest glade, so perfect and so peaceful till he came, a broken, ugly, torn-up waste.

'I feared so,' said Arawn. 'Your son has powerful friends, Goewin, and did well enough without my help. A good thing too. I could muster little enough to aid him there. And there will be much more waste to come.'

'But what of Hyddwen?' I cried. 'Deer cannot protect her from the forest itself...'

'Here comes news!' Arianrhod exclaimed, and I saw a long, tapering merganser, the sleek shape of a stretching water drop, fly towards us on fast-beating wings. It alighted on the grass by Arianrhod, as though reporting for duty, and looked up at us with blood-red eyes.

As I looked hard, and saw the black pupil swim and ripple, I found myself looking at the sea. I recognised the Daethwy tribe's port, where the river Cadnant meets the Straits. It's the only piece of still water that can harbour a fleet anywhere along their whole lengths, and my daughter, with Aneurin and their forces, waited to repel any landing that Gwydion might attempt there.

I saw across the Straits, racing forward on the current, a fleet of narrow boats, carrying a force bigger than all of ours put together. That was the end of the bird's vision. It had brought us all it had seen, at once. A warning.

I turned to Arianrhod. In that moment I let her see more of me than I had ever shown before. The desperation of a fearful mother. The weakness of raw need. But she needed none of that – she was already galvanised.

'They're mine,' she said, with something like joy, and she raised her jaw high and looked down beneath her lowered lids at the silver ribbon of the Straits. For a moment I watched her lip curl and twitch with mastered effort.

I had nothing to do but watch her, as I waited for news from the next bird. I longed to do something stupid – to fall at her feet to beg her to try harder, to do everything to save the most precious thing on the earth – or to run up and down the grassy sides of the dolmen and scream and cry and tear at the herbs and my own hair. I closed my eyes to stifle these useless thoughts, and when I opened them I saw a flight of swallows approaching.

Swallows were always my favourite bird – they remind me of childhood freedom in my summer meadows. The lilt of their trill means lengthening days and warmth to come, and I can sing it in my mind's ear whenever I need warming. And yet I have seen a swallow curl its toes around the rim of a crowded mud nest, and take up each tiny chick inside one by one, by the scruff of its exposed downy neck, and drop it to its death onto the stones below. I dreaded that these birds, skimming fast towards me, would treat my hope like that.

The gathering swallows painted a dome above in which I might see what had occurred five minutes since.

I saw a wave ground the foremost of the boats with a scrunch, and warriors hurl out of it and up the pebbles with a yell. More swarmed behind, powering forward as the stones flew back from under them. I saw Aneurin meet them hand to hand. I felt a sharp pang, realising how my mind had dwelt so much on the danger to my daughter that I had hardly thought of him at all. For a moment I was sure he would die from my neglect to guard him in my thoughts.

But there he was, swinging his heavy blade against the first man ashore, felling and pushing back with sickening success. To think that those hands had touched me as his had – butcher's hands, conqueror's hands – I had lain within the haven, the prison, of those iron-taut arms, which now cleaved up men, and dripped dark with taken life. His sweat swept the blood and dirt into the creases of his face as fast as he was splattered, and the lines in which I had so often traced tenderness were twisted into rage and bellowing triumph. He fought on, keeping my daughter safe, and I desired the monster in him. But no sooner did the first rank fold and die at his hands than another crop was there to take its place, like daisies, bold and stubborn in the sun.

It could not hold. I lost the conviction of his strength and invincibility that the sight of his rage had brought me. Now he confronted three at once, who I saw by the thonging on their arms were war chiefs from Conwy, the best fighters from those parts. Swinging at one, Aneurin caught his thigh, and killed, pulled back, and sent his sword's tip seeking the unprotected strip of belly below the armour of the second. But as he raised his head I saw it pulled back by the hair, and the blade of the third man at his throat.

Their eyes met, and locked the split-part of an instant still. And then, just the way that Venus pops into the dimming sky above the sea at night, an arrow tip pricked out from the Conwy-man's forehead, and he crumpled onto the stones. It was Hyddwen's dart – I saw her now, standing just a little way up the beach, stringing arrow after arrow as fast and sure as only she can, not far above the wall of struggling men.

But now something else was slowing the waves of warriors surging up the beach. The slippery stretch of wrack over the stones did not settle back into stillness after their boots passed over it. It stirred. A swallow had swooped low enough to untangle the sight – and I made out the slender coiling limbs of brittle-stars amongst the weed. Each creature, each of its legs, moved with a wilful independent life, but they were soon so massed and piled and shiftingly involved that they seemed to form one single seethe. They multiplied and grew and clambered sidelong up the beach, faster than the warriors ran. Their many arms whipped up sandalled legs, and if they tried to brush them off they only broke them up into clinging parts, which suckered up under their clothes and into their ears and nostrils and mouths and eyes. More and more crept up out of the weed, at last so many that they made a lapping, crawling wave, which sucked the enemy back bodily into the swell. And now a true wave came, and carried every one, dead and alive, out into the merciless bore of the Straits, and out to sea.

No swallows had waited to see more – not waited to show me my daughter and my lover safe again. The scene faded from the sky, and the birds, released by Arawn from their service, flicked off across the grass in search of flies. Arianrhod's face flashed for one moment in a noiseless snarl of glee. I saw sated rage in the movements of her clean white tapering hands. I traced hateful triumph, at her remote power to snuff out life, in the high set of the bones of her face. It was something more monstrous, more inhumane than I had seen in Aneurin as he chucked up windpipes and sliced through vein and sinew and muscle and visceral fat. And in that moment perhaps I loved her more than I did him. I saw Arawn look at her, and felt his love was far more troubled by pity and horror than mine. But then he had only territory and power and obligation in the fight – not the lives of his children. Though he took a lead part in all the goings-on, he could hardly know what they were really about. And so his mind moved on.

'What of Math?' he said. He said it again – intoned it this time. And now above us I saw a buzzard wheeling in the air, soon joined by another. As I watched their circling, my vision dizzied, and when I blinked, I saw my old friend Math, with Ystwyth, now his second-in-command, as close to his side as I would have been in her place, all those years. Their men were around them, and all seemed well – they were resting in the glade of a beechwood, spread out on the soft dry moss studded with little toadstools, that you find in the forests towards Penmon, over the grey limestone of those parts. I heard them sadly speak the names of their dead, but still congratulate themselves that they had not yet lost as many as one in five. The beech trunks were silken smooth and silver-skinned. The canopy sifted the falling summer light – and soon all were quiet, clearly glad to feel the roar of baited death die back to silence in their cooling brains.

Yet as they sat on, the bird's view made it seem somehow that the glade was smaller than it was at first. Perhaps it was not only the bird that saw this – I watched Ystwyth, leaning at ease against a trunk, suddenly dart a glance around her, as though something had snagged the corner of her eye.

The bird's attention followed hers – just in time to see the shuffle of a naked trunk. Its roots, like grey toes, curled and pulled it forward over the crinkling dry leaves and moss. As it inched forward, the trees behind it, and across the glade, began to creak and move, and one heavy limb reached stealthily towards the resting king.

Ystwyth leapt up to her feet, and every bare-skinned beech groaned into life. They moved slowly, grey forms of stolid cold, like dead arms and legs reanimated without will or goal or fear. The whole warband was on its feet now and running from the groaning giants, but the trees tripped them silently. Roots extended, creaseless knees dropped down on their backs, to break them with the weight of eighty feet of pallid trunk above.

The ranks of grey giants seemed too dense to escape. Some men used their dirks to hack the leaden limbs that reached for them. They slashed the wood, making jagged mouths, but then another limb would quietly press them onto the wooden teeth they'd made. Others found themselves in an elbowless hug, which pressed them tighter till they shared the trees' own stone-cold calm.

Math and Ystwyth had not tried to run, but stood in the very centre of the glade, while on every side naked limbs stretched out and blindly felt for theirs. They crouched down low, Ystwyth drawing a dirk, and Math his sword. I heard Arawn breathe hard, and mutter to himself, 'I have done all I can.' I could see that

Math believed he had no more centuries ahead of him, and was puzzling how he might go out of the world heroically when faced with such silent, stolid foes.

But now came a scream that echoed from the hill, a crash and rend and shattering screech rebounding from a thousand towering trunks, which made the buzzard launch in fear from his perch, and take for the open sky.

GOEWIN

43

There the buzzard wheeled above us, with all it had seen. But now it was joined by another, and another, which circled above, higher and higher, until my eyes strained to keep them within view – strained and strained until I saw right through the sky, back to the northern woods.

I seemed to see them from a thousand feet, and it looked as though two huge gales, which I couldn't feel, came suddenly off the sea on either side of Penmon's head, and swept together, so that in the place they met, they churned the wood, as two rapid streams of water meeting churn and boil. I seemed to look through glass, as long lines as pale as foam rippled out like swell across the stippled green of the treetops – the exposed underside of a million leaves.

Now the buzzard dropped off the thermal, sunk down, skirted the eyewall of the storm, and floated away, to where the wood was calm. There it drifted down with the golden light amongst the topmost branches – glided on through glowing shelves of cell-sealed sun – until again the dreadful sound ripped up the peace, spreading and advancing through the forest. I could now tease out the sounds of corrugated bark cracking and grinding, the shattering burst of a million twigs together, the snap of branches and the clonk and thud of heavy trunks. I seemed to smell the air, filled with the tang of soil and sap.

'The trees are at war,' said Arawn. 'Gwydion commands at least half of them I find. Math and Ystwyth may make their escape, as prey too small to notice, but I dread to think where such an evenly matched battle may end.'

For the next long hours many birds brought us visions, from right across that part of Môn before the river Cefni, through the vales off Braint, Cadnant and Lleiniog, from the dunes of Rhosyr to the cliffs of Fedw Fawr. They showed us alders locked in mortal combat, the rivers hurrying away their torn-off limbs, leaving sockets, pale at first, which soon grew bloody. Withy trees drowned each other in the streams, and rowans tangled with birches high on the cliffs, throwing one another down to smash their branches on the rocks below.

A crow followed a yew tree, and showed us how he stalked alone until he found a dark twin – showed us how the two of them, working together, drove hazels into fatal knots, and then fell on them, whitening the floor with cracked young nuts like shattered bone, showering sprays and drops of aril blood along the meadow's edge. The sparrows showed us how the cherries raged and took on sloes and damsons, until their limbs were gored with bursting fruit. Warblers showed us how the brambles and raspberries ramped low and stealthily, to snare and strangle one another in the dikes.

At last there was a sudden, silent pause, which we heard from the dolmen. A dove brought us the sight of it from a clearing close by, just within the fringe of the forest, and I set off to see for myself what might have caused it. Leaving Arawn and Arianrhod in whispered counsel, I walked down a little way into the woods. In the silence, light beamed through the shattered canopy in bars like green-gold harp strings, and the earth seemed to sigh, and play a tune on them – the saddest tune in the world, of lost things that could never come back or mend; a tune of peace which must find a home in every heart, setting there, swelling and bursting as true and soft as apple blossom.

As I reached the clearing, which was broad and opened into a ride, the rising tune seemed to stop my feet despite my will, and I stood quite still to listen. As I did so, I saw what I took for a mist drifting low above the churned earth and exposed roots of the trees on the other side. Onwards it floated, at last rising as though driven back and upwards by the brisker air of the clearing. But then still, on it came – until at last it shook itself loose of the green shade, binding the pale shafts of sun into its own form – the form of a woman, wrapped in one long sheet of vapour, her cheeks and hair paler than bone. She did not see me, but was turned away, looking down the ride.

At the other end, a bank of cloud seemed half-entangled with the uppermost branches of the trees. As I looked on, it shook itself free, and folded onwards towards the open stretch of bruised long grass. And when it reached the margin of the wood, it seemed gently to fall and pile into a tall shape, again weaving substance from the tremulous evening light. But this was a gigantic male figure, with legs as thick as the trunk of the most ancient oak, shoulders like hills, and a head . . . invisible I thought, but then I saw it – big as a moon, carried under one crag-muscled arm. As I watched, he placed it on his shoulders, and I saw a face obscured by a streaming beard of fog as thick as ever breathed from any humid ocean.

At the sight of him, the woman's face and hair and misty winding sheet began to seethe, as though at the mercy of winds from many quarters. The chill grey eddies shifted and writhed, turning in on themselves, until I saw in her the embodiment of turmoil, of unease beyond assuaging, and pain beyond relief. She seemed to be racked and ground, before my eyes, by every spiteful turn of chance, every unrighted wrong the sun had ever shone upon; ground down to the pale bone, ground finer still to a dust of pain, which would not scatter and diffuse on the winds, but instead formed a shifting tangled knot about the silent shafts of evening light.

And then she raised her arms, with their streaming sleeves of freezing mist.

Behind her, the roots of the trees came hissing from the earth like snakes from their holes, and the wood advanced across the clearing. The giant, watching her, shook his head, as though in dismay – his beard of mist floating after his movement, as if to draw out across the air his sorrowful disappointment. He hung his head.

And then he raised it once more, and raised his arms in turn – and bounding forward grasped a heavy, lead-bellied cloud from above his head and hurled it at the trees across the ride. Behind him the beeches now rattled their leaves, and moved forward as one in step with him. The tune, still playing on the sunbeams, now coaxed and ran and weakly flailed. A whimpering wan wind sighed and still pleaded for peace, but wolf notes pursued it, howling and gasping close on its heels.

The woods listened no more, but all took up the fight again. I turned and ran back towards Bodowyr, unnoticed by the fighting trees, though I fell hard into the trenches that opened as they wrenched free their roots, and was knocked down more than once by flying branches, until my face and hair were tangled with leaves and earth.

At last I was back in the open and climbing the hill. I looked back and could see the war raging again. Poplars tremblingly took on the chestnut hulks, who screwed submission out with corkscrew trunks, and in the higher woods, the ash trees clashed with burly elms, and the poor thornless broom was pricked to death by gorse.

I came back to find consternation in the camp, and my absence hardly noticed. It was clear that at this rate both armies would be utterly destroyed, and the island left tree-stripped and desolate. This was a victory I could hardly wish for. I began to tell Arianrhod what I had seen in the glade, but almost at once her attention was more urgently claimed.

On the next rise – which is called Caer Meini, and always had a bad reputation – we could see Gwydion's war camp, and himself, flanked by Lleu, Amaethon and Gilfaethwy. Arianrhod's eyes were constantly drawn towards her nemesis, and I knew she would never give up anything if he might gain by it. Much as I hated Gwydion, however, I knew he was no fool – and I doubted he would want to have the island so completely wrecked. So I was not surprised to see him approach us on his black horse, followed by a small party, and stop within hailing distance. His skin was ever pale, but now it and his black hair were silvered over with a deathly cast colder than that of age alone, and the depth of his mouth and eyes were more than ever like a skull's. I could well believe the mortal journey he had passed.

'I'd speak a little with my sister dear,' he said, his voice carrying strangely though the air without him taking much trouble to raise it. Arianrhod spoke up, taut and grey with hate.

'Say your say, and say it quickly. I am busily engaged just now in trying to kill you.'

Gwydion, however, evidently still loved the sound of his own voice every bit as much as Arianrhod might hate it, and now he was off, spinning out his words as calmly as though there were not deaths hanging on the space of each one.

'Did you never learn,' he said, with his very blandest smile, 'the lesson Uscia of Connaught used to teach? You remember Uscia, I'm sure, sister – that Irish Druid bitch – you used to love to empty and clean her chamber pot with your bare hands, and then to hide where you might spy on her as she undressed, to catch a glimpse of that flat chest of hers and the little spilled quails' eggs of her breasts – though I spied too, once or twice, and saw she was freckled and spotted all over like a toad. I had no appetite for her, even after I had killed her. She made the most bestial faces as she suffered the pain of my drug. Oh yes – I waited near and came back into the room when I heard her disgusting groans, and watched it all, to my great satisfaction. I was still there when you came. I was hidden in her bed – the blankets still warm with the last of her heat – I almost gave myself up with laughing, as I peeped out and saw your desperate efforts to wake her, and she as dead as a skinned rabbit. I began to think you were stupid after all.

Anyway – I'm sure you remember how Uscia used to weary us with a prophecy about a great war in times to come. If you are not in fact stupid, you will recollect she told us how the 'gilders of souls' would pit themselves against the forces of the fairy world, with Gwynedd as the prize for which they fought. Surely you've not forgotten that proud heart-warming day on which you so lovingly blessed your darling son, Lleu, with his name – how, when you came across us, we were making shoes of soft Cordovan leather, and gilding them, from arch to sole, with floating leaves of gold?'

I hardly dared to look at Arianrhod while her brother spoke. Her hate did not make her tremble, but the air itself seemed to shake about her, the sun afraid to light upon the set mask of her face. However, I could see she listened to what her brother said, and must have remembered what she had told me herself so clearly – how she glimpsed the beaten gold shift of itself within the opened box that day. Perhaps she remembered also the prophecy in Uscia's mouth.

At last she spoke, in a voice steady but hardly human.

'I have no need to hear her words from *you*. I remember them. She told us that Gwynedd would be taken by whoever guessed the name of a revenant who, thickly masked in mist, advanced and fought upon the other side. But this is all besides the point. I see no veiled warrior amongst your ranks, and so we have no chance to guess their name, and can reach no such agreement.'

'Yet here she is!' cried Gwydion, and stepped aside.

Behind the close ranks of his guard now stood the woman I had just encountered, still wrapped in the distant grey which I now knew for the caul of death itself.

'And,' said Gwydion, 'I see there fights with *you* another soul who's slipped the clutch of death for this long day.'

And indeed, in the midst of our army at the bottom of the hill stood the giant, twice as tall as any of the trees, the death mist all about him. Gwydion went on.

'Now shall we match our wills and wits once more, my sister dear? You know you never thought that mine were worth a curse. This prophecy – that fell from those thin lips you never dared to press – it shows our fate. Our only choice is struggle in its adamantine grip or yield with grace. A stubborn mare that bucks does nothing more than just invite the spur. Remember, Uscia spoke of this moment as a knot in time, never to be untangled.'

Now Arianrhod turned away from her brother. There was a spot of colour on each of her cheeks, and I thought she saw triumph within her reach.

I argued that Gwydion, foul cheat and coward that he was, would not suggest this course to us unless he thought that he would win by it. He might have sent the enormous, cloud-clad warrior into our midst, and know his name already.

'That would hardly fulfil the terms of the prophecy, which said that the revenants would fight of their own will on either side – not be placed there by the enemy. But it matters not at all, if we may take the first chance to guess. For my part, I know with certainty the name of that woman you see wrapped about in the clinging weeds of death. Before she died, I heard far more than Gwydion from Uscia of this augury. She trusted me much farther than she ever trusted him. Uscia has sent her wisdom to guide me when I need it most. I know it, and I know the name; I cannot doubt myself, or her. It's Achren: I told you already how Uscia honoured me by telling me the secret name, and all about the woman who bears it. In battle, many years ago, in a bitter war forgot as soon as won, she threw herself before Math's spear, in a vain attempt to save her youngest son from his unerring aim. It must have been that even in her grave she knew today might spell Math's end, and that a mother's hate and vengeance was strong enough to tear her through the thorny brake between ourselves and death, to lend her hand to his defeat. Besides Uscia told me that, in this struggle to guess the name, the pity of women would not be overcome. Gwydion is pitiless, and so the victory must be ours at last.'

I looked at Arawn. I plainly saw what I had all along suspected – he fought not for possession of the island, or for his roebuck or his lapwing or his bitch, but for Arianrhod herself. He would have needed grave reasons to defy her arguments.

'You loved and respected Uscia's wisdom more than any other on earth. I know your love and respect are not easy won. It may be that there is really no way of shaking off the destiny that she foretold – and in any case it seems to beckon kindly.'

I still had misgivings, but did not know how to argue against such fatalism. I was afraid to quarrel with my allies. I wasn't sure they would listen to me, and knew well that, if I could not persuade them, they could go on and do as they liked. And I could see no other way of saving my island from terrible desecration.

And so I hailed the rival camp. 'We will accept this fateful challenge if you will swear before our men and yours that true possession of Gwynedd shall be sealed in the instant that the name of either revenant is spoken. But on one condition. We must have first chance, and take some moments to guess the name, before you hazard any yourself: the time it takes for that cloud, shaped like a dragon, to range across the sun.'

'Done!' cried Gwydion. 'Let the heavens attest I swear it! You shall have your guess first, if you can make it before the cloud passes. But hear me – something else I swear as well. If you should name rightly the woman here behind me I will, according to my word, give you Gwynedd – but first, back at my camp, I will . . . relive . . . through this woman by my side, every pain I ever enjoyed inflicting upon the pair of *you*. I will do to her everything I neglected to do to the dead body of my sister's ugly Druid. Dead though her body is, and wrapped in shade, it shall be used by me, and all my men here, just at our will. Her grown children will die by my hands. And her grandchildren too, into the bargain. That would give me joy, all of it. I'm afraid she died before she learnt to take to heart the ways of men.'

The stunned silence was torn by a shriek from Achren, sounding deep as though tossed back from the hollow of the grave. She had been rudely grasped by Lleu on one side, and Gilfa on the other, and I saw her fade a paler shade of dead as men, who must be her sons and grandsons, were seized still more roughly from amongst the ranks of Gwydion's warriors.

At this sight we paused a moment, appalled by the horror that lay in the path of our victory. A weak, and fatal, hesitation. It makes no sense – such shrinking from the torture of one particular individual soul, when thousands more hang namelessly in the balance. It was a stupid human weakness. And yet, this echoing of our own past suffering in what Achren must undergo, before the sun sunk another finger's breadth towards the horizon, was almost impossible to hurry past.

I could not reconcile myself to the choice. 'Can't we hope that Gwydion may never guess the name of that cloud-wrapped giant in the woods below?'

'He must!' whispered Arawn. 'There's only one that ever lived to reach that size. I knew him at once. It's blessed Brân, the giant – properly called Bendigeidfran – brought right back from the dead! Did you never hear the songs of his battles?'

You know, stranger, that I have. I was appalled.

'Woman's pity . . . may not be overcome,' I said, and before any of us had gathered wits again to take our chance, a cold and dragonish shadow fell across the land, and we heard Gwydion cry gleefully the name of Brân.

'Of course I only knew him by the alder branches on his shield,' he laughed. 'I never noticed he was a furlong too tall, even for his mighty age! The day is mine.'

We three could hardly look at each other – still less speak. But I could sense that Arawn felt, as I did, the rage and humiliation that crackled from Arianrhod, in the rustle of her black clothes, the whipping of her hair, and the shallow rasping exhalation of her breath. She prided herself in her strength, and here was victory seized from her through a moment of soft-heartedness. I saw her resolving to be harder now than death until it might take her. It was left to me to think of the suffering of the land and its people.

'Wait!' I cried. 'The augury was of Gwynedd. Not a word of Ynys Môn. As we have sworn, we must allow your claim upon Arfon and on Llŷn. So go home now and revel in your spoils and leave my bleeding island here in peace.'

'I never promised that,' he said. 'I play for all! You listen now, Goewin, you slave-turned-toy-queen. Your men and mine heard what deal was struck: they saw how, in honour, I gave you every chance to guess the name of the revenant fighting in my ranks – and how you vacillated and quarrelled amongst yourselves, too weak to grasp the moment, until at last your advantage passed and I uttered the name of Brân – which of course I knew all along, not being blind or stupid. I won Gwynedd fair and square, and now fight on for Ynys Môn with my advantage, and my men well-cheered. Would you have me yield the day in mere compassion? Do you take me for a fool, like yourself? You were ever weak – weak, when you kept me close enough to win such glamourie by fucking and eating your beloved mare – weak, when instead of following your advantage, you lay still at Caer Dathyl like a milch cow, nursing your freakish children – weak, when you let my stupid brother take you, and spill your blood on the floor of the great hall, like the dirty baited badger that you are. Slyness is the weapon of the weak, but though it works for you with others, it never will with me. I know you. And I'll take your backward, inbred island for my own.' He raised his wand, and as he did so, the trees wrenched out their roots again, and the fight resumed more fiercely than before.

I had no more to say – and if I had, would have been gagged by the spewing force of Gwydion's spite. I turned, hopeless, to my companions. Arawn always looked sad, but now there was a terrible weight in his face. I saw that Arianrhod's will was still not broken – she spoke fast, close to his ear, of the magic of the wind and sea, no doubt, and what help it might still bring us – though from his face I doubted she gave him much to trust in.

As Gwydion rode away, I saw him turn, and fix his eyes upon his sister – watch her eager whisperings to the king of Fairy.

His horse rode on, but still he looked back, watching the lean of his sister's body – the trust, the respect, and the intimacy in it; the sympathetic symmetry between the stances of the pair, as if Arawn were Arianrhod's brother, or even more. He must, I thought, have seen in that moment that even if he won on Ynys Môn that day, those two would likely flit to Annwn quite unhurt, bound yet closer by their exile there.

Gwydion was ever decisive. And so he turned his horse about, and rode back towards us, raising his voice to a yell above the din of breaking branches and dying men.

'Arawn – king of shadows – nowhere's king – I find you less impressive than I'd hoped. You let the men of Gwynedd spill their blood while you stand safe, aside. Now, perhaps you and I should try whose knowledge, wisdom, power of mind deserves to reign this muddy island? Just dare to meet me at the henge – alone – two hours from now. I'll give you one last chance. Man to man we'll settle this at last, and no more boys need die for you today.'

I knew at once that this was the very chance Arawn could have wished for. He longed to lay his immortal life at Arianrhod's feet in penance for his imagined part in her pain at the death of her son, and to make Gwydion suffer a hundred-fold the suffering he had caused her. He rose like a hungry perch at Gwydion's words, confident in his magic, with strong hope he would prevail.

'Bring the lapwing, and the deer, and the hound your brother stole, so you may give me back your power over trees and land if I should beat you.'

'Of course I will!' Gwydion replied. 'I bring them everywhere with me, as they are *mine*.'

Arawn turned hastily to Arianrhod. It was nearly an hour's ride to Bryn Celli Ddu, and he said he must devise his plan of assault along the way.

'You take this guard, and go with Goewin to the palace at Rhosyr. If I should lose, you may sail safely from there towards the isle of Enlli, and so onwards to the south of Wales, to Erin, or even, with my escort, to Fairy, as needs be. But I shall not lose. I will see you there, by midnight, and tell you how I beat him.'

GOEWIN

44

Arianrhod looked over Arawn's shoulder at the retreating figure of her brother. For the first time, I saw her fear of him. It's not in human nature to have our tenderest places, our rawest spots, detected and jabbed mercilessly by another human being, without learning to fear that person, as we do the next lash of a whip. And now I saw her eyes flinch from her brother, and cling to Arawn, cling tenaciously, as though in compensation for the clasp of hands, or of tender arms, she still would not offer him. I saw her mouth search for words that might put off the parting just another moment, and her confusion when none came. Arawn looked at her in his turn – he must have seen all that I saw, unless he is stupid – I saw rising in him the impulse to crush Arianrhod to him, and beg for her forgiveness and affection to go with him. But I saw it forced down again by the white silence of her face and her straight black stance, and he turned away. Her countenance spoke things to his turned back that it had hidden deep from his gaze. And then she too turned away.

So while the light slunk from the sky, we went south to the ancient palace. We hardly spoke along the way. I was almost afraid of Arianrhod, so shaking tight seemed her control – I hardly knew what might lie behind it. And yet, as the night fell the darkness dissolved it. Her dress and her hair melted into shadow, and there was her face, thin and white as a moonbeam, and as transparent.

She let me see right through her, and what she was, now, was tired, harassed, and terribly afraid. I could see that Arawn was more to her than a lover. I could see she feared losing him as the final loss that would undo her, and it almost seemed that the dread of it was unravelling her mind.

Once we were safe and alone in the great hall, the flickering of our few candles and the shapes they cast as the light pooled and slid over the rough walls making the only movement in the room, she fidgeted and trembled and complained like a child or an old woman, and looked to me for help I hardly knew how to give.

'I feel so weak,' she said. 'Blind waiting kills. It turns my brain. Hush . . . do you hear that wavelet moan and murmur on the shore? Since Dylan died, the sea has mourned him bitterly, but never with a plaintive sigh like that. I have become used to training my anger to its roar, but here tonight, no matter how I try, I hear only enervating fear in every wave that crawls so up the beach.'

She left the portal towards the sea and sat down by my side, but was almost immediately up again, her hand clutching painfully at my shoulder.

'What makes that rustling whisper at the door?'

'A leaf,' I said, but she would not be calmed, and trembled at the very thought of leaves, and to spill out all her fear for the night in words.

'This storm wind strips and herds them from the boughs – they run from winter long before it's come. But the sound I hear is more like down, or cinders – I tell you, in my ear, it seems to say "What burst that sudden bloom of feathers there? And who has burned what down, to makes those palely puddling flakes of floating ash?"'

'Sit down,' I said, shaking my shoulder free almost impatiently,

for the tremor of her hand crept down my own spine, and her fear leached the warmth from my own courage. I began to think that she was growing mad.

But as I spoke, a shaft of moonlight, breaking past cloud and through the narrow postern, showed me – something – creeping into the room. It might have been a flurry of snow, but it had no sparkle, and the night was summer-warm. It might have been a puff of feathers plucked from bone-starved birds. The cloud advanced and snuffed out the moonlight for a moment, and I thought my eyes had deceived me – and yet, when it drifted past, what I saw was more definite than ever – definite, but indistinct. Of all the strange things I have told you, stranger, none have been as hard to describe as this. I can't say it piled itself in through the window, as it seemed quite weightless – I can't say it formed a pillar, as it seemed infinitely soft and hardly to hold a shape at all. But, softly, it drifted and shifted and clung into a form. I stepped closer, and could see that it was composed of faded, creased and wrinkled petals, and was something like the wraith of a woman.

I brought a candle, and set it near her. She looked so wan, so harried by the wind, that it felt wrong to feel anything but pity in looking at her – and yet I was filled with curiosity, and could not help staring. She was made to snare attention and to be gazed at. Her cheeks were blanched and wrinkled; they were made, I thought, of the petals of rock-rose and pale poppies – but the crumples themselves were silken and beautiful, shimmering quietly a lovely tale of fragility and transience and too-long constraint within a toughened calyx. Her very grief showed itself in downcast lily curves, the sadder for being so graceful, and she trembled with all the pretty tenuousness of the harebell on its filament stem. I would like to tell you of the way the deep blue four-sister-flowers of her eyes seemed to woo the darkness, and how the parting of her tulip lips seemed an immaculate opening to sweetness deep within – but the fascinations of beauty sit as awkwardly in a dark tale like mine as she sat, on the cold flags, in the grand and empty hall. It is the tale she came to tell us I should be speaking of. But I must admit that I could not see her without loving her, without believing absolutely in her innocence, and without wishing to right every hurt she ever suffered. Beauty, I know, is in itself neither good nor evil, but it involuntarily inspires in others the extremes of both. And her tale was a tale of beauty itself, tortured and purposely defiled.

She came to us weak from long and lonely wandering. She had killed Gwydion, with those innocent-seeming lips of hers, and then lain down, almost at ease on the earth, clasping her grief tight. But Gwydion's death let Arawn find her, and tell her of the danger of his resurrection. She couldn't bear that she might have to share one earth with him again, yet her will for vengeance was almost broken. She had heard of the strength of Arianrhod's magic, and of my own kindness, she said, and hoped we might do something to ease or end her suffering. And today, she said, she had felt the commotion in the roots, and answered the call for help sent out by Arawn. She hoped she had done her best – only grieved that it had not been enough.

We had to confess that we had lost Gwynedd to Gwydion, and that even Ynys Môn might yet fall to him – that for now there was nothing at all to be done. And so, as we asked to hear it, she poured out her dreadful tale – a skein of suffering as long and strained as either of our own, which we now saw was woven in with ours.

Her tale glowed with horror in the darkness, and left us speechless. Beautiful though she was, neither of us liked to look at her. I was grateful we could only see each other dimly through the gloom. Each of us had pain enough of our own, and almost dreaded another's claim. My words were shut up, like weak things not safe to be out. I knew that if we spoke all night we could yet never know the alien horror each had lived and borne alone, beyond repair. We were strangers there, in the dark, almost as though suffering had placed us each in individual cells.

Thinking of the other two, however, I saw a difference between myself and them. They felt no impulse to tap upon the rock walls, to send off vibrations to be swallowed by unhearing, unanswering stone and mortar, on the mere chance that a corrupted signal might creep through a crumbling channel and into the sleeping ear of a fellow prisoner. I examined this impulse. Was it only for myself that I wished such contact might be made? I knew that there was no remaining strength or sympathy in my silent companions on which I might lean. All they had was given up to their own pain. If I touched them, it would be in hopes of giving, and not of taking, a little breath of the relief that solidarity and compassion bring.

I got up, and took Blodeuwedd by the hand. Her fingers were petal-cool, crisp and soft, and as I held them infinitely gently in the curve of my hand, I was sickened by the thought of a fist closing tight on them – by the sense of men's capacity and urge to crush delicate, bright living tissue. From all she had told us, I had no reason to believe anyone had ever before touched her hands in pure kindness. Perhaps she might not know what it meant. I led her to the fire. It had almost died away with our neglect of bodily comfort as we listened. I sat her down by it.

Leaving go her hand – placing the little bloom back amongst the other smaller flowers of her lap – I set to feeding and chivvying the flames, trying to rouse fire out of the grey, crackling embers, feeding them what small light twigs their fading appetite might still consume without being smothered by my care. I blew gently through pursed lips onto the place where

I saw a shadow of a glow, and at last tiny flames peeped and then broke out and ran along the cindered crust. I carefully fed them chosen morsels, and then looked up into Blodeuwedd's face. I saw a warm flush on her cheek, as we sometimes see creep across a flower that we expect to find white, but it might have been a reflection of the fire's rising colour. I can't tell if she even felt the warmth – perhaps my small close efforts were beneath her notice, when she was used to being comforted only by the mighty distant blazing of the sun. I hoped at least she might feel the warmth in me that had prompted the paltry effort. After all, we are all of us sun-fed.

Except Arianrhod, I thought then – she always seemed to take her powers from the cooler beams of the moon. And yet when I looked at her, she was quite bereft of any light at all. That I could have forgotten her, even for a moment, in my care for Blodeuwedd, was a measure of the toll the day had taken on her. When I first saw her, her pale face seemed to command darkness itself, and even the black shadows in the room seemed to stream out from her hair – and from her eyes, dilating in her anger – and from her fluent-speaking, wine-stained mouth – like obedient familiars. Now the darkness pressed upon her, crumpling her, as her clothes were already crumpled. Her eyes were open, but vision did not seem to flow from them. Beneath the lashes I sensed only a blank – as though she were part of a race of creatures who, looking too long into absolute darkness, had felt the skin grow back into a sealed sheet over useless eyeballs. She couldn't see me, and I could no longer see into her. But her face now touched me more, through the comparison with the perfect flowery beauty of Blodeuwedd's. Beneath her command and her power, here she was: human, with a face of bare skin, made to show in its creases a more gratuitously intricate tracery of pain than that of any other creature. Fate, that sadistic and most creative artist, had indulged himself in every virtuoso trick on that soft fine ground. There were fractals of anxiety about the eyes, meanders of worry across the brow, crosshatches of conflict at the temples, and fanciful arabesques of agony about the mouth.

Her skin was made so thin it showed the lilac veins, like a map of the intricate falling streams and channels through which her blood had drained, leaving her paler, blanker and more lonely than the moon. This was the face of a mother who had cradled a dead son. Who might soon cradle a lover, dead, as she had never held him while alive. Reading all this in her face, I was more certain than ever that I could not comprehend her feeling, any more than I could accurately gauge the flutterings of Blodeuwedd's flower heart – that we three women might have been three stars, seen in the same piece of sky, but divided by unmeasured depths of freezing, pathless empty space. And yet, I took Arianrhod's hand now, too – something I would hardly have had the temerity to do, any other day – and led her also, unresisting, to the fire, where a coven of violet-hearted flames now leapt busily across the ashes, as though in a dance of invocation.

And there were Blodeuwedd's fingers, still lying useless in her flowery lap. I took them up again, and she, understanding the pattern, whether or not she did the feeling, reached out her other hand for that of Arianrhod. And we all three grasped, and held, and pressed – suddenly as though for life – until we formed a circle in the dark. And fear and pain and hate throbbed through the ring as though we shared one beating heart.

'You have killed him once,' I said. 'It must and will be done again, I swear. Though he returns relentlessly as winter, we'll dog his bloody heels as sure as spring. Tonight we wait. Tomorrow we run him down.'

In the pressing clasp of hands was an answer clearer than any words. I know we all three hoped, all three tried, though failed, to slip the sickly grasp of that waiting moment, and fold the night into tomorrow. Still we had nothing to do but wait, but we waited on in something more like company.

GOEWIN

45

At last the blackest depths of night were past. Its ink became a wash instead of a well, and we heard the birds stirring, though not yet singing. We were at strange peace, there, together, the three of us, and felt ready for the breaking day, as the silent forests and the waiting sea were ready.

At last the peace was broken by Blodeuwedd, who suddenly sprang from her seat and darted to the window. Hitherto she had been as soft and passive as a wind-scooped drift of fallen petals, but now at once she showed the courage of the sharp green spears of spring, arrayed against the frost.

'What new pain is this? I feel a tear – somewhere – in the nature of things. An unravelling of roots, and a dimming of the sun. What cry is that, that strikes my heart, so hard to answer, and harder to refuse?'

I listened, but could hear nothing. 'Sit down, my dear. Your mind is overstrained. It's nothing but the cry of little birds who've gone astray, and lost their fellows in the gale.'

'You cannot hear or feel it, with your dull human ears and sluggish soul. What thing could sound so sweet, but hurt me so?'

'The wail of wild lake swans on Llyn Rhos Ddu? Or perhaps a skein of geese, full stretched across the sky?'

'No! I feel a rent beneath the woods still more deadly than the wasteful fight between the trees – a breach behind the sky, beyond all it has looked down upon this last day past. Something dreadful comes – perhaps fate itself. Outside I hear petals rustle as they never should; soft tissues frozen or burnt in an opening void. I'll look.'

So saying, she hurried to the door, with Arianrhod and myself behind her, and flung it wide.

We peered through the fading dark. Our pupils widened. And we saw a heavy something, hanging there. We all three shrank back a moment, but then, seeing no threatening movement, peered closer.

It was Arawn, deadly pale, with one hand upon the post of the entry – seemingly lacking strength to knock. His tall shape seemed blacker than the dark itself, and broken, and the pallor of his face ready to fade back into night. He gave up, or lost, his hold on the gatepost, and sickly reeled and sunk into the room before Arianrhod could catch him.

'What's this?' she cried.

The silence beat like a pulse in the room while Arawn scraped together strength to speak. His speech sounded strange, like a voice's afterglow, painfully kindled up from embers.

'Ynys Môn is ours. Gwydion has resigned his claim, and all his fairy powers, and now heads back for Gwynedd in retreat.'

'But why then,' said Arianrhod, impatient again, 'do you look so sad, and . . . weak? Tell me everything at once. You owe your allies – your friends – that much.'

Despite her impatience, as Arawn tried to speak, I saw her watch him intently, and do all she could to make him comfortable – at first arranging under him some blankets that had been placed within the threshold for us, and at last supporting him in her own arms, with a hasty efficiency so much like possessiveness that Blodeuwedd and I had nothing to add. Once in his arms, it was almost as though her own nervous energy gave him strength. He looked about him – saw Blodeuwedd, and bowed his head solemnly to her, and thanked her for her past help and present attendance.

His voice was low but steady, and, as he spoke on, it seemed more as though he recounted a dream than conveyed urgent business. At times he sounded and looked as though he dreamed still.

'I came to Bryn Celli Ddu by the time appointed – I saw him approaching as I entered the yew tree grove, and the shadows that fell from the standing stones seemed long even for sunset. As always, I tried to read the maze-faced central stone, but it was inscrutable. I came to the dyke across the moat at the same instant as your brother, and stepped aside so I need not come too close to him. And then we each took up a place across the dial. Gwydion was insolent in his manner, and laughed, 'You go ahead – I'm curious to see what you can do.' I would not speak to him, but gathered up my first spell.

With all my mind, I flung at him darkness like the afterblow that dogs a lightning flash. That deepest dark, dilated and distilled, that seems to flow in through the eyes like swarming bees into a hive, or water into a whirlpool, ready to displace all sense inside the head. I held it over him, until he looked entirely lost.

But he rallied, and cast back at me a dreadful feeling – what a parent would feel, seeing a son climb too high, and watching from too far exactly how his hand begins to slip, exactly how he'll hit the ground before they reach the spot however fast they run.

I gasped, but shook it off in time to cast another spell. Now I made Gwydion feel as though each surface of his mind was bedded deep with muffling snow, which blanked and levelled all the impulses and meanings there to white. With all my mind's might, I made this feeling stretch and billow past the far horizons of his range of thought, till he turned pale as if he had nicked an artery.

But part of the pallor was anger, and in a moment he whipped across with all his force the shock a hurting child feels when he thinks he sees his mother come to take away the pain, but as she nears, sees her look of love distort into a stranger's face, which looks at him indifferently.

His magic is strong in these dark arts – he made me feel this moment all around, first as though I were the hurting child myself, and then as though I were the mother who wasn't even there, and then as though the child were Dylan, and the mother yourself, and I, both of you, and also neither of you, and no help to either.'

Arawn winced in pain, and struggled as though he would get up, but found himself unable, while Arianrhod, her face more tremulous than I had ever seen it, shifted her arms around him, holding him closer to her. He went on.

'Reaching deep for strength, I flung at him that feeling when you stand and peep earthwards from a great height, and feel your mind sucked down – that burning crawling itch to throw your bones into the void. I wound this feeling up, till it felt like a bolt through his crown, which left only a quivering consciousness behind. While he still reeled, I instinctively shot the nearest spell to hand – the regret you feel when June rain rots the spray of blowing roses; the tender weight of every petal that fell to form a drift without your taking note.

But this glanced off Gwydion's armoured mind and rebounded back on me. I felt it bitterly, and began to fear that, though my powers might be greater than your brother's, his mind, in its very narrowness and cruelty, was stronger than mine, and harder to hurt. He struck while I reeled – with the angry shock you feel when the tool you use twists round and strikes you back – but I parried this, and it struck Gwydion like a spear. He gasped, but so did I. We both knew that the end was near, as we knelt there on the mound and gathered up our hatred.

Gwydion struck first, with a novel and curious spell – a picture of a tall cliff face where scores of swifts were breeding, chicks all set to fledge, with just the one perfect chance to launch and fly, because they've only toes, not legs, and can't climb high to try again. The air looked blue and promising – and yet, from that warm rock face, there fell ten thousand baby birds, like rocks to ground. No single bird flew on, and I came to find the hidden reason – cradling one warm in my hand, I saw that in the under-down teemed ticks, their bodies plimmed as big as peas, and bluer than the sky.

I retched in horror, and the sense of despair and waste, and the ugly treachery of living things, swelled out and sucked the warmth from every secret nook of my mind. I thought it was all over. But thinking of the island, and of Goewin, and of Blodeu-wedd, and of Dylan, and of you, I gathered strength for one last desperate throw.

I made your cunning brother feel as though he were cast off at sea, and a wave dislodged his hold upon a rock, and shook him wide adrift, so that looking down he clearly glimpsed the dim heart of the sea – how, in heaving fathoms, thousands of lives passed aloft in automated shoaling hush, while millions more filed duly on below. I showed him how the broken edge of cliff begins its downward shelve towards the end of light, to a blind place of shapes and shapeless things innumerable, of infinite embellishment, with jaws and poisons which we never see. I made him truly see how all the beauty of our lives, just like the sea – the dazzling, azurite transparency – the lovely swell that seems so drenched in light – stacks up at last to suffocating dark, ready to cave our bodies and our minds if we slip down. I made him feel himself swept further from the shore, and looking back, grasp how small our desert island pocks the vasty weirdness of the wetter world – and know in any case it was too late to swim towards the shore. I made him feel the hopeless loneliness of swimming, with little flailing human arms, when adrift in the vast ocean.

With all my might, I made the void press heavier upon Gwydion till he saw into the depth of his own lonely soul. And at last, his head hung limply down, like a case of poppy swelled with the rain, and I knew that I had won.

'Yield!' I cried. 'If you haven't strength to defy me anymore, I'll hear your complete surrender. I'll not lift the spell until you free my beasts.' I saw he held the stolen lapwing in his hand. His fingers loosening, the plover stirred and burst into the air, its blunt wings beating back the curb that bounds the earth, and reeling free into the sky for home, and Fairy. Holding Gwydion still under my spell, I myself cut loose the fraying rope that worked about the roebuck's neck – it bounded away, captivity shunned behind it with each spring of its flying hooves. I undid the collar of Mai, my slender bitch, and her ears pricked bright as holly at the sense that she was free to follow me again – she wound herself about my legs, and I was comforted by her familiar warmth.

Gwydion only watched them go, and all his novel powers with them. As I raised the spell from his head, he turned about and slunk away. But the bastard is incapable of holding his forked tongue. He called back over his shoulder.

'Well . . . Ynys Môn, mother of Wales, is yours. And much may you enjoy the played-out bitch.' I had such contempt for his words, I did not notice in the moment that he cast something else with them.

'But I have no breath left. And I must rest.'

'Goewin,' said Arianrhod, 'you must go at once to oversee an orderly retreat – now that Gwydion has lost his hold on them, the woods and earth and marshes will be quiet as they should be, this time of night.'

'But perhaps – *you* would stay here with me?' said Arawn, looking up into her face. She looked away from him, but I saw her hold him close, and, I thought, only wished to find herself alone with him. I agreed to go, taking Blodeuwedd with me, and letting her know the way I would take with the army.

GOEWIN AND ARIANRHOD

46

I can't be sure how much I ought to fear for Arawn. He looked ill enough, and I will never again underestimate the power of Gwydion's malice. And yet – what can he do against an immortal king of Fairy? Should he recover, if he can ride with Arianrhod on his silver mare, they will overtake us easily. I hoped to catch a glimpse of them with the gathering light. In fact – do you see movement on the road, there above the bend in the river?

Whatever it is moves much too fast for a human cart, and yet too slowly, and too cumbrously, for the king of Annwn on his steed. I hope this is no bad news. I will go back to see. Stay with the men – I will catch up with you again along the way.

Well – Arianrhod it was – though at first I doubted it. Arawn's horse, with her on its back, but pulling a chariot containing what I thought at first was a bier. Arianrhod seemed to read my thoughts at a distance, and called to me, furiously it seemed, that Arawn still lived, and was only resting in the chariot, too ill to take his horse.

I was hardly reassured, and hurried to her, and as I neared I saw that she too was weak and about to slip from the saddle. I was just in time to catch her, though she did not quite faint, and we painfully slipped down between our horses in an awkward embrace. The horses understood, and stopped, and we sat down on the grass, which was silver with morning dew, and drenched our skirts.

Arianrhod, to my amazement, was still almost in my arms – and now she leant on my shoulder and began to sob.

'I have killed him, Goewin!' I heard her say, when at last I could make anything of her words.

'And yet you say he lives, and I know, despite you, that you love him, and so believe nothing of that story,' I said. 'Tell me what has happened.'

I hardly thought she would – but she was altogether softened, and began her story with something almost like obedience.

'I could see the king was in a poor way, but I hoped it was only fatigue from his great and triumphant efforts in the duel. As he told us of it, I searched with my hands for blood or wounds and could find none. And so I said, boldly, when you had gone, "Tell me at once, what hurt have you – what is the matter?" I tried to be very stern but I feared I was letting him see my feelings, with every touch and every word – I seemed to feel the crisp margins of my heart soften and melt, as when a haze drifts across the face of the moon. My light and strength felt tracked away from me – yet I was as firm and cool as I might be.

He hardly spoke, and I lifted him closer in my arms to find the matter in his face.

'I'm hurt,' he breathed, 'and likely now to die.'

'Likely! Likely's not certain,' I cried. 'Only say what needs to be done, and I will do it now. I have my powers too.'

'You've done . . . much already; and you can do more. Only . . . do not take your arm away, that feels so tender behind my neck.'

'Why should I? I know my duty to this world and the other. By the moon, I never will until I see you strong and well again.'

'Do you swear it?' he asked, with strange urgency, and I swore it again.

At this he shivered, as though a rising fever gripped and twisted him. I held him tighter, to stop it. But tight as I held, it would not stop – it grew . . . and changed.

At first his head hung down. And then his shoulders hunched, and there was a change in his neck, which had been soft on the skin of my arm. The ridge of his spine seemed to protrude and toughen. Looking at his face, bewildered, I saw an answering bewilderment – and then an impossible alteration I tried not to see.

The silence in the empty room stretched thin until it was split by the sounds of tearing cloth, and his clothing ripped from him and crumpled to the flags.

Beneath them were brindled bristles, a brutal bulk – and looking in his face, I saw his manhood flail and sink and drown – into the visage of a boar.

I was appalled, but, remembering my oath, clenched my arms about his neck, and let the fug of steaming breath fan my cheek. Knots of muscles heaved him like a sail, hard hairs bit my skin, and hooves kicked and panicked helplessly in my lap. I tried not to look as the long thick-stubbled tongue flailed the gash between the flayed-out tusks. I knew it was my king I held, and I gripped him tight, as though he were a rudder in a squall, until the wind that shook him died away and left him there, becalmed, though still a boar.

But now, quite quickly, just as choppy waves are flattened by the race, his bristled rucks and ribs were all sucked back into his hide – yet as soon as it was smooth enough to be his own again, it was too smooth. I saw a sleekness, that glided past the stippled, furrowed fieldscape that we love or hate in the skin of men. His neck now looked as slick as softly flowing glass, and a silky film, like the bulge of still water, smoothed his face. His body thinned and melted in my lap, until the mounds of muscle flowed as one, lithe and writhing in my arms.

A long tail lashed and flashed and curved, and the body of an eel wound round my waist. A cold fin slapped my face, but still I held him very tight, and looked for Arawn in the narrow, alien mouth and the sea-deep empty eyes.

At last the eel's muscle lost its tone, and the beast lay slack and flaccid in my waiting lap. I watched, almost calmly, as the water that made the surface of the skin seemed to ebb away, and held tighter.

Beneath shone a bone-dry coil of gleaming tiles – an enamelled shaft, that now moved stealthily and rasped my hands, as cold and parched as fear itself. An enormous snake now coiled about me twice, and curled its neck around to peer direct into my face. I dared myself to brave the frozen fire that burned about its diamond pupil, and as I met its eye, it stretched its mouth out wide. It was all dewy-petal pale within – with fangs, like two tiny tender rosy buds, each tipped with translucent, recurved thorns, and beaded with a gleaming venom pearl.

A black mechanic fork shot from the throat to taste my smell, and for a moment I was sure the dainty chops would close upon my neck. But now the snake's head snapped shut like an inlaid box. It tucked it in, and lay as still as stone – a neat tortile braid in my lap.

I saw another change was coming, but by now I minded less. Which of us, I thought, is not from time to time possessed by some beast or other – for a time it locks humanity so deep within us it can hardly see out from our eyes, but then, at last, the beast sleeps, and we lock it up again, safe and neat, until the next time.

Now the scales were melting, and the skin began to puff up like a bleb. Soon a swollen belly filled my lap, as soft as finest kid, and bloated fit to burst, marked crisply with a pale symmetric skull. I couldn't understand what it was, and that unnerved me. Then, through my clothes, a stealthy scratching against my thighs. From beneath the waxy globe something hairy tentatively protruded – and another and another, on all sides – dark-hooked little hooves, and behind them long articulated legs, which caught and tugged and scrabbled on my skirts, caught in my hair and scratched my face, in an uncoordinated clatter of turmoiled separate parts.

Now I saw the spider's downy head, which it pressed against me, like a baby rooting for the breast. Certain of myself now, I held it closer to me as though it were another son – could almost have offered a nipple to the lobed and bristled jaws, the darkly oiled, curve-honed crescent fangs. I gazed into eight crystal eyeballs, and looked for Arawn in each one.

And now eight eyes, eight legs, unbred to four, and then to two. The spider hair slid down towards the chin. The body thinned, and hardened back to ribs and hips and collarbone, and at last I clasped a naked man, who clung to me in his turn, like a child woken from a nightmare. I looked, with joy, into his face to watch it drift towards a look I knew. I saw the lips compose themselves, and bent my head to kiss him on the mouth, for the first time.

But then, before our lips could meet – oh, Goewin! – I let him go.'

GOEWIN AND ARIANRHOD

47

I could hardly conceal my dismay, and Arianrhod rocked herself, and pressed her hands hard over her eyes, as if to blot out scenes she relived behind her closed lids. I did not dare to touch her or to speak to her.

At last, in a clearer voice, she spoke again.

'I must confess it all. Just as the king seemed to be inhabiting his own form, I jumped up and pushed him from my lap. And as I did it, I saw his own eyes widen and flood with – abandonment – and despair.' She hid her face again, and spoke on from behind her hands.

'They were his eyes – Arawn's own – but for a moment I thought that they were Gwydion's. I swear I saw my brother's face, his black spyhole eyes watching me – felt it was his naked body drinking in my warmth, feeling me, insinuating himself deep within my trust. I could not be mistaken: for an instant it *was* Gwydion! Or . . . his form . . . an ugly prison for my love's. But then, within the pause of my heart, it was Arawn, like himself again – though also terribly like death.

I clung tighter to him and asked him what I had done to him. A pitiful shadow of my clutch was returned to me, as his body hung cold and slack in my lap. When he spoke it was with terrifying calm.

'You almost saved my life.'

'But by the moon, explain!' I cried. 'Almost! Don't say that single moment was enough to kill? Death is not at hand?'

He smiled at me, so lovingly that I might have abandoned myself then, as I have now.

'Perhaps not yet. But life feels hardly closer. I've no more footing in this world, and cannot stay.'

And now all my control was lost, and I began to beg him, as though he could help me –'You cannot go! I can't be left alone *again*!' – but he did not hear. He had fallen into a deep faint, from which he has not yet woken. I . . . dare not hope.'

I thought a moment. And then said,

'And yet he is a king of Annwn. Death is not to them the simple thing it is to us. There are realms there between life and death, which thousands inhabit. And besides – none of this is simple. He is a king, but not a god. He can't know the future. Perhaps he is affected by the terrible sufferings he endured in his duel with your brother, and judges his own chances too gloomily. Climb up into the chariot and lie down by his side, and hold him, and watch over him. You might even tell him you love him. He will be better kept still. I will go on as fast as I can and send messengers to fetch old Owena, the witch who has saved my life, and those of many others I love, when hope seemed lost.'

My words hushed her for the moment, and she climbed up, as obediently as a little girl, beside Arawn in the chariot. She must need the rest almost as much as he does by this time – I feared she would break down entirely and lose her wits without some immediate respite.

And now, as the sun is up, I must go on as fast as I can, to keep my word to her, and to make sure all is well with my men. Perhaps you could stay here, or hereabouts? Knowing all Arianrhod's story, you might prove of some use when she comes to herself. Blodeuwedd, also, is somewhere – she followed me from

Rhosyr, but is ill-suited to march with an army, and drifts off into the forest and meadows along the way. I can't tell whether she's before or behind us by now. Perhaps you'll come across her, or she across you. But you must be tired yourself. If you look, up there – that old thorn tree on the broad cliff ledge, just below the edge of the forest, has a lovely bed of moss and wood sorrel beneath, spangled with wind-flowers white as wax, where I have napped many times. These are my own home meadows and woods – safe again, and out of Gwydion's power. But farewell, stranger; I hope we meet again when my business is wound up.

BLODEUWEDD

48

Sleep or wake, stranger? I like humans best asleep. They are a little nearer to being flowers, especially when they doze outdoors. They are mercifully still, but for the little hairs on their skin, raised by the breeze, not like those the stems of flowers bear – and they feel the sunlight brightening their cells. For the time, their impatient, roving eyes see only light, in the colour of the pimpernel. The broken ticking of their brains is slowed or stilled, and, from what I hear, they sometimes dream the dreams of flowers – dreams where life appears in its true colours, vividly. Their misty perception is unveiled a while, just as the clouded blue of the sky streams down and distils its essence in the waiting speedwell flowers. For a moment, they may grasp the saturating presence of the light – how it cascades and glows, in one illuminosity, through everything that lives, and gives it more than meaning. If you have ever dreamed the secret emerald of the moss, the violet incandescence of the heather, the sap green of the canopy, billowing in the spring – and felt the colours float free, lighter than the atmosphere of thought, diffusing through and beyond the narrow limits of significance – you have come close to dreaming what the earth and flowers dream, which is only light.

But I have not dreamt so for many a year now – and I could grudge any man or woman such a dream, after what has been done. Oh, the shattered flowers! Sleep or wake, you must share the nightmare. The blossoms of the woods are shaken down and crushed into the mud, roots stretched and snapped, and a million trunks and branches killed. In the river, poor shattered trees are clogged and chaffed with bloating human dead, and tender grass is minced and dark with ugly gore.

You'd think he would have been content with this! But as Gwydion led his armies back towards their ships, he lit a racing fire among the sedge which licked along the poor battered bank like a hound catching blood. All the tortured trees burst into copper flames, as though run down by autumn on the longest day. The withies bloomed as funeral flowers – fire-lilies against the smoke-dimmed canvas sky – and the rushes flickered, like rows of candle flames before an icon with a slashed-through face.

Poor Afon Braint! Such desecration of her flowery shrine. The lacy skirts of ragged robin and the lady's smock caught sparks and burst out into floating trains of flame – I could hear the tiny screaming on the wind – and the soft petals of musk mallow shrivelled and paled, like cheeks aged in a moment, as their stems contorted and their seedpods burst. The alders and the birches sprang up into spires, so briefly, before shrinking back as shuffling columns of ash. The long leaves of the willow curled and paled, then hissed like tempering tears into the stream, until the frogs and fishes gasped, and eels twisted in death's grasp. The stream was clotted with the trunks of trees and men – the water slow with mud and blood. Half-choked, the river tore at her own banks, and her broken heart turned black.

But you humans, even the best of you, care little for all this.

You have slept all day, careless, as that fire raged – all through the last day, until now the sun has almost set. How can you sleep when the world burns around you?

At last the fire spent itself, and as the smoke cleared, I saw the dregs of Gwydion's army, and the evil man himself, finally filing away towards a wide bridge across the river Braint, built where the bank is highest, which crosses it with three spans, bearing on its rounded back the path from the island's inland plains towards the sea. It is the only crossing fit for bands of war and carts, and so there also, on their way to court at Llanfaes, came Goewin, with Math and his train, and all her children approaching. Neither force wished to grant right of way to the other, and so the rival bands jostled each other on the bridge, and Gwydion himself endured the taunts of battle-dirty men, and the hard glare of his uncle Math, quite close at hand.

I saw that Goewin would not look at him. She greeted me, sadly enough, but hardly knew what to say to me of my new loss – burning flowers are perhaps beyond words. Yet as she spoke to Ystwyth she could hardly conceal the joy of relief in her face, and her voice bubbled out like a spring which nothing could stop up.

'A dark and bitter day . . . More than half my kingdom lost, the island scarred, and Arawn perhaps killed – the waste of so much life and pain and blood. Yet when my eyes rest upon these three babies of mine – for babies they still seem, although I watched them pass right through the heart of such a furnace as this war has been – they glow like little nuggets, newly smelted. What relief, to crawl out from the hollow-sounding gorge of death into the sun; although it sets, it shines on these three darling faces, all alive and well! I'm not fit to be any sort of queen – I can't deny, I'd lose a hundred kingdoms, twice, to bask for one moment in a sight like this.'

She turned to her daughter, and took her hand, as though she would have praised her part in the battle, but seemed to find her heart choked up her words. Seeing Hychddwn close, she beamed into his dirty face, and kissed his forehead through the sweat and blood. And her son lifted her in his arms, and set her to ride high on his shoulders, as he must have ridden on hers a thousand times, kicking his legs, back when he was a tiny tired-legged child, instead of a burly, bloodied youth. And all the weary men, who had spent days in killing and desecration, seemed strangely moved at this, and cheered the sight of her, until Hychddwn set her down, still smiling. And there stood Bleiddwn, her other son, who seeing his mother's face, put off his wolf form and armour both, so that she could cling to his neck. I seemed to see relief pour through her fingers as she touched his cheek and childish ruffled hair, and spoke to him.

'My dearest pup: has your tender paw batted away the brindled dogs of war, and brought you safely back to me at last?' She turned aside, and moved onto the bridge, to hide the tears that I saw glinting in her eyes, making them almost as pretty as flowers.

I thought her tears more fitting than her joy. But Gwydion did not. Just now, moving onto the bridge himself, he saw and hated all this, and felt each loving drop like molten lead upon his heart. That tinder heart seemed to blaze white, and seizing up a spear from the ground, he aimed it true at Bleiddwn's frank and undefended back.

His mother saw, and foresaw that the spear would hit its mark between Bleiddwn's shoulder blades. She sprang at Gwydion faster than a hare, so that his spear flew wide and stabbed the earth, still quivering with flesh-hunger. Gwydion, clutching Goewin for his life, stammered in the air above the bridge's parapet. Goewin's face was filled only with triumph, though she must have felt the fall come, sure as the dogrose petal as the hip begins to swell. Gwydion grasped her arms with hateful force, as though that could have saved him. And then I saw them fall, and their eyes lock, as they plunged into the raging slake.

Fast, I let Braint know all the evil wreaked by that man now within her current's grasp. I cried to the marsh trefoil and pale lobelia, and with their roots they carried the tale to the river's heart – I called to the flag irises in the shallows, and their swords sung of his sins as the wind blew through them. I screamed it to the loosestrife and marsh marigolds, and they bent their heads and whispered it to the water. And the water recognised the tale – for Arianrhod, mistress of the sea, its source and end, had also suffered wrongs as deep at Gwydion's hands.

So as the Braint felt Gwydion's presence, she roared, and surged high to leave her burden of bodies along the shores, that she might hunt him unencumbered. She grasped him in an eddy, ducked him – but he bobbed, and seized for his life a half-burnt elm that hung above the tangled flood. Yet its roots had no purchase on the flood-breached bank – it toppled with his weight, and jammed across the fierce flow. Gwydion, clinging still, dragged his body from the stream, and found footing back upon the land.

But my sister Braint would not be baulked. She now rose in towering anger right up from her bed, and raced after him across the plain – past and through the campion and gentle cuckoo flowers, who cheered her on. He felt the water race past his knee and murmur at his heels, and now, at my command, the docks and cowslips beneath his feet smoothed themselves flat and made a slick – he slid, and staggered, and the ravaged water beat on his back, and burst over his head, and sucked him down, and back into her bed.

When I came to the bend in the river afterwards, the water lilies told me what became of Gwydion after the air was freed of him. They showed me what they saw. I watched the Braint hold him tight, bound with currents, wrapped about with eddies, and suffocating in her tight embrace, until the water was all he breathed, and he was dead, and could never live again. Flowers and water would make sure of that. Amongst the lily roots, his muscles tensed, then sagged, then locked, and then began to bloat. I watched them guard him, until his dead flesh was paler than their faces – until it swelled to jelly, and the little fishes gulped it up with their chilly boneless lips, and eels, with rows of rice-grain teeth, tore ribbons loose, to show the lace of fat around his organs. These they peeled away in sucking clammy mouths, to melt him down to broth. And the river now will roll his bones, and drive him deep into a sink of mud – pile silt on silt, and clay on coldest clay, and gravel layers in ascending grades, so not a grain of his hideous foulness shall ever taint the lovely blooming waters of the Braint again.

BLODEUWEDD

49

This is my last day of flowers – the last time I shall lie like this, and watch the lengthening shadows of the blades of grass and buttercups. But, you know, trapped in this woman's form, I have long been separated from my sister blooms. I wish to boast that I feel the ravages of the last days in my own body – that it is my flesh that is torn, my veins rent – and that the healing, too, will be mine. But it is not so – I can only watch, from outside, as you might do – and it is nothing like life, to be separate and alone like that. And so I made my last bid for escape.

With Gwydion dead once more, I could again feel directly the presence of the king of Fairy, which dark magic had so long hidden from me, as it had hidden my plight from him. He was badly, perhaps mortally hurt, though as he is immortal I hardly knew what that might mean. And now the surviving flowers led me to him – the daisies traced a starry path through the short grass, orchids stood to attention where it grew taller, and through the heath the mounds of heather and bilberry shuffled apart to show my way.

And there he was, lying pale as sickly arums, on a death bier, with Arianrhod silent at his side, her head bowed like a little nightshade bell, his lifeless hand crushed in hers. For a moment, proud human though she is, she reminded me of my own last hopeless hopes, as I clasped my darling's body.

But here, I thought, the healing of the flowers might not be all in vain. I summoned foxgloves to set a steady pulse, yarrow to ease his fever and meadowsweet to help his blood run steadily; valerian to calm the torments of his mind and amber weed to cheer him. I thought I saw a timid seep of colour in his face – like that which flushes buds of apple blossom as the rising sun drinks up the dew – and saw his eyelids flutter like butterflies hung in shade beneath a flower, just warmed by dawn. But still his eyes were closed – he did not move.

I turned angrily to Arianrhod.

'You see what flowers can do – they have all but undone the harm made by you humans, and your meddling with the powers of earth, and your petty rivalries and pride and resentment. More than your own fate hangs on the life of this king here – he is guardian of a realm which you know almost nothing of – and besides that, he is my only hope. By every wave that creeps across the sea, by every leaf that drinks the sun, and all the grains of pollen dancing in the air – do your part. Let the fairy king know your love. Just for once, I conjure you: show him the tenderness of lush woodbine – of sweet musk roses and of eglantine.'

I know little of humankind, but enough to be sure that I must now turn away. I went into the wood, and spoke with the quiet flowers of the briars and hellebore of our mutual bereavements. When I returned, little to my surprise, I saw Arawn in Arianrhod's arms, his cheek still blanched but animate again, his eyes open and intelligent.

Now I did not hesitate to press my cause with him, arguing

the useful part I had played in the war, and the good I had done him even now. I saw he would give me all the help he could – though I believed him when he told me that, my spirit having been caged as it had, I could never return to what I had been before. But he could at least ease my loneliness.

He summoned all his powers, and sent them out as a cloud of crackling storm. At last it came to hang above the hill of earth which weighted down my darling Gronw's pale body; the lily vessel that once gushed green with tides of spring's sweet sap, and now lay hollow as a winter stem. I had lain long there, in my love's dissolving arms, in the place where Gwydion had buried him – the worms and woodlice weaving us as one once more – only leaving him to fight in Arawn's war. Even the king of Fairy could not heal the hole struck through my Gronw's heart – but he raised his spirit in the form of an owl, and he promises, tonight, I shall be made his counterpart.

I shall be condemned to the darkness, and never more shall drink in the sun with my sisters. I shall no more have glowing petals, to glisten in the light, but only dull and downy feathers, speckled like the earth, to hide me from the noon, and let me float between the daylight and the dark. I must no longer drink sunshine, but instead skewer little mice and eat them whole. But if you peer into descending shade, you perhaps may see me – alone no more, but with my love. Though mobbed and shunned by all the pretty birds, we'll sit there, fan-downed cheek nestled to cheek, upon one single noon-time shaded branch. And in November nights you'll hear our coos of love, as sweet as summer's long. In the meadows I can never dance again, but with the darkness I will drink the tang of ransoms, and the musk of sycamore, and never feel this broken loneliness again.

I asked Arawn what had become of Goewin – I hardly thought

of her, after the fall from the bridge, I was so engrossed in watching Gwydion die. But as women go, she was a good one, and I did not dislike her – she had something of the toughness of the blackthorn-may.

He told me how, locked behind his closed eyes, almost powerless with fever, he had nevertheless seen in his mind all that passed there by the Braint. He sent out what he thought was his last strength – made what would have been, but for me, his final effort. Goewin would have drowned with Gwydion, but in the very nick he changed her to a little trout, with bold spots haloed on her sides.

And now, when the sun is high, she will hide in flowing light, her body's curve flickered by ripples as they pass; shadowless, with skin as bright as water. If you wish to see her, go in the afterlight – you still may glimpse her whole, her muscles flashing amber as she leaps, to scatter dazzles across the sunset air.

She is made of fairy stuff now, and part of the whole earth. In her vaunting leaps her soul may flutter onwards as a damselfly, her bold spots now impressed on silver wings of shivering film, their beat a throbbing pulse which lights and passes on into a hare, and bounds off onward through the rising grass.

I come to you from the stony shore below – I went there because I could bear no more death. There, on the margins of the land, many flowers have been saved. There are bees, even now, drawn from afar by the sea holly's electric blue . . . though I fear when they carry home their panniers of nectar they may find their hives burnt. The campions still glisten white, marked only by the black lace of their own stamens, and the lavender and the burnet rose gather the last light from the fading day.

There, just now, I saw a boat rock on the waves' silky lap. It was softly stilled by a tall woman – she was followed slowly by a man, whose grey cloak seemed to flow into the mist that now rose off the sea, and the mist into his face. He had the look of Arawn, and the woman with him, of Arianrhod. They sat side by side across the centre of the boat. Each took an oar, and pulled away without a sound, along the glittering pathway of the moon.

AFTERWARDS

50

Ynys Môn was badly hurt that night. All over the island, but especially along the passage of the Braint, trees and men lay side by side. The eroded river was choked with branches and bodies, its water flowing muddy. Flakes of ash hung in the air. And in every house, come night-time, there were eyes kept wide with loss.

But slowly, the island healed. Young saplings found new space in the tears in the canopy, and the forest floor was quickly darned with bramble and stitchwort and cleavers. And in the green shade in the storey in between, young leaves flickered, and the bees hung.

The Braint rubbed away the crumbling broken banks, and laid them down again in gradual slicks of silt, so that the river flowed as evenly as ever. By the time tasks were undertaken cheerfully again, some of the young cherries were as thick as an arm – and by the time the new oaks were as thick as a leg, no one stayed awake at night to think of that day's dead.

Even with Gwydion gone, his brothers still retained control of Gwynedd. Gilfaethwy, as the taller, named himself high king, but had neither will nor brains to do much other than hunt and eat in his high hall, and practise uninventive cruelty with his nephew Lleu. Amaethon, though he was seen little in the hall, was the real power. He made sure there were plentiful harvests in the plains and valleys, though the high hills and distant *cwms*, far beyond the reach of the plough, soon echoed with the low rumble of discontent. But gentle earthquakes are common in those parts, and often come to nothing.

Hyddwen, daughter of Goewin Bach, became queen of Ynys Môn, counselled by Math until he died soon after, and then by old Aneurin, whose love now flowed all towards his land. Her brothers, knowing how Goewin had prized Hyddwen's wisdom and decisiveness, and too young to wish for such responsibility themselves, were strong in advancing her claim. There was now no one of determination to oppose it.

With the departure of Arawn, communication with his fairy land of Annwn all but ceased. Sometimes a child would glimpse its greener shade through the spray of the white water as it tumbled down through the wood, or a tired worker, half-waking from a stolen nap under a solitary thorn, might see its ever-blooming meadows glow behind the springing grass. In heavy mist, the lonely traveller sometimes wandered into fairy land and out again, with no certain knowledge of where they'd been, beyond the sense that the journey had been longer and stranger than expected. The deer, weaving among the shining trunks of the birches, often slipped through the warp into Fairy and back again in safety. The lapwings rowed to and fro with the season, piping always of what they had seen, though no one understood the language in which they sung. And every night, Blodeuwedd and Gronw floated between worlds on muffled wings, with shrieks that pierced the film between the two, so that the sleepers they roused hardly knew into which world it was they woke.

Lapped in the warm Gulf Stream, the island healed well – but not completely. Scars remained. The sons and daughter of Goewin Bach mourned their mother bitterly for many years, as did the people. They did not know they need only peer into the river when the light shines deep, or watch at dusk when the fish begin to leap, to catch a glimpse of her again.

Goewin was the last queen that we know of to rule all of Gwynedd and Môn together. The banks of a river, once so breached, never closed to the same muscular channel, and the water murmured a lower and a softer tune. The young trees were not like the old ones – the upward twist of the chestnuts told of different droughts and storms, and the arms of the oaks rested in a new attitude. Above Goewin's home meadow, there was now no tree to climb with a view across the Straits. No other grew high enough above the rest. You could no longer look out across the receding mountains, and down, past Carreg y Llam, along the far blue falling rhythm of Llŷn, to Enlli, marooned in mist alone. And when the hares ran, it seemed with new alarm.

Note on the Text: The Collective Imagination

This novel is based on the fourth 'branch' of the Mabinogion – the earliest British written narrative, set down on paper around the twelfth century, but based on oral traditions stretching back to the Bronze Age. The story told here is unfinished in the Mabinogion, but the events of Part III can be found in the medieval sources of the bard Taliesin's poem 'Cad Goddeu' and the Peniarth manuscript 98B. The story was written in Welsh – the language of northern England and much of Scotland as well as Wales until the Middle Ages, which descended from the Cumbric language spoken across all Britain until the invasions of the Gaels, Angles and Saxons. This narrative – not *Beowulf*, which is written in the tongues of Dark Age newcomers, and tells of the heroes and landscape of Scandinavia – is our island's oldest story.

The narrative, as recorded, is brief, and gives little idea of the emotions of the characters. There are many holes – events which lack explanation, and leads which come to nothing. This leaves many interpretations open so that in more recent retellings Gwydion has been presented as something like the hero; though the bare facts of his conduct are as I have presented them, and I think they speak for themselves. I have darned the holes and filled in the detail with other narratives taken from traditional songs and stories across the Celtic tradition.

The Mabinogi's stories are closely related to versions told across the British Isles and far beyond. The children of Dôn have more thoroughly supernatural and fairy counterparts, not only in the Hindu children of the primordial goddess Danu, but closer to home in the Gaelic Tuatha Dé Danann, who are reincarnations of the most ancient Celtic deities, and who live on as the *aos sídhe*, the fairy inhabitants of hollow hills in Celtic folklore.

The bards, fili and seanchai – the musicians, scholars, poets, storytellers, historians and prophets of ancient and medieval Celtic Europe – claimed descent from the Danann. Their task was not to sing a new song, all their own, but to convey the history, dreams and wisdom of the past to the present – and to cast the long beam of this vision into the future.

I would like to do the same. And so although this is a novel, it is not all new – my voice, and my vision, are not all my own. All the places, and a surprising number of the events in the novel, are framed by my own experience, but that experience, in turn, was coloured by the tales and songs I had already heard. I am proud to know, to repeat and to build on the traditional stories, metaphors and lore I heard sung and spoken in my childhood, and all the poetry and fiction of more bookbound 'literary' culture which draws its influence from that folk tradition. Far more of our great books do so than is commonly understood.

You may find fleece from which I spun this Welsh tale in ancient classical text – in Homer, Ovid and Aeschylus, in Virgil, Tacitus and Lucan, as well as in the oldest Gaelic narratives, such as that of Cú Chulainn and of Deirdre. You may follow my thread through both English and Irish writers – Shakespeare, Tennyson and T. S. Eliot; Emily Brontë, Synge, Yeats and Beckett. But the shepherds who followed and sheared the flocks from whom the fleece first came are the nameless, or many-named, composers of dozens of folk songs and ballads, such as that of 'Yarrow', 'Tamlin' and 'Little Musgrave' – and of many oral legends, such as that of the seven whistlers, the water wife, and the washer at the ford. There is an homage to one or other of these imaginative progenitors on almost every page, because I couldn't help it; I hope others who love them will enjoy looking out for them.

Brigid Lowe, 2026

Acknowledgements

In writing this book I've been taken aback by the unstinting encouragement and help offered to me along the way, even by those with their own lives still to live. Gore Vidal and Scott Fitzgerald were wrong. Generous hearts who never grudged me – you know who you are. I would never have gotten started without the hyperbolic faith in my writing displayed by Bina Widdowson and Don Paterson, or persisted without further confirmation from Rod Dalrymple and Matt Jackson, whose critical feedback shaped the story in a hundred ways. Another slice of good fortune came in the shape of my agent Philip Gwyn Jones – Stakhanovite, canny and kind as they come, and shamelessly bold in his commitment to writing as a serious business. He found me the perfect editor and publisher in Liz Foley, who seemed to recognise and value exactly what mattered most in the tale, and never asked for compromise, but only that I rise to the occasion. Thanks also to the rest of the team at Vintage, especially Chris Sturtivant, Sam Rees-Williams and Jessica Spivey, who poured so much of their own professionalism, passion and flare into making the book a real thing and launching it into the world, and to my all-seeing copy-editor, Hayley Shepherd.

Writing a novel creates externalities – before you ever set pen to paper, and long after. Loving thanks to Sean for his unqualified faith in me. Thanks to Andy Smith and to Michelle at the Jobcentre for their trust and support. Thanks to my dear friend Isobel

Breton for looking after me and keeping my eighteen mythical children so well fed. Thanks to Charlotte, who, when I was six and she was ten, lit up the lanes around Bryn with racing imaginative fire, and to my teenage gang, Vic, Jess and Willow, with whom I saw so much, real and visionary, in the darkened cliffs and fields of Ynys Môn. And to Simon – 'Quien a buen árbol se arrima, buena sombra le cobija.'

My debt to my late father is in the story, just as it happened. There too are my mother and all my children, who showed me both sides of the mighty mysteries of motherhood – the great force at the heart of this story. Thanks to Cati for exemplary lessons in sisterhood, as well as meticulous proofreading. And to my daughter Ide Crawford, my most exacting editor. The scenes, stories, feelings and ideas behind the book were teased out between us, walking the crests of our little mountain, finishing each other's sentences. And thanks to you too, stranger, for picking up the book. You're the loom.

Brigid Lowe grew up in a remote Welsh-speaking community on Ynys Môn, with her younger sister and Irish immigrant parents. She now lives with her children in that part of Scotland known as Yr Hen Ogledd – The Old North – formerly joined with Wales in one Cumbric nation. She studied literature at Bangor, completed a doctorate at Oxford, and went on to teach and research at Sheffield and Cambridge universities, publishing a book and many essays on the art of fiction. Brigid traces her descent from travellers, circus performers, mill workers and gallowglass warriors. She takes photographs of flowers, forages her food, clambers pinnacles, and swims in ice caves and bottomless pools.